THE VOICE AND THE MIND

Book IV of the Shapewalker's Song

JH Tomen

Dedication

For Janis & Helen
Even at the end, love remains

And for Karl
You paved each step back to Berill
To this journey and the ones that follow after

These hands of infinite promise,
Intertwining like so many vines;
May we turn them to gardens,
Where the shade and soil remind us,
That we are one.

Cover by Karl Nilsson (@sigvardnilsson)
Map of Ekosinar, the Isles of Dawn, and Berill Detail by
Matt Dye (@mattdyedraws)
Map of Wellonai & The Three Sisters by Jeremy DeBor
(@jeremydeerboar)
Editing by A.K. Edits (@AdotKEdits)

et tui amóris in eis ignem accénde
renovábis fáciem terræ

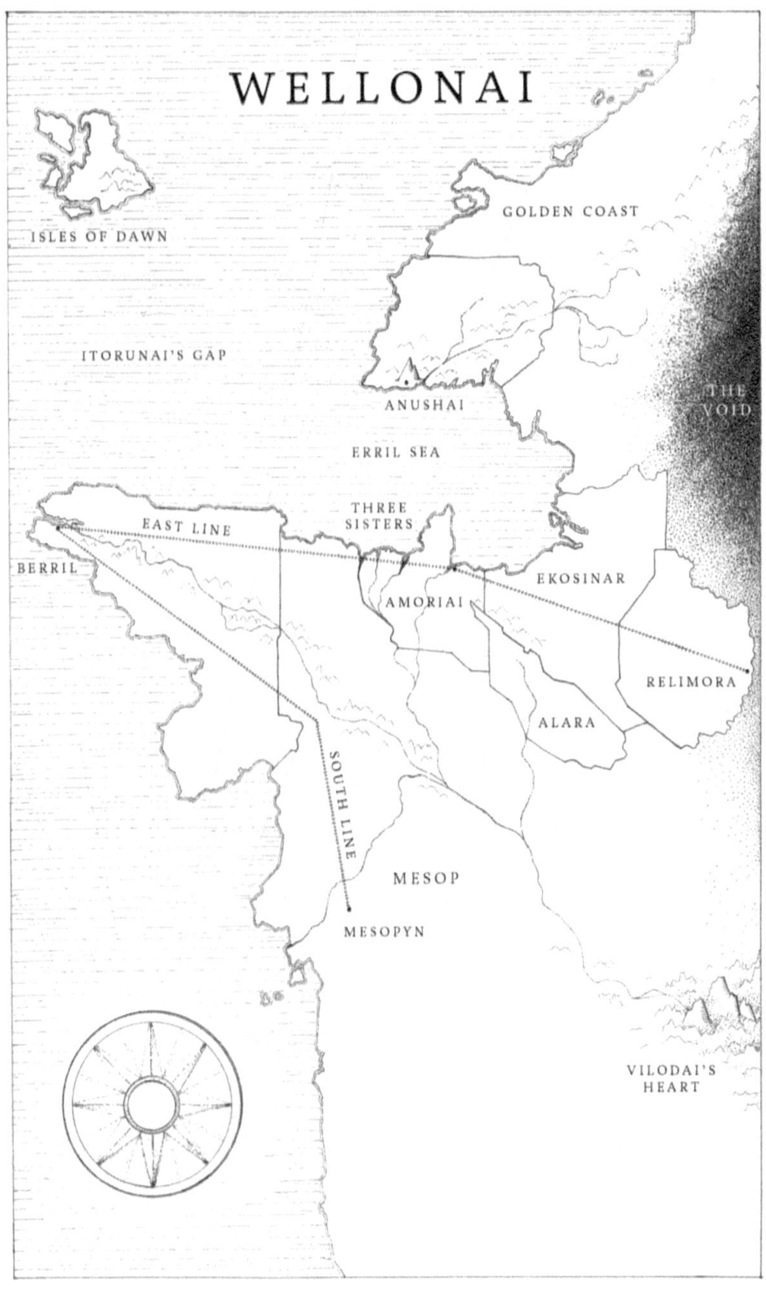

WELLONAI
ISLES OF DAWN
GOLDEN COAST
ITORUNAI'S GAP
ANUSHAI
THE VOID
ERRIL SEA
THREE SISTERS
EAST LINE
BERRIL
EKOSINAR
AMORIAI
RELIMORA
ALARA
SOUTH LINE
MESOP
MESOPYN
VILODAI'S HEART

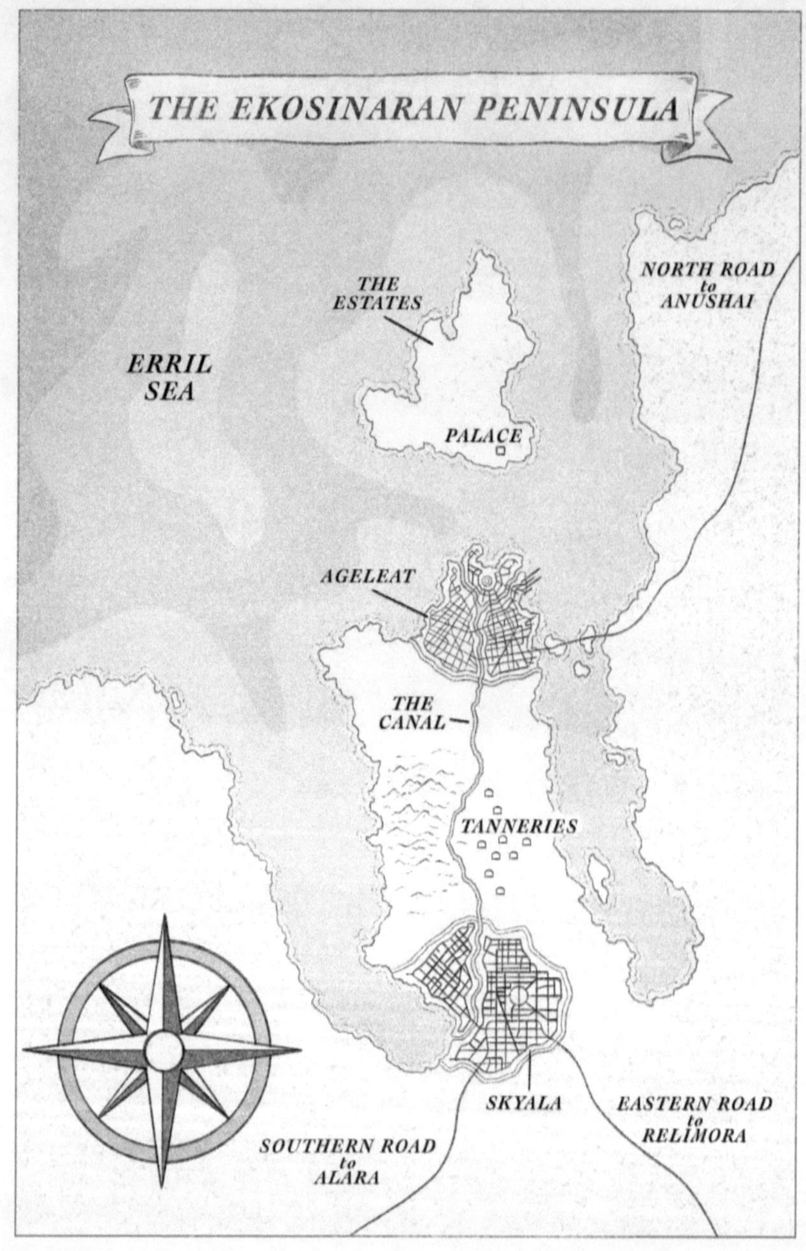

THE EKOSINARAN PENINSULA
THE ESTATES
NORTH ROAD to ANUSHAI
ERRIL SEA
PALACE
AGELEAT
THE CANAL
TANNERIES
SKYALA
EASTERN ROAD to RELIMORA
SOUTHERN ROAD to ALARA

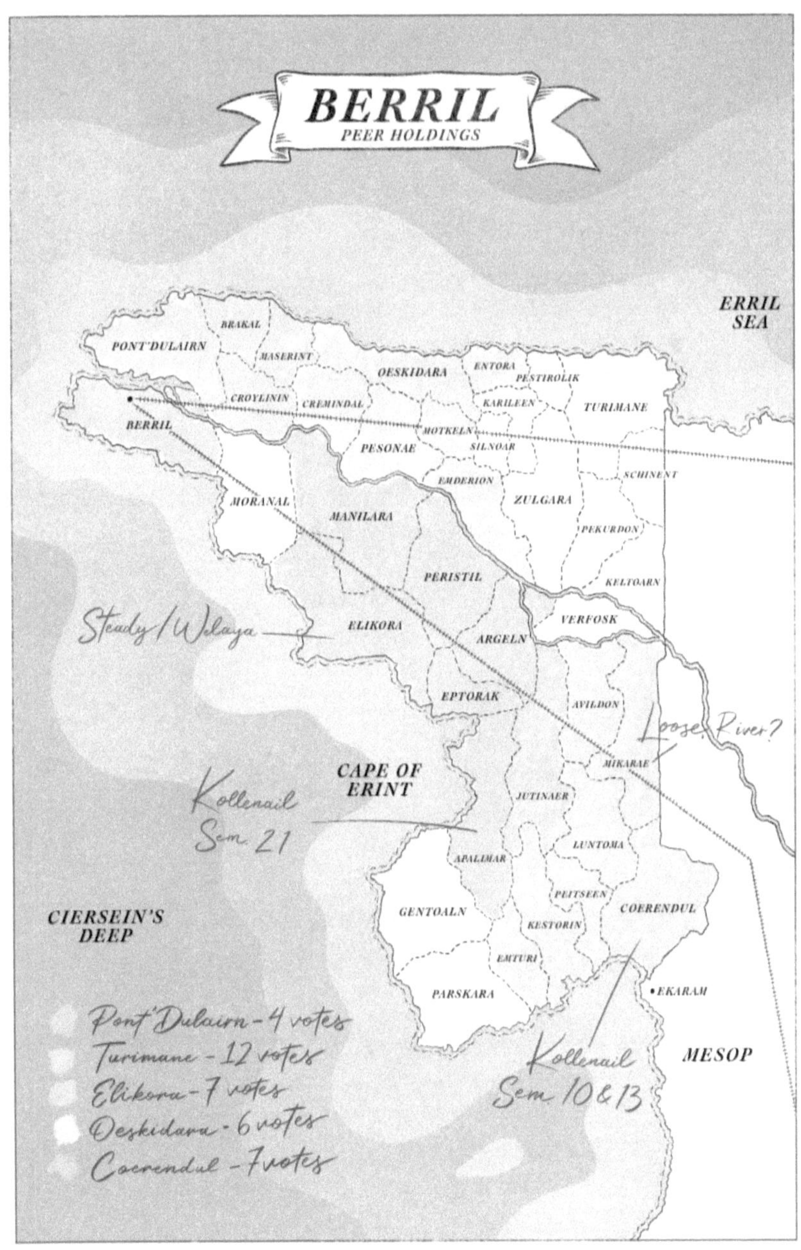
BERRIL
PEER HOLDINGS
ERRIL SEA
PONT'DULAIRN
BRAKAL
MASERINT
OESKIDARA
ENTORA
PESTIROLIK
CROYLININ
CREMINDAL
KARILEEN
TURIMANE
BERRIL
MOTKELN
PESONAE
SILNOAR
EMDERION
SCHINENT
MORANAL
ZULGARA
MANILARA
PEKURDON
PERISTIL
KELTOARN
VERFOSK
Steady / Welaya
ELIKORA
ARGELN
EPTORAK
AVILDON
Loose River?
MIKARAE
CAPE OF ERINT
JUTINAER
Kollenail
Sem 21
LUNTOMA
APALIMAR
PEITSEEN
COERENDUL
CIERSEIN'S DEEP
GENTOALN
KESTORIN
EMTURI
PARSKARA
EKARAM
Pont'Dulairn - 4 votes
Turimane - 12 votes
Elikora - 7 votes
Oeskidara - 6 votes
Coerendul - 7 votes
Kollenail
Sem 10 & 13
MESOP

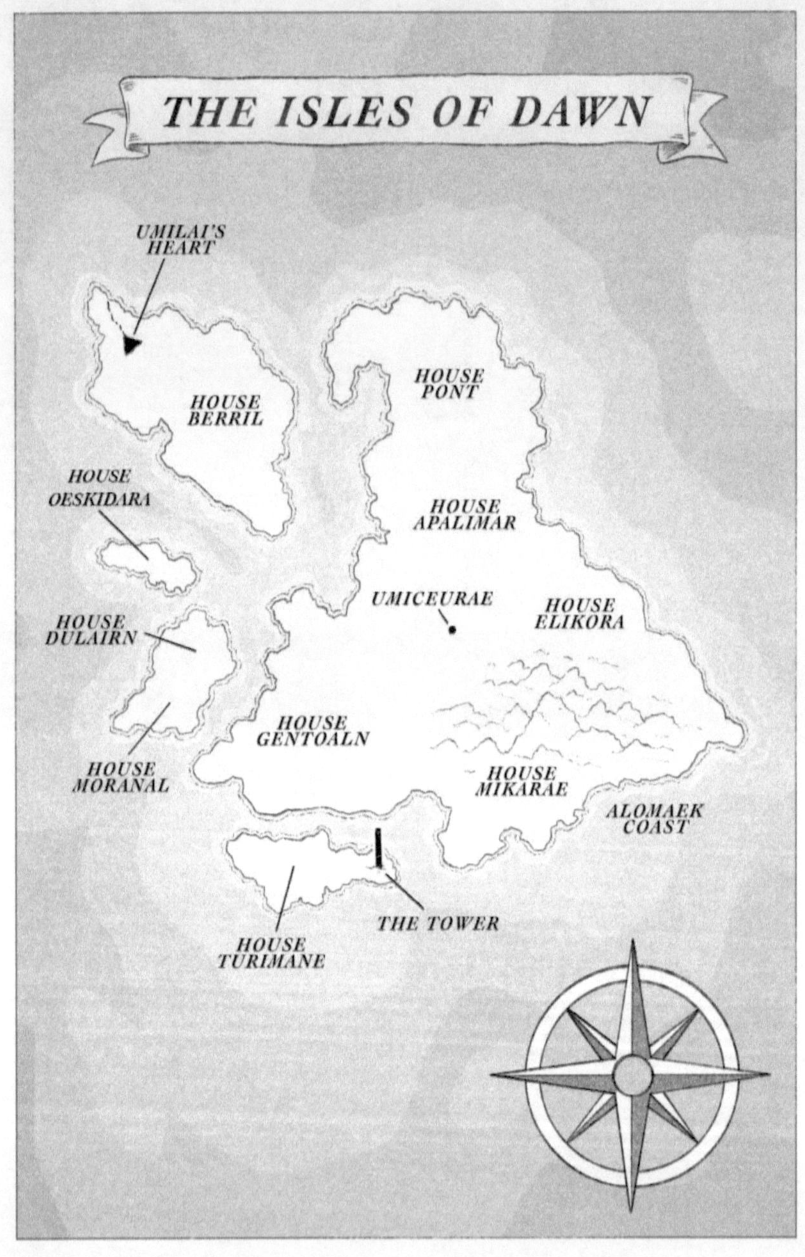

THE ISLES OF DAWN
UMILAI'S HEART
HOUSE BERRIL
HOUSE PONT
HOUSE OESKIDARA
HOUSE APALIMAR
UMICEURAE
HOUSE ELIKORA
HOUSE DULAIRN
HOUSE GENTOALN
HOUSE MORANAL
HOUSE MIKARAE
ALOMAEK COAST
THE TOWER
HOUSE TURIMANE

THE THREE SISTERS
VOLNEERAN PENINSULA
CÖTTHURN
HAFANELLE
STRUSSFARAN
CAPE OF V'INIEL
BERRIL
LUTERRIN
KASELDA
ENOZEIRA
KOLBENZ
AMORIAI
ELTIMEIR
KO'LESTA
MESOP
MALDEGURN
MIEDARAL

PART ONE

1

It appears I'm to be secretary for this quarter. The ciphers are murder, but I suppose someone has to take the bloody notes.

-Monthly Meeting Minutes of Dialasera's Rose
Handwritten Excerpt from the Margins
Sienomon 812 PD

—:—

Erso dropped his forehead into his palm and groaned. The dice on the table were most certainly *not* winners. Not that he cared. In fact, he had shaped one of them to come up with a losing number no matter what. He pushed his money over to the sailor who'd just won, taking the opportunity to slip the guilty die back into his pocket. Then he raised his head, laughing with the men as they slapped him on the back and poured him another drink.

It was probably time to call it a night. The drinks were still tasting pretty good, but he'd lost ten crowns on that last roll. Sumi hadn't said anything about him gambling below deck yet, but it wouldn't do to come back with an empty purse too often. Knowing her, she might even find him more charming as a degenerate gambler. But if it meant explaining the truth behind his little nightly ritual… Well, he may not have the strength to tell her just how powerless he felt.

"Where'd you learn to gamble, mate?" Pejm asked him. "At the three-legged dog track?"

The other men burst out laughing. They were all good-natured, really. They didn't like laughing at him losing so much as at what a good sport he was. Not that they minded the winning either, of course…

Erso smiled, nodding. He was a good man, Pejm, classic Amoriai stock, even if they all spoke Berillai on the ship.

"Actually," he said, "my mother taught me to gamble. She was an actress, right? And they'd all get one big paycheck at the end of each show. She'd always sneak off with me without my pa knowin', and we'd gamble on the turtles at the docks. She was bloody awful at it, too, lost even more than me, but it was a hell of a time."

The men laughed, swapping their own stories of who had taught them to gamble. For once, though, his story was actually true… How had that come out so easily? He supposed it was a good thing, learning to face his regrets. Maybe if he took his own advice like he'd taught Parimu, he'd come out the other side a better man. Or at least slightly more prepared for what lay ahead. It was the future that bothered him now, not the past.

Everything had changed up in those mountains. He hadn't gone into the cavern, but he'd felt the earth shake sure enough. And then, Sumi had returned, looking like a goddess herself with another apparently tied around her neck. She looked…perfect, determined, ready. But for him, it felt like the beginning of the end. He'd been content thinking they would fail and he'd — as much as it went against his deep sense of self-preservation — get the privilege of dying by her side. But now, unfortunately for him — and perhaps luckily for her — it made him realize once and for all he was no good for her.

He loved her, true. Loved her so much he could hardly think straight, but it was time he faced facts. He was a drunk, a coward, and a fool. Maybe he could have gone his whole life without admitting that to himself, but that's what happens when you fall in love; the truth comes out, whether you like it or not. This woman was a literal goddess — or near enough, anyway — and he wasn't about to drag her down into the muck with him. When this was over, when she succeeded, he'd have to learn what came after running. But it sure as shit wouldn't mean saddling her with a heap of a man. He would stand by her now, fight for her, but then he'd have to find the strength to let her go.

He shook his head, shooting back another drink. That's why he was really down here after all. Not the booze — he could drink just fine on his own. He was here to make friends. Maybe they'd run into a customs officer asking too many questions, and a sailor would agree to hide Sumi in a crate for an hour. Or maybe the captain would sell them out, and they'd get a few minutes of warning. It didn't matter what form the friendship came in, so long as it arrived before the pinch. Maybe that wasn't much, but it was the only currency he had, the only kind of magic he alone could do.

He poured another round for the men and shot his own drink back with a grimace. How did he convince himself this stuff tasted good every morning? It tasted like motor oil now — worse than that, actually — not that it would keep him from it. Even when it went down like fire, he couldn't deny he loved the feeling. Only here, losing his money to a bunch of bloody cargo men, could he feel like he *mattered*, that he had something to offer other than lies and bad jokes. The seedy pub, the back door deal — the grimy side of life had always been his stage, and he'd be damned if he didn't nail his lines now.

He looked in his wallet and found a single ten-parse bill. There were still a couple odds and ends in coins, but he was getting awfully short… He'd have to recoup some of this eventually, ideally before he went to Sumi for more, but not tonight. Tonight, he was the king of clowns.

"Al-right," he said, slapping the bill down as he forced his speech to slur — not that the others would notice, two yards down the wrong hallway as they were. "I…wanna start doin' some proper winning now. What do you lot say to…to that!"

At least he wasn't addicted to the gambling too, right? He still disliked losing too much — not like his mother, bloody fiend for the rush. He was never willing to bet past the point of no return like some blokes. No, what he was addicted to was the way Sumi smiled when he told her he'd run out of money. All she did was roll her eyes — maybe try to hit him with a shoe or something — but then she'd laugh. He made sure his losses didn't get *too* out of hand, of course, but still, the woman really was a saint. And in those moments, her presence was all he craved. When you could tell there was no goddess in her head. Just herself, completely and utterly perfect.

He'd thought he was making good progress on keeping Sumi present. When they first reached the woods, she'd looked like that sage his ma used to play on stage — with flowing robes and brambles in her hair — constantly communing with Essomuai or disappearing on the wind. But that all seemed to change when they joined the caravan, at least for a time. But ever since the mountains… She didn't even look like a sage anymore, someone who at least had the peace of a woman in the wild. Now she looked…worn. Still the most beautiful woman on the bloody Continent, of course, but tired. Weight of the world on her shoulders.

But sometimes she laughed, as long as she was laughing at him. So here he was, gambling with a bunch of river rats and doing the little bit he could to keep her whole. He just had to hope these bloody goddesses were better gamblers than he was. In the end, they were sending a beautiful woman and two lost souls to undo a thousand years of war and misery. It was either the most ridiculous thing he'd ever heard, or it was pure genius. But either way, when the time came, he wouldn't let Sumi get caught holding the bag, no matter what it cost him. And when they were done, she would be truly free.

———

Vice Peer Pont'dulairn sat in his carriage, trying to get through his letters as they wove toward *The Elinark*, some new hoity-toity tea shop on the east side of the city. It usually wasn't best practice to meet in public, of course, but there were only a few weeks left on the crown stay, and he'd roll around in dirt if it meant getting the votes. This morning he was meeting Mikarae, vile man, a volatile mix of ego and desperation like every other hapless fool in Coerendul's camp. And not so different from his favorite tea shop, at that…

Unable to live in the city center, many of the newer peers seemed to be trying to colonize the eastern side of the city, building a new neighborhood along the bay from their own coin. That was all fine and well — it was good for commerce, after all — though it did smell a bit mercenary to him. Still, Mikarae wanting to meet in public sent an important signal — he could be bought. And meeting publicly, he almost certainly wanted word of this meeting to leak out, likely in hopes of a bidding war for his support. Coerendul couldn't come up with that kind of coin himself, of course, but with the Thorns circling about, anything was possible.

As much as it galled him, he'd agreed in principle to imposing a new river tax on the commerce coming out of Akashan. Mikarae's lands were on the far eastern border with Mesop, flanking the river, and the tax would be paid equally between him and Keltoarn. Still, it was a small price to pay with the wolves prowling about. It seemed every other man and woman on Elikora and Coerendul's list had been receiving non-stop visitors. Not to mention how busy Commissioner Kollenail had been of late…

Pont'dulairn couldn't have the man followed all the time, but he'd been meeting with the admirals more regularly, and then there was that sleight of hand in Ekosinar… He'd had it on good authority that Welaya was going to send a whole passel of navy ships to Ekosinar, all in the name of hunting Shapewalkers. Then, at the last minute, a half-dozen merchant vessels were attacked by pirates off the coast of Perous, just in time to give the navy a pretext for sailing east.

It seemed Kollenail was content to keep the Queen's mistakes from pushing the other Peers over the edge. It was sensible enough — the Thorns certainly wouldn't like the Peerage controlling the navy anymore than Welaya — but why meet with the admirals so often when the Queen could do that herself? It smelled like a barrel of fish, and not the fresh kind. Unfortunately, he needed to know more before he could act, which left him stumbling around in the dark like every other bloody fool in this fight.

His driver knocked on the roof to signal their arrival, and he looked out the window with a grimace. *The Elinark* was even uglier than he'd feared, shaped like a boat of all things and gilded like an emperor's funeral pyre. He sucked in a deep breath, closing his eyes. Compared to everything else he'd done, what was an hour of tea in the most unbearably gauche place on Wellonai? What he did was for the good of Berill, Welaya included. Hopefully, he'd make her see that someday, but first, he needed to guide their careening vessel through the shoals.

2

I understand your point, and I don't deny your royal prerogative, but let me just say this — every step toward the battle line makes the whole thing harder to unwind.

-Excerpt from the third letter Essolurei to Hiyelleom

—:—

Parimu looked out at Akashan from the edge of the ship. The town sprawled clear across the valley to where the mountains had put a stop to the rampant growth, though there were still plenty of little houses dotting the hillsides. Most of the structures were made of iron, sheet metal rooftops over quickly constructed frames. He had heard of the town, of course; everyone probably had. Still, it was baffling that a place could spring up out of nowhere like this. Even Berill had at least eight centuries under its belt. None of these buildings could be much older than he was himself, and yet, here it was.

It reminded him of a sailor, Neran, who'd retired the year before him, saying he was moving to Akashan to open an inn. It had been the talk of the ship, everyone dreaming of ways they could make their own fortune in the new factory towns. Even a few months earlier, everything about the place would have screamed progress to him, but that was before Sumi... Akashan was a non-place — within Mesop territory but managed by Berill — and was just another mark of the endless fight between the gods. Beyond the mountains, the Mesop grasslands seemed to stretch into forever, but here, the smoke belching from the Berillai factories told you who really controlled the land.

He'd known for a while now how wrong his thinking used to be, of course — he'd spent his whole life hunting his own kind. But ever since Sumi emerged from that cave, his mind was consumed by thoughts of the gods — if he could even say *gods* now that he knew the true goddess — thoughts that were somehow at once both reassuring and unsettling. On one hand, being children of Vilodai meant his people really did belong on the Continent — which didn't take away an ounce of his own guilt, of course, though there was hope enough in the fact. On the other hand, though, it left the three of them alone to undo the work of centuries and somehow seal a pact between the gods.

He had designed his entire life around his father's principle that one man's duty would be enough. He had never seen himself as more than a cog in the wheel, but he had found solace in that. But now, he'd been enlisted for a job far above his rank. If they failed, at least he would die serving his creator, but what came after? It actually made him sad to think there was no underworld where he'd at least hoped to see Jalicyne again. Though maybe she would be waiting for him, wherever she'd gone, whether it was in the fountain or that hallway of Erso's. He just couldn't believe she was gone. That much light couldn't disappear, it could only change shape, becoming something else...

He nearly jumped when Sumi put her hand on his shoulder. When had he closed his eyes? It wasn't reassuring, knowing how precious the woman he had to protect was...

"Relsenair," she said gently, smiling. "We're going into town now if you'd like to join us."

He felt his face mirroring her smile back at her, but he likely would have smiled anyway. This woman, even more than the gods, was who he followed, a leader worthy of any battle. She would likely never think it of herself, but no one had ever made him feel so...needed. She was a queen in shopkeeper's clothing, and as long as he served her, he knew they'd have a chance.

"I wouldn't mind seeing it, actually," he said. "But do you really think we'll be alright without disguises?"

"We'll have to be," she said, glancing toward town. "They have no reason to expect us on the river, and we can't very well change our forms in front of the crew. Let's just be glad the Berillai don't know how to spot keyholes, eh?"

"Right," he said, nodding slowly. "And you're sure about that? I didn't know what I was, but it doesn't mean no one does." He thought of Drekkles again. What had he known when he recruited Parimu, and how could he have known it?

Sumi let out a sigh, nodding.

"I have wondered about that," she said. "It's possible, but I guess part of me has to believe that if our government really had Shapewalkers in it — ones that knew what they were — we'd already live in a very different world."

"I suppose so," he said, nodding. "And you're…alright?" he added, gently touching her shoulder. She was still always smiling, of course, but ever since the cave, her worries had seemed to multiply, the bags under her eyes growing darker and her brow always furrowed. There would be plenty to worry about in Berill, but his first job was to keep her whole.

She chuckled at first, her usual response to anything, but then she sighed, turning against the railing and leaning into it with her arms folded.

"I'm sorry," she said. "I know you're both worried about me. I promise I'm alright, just having a little trouble sleeping."

He shook his head; there was nothing for her to apologize for, of course. Besides, he was an expert worrier himself. Like his mother used to say, he'd probably worry about the sun if it weren't stuck in the sky.

"Before the cave," she continued, "I could focus on reaching the fountain. I mean, a *real* goddess waiting for us, you know? I just wanted to see her, to reach her, but now… I guess I just feel small. I *believe*, but how am I supposed to do something so huge?"

He turned too, leaning against the railing, as he stared into the river on the other side of the boat. He wanted to add *something* supportive, but what? She was worried about being enough? She was a messenger of the gods who could hear the songs of Wellonai. If she wasn't anything, then what was he?

"You're not nothing to me," he finally said, forcing himself to smile.

"Thank you," she said, turning toward him with her own sad smile. "I don't want to seem ungrateful. Having you two, it's…everything."

She took a deep breath, raising her shoulders.

"It'll be alright," she said, "we'll figure it out together. Speaking of which, maybe you'd be willing to do me a favor?"

"Anything," he said, nodding eagerly.

"If you think you're ready," she said slowly, "I want to teach you to hear the songs. I think I'll sleep a lot better knowing these secrets aren't resting on a flimsy girl."

He wished he could reassure her, tell her she was anything but flimsy, but instead, he only gulped, his concern swept away by his own fear. It had taken him so long to figure out his own powers; could he really hear the songs, too? Erso's advice *had* helped with his Shapewalking, of course — talking to Jalicyne, facing his failures — but would this power work the same? Maybe all he needed was to open his heart a little wider, but how wide could it really go?

"I promise I'll try," he finally said. Whatever your commander's orders were, you had to see them through one way or another. But where to practice? He glanced around the boat, eyeing the sailors. Verasa's boat was a long way from the caravans.

"Maybe we…find somewhere on land to practice?" he asked.

"Yes," she said, grinning, "that would probably be best."

———

Sumi followed Erso and Parimu down the gangplank into Akashan. Captain Verasa — who clearly couldn't wait to be rid of them — was barking orders at a pair of men tying ropes, but a few of the sailors watched them go, calling after Erso to bring back whiskey. He chuckled, shaking his head as he waved them off. At least he was having his usual luck making friends, though that did make her wonder if he'd gambled away his pocket money again…

As small as Akashan was, it seemed to bustle like Berill, teeming with workers who were pouring out of the factories as the lunch hour was called. Many of them stopped to buy food from vendors lined up along the walls, though others simply perched on the curb, eating whatever they'd brought in their bags. There were so many different kinds of people; Amoriai, Ekosinarans, and even some Relimorans, all of them somehow drawn to a field in the middle of nowhere for work.

"Well," Erso said, pulling them to the side as he looked at his watch, "according to Lord Verasa, we have an hour. I'm not keen to test the man after Puyuln, but maybe we grab a bite to eat and look for somewhere to practice?"

"Sure," Sumi said, looking around. There seemed to be factories and houses in all directions, though they'd passed some empty fields back along the river. "You think there's anything quick?"

She eyed the row of vendors, doing a double-take as she caught sight of a man handing out grilled squid.

"Well," she said, grinning at Erso, "I know what I'm getting." She marched off, not stopping for Erso's groans when he realized what she was after. Apparently not one for squid either, Parimu followed Erso toward a pie stand before they all met back on the corner.

"It's like bloody Puyuln all over again," Erso said, shaking his head at her fanned-out squid skewers. "I still have nightmares." She took a hearty bite from one and smiled.

"You can take the girl out of Berill," she said with her mouth full, "but you can't take Berill out of the girl."

"I guess I knew the risks," he said, chuckling as he bit into his pie. "Bloody pirates, the lot of you."

She watched him for a moment longer after he looked away, searching his face. It seemed easier than ever to joke with him, but it was almost like they were acting, hiding the fact that something had changed. She'd noticed it before, that strange…distance, but it was worse after the mountains. There was something missing, some vital thing they'd lost when their eyes met. Perhaps he was just worried like they all were, but what if it was her? Would he tell her when he realized she wasn't enough? Would she even matter to him when their work was done?

"What'd you two get?" she asked Parimu, forcing herself to look away. There would be time enough for Erso when this was over…right?

"Lamb stew," Parimu said, "not bad for this far from home."

She shot Erso a look. Complaining about her squid when he hated lamb just as much!

"I know, I know," he said, raising a hand in surrender. "I was hoping for something better with all these outlanders, but the menu was Berillai all the way down."

She chuckled, jerking her head toward the east before leading them out of town. Akashan had seemed endless in the center, but it only took a few minutes of walking before they reached the end, the dirt road suddenly giving way to endless fields. They crossed over a short ditch and were back in the wild again.

Sumi took a deep breath, the smell of grass swimming through her head like perfume. The grass was already knee-high, eagerly drinking in the spring rain as it reached into the wind. At first, as she listened to songs, the fields sounded like an ocean, endless and divorced from time, the grass pouring out happy memories of their centuries waving in the wind. But there, in the middle of the song, were tiny, bloody blips. Battles had been fought here, the Berillai eager to capture this spot by the river so many hundreds of years ago.

She gritted her teeth, her mind unable to escape the sour notes of death, the Mesop laying down their lives for their home. It seemed no matter where she went she'd be reminded of that pain, the immensity of the task laid before them. But hearing them only made her feel more lost. If even those warriors were nothing but a blip in the memory of the grass, then what was she? She was less than that, nothing more than a speck, and she was meant to stand up to the Berillai?

Sumi led the others through the grass for a ways until they came to a clearing. There was a small rise in the ground where a tall sycamore tree stood by a tiny stream flowing north toward the river. The tree had wide branches for shade and thick roots, so they perched on them, finishing their lunch in silence while a chorus of birds sang from all directions. For a while, she focused only on her squid, letting her troubles slip away.

It could just be the lack of sleep, but lately, she'd felt hungrier than she ever had in her life. Though thinking of sleep only made her wish she could curl up under this tree for a bit… In addition to all her other worries, it felt like her dreams were getting more…visceral. Last night, she'd dreamt she was a mouse running through the grass. Even when she'd woken up, it had felt real, like a memory, but was it hers or Essomuai's?

Erso crunched through his pie in a matter of minutes and was the first to speak, breaking through her daze.

"Well," he said, standing as he brushed the crumbs from his coat, "seems like as good a place as any to make a fool of myself."

He faced her, bowing deeply.

"I am ready to learn from you, oh great Master of the Songs. But please have mercy, for I am but a fool, and there is only so much of your wisdom my meager vessel can hope to hold."

She threw one of her empty squid skewers at him, though he caught it, of course, flourishing it like a sword.

"Thank you both for trying," she said — more to Parimu than the court jester. "Just don't be too hard on yourselves. I have no way of knowing if this will work, and it won't be your fault if it doesn't."

Parimu nodded. "I'll give it everything I got, I promise you that," he said. "How do you propose we start?"

Sumi looked around the clearing, at the field, the tree, and the babbling stream. There were just so many songs! And how was she supposed to teach something so infinite, anyway? She hadn't even realized how much she was opening herself to Essomuai before she'd touched her, and now she'd been listening to the songs for months. It was like teaching someone to run before they'd taken their first step.

"Well," she finally said, bringing her attention back to the men and their own noisy songs, "they're all around us. Maybe we just pick one, and you both try to hear it?"

"Sure," Erso said, nodding. He looked around, his eyes narrowed as if the songs might pop out and say hello. "What about that?" he asked, pointing to a small patch of flowers between the roots of the tree. They were periwinkles, their tiny blue stars shining against a bed of green.

Their song was brief, a little circling melody telling the story of the flower's life so far — which wasn't long given how recently the snow had melted. Still, underneath it, there was a sort of bass line which held the profound memory of plants as if they'd sucked up their stories from the earth.

"Good idea," she said, nodding. "It's a simple one, but it should be good for practice."

They stared so intently at the periwinkles that if the stakes weren't so high, she probably would have laughed — two grown men staring daggers at a patch of flowers. Erso eventually slid his back against the tree trunk, leaning forward with his elbows on his knees.

"I'm sorry," Parimu finally said, shaking his head. "I hear absolutely nothing. A slight buzz from you two, keyholes, I guess?"

"That's it!" she exclaimed, bolting to her feet.

If they hadn't looked so different, she would have thought them twins the way they both cocked an eyebrow at her.

"The keyholes," she said quickly. "Those *are* the songs. If you learn to listen closely enough, they're all different, and the buzzing you hear is a melody for me."

She stood eagerly, stepping away from the roots of the tree and planting herself beside the periwinkles, a plan forming in her mind. It was like Grandpa's books on engineering; the easiest way to learn about a thing was to watch it change. A new shape would never completely change your song — you were still you, after all — but the rhythm would pick up fragments of the real song. Hopefully, that shift, however subtle, would help them hear the difference.

"Right," she said, her face flushing, "focus on my keyhole. But really listen to it, close your eyes and go to your pools. When you think you've got it, tell me, and I'll switch to something new."

They both dutifully shut their eyes. She didn't need to do that herself anymore, of course, but she still opened herself up to Essomuai, listening to her own song while she waited for the others. It was strange now to think there had been a time when she hadn't been able to hear her own keyhole. But now that she *could* hear it, it was strangely soothing to have her own memories set to music, like seeing home all lit up from the outside.

"Alright," Erso finally said, "I think I've got it." Both their eyes were shut tight, but Parimu nodded too.

"It's…subtle," Erso said, "but it feels different. It's not just a random buzz; it's lighter?"

"Good," she said, smiling. "Now, keep your eyes closed and pay attention."

She already had a form in mind, a rat, though whether it was from her dreams or Erso's general demeanor was anybody's guess. As she pictured it in her mind, Essomuai attuned its song, furtive and high-pitched, like a violin being plucked. She stepped through the door and reappeared on the grass as a rat.

For a moment, nothing happened. She stared up at the others, their faces pinched in focus. But then, Erso clutched his chest, laughing.

"Bless my bloody halls," he said, "I hear it!" He opened his eyes, his jaw dropping. "I *do* hear it, and it's a bloody rat of all things!" He laughed again, wiping away a tear. "Oh, those poor bastards, so much worry for just a little bit of cheese."

Sumi flashed back to herself, and he grabbed her, swinging her in a circle. For a moment, she felt the familiar bliss from Anushai when they'd first kissed, before the tension, before the gods.

"I can't believe I never realized," he said, putting her down. "And I swear I didn't peek. It's just like what I heard in your head in Puyuln, only…in *my* head now! A big rat appeared in my mind, and, I don't know, I guess I really could hear its keyhole!"

For a moment, his face fell, and he looked unbearably sad.

"You're amazing," he whispered. She was about to reply when Parimu stepped up, scratching the back of his head.

"You couldn't hear it?" she asked.

"I'm afraid not," he said, smiling sadly. "I felt…something, maybe a tiny ripple? But no song. Hopefully with some practice."

"I'm sure you'll get it," she said, smiling. "Give me a minute, and I'll think of another exercise."

He nodded, moving back to his spot on the tree as she turned away, tapping her chin. Parimu was a bit behind in his studies, of course, but he really did seem to be opening up to Essomuai. Perhaps if they tried a joint transformation? Erso had been able to hear the songs through her mind, and maybe if he had the chance, too…

She was staring off into the distance, thinking, when she felt a buzzing against her chest. She put a hand to her blouse and found a sort of…hum coming from Vilodai's stone. Why hadn't she felt that before? She pulled it out by its cord, holding it in her hand. It felt like the thrumming of the cavern when the quakes had stilled, the vibration in tune with her song. It felt almost like Vilodai's, only without any words, its rhythms deep and interconnecting, completely different from Essomuai's songs, and yet somehow familiar.

She lost herself in it, swimming through its vast texture, when she suddenly felt it again somewhere beneath her, an echo or a copy. Was it coming from the ground? She could hear the song of stones beneath her, of course, but this was deeper than that — as if the bedrock itself had picked up Vilodai's voice. And behind it, there was a...presence, as if the stone was coalescing around the rhythm, as if she could almost—

"So," Parimu asked from his seat on the root, "any suggestions?"

Sumi blinked her eyes open, starting at his voice. She squinted her eyes at Parimu, forgetting the vibration of the stone. But there had been an echo of that rhythm in front of her, too, hadn't there? Had it been coming from...Parimu?

"Sorry, what?" she asked, shaking her head to block out the strange sensation.

"Any thoughts on other exercises I should try?" Parimu asked.

"A few," she said, "though they might require a bit more time."

Parimu nodded, his mouth forming a thin line.

"But really, don't worry," she added quickly. "We're in uncharted territory, and this isn't necessarily something that's supposed to come easy. Besides, you have the most important job. Erso showed me it could be done, but you're gonna help me figure out how to teach it."

"Okay," he said, smiling sadly. "I'll follow your lead."

Speaking of Erso... He was still zipping around the field, apparently checking every single plant to see if it had a song. He dashed over to a large clump of dandelions and knelt down, turning his ear toward them.

"I can hear this one too!" he shouted, his eyes lighting up.

"I don't think you need your ears," Sumi said, raising an eyebrow.

"Shush," he said, waving her off. "I'm beyond your lessons now, Wise One."

While she was still busy rolling her eyes, he stood, holding his hat to his chest as he shook his head.

"That really is something," he said. "Thank you, Sumi."

"Don't thank me," she said, smiling, "they aren't my songs."

"Maybe," he said, "but no one else has sung them for me." He pulled out his watch, sucking in a breath as he glanced at it. "I could do this all day, but we'd better shove off if we still want a boat to ride."

She nodded, waving Parimu over. As he joined them, Erso clapped him on the back.

"Don't worry, mate," he said, "you'll get it just like you got the Shapewalking."

"You're right," Parimu said, "thanks to the two of you, of course."

Erso stepped ahead, taking the lead as he walked backward, facing the two of them.

"How about a smoke?" he asked. "See if we can't hear the leaves singing." He started to pack his pipe but stopped, his eyes widening. "Wait," he said slowly, meeting her eyes, "will I hear them…burning? Isn't that cruel? Heavenly halls, how do you eat?!"

She laughed. This was probably only the beginning of a very dramatic set of questions from Erso.

"Don't worry," she said, "it's not as bad as all that. By the time something's in a dish, it's singing a different song."

"Phew," Erso said, sticking his pipe in his mouth before taking Parimu's. "And here I thought I'd have to start eating squid."

"Don't you hate squid?" Parimu asked. "Why would a song make it better?"

"Well," Erso said, nodding sagely, "if I gotta hear a sad song, might as well be sung by something I loathe, eh?"

They continued on through the field and back toward town. She breathed in deeply, feeling lighter than before. She could still hear the faintest buzz from Vilodai's necklace, but that could wait. For now, walking in the sunshine, she felt at peace, and she didn't want to give that up just yet. Despite the battles of the past, the field was just a field again. Even if she was just a blip in history, she was alive today, and she had a song to sing. And whether they won or lost, she would sing every note.

3

Domelgaine called the meeting to order, seconded by myself. A quorum was accounted for, despite the chair's absence on business.

-Meeting Minutes of Dialasera's Rose
Umildinom 788 PD

—:—

Commissioner Kollenail left Admiral Heller's house, sighing as he walked to his carriage. *Just let the man be firm*, he thought. Heller seemed to have a stronger stomach than most, but you never did know if the vase would crack before you put it in the kiln. Still, the gods alone knew just how many chances they'd have to crack in the days ahead. After all, it wasn't every day you decided to kill your queen. It was still strange to even think the words — even stranger to have said them out loud to Heller after so many weeks of dancing around. But it was time, and he, for one, certainly had the mettle for the work.

Part of him still wished Welaya could live, of course. She had pushed for him to be Commissioner, practically placing the ring on his finger. Still, only a fool let sentiment keep him from cutting off a limb once the gangrene had gotten it. And in Welaya's case, she was far beyond reasoning with. Even after everything he'd done to smooth things over in Ekosinar, she was insisting on sending a full company into the city. As if a few hundred soldiers could just fan out and find a Shapewalker! Maybe the Ekosinarans could stomach a few Berillai ships off their coast — provided they were out of battery range — but they'd never take foreign soldiers wandering their streets.

He shook his head; there was no point getting upset about it all over again. He'd made his decision, and all he could do now was grit his teeth and see it through. He reached his carriage, nodding to Serkis as he opened the door. It was lucky having Serkis on a night like this, not to mention Belarin driving. They were his best — Shapewalkers both — and it just felt…safer being in their company, especially now that things were getting truly dangerous.

"Take us to Coerendul's," he said to Belarin as he climbed into the carriage. He pulled out his papers, eager to get through at least some of his letters before the next meeting. If he had thought there was a lot of work to do before, it would be a monsoon now with this operation to plan… Serkis climbed in after him, shutting the door as the carriage left the curb.

Kollenail leaned back, tapping his pen against the paper. He needed to shore up support from the Peers who were still on the fence. If only he had more of them to work with! Unfortunately, the way Pont'dulairn had drawn the battle lines, there were really only fourteen up for grabs. Coerendul was easy, at least — his family had only achieved the peerage in the 550s, and the man was always looking for the crown to pad his estates.

The others, however, presented a challenge. Elikora, for one, would never take a bribe, no matter how enticing. As bitterly as the man hated Pont'dulairn, his family was one of the original ten from the Isles, and he'd become an outright enemy if he realized what they were really planning. And without enough peerage support… Well, it would leave him with a lot more to do than one assassination. Still, at least he had the admirals, and as father used to say, if you were in for the sheep, you were in for the wool.

"Serkis," he said, "get me Apalimar's cipher. We need someone close to Elikora we can reason with."

Serkis nodded, digging through his leather folio. There were too many ciphers to keep straight these days, but at least his men could be relied upon. Not that they ever left enough information on the cipher to cause trouble if it were misplaced…

"Sir," Serkis said, handing him a long sheet of parchment. Kollenail nodded his thanks as he lined it up next to his letter. "Oh, by the way," Serkis added, "this came for you from Pont'dulairn."

Kollenail looked up just in time to see a knife darting toward his chest. He cried out, reaching with both hands to stop it, but he failed, the blade slipping in. His mind whirred, trying to calculate how much time he had. It wouldn't be long with a knife under the rib like that. He tried to fight back, but Serkis's hand was like a boulder as he pushed the knife in deeper. No…that couldn't be Serkis. His mind began to slow, growing cloudy with shock. Serkis…would never.

"Seems the Thorns won't have their way, after all," the man said. "Hard for them to bite without their head."

"There will be another," Kollenail spat, coughing on blood. He tried to speak again, but the words wouldn't come. His vision was swimming, the darkness creeping in. It would feel so good to sleep, so good to let go. He closed his eyes, and he was gone.

———

Pont'dulairn knocked on the roof of the carriage, signaling the deed was done. He maintained Serkis's form but took off his jacket, unbuttoning his shirt. There was still a great deal of work to do this night, and none of it would be easy. Disappearing someone as high up as Kollenail was no simple task, and it required perfect secrecy on top of everything else. It wouldn't do to have Welaya find out, even if it had saved her life...

He leaned forward, pulling out the knife and wiping it on the other man's coat. Then, he carefully took the ring from Kollenail's finger before folding the man's hands. No matter what the man had done, he'd surely thought he was a patriot, and he deserved what respect they could give him. Still, there was no room for regret. Welaya didn't deserve an end like that, and if Kollenail had succeeded, generations of work would have been undone in an instant. Shapewalkers may not be much safer under Welaya, but they'd be doubly cursed if Kollenail got his war with the Continent.

He sighed, rubbing his forehead. There was still plenty to do if they were going to avoid the worst. First, he'd need the admirals to back down. That shouldn't be impossible with Kollenail dead — Heller was an opportunist, after all, not a demagogue — but it would still take finesse to ensure the man didn't make the wrong choice. Still, that wouldn't be the end of it. As Kollenail said, there would always be another: another head of the Thorns, another man with dreams bigger than the boundaries of the kingdom.

His thoughts continued like that, winding about in circles until the carriage finally stopped. For a moment, it was silent, but then Terosan knocked on the roof three times, signaling they'd reached the forest without being seen. At least the first part had gone smoothly, then... Terosan stepped down from the box and opened the door, still wearing the driver's face as he nodded.

Pont'dulairn stepped out, Kollenail's folios firmly in hand. It was pitch black outside their circle of lamplight, the trees silent save for the far-off hooting of an owl. Terosan got to work, filling the carriage with kerosene. When he was done, he threw the lantern inside, the fuel-soaked cloth bursting into flame. They needed to leave, of course, on the off chance someone rode through the woods. But they both stood, watching for a moment as they gave Kollenail a brief witness to his end.

Pont'dulairn stared into the flames, promising himself he'd be done with all this someday. When Berill was redeemed, when he had his grand bargain, he'd move to his estates and never look back. He would see it through to the end, of course, but gods, was he tired. All the maneuvering, all the casual cruelty; on nights like this, the cost felt higher than he'd been hoping to pay. Still, the butcher would bloody well get paid. This wasn't the first man he'd killed, even if he sincerely hoped it'd be the last.

4

Need I remind you that your own great-grandfather led the second charge at that battle? You think him wrong for his choice?

-Excerpt from the second letter
Hiyelleom to Essolurei

—:—

Sumi lay awake on her cot on Verasa's ship, Vilodai's stone dangling above her face. She let it spin slowly on its leather cord, the sapphire center glowing like an eye in the dawn light shining through the porthole. Ever since she'd...*awoken* the stone in Akashan, she'd been trying to understand its strange rhythms. She put her thumb and forefinger over the center of the stone — it seemed to work best when she got close to the sapphire — and closed her eyes, letting the rhythms enter her mind again.

Perhaps she shouldn't be calling them rhythms? They did have a sort of cadence to them — albeit a seemingly random one — though she may just be trying to apply her understanding of Essomuai's songs to this strange new feeling. They could be related, of course — the goddesses were sisters, after all, though she really didn't know much beyond that.

On their own, the vibrations weren't so strange — the stone *was* a part of Vilodai — but those...echoes. The goddess had implied this stone wasn't a weapon, but had she been wrong? Not only had it harmonized with her pendant, but she'd heard it in the stone beneath her feet too. Now, the more she listened for the echoes, the more she seemed to sense them. The metal of the hull, the coal in the engine room, everything seemed to quietly thrum with it.

And then, when she truly lost herself in the vibrations, there almost seemed to be a...*presence* there, a whisper behind the rhythm, a whisper of something giant. She could almost feel the necklace trying to reach out to it — though, to what purpose, she couldn't be sure. Each time the vibrations were about to merge, she pulled her hand away, pushing it from her mind. Perhaps Vilodai was just trying to 'see' the world through the sapphire, but with a goddess that powerful, she couldn't risk unleashing her power without understanding it first.

Not that her sleepless nights were getting her any closer to figuring it out... For one, she could have sworn she'd heard the echo in Parimu that day, but why would that be? What did he have to do with the stones? She wanted to try it again, of course, but she couldn't exactly go into a trance with the crew around. At least they were leaving the ship today, though that would mean telling the others about this strange new phenomenon — and admitting she hadn't told them about her new necklace yet. She hadn't thought anything about it at first. What was one more goddess around your neck anyway? But if it *was* a weapon...

She opened her eyes, rolling herself over before scrambling off the cot. At least a few more days in the woods would give her time to think. Not that she had the time... They were deep into Berill now — in Manilara lands, only fifty leagues from the capital — and she still didn't have much of a plan for what they'd do when they got there. Verasa would be dropping them in Oeron, and they'd go the rest of the way on horse. But they'd be there soon, and she still felt far too small for the task she'd been given. So, for now, she'd keep lying awake, listening to a stone and praying they survived this mess.

————

When they finally made their way up the ship's stairs for the last time, Verasa was standing at the top with what could only possibly be described as a grin on his face.

"Well, lass," he said, "I thought we'd be leaving you down there in those mountains, but here we are. If you'll make the final payment, it looks like a...lovely day to be in Oeron."

Sumi looked over her shoulder, finding the village straddling the river. It was small, about two dozen buildings and a town square with sheep fields on either side.

"Well, thank you, Captain Verasa," she said, turning back and handing him the money. "I appreciate you getting us so far."

"A pleasure," he said, his smile growing wider as he stuffed the money into his pocket. "Next time you need a ride, you know who to ask for."

"Captain," Erso said, giving him a little salute. "Buy the boys something better than beans with that coin, eh?"

The captain's face turned slightly purple, but all he did was nod, turning back toward the wheel room without saying goodbye to Parimu.

"What was all that?" Parimu asked, stopping next to them with his saddle bags.

"Just trying to save the boys from another week of slop," Erso said, chuckling.

As they made their way down the gangplank, the sailors started to appear on deck, waving and whistling — with more than a few calling Erso names.

"Sure you don't want to stay?" she asked, chuckling. "Plenty for a rat to do on a boat."

"My dear," Erso said, "if I have to spend one more day on that bloody thing, I'll sink it."

"Assuming the captain doesn't strangle you first," Parimu said, grinning.

Apparently, though, Verasa was happy leaving them to their fate. As soon as the gangplank was pulled, the boat pulled back into the river, Verasa's shouts carrying to them over the water until the ship was gone around the next bend. They didn't wait much longer themselves, one of the dock workers pointing them in the right direction — not that there was much of the town to navigate. And after another hour and some painfully dear reserves from their purse, they were riding out of town again.

There was a small copse of woods behind the town, and they followed the narrow dirt road through them, returning easily to their single file from the north — Parimu in the front and Erso behind. For a moment, it felt strangely familiar, as if everything after Ekosinar had never happened. As Sumi closed her eyes, though, the songs seemed to tell a different story. These were Berillai woods, with Berillai stories, and her horse didn't even seem to know its true name. It made her miss Eto, though Porridge did seem like a sweet mare…

As they left the woods, the view opened up before them, the trees giving way to seemingly endless fields flanking the Eltimeir. It was more or less the same horizon they'd seen from the boat, but now that they'd climbed a ways, it felt like they could see for a hundred miles.

"Wow," Erso said behind her. "Even for Berill, that's not bad."

She turned, smiling at him, though her smile disappeared the moment she turned back, Parimu guiding them up the next hill. Erso still cared for her, that much was clear, but something *had* changed. His eyes would still watch her when they were together, their usual warmth still there, but he seemed…distant somehow. Could it be her? After all the time they'd spent together, was she not what he'd hoped? She was horribly inexperienced, and no woman looked her best on the road, but where to draw the line between his love and her insecurity?

She sighed, shaking her head. She had plenty of other things to worry about, of course. Still, unfortunately, love had a way of making itself loom large in your mind, even when the fate of the world hung in the balance. Like *The Borimol Plains*, when Vorseyai made the Duke stop his carriage in the middle of the street. Sometimes, when you were in danger of missing out on love, nothing else in the world seemed to matter.

They rode on, slipping into the familiar meditations of the road. Now that they were away from the crew, they could talk about anything, but they kept their silence. It was as if their bodies could feel Berill's presence on the horizon, pulling them in even as it threatened to destroy them. For every one of them, Berill would be the place where fate decided if they were enough, if the tools the gods had chosen were worthy of their task.

————

Eight hours later, they finally stopped in a meadow to set up camp before they lost the sun. As the others worked on dinner, Sumi sat on a hill nearby, a half-formed letter on her lap. She really ought to be helping, of course, but the others had shooed her away, convinced she had something important to do. Still, it wasn't as though they couldn't handle dinner without her… They'd bought a bag of beans from Verasa's cook and a bunch of potatoes from the horse trader. It wouldn't be much of a break from hot mush, but it wouldn't be hard to cook, either.

She sighed, looking around at the meadow as she listened to its song. It sounded almost like the ocean had in Ekosinar — practically endless and nearly divorced from time, the grass filled with happy memories of waving in the wind season after season with no regard for history. The grass rolled gently toward the river in waves of green that made winter seem like it had never occurred. Normally, this kind of view would do wonders for her spirits, but it only seemed to be a reminder of how quickly time was slipping through her fingers. Somewhere far to the north, past the horizon, the Isles of Dawn would be starting to thaw, the cycles of Itorunai's treaty pushing ahead while she struggled to undo all the pain they'd left behind.

She shook her head, forcing her eyes back onto the paper. She'd been trying to write this letter to Empress Hiyelleom for a week, and if she had no other way to be useful, she may as well finish this one thing. First and foremost, Hiyelleom needed to know about the Anushai stuck in Vilodai's Heart. She had tried to get them to leave when she came up from the cavern, but even with the shaking stilled, they were still afraid to leave their post. It would never be easy, leaving for a world they'd hardly recognize after thousands of years, but if their Empress sent for them…

Even more than that, though, she *needed* Hiyelleom. If they were going to have any chance at peace, the Berillai alone wouldn't be enough. There were two sides to this war, two memories of pain and hurt. But she wouldn't be easy to convince — reading Nela's letters a hundred times over proved that well enough — but she had to try. She knew too much now to simply leave things as they were. Part of her wanted to just tell the Empress to open Geomongiar's grave, to see for herself the contract with Itorunai. But in truth, even that paled in comparison to the truth Hiyelleom needed — the truth they *all* needed.

Human history could only tell you so much, could only repeat the patterns it had been taught. Until you saw Essomuai dancing among her plants at the beginning of time, how could you see another way? Until you broke the cycle of fear and greed, violence could never be anything but logical. And if you were trapped on the Isles of Dawn…well, the only rational thing to do was conquer the world in search of warmth. No, now they had to learn to really live, to dance amongst the flowers instead of trampling them. If only she could show them…

Parimu finished putting up the tents — far flimsier versions than the ones they'd left behind, unfortunately — and he came to the edge of camp, scanning the hillside for Sumi. When their eyes finally met, he waved, smiling shyly before he began to climb the hill. He stopped just a few feet beneath her, leaning against the slope with one knee.

"Still writing your letter?" he asked.

"Trying, yes," she said, pursing her lips. "At least there's a nice view."

"There certainly is that," he said, nodding as he turned around. He stood there for a while, looking out at the river with his hands on his hips. She looked with him, still hoping for some kind of inspiration. But dinner would be done soon, and she'd probably go another night without helping the others at all.

"I'm sorry I've just been sitting here while you two do all the work," she said, "…again. I'm just having a hard time deciding what to say. The first time I spoke to her, I sounded like a wool-headed child. But this time, I really have to convince her. I *need* her to see that things can be different."

"About that," Parimu said, turning back toward her. He paused, taking a deep breath. "There's something I should have told you...about Hiyelleom.

"It isn't something I kept from you deliberately. It's just that, well, after you saved me, everything from before didn't seem to matter anymore. Even seeing you read those old letters didn't seem to put the idea in my mind. But now that you have to write to her..." He shook his head quickly, waving one hand in the air. "Anyway, sorry. Just...be careful with her, Sumi. She was the one who told me where you'd be in Anushai. She gave you up to us to save herself."

Sumi blinked. She tried to speak, but her tongue suddenly felt glued to her mouth. Of course, it probably shouldn't have come as such a surprise. The empty street, Parimu waiting — none of that happened in a city like Anushai without help. But to think the woman from her letters, Nela's best friend, could do that to her... She forced in a deep breath of her own, stilling those thoughts.

It changed nothing. Hiyelleom had *always* been that person. In the letters or otherwise, she had always promised she would do anything to protect Anushai. If she had learned anything on her journey, it was to accept the fear that people felt, the fear that drove them to become darker versions of themselves. If she was ever going to convince anyone to imagine a different world, she had to look past that darkness. Suddenly, a line from Nela's letters came to mind, a quote from some poem she didn't recognize:

"*Daowel nelm duyel jiyen, kelshem bulneng siom duln,*" she muttered.

"Pardon?" Parimu asked, raising his eyebrows.

"Sorry," she said, finally finding the strength to smile. "Something from the letters. 'A sword can become sharper, but it can never become a shield.' Thank you for telling me. We do need to be careful, but we can't blame Hiyelleom either — no more than we can blame ourselves. If we want to change the world, we'll need her — we'll need everyone."

"Thank you," he said, nodding as he turned to go back to camp.

"Wait," she called out, "that's it?"

"Yep," he said, smiling. "You saw the good in me, after all, and I'm ten times worse than Hiyelleom could ever be. I don't know what's waiting for us in Berill, but it feels good to serve a Queen again."

She cocked an eyebrow, chuckling as she shook her head. He certainly had some funny ideas about her, but at least she'd been right about him. Even if he thought she had redeemed him, he'd done it himself. She returned to her notebook, suddenly seeming to find the words:

'Empress Mother,' she wrote, *'I hope this letter finds you well. I want to thank you for everything you taught me in Anushai. I hope you know there are no hard feelings for what you felt you had to do. Let's consider that water under the bridge. I hope you'll read this letter carefully. There's so much for me to tell you, but I suppose I'll just begin.'*

She continued to write on, the smell of the fire and the river wafting up to her. She was no queen, she was no one, really, but still, she wrote. She'd seen the truth, glanced behind the veil. And once you'd done that, how could you do anything but try to tell the others waiting on the other side?

5

There were three new members at today's meeting, each of them vetted by the committee. Unusual before the holiday, but they all took the oath, promising further attendance.

-Meeting Minutes of Dialasera's Rose
Shaffinom 793 PD

—:—

Queen Welaya walked into her war room, twice the usual number of guards flanking her. Normally this was one of her favorite places in the palace, a sacred space, and one she'd never had access to before her coronation. Today, though, it brought her no joy. With Kollenail missing and enemies on all sides, it was hard to feel anything but fear — and a seething rage fit to burn the world down.

There were a dozen men around the table, and they all stood as she entered, their eyes beady and nervous. These were not admirals, men accustomed to privilege and access. These were cautious men, and their desire for anonymity had only added to the headache of getting this meeting together. The governing council of the Thorns, a group that should not exist. Mostly, they had served at Kollenail's beck and call, but now that they had no master...

"Thorns," she said, taking her seat at the head of the table and waving away the punch her servant offered her. "You have had several days to gather information. Where is Kollenail?"

Gerinom spoke first, little weasel of a man. He was the slimiest of them all — and the most ambitious after Kollenail. It certainly wasn't lost on any of them that the events in this room could very well decide

Kollenail's successor if he had indeed defected…or worse.

"Your Majesty," he said, standing from his chair and bowing at the waist. "My unit covers the trains, and there has been no sign of him leaving via rail."

"Your Majesty," Keppinor said, raising a hand as if she were his bloody schoolmarm. "I cover the boats, and unfortunately, I have to report the same. Unless he left in a crate, there's no way he left Berill by sea."

"Your Majesty," started another of the twelve, but she held up a hand, silencing him.

"Enough with the 'your Majesty' business," she said sharply. "You'll all get the chance to backstab each other for Commissioner soon enough. Just the information, if you please."

"Your — uh…yes," Ferrinos began, "I was sent to search Kollenail's house. His coach was not there, and there was no sign he'd left. Luggage, clothes, everything was intact."

Welaya put her fingertips together, leaning on them as she stared into the table.

"What of his papers?" she finally asked.

"Usually kept on his person," Keppinor said. "They were ciphered and maintained by his lieutenant, Serkis, though no one has seen him either."

Welaya looked at the military map stretched across the table. The ships she'd been moving were far deeper in the Erril Basin than when the month had started. Perhaps the Anushai? Though, if they'd been able to suss out Kollenail's identity, she was in much greater danger than she'd thought. Still, it wasn't as if an assassination would be a challenge for those filthy creatures…

"Nesarin," she said, calling for her head guard. The man stepped up with no expression on his face. If only her spies could be so calm.

"Ma'am," he said, nodding, notably avoiding a 'your Majesty.'

"Triple your guards around the palace. I also want a company of archers brought up from the garrison. Set up the bow stands according to our emergency plans."

"My Queen," Gerinom said, "are you sure that's wise? Wouldn't it be best to avoid advertising weakness with the end of the royal stay at hand?"

She kept her eyes on the guard, her voice icy.

"Do you think me weak, Nesarin?" she asked.

"No, ma'am," he said simply.

"Good," she answered. "We'll use my father's birthday as an excuse. Drape the bow stands in navy and put the archers in full regalia. Just make sure they have plenty of arrows, silver tips."

"Ma'am," Nesarin said, stepping back to his place by the fire.

"Very well," she said, turning back to the Thorns before any more of them could pipe up. "Here are the rest of my orders."

———

Pont'dulairn hurried toward the kitchens, the lad who'd been sent to fetch him struggling to keep up. The man waiting for him was not the type of guest you kept waiting. Not that he wanted to walk so quickly he broke a sweat...but hopefully, he'd land somewhere in the middle between composed and harried. They turned down the last corridor where the marble gave way to rough flagstone. At the last moment, he stopped, turning toward the kitchen boy.

"Why don't you go check on the hens, see if they have any extra eggs?" He opened his free hand, revealing a silver coin, which the boy pocketed.

"Sir," was all he said, nodding as he turned back down the hall. Well, at least Pendulen knew how to train his staff. He pushed his way past the thick wooden door and into the kitchen. There, by the back door, was Admiral Heller, sitting on a stack of boxes with his cloak still around his shoulders.

"Admiral," Pont'dulairn said, extending his hand, "thank you for coming." He did a once-over of the kitchen, but it was empty save for Pendulen, who was carefully gutting a fish by the ovens. The chef looked up for a brief moment, nodding before he went back to pretending nothing existed but the fish. He may be the most expensive chef on the bloody Continent, but the man's discretion was legendary.

"Well," Heller said, blowing out his mustache, "I didn't really see much choice, but I'm here now, even if you shuttled me through the bloody kitchen like the help."

"Of course," Pont'dulairn said calmly. "And I'm sorry about the cloak and dagger. I just wanted to respect your desire for...privacy. Please, have a cup of tea, and we'll have you on your way. Perhaps a nice cut of fish for the wife?"

Heller continued to grumble as he led him to the servant's table where Pendulen had put out tea. Still, the man did seem strangely mollified. Was it the fish, then? Was it really so easy? No wonder Kollenail had such an easy time netting the man...

"So," Heller said as he picked up his mug, carefully sniffing it before risking a sip, "what have you really brought me here for? I have important business for the Queen, and I can't very well be seen tromping around Lournoy with the old fops for no reason."

Pont'dulairn kept the smile glued to his face, but it took a great deal of restraint not to laugh. Even with the weaker position had, the Admiral still behaved like the caged tiger he was, snapping at whatever strayed too close.

"Yes, well, I'll skip the niceties then," Pont'dulairn said. "I know what you were planning with Kollenail." The Admiral's eyes bulged — his letter had hinted he knew something important, but apparently, the man hadn't guessed as much. "Don't worry," he continued quickly, "I don't blame you. In fact, I understand your predicament entirely. However, it appears our interests have aligned, and I thought I'd offer you something better, seeing as how your plans have…changed."

Heller narrowed his eyes, his sword hand twitching on the table. Pont'dulairn sat completely still, his smile unchanging. After all, this was the man who'd single-handedly cut off Black Wave's head as a cadet. It wouldn't do to make any sudden movements.

"And what do you think you can offer me?" Heller asked. "It seems you're not too keen on navy blokes."

"Now, see, that's why I'm so glad you've come," Pont'dulairn said, carefully picking up the teapot and refilling Heller's cup. "I'm not sure how I picked up that reputation, but I believe the Berillai Navy is the gem of Wellonai. I simply want what we all want — more balance in how we deploy that incredible resource. You know the old saying, 'if a snake had no eyes, he'd just be leather and teeth.' I'm sure you've heard my bill contains a provision for a Minister of War? It'll be quite the responsibility, leading the army and the navy, but I'm sure we'll find someone with the right qualifications."

Heller leaned back on the stout wooden chair, folding his arms.

"So, you think I can be bought, then?" he asked.

"Nothing so crass as that," Pont'dulairn said, waving his hand in the air. "You see, Mr. Heller, this isn't about prestige but *stability*. With the right person guiding the ship, I feel confident we can strike the right balance. Take the situation in Ekosinar, for instance. I'd be fascinated to hear your ideas on how to keep that pot from boiling over."

Heller began to scratch his chin, nodding slowly.

"And you don't think it foolish to take those wonderful ships and put them in the hands of a bunch of gavel-swingers?"

"No more than the situation we currently have, my friend," Pont'dulairn answered. "You see, a man of character and experience — like yourself, for example — would still be at the helm of those ships. The only difference would be who calls the Writ of War. It could be in the single hand of the Queen, as it is now, or it could be in…steadier hands, say of nearly thirty Peers. Gavel-swingers, surely, but with the temperament to keep things at the right temperature."

"And let's say I do agree with you — in principle, at least. How am I to know you aren't going to throw me over the moment I stand down?"

"You've seen the bill yourself," Pont'dulairn said, shrugging. "Someone is going to have to be Minister of War. The only other candidate would be General Seridon, and I personally don't think he has the experience. Although, based on our conversations, he certainly does seem to at least agree with the concept of the bill."

A flash of hot fire crossed over Heller's eyes. He almost certainly wouldn't be choosing Seridon for Minister of War, but Heller didn't need to know that with how much he hated the man.

"Fine," Heller said, reaching out his hand. "Just do your part. There's only two weeks on the crown stay, and I won't have you sinking us when we can see the shore."

Pont'dulairn took his hand, shaking it firmly.

"Trust me," he said, "I'll hold up my end, Admiral. Just remember, we're similar creatures, you and I. I won't let the ship keel, no matter how rocky the seas get."

Pendulen stepped up to the table on cue, placing a large cut of sera fish in front of Heller with a bow.

"For you and your family, Sir," Pendulen said, turning back toward the ovens. Sera fish was notoriously expensive, and if the man's ambition wasn't enough to keep him in hand, his greed should be. Heller's wife would almost certainly have her servants crawling around the neighborhood with dinner invitations by morning. You didn't eat gold caviar because it tasted good after all; you ate it so your lessers could watch you.

"I'm sure we'll be in touch," Heller said, standing with the fish in hand.

"I dare say so…Minister."

Heller didn't turn back, but he seemed just a bit taller as he walked out. Pendulen returned, a bottle of whiskey in one hand and two glasses in the other.

"Either we're celebrating a job well done or drinking to our troubles," the chef said, "but my pa always said he couldn't find an occasion that didn't call for whiskey."

"No, I suppose not," Pont'dulairn said, chuckling as he accepted a glass. "To your father, and to hoping I know if I'm celebrating soon enough."

6

I could never get you to read the old philosophers, but Peyolguln had a phrase I find fitting here — 'drinking from the spring while neglecting the rain.'

-Excerpt from the fifth letter
Essolurei to Hiyelleom

—:—

Twenty-seven Years Ago

As painstaking as the Trierlien had been, Kemarin spent another two hours in the library, reading the treatise Elisal left behind. He read until the light began to fade from the windows, and a servant came to find him. His head had shot up when the door opened, hoping she'd decided to return, but it was only a footman, wearing the strange Miedaral livery, his olive green trousers stitched with tiny pink flowers.

"*Sohnleist* Pont'dulairn," the man said, bowing, "your presence is requested in the drawing room by the Lady Tauschfeig. She would be honored if you'd join them for drinks."

He nodded, closing the book and standing.

"Time to shear the sheep, eh?" he asked.

The man furrowed his brow, struggling to understand the Berillai phrase.

"Excuse me, *Sohnleist*, I'm afraid I'm not familiar with that saying."

"Pay the piper?" Kemarin asked, trying the Three Sisters version.

"Ah, yes," the man said, smiling and nodding. He was very gracious, though it was the kind of smile a servant would give anyone, no matter how foolish the things they were saying.

"If you'd follow me, sir," the man said.

"With pleasure," Kemarin said, gesturing toward the door.

He struck up a conversation as they walked, trying to glean what he could from the man. The servant — Gelheim or some other hard-to-pronounce thing — was a first footman, and while he didn't reveal anything that he hadn't been force-fed by his mistress, he gave a much better impression than any briefing book could. Lady Tauschfeig was the one to watch out for, obviously. Her husband's name may be the one officially going on the treaty, but she was the true organizer behind their visit. More importantly, she had two supposedly eligible daughters, and avoiding being muscled into marrying either of them without giving offense would likely be his greatest challenge.

After traveling along another series of nearly endless hallways, they finally reached the drawing room. Like so many others in the palace, it had another large statue outside the door, though it wasn't quite so primal as the lion outside the library. He liked it more, actually, if only because it raised far more questions than it answered. It was of a large turtle, its fins splayed into the air with a fish riding on its back as it played a flute. It was entirely strange, which was far preferable to the hunter's bravado of every other statue they'd passed.

"*Sohnleist* Kemarin Pont'dulairn," the footman announced, bowing and standing to the side so he could enter. Kemarin stepped through to find a good portion of the party already assembled. The room was much like the library, only without the books. Instead of shelves, there were twice as many chairs and settees, and the walls were lined with great mounted beasts from generations of what the locals no doubt thought were legendary hunts. There was a roaring hearth at one end of the room, with some two dozen men and women divided into little groups throughout.

He finally spotted Elisal by the fire, talking quietly with what must be two of her cousins, in a group with no men and no foreigners — and no drinks besides. He had half a mind to walk right over to her, but almost as soon as he was through the doorway, a thickly accented voice rose above the din of the party.

"There you are," Lady Tauschfeig said. She was on a settee in the middle of the room, flanked by two girls and surrounded by standing men. "You simply must join us, Kemarin. I have been raving about you to my daughters."

He raised an eyebrow at hearing his given name, but he smiled all the same. As a queen, she technically didn't have to use his title, even if the reality of their...situations dictated otherwise. What she had to rave about, however, was another question. The two younger women, presumably her daughters, Estairin and Lilara, sat up, turning their heads coquettishly as they smiled.

"Thank you for including me," he said. "And my apologies for my tardiness. I was delayed in the library."

He shot a glance at Elisal and found her looking at him, though she stared hard into the fire the moment their eyes met. His smile grew as he turned back toward his host.

"Not at all," the queen said, gesturing to the settee. He sat by her younger daughter and was promptly given a cigar by one of the men — a duke if he had done his homework correctly. "Estairin has been practicing her Berillai most religiously," she added, "you simply must let her tell you one of the jokes she's learned."

The evening went on like that, a mind-numbing deluge of meaningless drivel. He could manage it well enough — he'd spent a lifetime in parlors just like this, after all — and he could play their little game with only half a mind, even if the language and decor had changed. After moving to the dining room for a tiresome pheasant dinner, they were finally released from their bonds into the freedom of the gardens. This, at least, let them breathe a bit, getting out of the palace and into that 'famous' Miedaral mountain air.

The garden twinkled with lantern light as music floated on the air, the crickets in the bushes chirping alongside a brass band. It was a military band, apparently — the players resplendent in medals — though in which conflicts they'd been won was questionable… There was a bit of waltzing to the oom-pah-pah, though, thankfully, the Tauschfeigs were occupied with the diplomats under their tea tent, leaving him free to wander across the grass.

A few people tried to flag him down, but he simply smiled, acting as if he were on his way to the dancing. Finally, he reached the other end of the garden. Elisal was there, standing with one of her cousins and the youngest peer in the group, Emdirion. They'd grown up together, their fathers already allies, and their lands not far apart. With luck, when they both took their titles, they'd pass some bills together.

"Pont'dulairn," he said, nodding over his raised glass. By the flush on his face, it likely wasn't his first drink. At least it seemed to be working for him… He was also of marrying age, and his arm looked far from uncomfortable around Elisal's cousin. His parents supposedly had plans to marry him to some shipping mogul's daughter from Ekosinar but judging by the rank of the princess he'd chosen, his mother wouldn't be displeased.

"Emdirion," Kemarin said in return. He stationed himself carefully between his friend and Elisal. She stood with her arms folded, looking out at the dance floor. "You always liked dancing," he said to his friend. "Think your fetching friend could teach you the steps?"

The princess tilted her head back and laughed, answering for him.

"I don't think he could walk," she said, "let alone step. My shoulder is merely here for balance."

She laughed again but smiled warmly, apparently as eager to escape her parents as they were to be rid of her. The Three Sisters was overflowing with princesses, every one of them for sale in exchange for protection. At least with Emdirion, she'd be in good hands. He was a bit wanting in the brains department, but he was a good man, and you certainly couldn't say as much for every other bachelor from Berill.

"I'll show you dancing," Emdirion said with a humph, taking his hand off her shoulder and dragging her toward the dance floor.

"Well," Kemarin said, glancing over at Elisal. "That was easier than I'd hoped. That was the most dreadful dinner, wasn't it?"

She said nothing, simply humming the barest trace of an assent, her eyes never leaving the dance floor. Perhaps he'd gotten more under her skin than he'd thought…

"Since we're friends now," he added, stepping closer and gently touching her elbow, "why don't you teach me how to waltz, too?"

She jerked her arm out of his hand and whirled around, sticking a slender, dagger-like finger in his face.

"I am not your friend," she spat, her accent once again thick with anger, "and I cannot be bought like one of your…your trinkets. You may have surprised me in the library, but I'm no fool. Just because your papa built a train doesn't mean you own the world, little prince."

She stopped for a moment, her chest heaving. She was about to say something else, but then she spun on her heel, storming back toward the palace. He stood there for a moment, his face like a furnace as his jaw hung open. He looked quickly around the garden, but thankfully, everyone was still busy with their dancing. He raised his drink to his lips, taking a large swallow.

Well, perhaps he had miscalculated slightly, but he *had* gotten under her skin…right? Before he could be seen bumbling like a fool, he wandered toward Lady Tauschfeig, the punishment of that woman's company somehow more inviting than this strange feeling. His mind slowly churned over her words, burning far more than the slap she probably wished she'd planted on his face.

7

Peace is not a destination, but a state. What is Anushai if we fail to stand for that? Do you think the ancients were just trying to cover our eyes with flowers?

**-Excerpt from the eighth letter
Essolurei to Hiyelleom**

—:—

Sumi sat on a log in front of a fire, finally finished setting up camp for the night. After two days on the road, they were in the forests south of Berill, only ten or fifteen miles from the city. She was tempted to fly into town as an owl just to get a glimpse of home. She could still picture it; the stones, the garden, all of it tantalizingly close. Unfortunately, though, every step toward town brought them closer to danger, too. They were all wearing their disguises during the day, only taking their true forms at night. In the morning, they'd ride for Parimu's, staying as far from the city center as they could while they figured out the rest of their plan.

She sighed, looking back at her notebook. She would love to think about the terrace all night, homesick as she was, but she had a good bit of work left if she was going to take her plans from harebrained to actionable. She'd been drawing wobbly little sketches from her horse during the day, and ideas were finally starting to take shape. Her mind kept circling around the old stories from Anushai when the elders had joined together, turning Elomikarus back with the shapes they wove in the sky. She needed something similar, something incredible. Not to scare the Berillai but to show them how beautiful Shapewalking could

47

be.

Unfortunately, for that, they'd need more Shapewalkers, and there was no telling how many they'd be able to find in Berill. It wasn't like she could take an ad out in the paper. Still, it was a better plan than she'd had before, even if she'd still only managed to teach the songs to Erso. Berill was her home, and after risking so much to return, she had to believe the answer would be waiting for her there. Whether they liked it or not, her people were tied to this land now and the magic that came with it.

She went back to her sketches. She wasn't much of an artist, of course, but she at least needed a vision if she was going to be recruiting others to her cause. She had gone back to the very beginning, to the first shapes she'd ever written down, and she was drawing them in a row, like a parade marching across the page. Boats, horses, even a rainbow — these things had spoken to her heart when her powers were new, and hopefully, they'd be enough to inspire someone else.

She put the finishing touches on a pack of horses' manes before glancing up at Erso. He was kneeling over the cooking pot, stirring the beans rhythmically as he made a drumbeat sound under his breath.

"*Bum - ba - ba - Bum - ba - ba,*" he went over and over, nodding his head to one of the many songs around them.

"And what's that one?" she asked, cocking an eyebrow.

"Why, the cooking pot, of course," Erso said, looking up. "Let me do it properly for you."

He dropped his spoon and began singing more loudly, putting his feet wide apart and stomping around to the beat as if he were a giant beast. "*BUM-BA-BA-BUM-BA-BA,*" he chanted.

Sumi chuckled, looking over to the pot itself. She narrowed her eyes, focusing on its song. He wasn't wrong, per se — the iron in the pot had a metallic rhythm to it, thick and resonant. He'd just…dramatized it about a hundredfold. She smiled, marking the rhythm in her notebook. She'd been stuck on seeing the songs as this massive, somber thing, but with Erso, it was just another chance to laugh, a chance to show the world how wonderful life could be.

He finally stopped dancing, looking to her for approval, and she carefully dropped her smile, rolling her eyes. She may love his antics, but it was best not to give him too much leeway — he'd get lazy otherwise.

"Well, la-dee-da," he said, dismissing her with a wave of his hand as he knelt back down to stir the pot. "Complain if you want, but it's a much better song than the one the bloody beans are singing. Disgusting little bastards."

She chuckled quietly, shaking her head as she went back to her notebook. She heard a cracking twig in the woods, and her eyes shot up, finding Parimu returning from his loop through the woods. The closer they got to Berill, the more determined he was to keep watch. He nodded when their eyes met, crossing the campsite and taking the spot next to her on her log.

"Anything?" she asked.

"Nothing," Parimu said, wearing his father's face. "Well, actually," he said, pointing to the west, "there was a burned-out carriage a mile or two that way, but I stayed clear of it. We'll be keeping east of it, straight through the woods, so hopefully, whoever left it there won't give us any trouble."

"How about you?" Parimu asked. "I'm excited to see what you've come up with."

She pulled back her pencil, handing him the notebook. She'd been embarrassed to share her sketches at first, but he was always suspiciously kind with his praise. Still, it was the least she could do for the man who was willing to follow her with barely a plan to guide them. His eyes moved quickly over the page, darting back and forth, even a silly sketch bringing out the policeman in him.

"This is good," he said, nodding as he handed back the notebook. "I'd certainly want to see something like that as a kid. We never had any parades in Emillon, let alone a bunch of Shapewalkers."

"Thanks," she said, smiling, "it's all thanks to you I've made it this far."

She'd told him the basics of her plan the night before, and he'd just started calling it a parade. They'd all seized on the word then. They weren't going to war, and they weren't trying to scare anyone, so why not a parade? The stories in Berill treated them as monsters, but that lie would be impossible to maintain if they could make the children laugh, dancing their forms in the street before thousands of witnesses.

Erso banged on the metal pot with his long spoon, pushing himself up from the ground.

"Beans are done, I guess," he said, shrugging.

"You guess?" Sumi asked.

"I mean, they're beans…" he said, cocking his head at her. "We can leave them on the fire if you want, but I suggest eating them before they become any more bean-like."

She rolled her eyes again, the motion becoming well-practiced as she pushed herself off the log.

"What do you say, Relsenair?" she asked. "How would our chef fare in the navy?"

"Better than you think, actually," he said, chuckling. "On my second ship, our cook — Old Jurin, they called him — heard one of the officers complaining about the food and put a roach in his stew. Laughed all the way to the brig."

"See?" Erso said, spreading his hands over the pot as if it were filled with gold. "I present to you roach-free beans, the culinary talk of the Continent."

They went on like that until the beans became tea, and the forest turned dark, until the only thing visible was the glow of the fire and the smoke from the men's pipes. Sumi's eyes were bleary with exhaustion, but she forced herself to stay awake. Even if she managed to fall asleep now, she'd be up half the night anyway, her thoughts bouncing between Erso and Berill. She watched him from across the fire, losing herself in his face as he laughed. No, it was time she dealt with at least one of her problems.

Finally, Parimu stretched, stifling a yawn as he stood from the log.

"Well," he said, "if I'm taking the second guard shift, I'd better get a few hours in." He nodded at Erso. "Wake me whenever you're ready."

With that, he walked toward his tent, barely ruffling the flaps as he slipped inside. Sumi stared into the fire for a few more minutes, trying to give Parimu time to fall asleep, but it was Erso who spoke first.

"You might want to get some sleep yourself," he said, his smile warm despite its distance. "There's too much on your plate to be whittling away the hours on guard duty with me."

"Actually," she said, her voice catching in her throat, "I think we should talk." She looked back at Parimu's tent. None of the shadows on the canvas moved, but she still worried her voice would carry. "Would you mind going over there?" she asked, pointing. "Just to the edge of the clearing."

"Alright," he said quietly, no joke, no smile.

Sumi nodded, leading Erso into the darkness. He followed a few feet behind her, not reaching for her hand as he had so often done before. Finally, she turned, folding her arms with her back to the forest. A few months ago, the dark trees would have sent shivers up her spine, but now it seemed…ordinary. Besides, she knew the songs well enough now to hear anything dangerous while it was still miles off. What really scared her was right in front of her. Still, after so many nights thinking the same thoughts, she was ready to begin.

"Listen," she said, "I know things have been different since Vilodai's Heart. I don't really know anything about love, but I know you." She took a breath, memories of Erso's song drifting through her mind. "I know there's people you had to leave behind, and if you want to leave me, I don't blame you. I just…want you to be happy, and I know I'm not much of a catch. I promise I'll always be your friend, but where we're going, we need our minds to be clear." She met his eyes in the darkness, his face barely visible in the distant glow of the fire. "Please say something."

He chuckled, pinching his forehead, and for the first time, she felt a flash of anger. Did everything have to be a bloody joke with him?! But then, he reached out, grabbing her hand and squeezing it, the warmth of his palm soaking into her fingers.

"Sumi, you're the best damned catch that ever came out the bloody sea, alright? No matter what happens to me — to us — don't *ever* let yourself think like that." He let go of her hand for a moment, taking off his hat and running a hand through his hair as he sighed. "I'm sorry I've been a bit…off-kilter. I think this goddess business is a bit much for me, to be honest, but don't let it worry you. I'm with you in this, no matter what happens. I promise I will never love anyone as much as I love you. But for now, just stay focused on what's ahead; everything else can wait."

Her heart did a somersault to hear he loved her, though it didn't still the worry in her mind, not like it would have before.

"I love you, too," she said, "and if you don't know that, you're a bigger fool than I thought." She earned a grin from him at that, at least. "But what does 'everything else' mean? What aren't you telling me?"

He took her hand again, staring into her eyes.

"It can wait," he said firmly. He took a breath, breaking the spell. Still, he looked back at her with…sadness in his eyes.

"You've seen my life; you know the ghosts chasing me. You know they aren't new, either. But I guess now that you've opened the creaky old door to my heart, they're looking to escape. But that isn't your burden. I'm here now, no matter what. We have wider halls to walk, and I can lick my wounds after we're done."

Looking at him then, she knew it was the truth.

"Alright," she said. "Take as much time as you need. But if this all becomes too much for you, promise you'll tell me. Relsenair and I will figure something out."

"I'm here 'til the end," he said without hesitation. "Even if it ends on the docks, I'll be by your side."

He touched her shoulder, cocking his head toward the fire.

"Come on," he said. He took her hand, leading her back. It was warm like it always was, though it felt stiff as if his fingers were hesitating. She had a sinking feeling of what would come after their work was done, but for now, what they had was enough. She looked out at the woods, listening to the voices in the darkness and wishing creatures in the night were all they had to fear.

8

The record stands at eight votes for and nine votes against, though the Chairman's votes allowed for his side to prevail.

-Meeting Minutes of Dialasera's Rose
Oruminom 782 PD

—:—

Parimu led the line of horses, picking his way through the underbrush toward Berill. It was hard to tell exactly how far they were, riding away from the road, but they had to be getting close. They'd ridden out of camp around sunup, and it was already well into the afternoon — or at least it should be by his watch. It had been raining steadily all day, and the sky peeking through the canopy didn't seem any brighter for the sun's effort.

Still, it was probably for the best. It was harder to spot trouble coming in the rain, sure, but with a party their size, it would make them just as invisible. Not that there was anything for someone else to see… He ran his hand through his father's beard, pulling the water off of it. Odd how normal it seemed now to spend a whole day as his father. And with Erso's advice, he barely even felt the strain of Shapewalking anymore. So, at least he was doing something right…

He shook his head, tightening his grip on the reins. It still bothered him that he couldn't hear the songs, of course, but he pushed his worry to the back of his mind. He had to focus on getting them home safely. Besides, Sumi would figure it out; she always did.

He pulled out his map again, holding it against his saddle with one hand as he blocked the rain with the other. Once they came out of the woods, they'd trace the city wall to the west, picking up Seris Road. There shouldn't be anyone out there — just a bunch of old sheep farms — and from there, it was just another hour of riding to his house.

Now that was a strange thought… He'd never once had guests stay there, but they'd agreed it was the safer option compared to Sumi's cottage — not to mention the Thorns likely watching at the inns. Still, would the others find his place comfortable? Would the beds be alright? It was a silly thought compared to everything against them, but he couldn't help but wonder. The place had been bought for Jalicyne, and with so many years with no purpose, it was a lot to take up such a sacred task…

They came up to a short rise in the forest, and Parimu nudged his horse's sides, urging him up the slope. As he crested it, the trees suddenly stopped, and he finally saw Berill stretching out below him as it hugged the bay. His breath came up short, and he reined in his horse, suddenly incapable of doing anything but staring. It felt like it had been years instead of months. In a strange way, he almost hadn't expected it to still be there, his home somehow shifting as seismically as his own life. But here it was, smoke rising from chimneys like lungs that had never stopped breathing. Even the sun seemed to know what this moment meant, finally cracking through the dark underbelly of the clouds as it lanced a few golden rays down through the misty rain.

The cracking of branches broke him from his reverie, and he turned just as Sumi's horse pushed its way through the tree line.

"What's happened?" she asked. "Why did you— Oh…wow."

She was wearing her friend Seriai's face, but her jaw nearly hit the saddle.

"I know," he said, smiling. "Makes you want to pinch yourself."

Erso rode up a moment later, holstering his rifle.

"Well," he said, his face grim despite his smile, "welcome home."

Parimu nodded, his face suddenly hot with shame. While he was staring like a child, Erso was considering a maw where Shapewalkers were swallowed whole. And for most of his life, it had been Parimu himself doing the swallowing. It was a wonder Erso could stand him at all, could go a day without spitting in his face. And still, he smiled… He took a deep breath, shaking his head. He refused to wallow in it any longer. If Erso had taught him anything, it was to live into the man he wanted to be. Every day he lived was another opportunity, not to make it 'right' — nothing could ever take away what he'd done — but to turn around, to choose a different way.

"We'd better go," Sumi said quietly, breaking through his thoughts.

He smiled at her, picking up his reins. He met Erso's eyes, nodding as he turned his horse toward the west. It wasn't much, but hopefully, it conveyed just a fraction of care, of…appreciation for Erso coming back to this place he could never love. Perhaps he wouldn't have seen it before with all the cursing and drinking, but Erso really was an astoundingly good man, a man worthy of Sumi. Not that he had any right to give opinions about her affairs. But strangely, when he didn't feel like her soldier, he almost felt like her uncle, and he wanted to see her happy. And that thought alone was enough to make him want to laugh, to jump from his saddle and dance. He had a family again, and he would protect them, no matter what it cost.

He rode on, bouncing in the saddle on the steep hillside, but he still found himself looking over his shoulder every so often, meeting Sumi's eyes and smiling. This wasn't the place he'd left behind, or maybe he wasn't the same person who had left it, but it felt good to come home all the same.

———

Erso followed the others down a street on the west side of Berill, their horses already sold to a nearby stable. Sacred halls, but it was strange being back in a city! Not to mention good old bloodthirsty Berill… He found himself staring almost as often as Sumi and Parimu were. It was a good thing they hadn't started downtown. He'd probably walk right in front of a trolley, his eyes wide as a woodpecker's! Lucky for them, though, Parimu's neighborhood was somewhere in between the city and the country. The roads were still paved with cobblestones, and there were street lamps and all that, but every house was set back behind a large garden, and some of the cottages weren't even visible behind tall hedgerows.

Halls knew they could use the privacy. Not to give the bastards too much credit, but after the Thorns found them in Ekosinar, there was no telling what they were capable of. Besides, what was that old saying again — 'Best not assume the lion wears dentures?' Anyway, it was better than Sumi's terrace, where the neighbors were practically breathing on each other, everyone probably just trying to lean over their garden to get a look at Sumi's beautiful face.

He glanced at her. She was still in disguise, but even after so long in the woods, she still managed to look like she'd just gotten out of the bath. Her eyes were bright, darting around as they soaked up Parimu's neighborhood like Peritrine's palace. He sighed. It was going to be impossible to leave this woman behind. But somehow, that made it feel even more like the right decision. Whenever he'd left women in the past, he'd had the same nugget of fear, the need to escape overwhelming anything he felt for them. Now, all he felt was loss, knowing he'd be giving up the single greatest gift the gods had ever bestowed on his wretched little life.

He sighed harder, and Sumi glanced at him, worry already creasing the sides of her eyes. He forced a smile on his face, waving her off. Sacred halls, this would be the hardest thing he'd ever done, playing a role he was no longer worthy of. Still, all he had to do was hold out a little while longer, just long enough for Sumi to seize her victory, for the goddesses to be done with her so she could move on to a better life, a life without him weighing her down.

They made one last turn, entering a narrow lane that dead-ended on the shoreline. About halfway down, Parimu pointed out a tall clapboard captain's lodge. It looked oddly like his parents' house, actually, so much so he laughed out loud. He'd always prided himself on having a well-developed sense of irony, of course, but this felt a bit much, even for him. A baby couldn't even be born in the time it had taken him to change from being the detective's prey to being his houseguest. Still, it wasn't a pub, and it wasn't a leaky tent, so he couldn't blame himself for being excited.

Parimu unlatched the front gate, letting them into the garden. The beds were grown over with spring weeds, but the lawn still had a nice shape to it, and the house looked like it had been repainted every summer.

"Sorry about the mess," Parimu said, guiding them to the porch. "I suppose I thought I'd be back sooner."

"Believe me, mate," Erso said, clapping him on the back, "I'm plenty glad you didn't make it in time to plant flowers."

Parimu grinned nervously, digging in his pocket for the key.

"How'd you come across this place anyway?" he asked, leaning his back against the house so he could watch the street.

"It's a pensioner's cottage," Parimu said, finally unlocking the door. "I applied just before leaving the navy, thought I'd live here with Jalicyne, I guess."

"Not bad," Erso said, still looking around the garden. He noticed a faucet on the side of the house without a pump on it. "Do you not have to pump your water here either?"

Parimu swung open the front door before turning to look.

"Oh, no," he said, pointing to the west, "there's one of those windmill pumping stations a few blocks over."

Well, the bloody Berillai did think of everything, after all. If Sumi could get them to stop being so bloodthirsty, maybe it wouldn't be such a bad place to live. Sumi was staring at the faucet, too, tilting her head in surprise, so at least the terrace folks were still like everybody else.

They followed Parimu through the door and into a narrow hallway. There was a staircase to the left and a sitting room on the right before the hallway ran back to the kitchen. Large windows showed a decent-sized garden behind the house, and beyond that, you could actually catch a glimpse of the bay.

"So," Parimu said, turning to face them as he dropped his luggage. "Unfortunately, there's only two bedrooms. Sumi, you can take mine on this side of the house; it has a bigger bed." He turned to Erso, wringing his hands together. "I figured you and I could bunk up in the other," he said, "at least it's better than sleeping on the ground."

Erso laughed, smacking Parimu on the shoulder.

"Mate," he said, "I may be learning to love you like a brother, but I'll be just fine in the sitting room."

"Oh, well, alright, sure," Parimu said, finally smiling himself. "I'll get you some blankets, then. Now, how about I get some tea started while you two make yourselves at home?"

They all scrambled about the house, each person going to their respective corners. It always felt strange to unpack after a long time on the road, his hands seeming to balk at spreading his items out of easy reach, any form of permanence too much to bear. Still, he forced himself to do it, organizing his things into neat little rows alongside the settee. He wasn't running anymore, and so long as Sumi stayed in this house, so would he.

As he finished laying out the last of his things — the tableau surprisingly cozy — Erso heard a creak on the stairs and turned to find Sumi waiting for him.

"How about a cup of tea then?" she asked, smiling.

She was still in her disguise, but as he followed her to the kitchen, he listened to her song, her true form bubbling up from underneath. It was so much more…*expressive* than the old keyholes. He'd spent his whole life getting used to those, sure, but it was a welcome change. It was like smelling someone's perfume, knowing they were just around the corner.

They walked into the kitchen, finding Parimu fiddling with a pot on the stove. Unsurprisingly, even the kitchen was beautiful, filled with white tile that sparkled in the sunlight from the garden. Maybe he should've been a bloody Berillai sailor… The room was big enough for a family of twelve back in Amoriai, and there was a countertop dividing the eating and cooking areas, the whole thing lined with pub stools. He sat on one, leaning his elbows on the counter. It would be a hell of a place to sip an ale, looking over the garden like that. Or, you know, whatever wholesome folks did.

Sumi sat beside him, running her hand through Seriai's short hair.

"I guess," she said, "as long as we're alone, we might as well be ourselves, right?"

Erso looked out at the garden. The hedges were thick, and there was absolutely no view of the east-facing street beyond. He nodded, glowing as he returned to his own form. When he opened his eyes, the others had done the same, their usual trio reappearing out of thin air. He turned to Sumi, his heart wrenching just a bit at finding her as beautiful as ever.

"Well," Erso said, yet again forcing a smile onto his face, "I guess we made it this far, boss. What's next?"

"Right," she said, reaching in her pocket for her notebook. The kettle started to whistle, and Parimu poured the tea, setting some mugs in front of them along with some stodgy-looking biscuits. "This is the part that might take some time, but I guess so long as no one recognizes us, we aren't really in any rush. What we need is to find more Shapewalkers. Any ideas?"

"Not really," Parimu said, leaning against the other side of the counter and running his hand over his chin as if his father's beard were still there. "It bothers me how little I knew as the DoR. I guess Drekkles must have known, but he never told me, which, of course, I'm glad for, really. Still, there must have been plenty — like your Nela — we left alone. As much as I hate to admit it, we never really patrolled in the…respectable parts of town."

"I agree," Erso said. "Didn't see a lot of stray keyholes before. I always assumed whatever mu'amashdar there were knew well enough to stay hidden. But I never thought about it much since I was here to train the youngers. Suppose we just have a look about?"

Sumi hummed in agreement.

"I guess you're right," she said, tapping her chin. "Maybe we can be more methodical, though? I don't want to scare anybody off going up to them on the street. But maybe if we did some research, made a list; birth records, marriages, and things. There'd have to be some sort of clue, right? Still, it's not a bad idea to have a look around. Now that we have the house, we can go out one at a time, report back every few hours."

He and Parimu looked at each other, the same thought likely crossing their minds at the same time.

"I'll be fine," Sumi said pointedly, raising an eyebrow. "And I'm taking the first shift."

She cracked a smile.

"You can't chaperone me forever, however much I appreciate it. But…" She paused, taking a breath. "I'll be in disguise, and I promise I'll be careful. I want to check on the cottage, see if Nela left anything useful behind. And while I'm at it," she added, looking at Parimu, "I wonder if I might ask a favor?"

"Anything," he said, nodding eagerly.

"Would you mind…if I brought my cat home? I don't want to intrude, but…well, if I stay away any longer, I'm not sure he'll forgive me."

Parimu looked around the house as if gauging what it would look like with a cat in it. Still, after a moment, he shrugged, nodding.

"I suppose I don't see why not," he said. "If we're going to liven up the house, we may as well go all the way. Besides, you know what they say, 'nothing kills a sailor like a rat on a ship.'"

Sumi laughed at that. Erso shook his head, taking a sip of his tea. He supposed he was the only rat on this ship, but for now, his little friend Amis would do just fine.

9

*It's easy to say such things. I know your heart is in the right place —
you're truly incapable of doing otherwise — but wandering about with
your head above the grass will only leave you stubbing toes.*

*-Excerpt from the sixth letter
Hiyelleom to Essolurei*

—:—

Sumi hurried up Fort Hill, looking over her shoulder every few seconds. Although, that probably only made her look more suspicious... She was wearing Seriai's form, of course, but that came with its own risk in the terrace districts — and pre-canned lies to tell for why Seriai would be home. Still, it was hard to think of a more reliable disguise. More importantly, if she arrived as someone else, her poor neighbors might think the place was being burgled. She'd just have to add it to her list of things to apologize to Seriai for when this was over...

She pushed on, more scurrying than walking as she climbed with Seriai's little legs. She was taking the western hill to avoid Fort Street, and even though the switchbacks had her sweating, the view more than made up for it. The terrace stretched out before her, the cottages standing out like jewels on a crown as they caught the sunlight through the clouds. More than Grass House, more than Berill, this was her *palace*. The place where everything had begun. The place Nela had *chosen*. And she needed every ounce of strength it could give her.

Finally, she reached the top, the fort wall curving toward her as it made its way back down the hill. She probably shouldn't risk drawing attention to herself, but she couldn't help walking up to it, putting her hand against the mossy stone. It felt familiar, like an old friend, albeit one whose dark past you've finally learned… It was this wall, after all, that had helped the Berillai hold this stolen land. Still, the stones were more than the wall they'd been formed into. The stones *were* the land, and the sooner she could make it safe for anyone to live there, the sooner it would return to how it was meant to be.

Without thinking, she reached for Vilodai's Eye and put her fingers over the blue center of the stone, a rush of strange voices filling her mind. Only, unlike on the boat, she could hear thousands of them, each stone in the wall beating out its own slow rhythm. Sometimes they seemed to overlap, but it wasn't quite like the harmony of the songs. It was more like a room full of people, each voice vying for attention. And yet… There was one vibration beneath them all the eye seemed to latch onto, the necklace thrumming in a way she hadn't noticed before. It felt like if she only gave it a tug, following that note to its end, she could even—

Sumi shook her head, dropping the necklace as if burned. Those had felt more like…Vilodai's thoughts than her own. The goddess had claimed to only want to see the world, but that had felt…*powerful*. It was almost as if they were about to connect the voices of those stones, turning them into something else. But then what would happen? Or the sound she'd heard from Parimu. What was this necklace really capable of?

She shook her head again, continuing down the terrace. She needed to be careful with Vilodai. She believed in the peace they'd agreed to — could a goddess even lie? But she was still dealing with a power — and an immense one, at that — she didn't fully understand. And like everything else on this journey, there wasn't much to protect her outside of her own caution.

She finally reached the cottage and went into the front garden, the fence creaking as she pushed it open. She didn't bother with the front door, slipping along the side fence toward the back. Honestly, she was a bit shaken from the necklace still, but once she was safely out of sight, she stopped, forcing herself to take in the view. The bay seemed to glisten under the clouds, its water a perfect sapphire as it shed its winter grey.

She had certainly missed this. No matter how many incredible things she'd seen across the Continent, they could never compete with this view. The garden, on the other hand… She turned, finding the vegetable beds even more weed-filled than Parimu's, some of them already waist-high as they fed on the spring rains. Still, they were beautiful in their own way, their buds popping with thistly flowers, quietly singing their own songs.

She crossed to the old oak tree by the fence and reached into the hole in its trunk, fumbling around until she found the key. She and Erso had hidden it back there the day they left, deciding it was safer than the old jar she'd normally hidden it in. As she approached the back door, to her relief, everything still seemed just as it had been. She hadn't thought to ask Parimu until this moment, but she had certainly worried enough about the police tearing the cottage apart. By the looks of it, though, he'd simply gotten on his train to give chase. Though she would have to ask him what became of her purse someday…

She unlocked the door and stepped through, the house eerily quiet. It seemed that without her in it, the house had finally settled into stillness. She put down her bag and walked through the kitchen, running her hands along the counters. She stopped by the stove, playing with the oven compartments. Then she walked to the cellar stairs, peering down into the gloom. Even if it was a spider-filled dungeon, she somehow found she missed this part of the house, too. She turned to the rows of canned goods sitting on their shelves proudly as they awaited her return. She pocketed a jar of pear jam to share with the others, one of the last batches made by Nela.

She moved toward the front hall, where there were a hundred different artifacts to stop her: the mirrors, the paintings, the blank spot where Nela's picture used to hang. There was even the etching of Grandpa's first boat, *the King's Oath*, all of it seeming to take on so much more meaning now that she knew how her grandparents had met. She turned toward the office when she stopped, finding a half-dozen letters sitting on the floor by the mail slot. She felt a lump in her throat, all the people who could be angry with her for disappearing flashing through her mind. Still, she stooped down, grabbing the letters and flipping through them.

The first one was, as expected, from Mr. Furttenhur. The next two were from the bank and the milk service. She chuckled, thinking of how the milkman must have felt when a week's worth of milk piled up on the porch. The next was from Seriai, and then, finally, she found a letter in a hand she didn't recognize. She turned it over, looking at the return address. It was from Barine! She'd nearly forgotten in all the chaos of the past few months, though she'd always hoped she'd hear from her again after helping her outside Wembly.

She ducked her head into the sitting room, grabbing Nela's address book before dashing back into the kitchen where the light was better. She couldn't stay long, but now that she'd seen Barine's letter, she couldn't wait to read it. Still, as soon as she sat at the kitchen table, Mr.

Furttenhur's letter peeked out from the stack, and she forced herself to open it. As Grandpa had liked to say, it was always better to shear the ram before the sheep.

Dear Sumi, the letter began, *I'm very sorry to hear about your great aunt. Of course, take all the time you need. I wish her a speedy recovery and know how important it is to care for family. As you know, my family is also distant, in Strussfaran, and when duty calls, you simply must answer. It will be very difficult without you, though, so please write to me when you can.*

That wasn't so bad, right? She'd been gone for months already, though, and it did make her wish she'd written him some kind of update. Although, she hadn't had any hope of returning home at first… At least he didn't seem angry. Hopefully, it hadn't been too hard on him without her. She'd have to find some way to make it up to him when all this was over, whatever that looked like… Survive the Berillai, and then what, go back to being a shopkeeper? She chuckled. That was about the extent of what she'd planned for her life, but it seemed a little silly now.

She tossed the letters from the bank and the milk company into her bag, unopened. The milkman would just have to line up behind the headsman and everyone else in town. Even Seriai's letter went into her bag. She felt a sharp pang of guilt at that, but there was also basically nothing she could tell her, not yet, anyway. Once this was finished, though… Well, then she could figure out how to explain it all. At least she'd have good news to share as well. After all the afternoons they'd spent shut up in her room reading *The Borimol Plains*, Seriai would die of shock when she heard about Nela being a princess!

Finally, she grabbed up the letter from Barine, eagerly tearing open the seal.

Dear Sir, she wrote,

I hope you remember me. My name is Barine, and you did me an incredible kindness a few months back at Wembly Market. I wanted to thank you again from the bottom of my heart. You were so incredibly valiant to come to my aid that night. I also thought, if I'm not being too presumptuous, that I could invite you for tea. You see, it's most lonely here without my brother, and I thought you might enjoy some company as well. You deserve a proper tea as thanks, and I'd love to have you on any day you find convenient.

I also wanted to mention to you that I had trouble finding your neighbor's niece. I stopped in at Furttenhur's Flowers, but the owner said she'd gone away to help a sick relative. I suppose you know as much already, but I was wondering if you might have an address for her abroad. I hope this isn't too forward of me, but I'd love to have a friend, and by your description, it appears we may have quite a bit in common.

Yours truly,
Barine Sepolimarne

Poor Barine. They'd both been so alone… She scanned the top of the letter and found it had been dated on the first of Ewannin, nearly a month ago. That settled it — as soon as it was safe, she would drop by Barine's place. She couldn't give her much, but she certainly had plenty of friendship to give.

She gently folded the letter before putting everything back in her bag. Then, unable to risk staying any longer, she quickly moved across the kitchen and out the back door. She locked up and was turning to go, but she stopped, putting her hand against the side of the house.

"This isn't goodbye," she said to the old cottage. As long as she lived, this would be her home, and she would care for it. She hurried back to the street and into the city, her heart starting to flutter as she headed toward Amis. He may be grumpy with her, but they were family, and he was stuck with her whether he liked it or not.

10

*Could you walk down the street of your own city with such confidence?
I'm not asking you to abandon your cloak in the rain, just remember
that getting wet can serve a purpose!*

*-Excerpt from the fourth letter
Essolurei to Hiyelleom*

—:—

Erso walked down Laeryia Boulevard with his hands in his pockets, his teeth clamped firmly around his pipe. A trail of black smoke drifted behind him, though it didn't seem to be helping. Bloody Berillai tobacco. After everything they'd gone through in the wilderness, he'd finally run out of polis leaves, just when he could use them the most. That familiar knot was forming in his chest, like a cage closing on his soul as Berill loomed around him.

He thought about heading down to The Grainer to see if Dulkhen could spot him some polis, but hitting the bars wouldn't exactly be keeping a low profile… Besides, it had been hard enough to convince Parimu to let him leave with Sumi gone, and it wouldn't do to go losing his prison pass now. But it *was* the right call. If they were really looking for Shapewalkers, the more eyes, the merrier.

He shook his head, putting his attention back on the street. He'd almost run into a sailor while he was lost in thought, but luckily his face looked like a storm, and the bloke had scrambled out of the way. Bloody low profile, indeed… Still, the street was dry, not a keyhole in sight. He'd thought he felt one coming from a fancy carriage a few blocks back, but it had zipped away before he could get a look. Funny thinking there could be more Shapewalkers hiding here. His kind could be anywhere, of course. But if they'd been here this whole time, and rich to boot... Would they really be keen to tip their boats over for Sumi's plan? They would when they met her, of course; Sumi was like that. He'd just have to make sure the bastards took the meeting.

He leaned against a lamppost, letting traffic pass him as he watched. Berill wasn't all bad, of course. They were a bunch of stodgy sheep sailors, sure, but they did like their liquor strong. Not that he was supposed to think of that as a perk anymore... If he were a different person — if he were even a tiny bit worthy of Sumi — would he have been able to make a home for himself here? He did like how quickly the city changed. Even back home, people still walked over the same bridges, lived in the same buildings they had for millennia — until the fellerhurns burned them down, of course. But Berill felt like it had no memory, hurtling into the future with its eyes closed. Maybe he should stay. If Sumi succeeded, he could probably even be here legally. And...if she ever forgave him for breaking her heart, he wouldn't mind seeing how her life turned out.

He suddenly had a sour taste in his mouth, and he took his mouth off the pipe, spitting on the cobblestones. Best not to think about all that yet. He still owed her a good performance, and it wouldn't do to dwell on what came after. If only he didn't love her so damned much! She was perfect, and he was a bloody fool to let her go. But that was exactly why he had to. Only Sumi could have gotten him to believe change was possible, and she was too perfect to have him ruining her life.

He tapped out his pipe, grumbling to himself as he ground the smoking dottle with his heel. It was a real bloody mess he'd found himself in this time. Still, it was his hall to walk, and he'd march through it with his head held high until the final door. She deserved at least that much. He could walk around Berill, he could wear a mask, and he could sure as smoke find some bloody Shapewalkers.

———

Finally, Sumi reached Alip Tellemuir's house, her own face reflecting back to her in the window. She'd flashed back into her own form a block away, rushing to his door with her hood up. She couldn't risk too much time wearing her own face, of course, but she wasn't sure if he knew Seriai, and hopefully, he wouldn't be too keen to hand her cat to a perfect stranger... She knocked, turning to watch the street before Alip appeared, his eyes widening as he recognized her. He opened the door, a wide smile appearing on his face. How had she ever been afraid to run into him at the market? Now, seeing his face felt like home.

"Sumi!" he said, leaning in to hug her with his massive arms. "I can't believe it's you!"

She'd never hugged him before, but it felt oddly familiar, even if her own arms only made it halfway across his back. He pulled away, reddening as if he just realized the same thing.

"It's good to see you," she said, smiling. "Sorry I was gone so long."

"No trouble at all," he said, running a hand through his hair. "You just get back?"

"Only just," she said. "I came to get Amis as soon as I could. I can't tell you how much I appreciate you watching him. He didn't misbehave or anything, did he?"

"Nah," Alip said, chuckling, "big softy, that one. He'll be happy to see you, though, I reckon. Looked for you for a month straight. Why don't you come in? You should at least have a cup of tea while you tell me about your travels."

Sumi looked back at the street, the other homes still perfectly quiet.

"I suppose I could," she said, smiling, "but only if you're sure I'm not wasting your Queen's Day."

"Never," he said, moving to the side and ushering her through the door. "Pa and Aliern aren't here, but Ma will just about pop when she sees you."

She walked in, standing to one side as Alip shut the door. She hadn't been inside since she was a child visiting with Nela, but it seemed bigger than she remembered. There was a large parlor to the left of the door and a hallway leading to the kitchen. They had a garden out back, and behind her was the stairway to the second floor. She could just remember climbing those stairs to bring him his soup. Alip turned toward the kitchen, waving for her to follow as his mother called out.

"Alip, who's at the door?!"

They came around the corner, Mrs. Tellemuir looking up from a forest of pots and pans, her daughter, Andeli, beside her. They were both wearing aprons, their hands covered in flour. Even though she'd eaten the woman's bread nearly every day, it suddenly dawned on her how many years had passed since they'd seen each other, Mrs. Tellemuir's hair already entirely grey. And Andeli… She'd grown about a foot since Sumi had seen her last, but she looked like a copy of her mother, albeit with Alip's cheekbones. They all stared at each other for a second before Mrs. Tellemuir's mouth dropped open.

"Sumi Elerair?!" she cried out, rushing over. She rubbed her hands on her apron before grabbing Sumi in a tight hug. She had missed hugs like these. Like hugging Nela, the woman's arms seemed strong enough to snap her in half even as she was pressed into her soft, matronly chest. Up close, she also couldn't help but listen to her song for just a second. It had the tone of all human songs, its central note reminding her of Vilodai, but it was rich and warm, like the oven where she baked her bread.

As Mrs. Tellemuir let go, Andeli smiled, waving from the counter.

"Lovely to see you," she said. "It's been ages, but the whole family talks about you loads."

"All good things, I hope?" Sumi asked, shooting a glance at Alip. "But it's great to see you, too; your father's always raving about you."

"Well, come in, come in!" Mrs. Tellemuir said, pushing Sumi further into the kitchen. "It's a lovely spring day, why don't you two sit in the garden while I make some tea?"

Sumi turned to protest; the last thing she wanted to do was put the woman to more work on Queen's Day, but she was promptly shushed and pushed toward the door. As soon as she stepped through to the garden, though, she saw Amis, and every other thought was pushed from her mind. He was laying in the grass, a giant grey lump surrounded by green as if he'd become a grass cat while she was gone. She hurried over, kneeling down beside him.

"Amis," she called in a quiet voice, not wanting to startle him out of his nap. He lifted his head, and when their eyes met, he started meowing, heaving himself upright as he tried to climb into her lap, running his whiskers along her dress and hands.

"Aww, so you did miss me!" she cried out, trying to pet him as he crawled about.

"Told you," Alip said, laughing as he stepped up behind her. He crouched down, too, reaching to pet Amis's tail as the cat shook with purrs. They stayed that way for a few minutes until Andeli came outside with a tea tray. Sumi decided to just grab the cat, carrying him over to the little tea table on the patio off the kitchen. Amis squirmed for a moment, but he had never been one for biting, so she just held him tighter.

"Thank you," Sumi said, "this is really too kind."

"It's no trouble," Andeli said, smiling as she wriggled a finger at Amis before setting out a pair of plates and mugs. The tray held a fine porcelain teapot and a large plate of Mrs. Tellemuir's biscuits.

"You sure you don't want to join us?" Sumi asked, realizing there were only two of everything.

"Oh, no," Andeli said, grinning. "Ma certainly wouldn't like that at all."

She shot a look at her brother, who shooed her away.

"Back inside with ya then, eh?" he said, his cheeks darkening. He took a chair, motioning for Sumi to do the same.

What's that supposed to mean? Sumi thought, her eyes narrowing. She planted Amis on her lap, grabbing a corner from one of the biscuits for the cat so he'd sit still.

"Well," she said, smiling at Alip as he poured the tea. "Sorry to cause such a fuss. It's nice to see you, though."

"It's me who should apologize," Alip said, shaking his head. "I'm afraid my family can get a little carried away where you're concerned."

Before she could ask what he meant by that, he passed her a mug, asking her about cream and sugar. When everything was laid out, he leaned back, crossing his arms.

"So," he said, "tell me all about your trip. I've never been farther than Moranal myself. I'm sure you've seen things I couldn't even imagine." He smiled for a moment before he frowned, raising a hand. "I'm sorry, listen to me, going on like you were on holiday when you had a sick relative. Are they alright?"

"Yes," she said quickly, remembering her lie, "my aunt. But don't worry, she's alright now. Thank you for asking." She took a sip of her tea, her throat suddenly dry. "Honestly, though, outside of her getting sick, it was sort of lovely. I'd never been to Anushai before, and it's just beautiful. They have all these brick buildings and a giant temple for their goddess, Essomuai. It was…well, sort of life-changing, I guess."

He leaned forward in his chair, rapt as he listened to everything else she could safely tell him about Anushai. It was still hard to believe herself that she'd seen so much. She would have felt just like him only a few months ago, struggling to imagine a world she'd never seen.

"I'll bet it was beautiful," he said as she finished, smiling warmly. "None of us know head from tail on the Continent, but the whole family talked about you seems like every day, trying to imagine what you were doing over there."

"I'm sorry I kept you waiting," she said quickly, bowing her head low in apology. "I hope your family isn't cross I left the cat so long. I promise I'll make it up to you somehow."

"No, no," he said, waving a hand. "It isn't that…" He flushed again, looking away as he scratched the back of his head. He stared at the garden as if the words would be growing out there. "You see…" he finally said, almost to himself, "since you dropped off the cat, my ma just couldn't stop gushing about you. I guess she got this foolish notion in her head that if you trusted me enough with your cat, you might…want to marry me or something."

She watched him, her eyes widening.

"It's silly, I know," he said quickly, grabbing his tea and taking a gulp. He sighed, shaking his head. "Though I guess I can't blame her, especially…well, especially seeing as how I always loved you."

She coughed, seeming to forget how to breathe for a second.

"What?" she asked, suddenly blinking more than normal. "You…what?!"

He actually laughed, which was good, his normal color returning somewhat.

"It's alright," he said, waving his hand again. "Unlike my ever-hopeful mother," he said, cocking his head toward the kitchen, "I know it's never gonna happen. You're much too good for me. I just thought I ought to give you an explanation for how strange everybody's being."

"Whoa, whoa," Sumi said. "I don't know what you're thinking, saying I'm too good for you! Alip Tellemuir, you're the talk of the terraces. Every woman — and her mother — sighs after you!"

"I don't know about all that," he said, scratching the back of his head again. "Though I'm sorry I've always looked like such a scamp. I promise I'm not trying to nab your sheep for laughs or anything." He looked down at his hands, sighing as he nervously spun his spoon around his teacup. "Truth be told," he added, "I never would have dated those other girls if I thought I had a chance with you. It's just…well, you were always so smart. Your grandmother — your…*Nela*, right? — she always raved about how smart you were, reading and speaking Anushai and all that. And you were so *kind* too. You never gossiped like the other girls or hung around the pubs — you were always off with your nose in a book or working with the charity folks. I just knew I'd never be worthy of that."

Her mouth had slowly drifted more and more open as he talked, and she finally realized, clamping it shut as the back of her neck blazed with heat. *Alip Tellemuir…liking her?!* That was almost stranger than realizing she was a Shapewalker or a Saldalgiar. She was mousy, frumpy, uninteresting — not exactly the stuff dreams were made of. Although, she never would have dreamed of Erso loving her either. That was if he still did… But in spite of everything, she was still just a shopkeeper and a sailor's daughter. But maybe that was the point… Like Nela, moving to Berill even though she was a princess. The world could tell you what you ought to want, but in the end, all your heart longed for was a home.

He looked up, grinning.

"I hope you're not angry," he said. "Don't let this come between us now that you're back. I'd feel awful if you had to get your vegetables somewhere else because of me. I just thought you should know, but I promise, on my Ma, I'll never mention it again."

"No, no," she said, shaking herself out of her wild jumble of thoughts. She reached out across the table, grabbing his hand. She squeezed it, shaking her head as she sat back.

"I'm just a bit shocked, is all," she said. "You're a good man, Alip. Better than I could have ever dreamed of before I left home." She looked up, grinning. "With how hard Nela pushed, I can't believe you never asked!"

He laughed, their eyes meeting. There *was* something there, but he deserved the truth, too, didn't he? By all indications, Erso might well be done with her. But no. It wouldn't be right to string Alip along when she was already in love. And she did love that silly man. Even if he was going to leave her, he could do that on his own. She took a breath, forcing herself to continue.

"It's just…I've met someone, in Anushai. I don't know if it'll work out, but part of me still hopes it does. But you're worthy of any woman in the kingdom, Alip. I just hope you find one worthy of you."

"Well, that's alright, isn't it?" he said, chuckling. It was genuine, a happy sound that made his song twinge with mirth. "Even knowing that, I feel…lighter, somehow. Thank you, Sumi. I missed the boat on a lovely girl like you, but maybe I don't have to miss the next one." He smiled brightly, like a big electric lamp. "I hope we'll be friends, and if it works out with your special someone, I hope you'll invite me to the wedding."

"I'd love nothing more," she said, smiling back. A weight seemed to drop from her shoulders. A few months ago, it had seemed impossible that anyone would ever love her. And she certainly hadn't ever imagined being the one doing the rejecting. But this felt…different somehow, less final. There was still love here, albeit of a different kind, and she had the feeling she might know Alip for a long, long time.

"Besides," she added in a sly voice, "you never know. Now that I know what you're after, I might just have to keep my eyes peeled, see if there are any other mousy girls hiding in the library."

He laughed, and they finally fell back into a more comfortable rhythm, joking like they'd always done at the stand, sipping tea and taking the first few steps into a deeper friendship, the start of a duet where two songs could make a symphony.

11

You asked me why I'm resigning. I suppose I'm no longer comfortable straddling these two ways of thinking indefinitely. How can we know so much and yet do so little?

-Monthly Meeting Minutes of Dialasera's Rose
Letter stuffed between two pages
Puralmon 803 PD

—:—

That evening, Sumi sat at the kitchen table at Parimu's, Nela's address book spread out before her. She'd gone through the book twice — not to mention each of the men giving it a look — but nothing in it seemed to hint at other Shapewalkers in Berill. There were plenty of notes in the margins — mostly in Anushai, of course — but it seemed to only have reminders: birthdays, names of daughters-in-law, a few snide comments...

Parimu walked over, his hands clutching a steaming pan between thick towels where a roasted rack of lamb simmered in its sauce.

"That smells amazing," she said as he placed the pan on a corkboard. "Remind me why you weren't our cook before?"

"Har-har," Erso said, looking up from his notes. "I could have made a name for myself too with some better ingredients, but noooo, beans every night!"

"They *were* good beans, all things considered," Parimu said. He shrugged, leaning over to cut the lamb. "Honestly, though, this is the only thing I know how to make. My ma taught me how to stoke the oven and how long to leave it in, but mostly it's about leaving the meat alone."

"Well," Erso said, leaning toward the meat with his elbows on the table, "it smells lovely, even for a lamb. Bang-up job."

His eyes shifted toward her for a moment, and he smiled. It was a handsome smile, of course, and part of her melted at the sight of it. But how much of it was an act? He still seemed distant — he was even sitting on the opposite end of the table — but what was there to do? She was meant to be looking for Shapewalkers, but the only one who mattered was drifting away.

Parimu dropped a plate of lamb in front of her, and she shook her head, finally realizing she'd been staring in a daze.

"Wow," she said, "this looks incredible. I guess we really are home."

They tucked in, eating like it was their first meal in months, with only the sound of forks to break the silence. As she was taking seconds, Erso finally piped up.

"So," he said, "looks like the address book might be a bust. Did anybody see anything while they were out and about today?"

He had told them about the keyhole he'd seen passing in a carriage, but that was still little more than a mystery.

"Not me," she said, wiping her mouth as she shook her head. "I think I'll try the library tomorrow, though, see if I can dig up some old records or something. How about you, Relsenair?"

He had left briefly to get some groceries once she and Erso had gotten home, but he hadn't traveled far, going to a nearby greengrocer's instead of walking all the way to Wembly.

"Nothing in the way of keyholes," he said, "but there was this."

He leaned back in his seat, reaching for the newspaper he'd left on the counter. He turned it around before sliding it toward her.

Two Weeks Left on Royal Stay, it read, *Will the Goat Pin the Queen?*

She narrowed her eyes, trying to make out the tiny print in the soft light of the kitchen lamp. The article was from the *Naval Officer*, a paper her Grandpa used to read, though she and Nela had always read *The Berillai Standard.*

"What does this mean?" she asked, stroking Amis as he came meowing for a bite of lamb. "Who's the Goat?"

"That's what they call the Vice Peer," Parimu said, shrugging. "Goat of the Northern Shore. Something about being stubborn, I guess, but I'd always thought the *Officer* printed classier lines than that. Anyway, it seems the Vice Peer has a bill in the Peerage right now, aims to strip the Queen of her war powers."

"Well, thank the gods for that," Erso said, leaning back in his chair as he crossed his arms.

Parimu stared at the paper, shaking his head.

"I don't know," he said slowly. "I mean, obviously, knowing what I know now, I'm for peace. The papers all say Pont'dulairn will do anything for commerce, but I worry that won't change things either, not really. I just worry we're going from the barn to the field without checking the weather, you know?"

"Hmmm," Sumi hummed, drumming her fingers on the table. The paper had an etching of Pont'dulairn on his dais. The image of the Queen was never shown, of course, but she could see where the Vice Peer had gotten his nickname. In the sketch, he had his hands raised, shouting to a room full of Peers.

"I wonder," she said, "if any change is a good thing. Maybe not this bill in particular, but if Berill is ready for something new, maybe the changes we're hoping for won't be so hard? I just wish I had followed politics more closely before I left. It feels like sailing into a storm."

Parimu nodded, rubbing his hand along his chin as if his father's beard were still there.

"You have a point," he said. "It's not like the Queen would like what we're doing very much either."

"If an Amoriai can say anything," Erso said, "it's that change isn't always for the better. But I do have a good feeling about the Pont'dulairn bloke. I have met his wife, after all, in a manner of speaking."

Somehow, they all laughed, cutting through the tension of their worry. Erso had come clean about impersonating Elisal Pont'dulairn to try and get Parimu fired, and even as it brought up memories of Erso's friend Aelibis, somehow, the pain had transformed into hope.

"You know," Sumi said, arching an eyebrow, "if you like blondes so much, I got a letter from my friend Barine today. She's not even married yet, so you won't have to fight a Vice Peer to win her heart."

"Yeah, yeah," Erso said, rolling his eyes. "Just pass the lamb, eh? And keep your letters to yourself."

––––––

Long after dinner, with the house asleep, Sumi sat in the garden, scratching Amis's chin as she listened to the waves beyond the garden hedge. They'd sat talking at the kitchen table for a few more hours, but in the end, she was the last one awake, sitting in the dark with her mind swimming. She never would have imagined herself as a night owl — especially when she was up before dawn for the flower shop. But now… Every time the sun set, her worries seemed to hunt her, like lions prowling in the night.

For whatever reason, the thing bothering her most was how to teach the songs. Even her worries about finding other Shapewalkers — which didn't seem especially feasible at the moment — were somehow allayed by her infinite confidence in the library. And the parade, as absurd as it was, felt like it would simply fall into place once she had the right people around her. So that left the songs and endless hours trying to understand how they worked. Suppose she couldn't ever teach anyone besides Erso? Where would that leave the parade or any of her other plans?

She picked Amis up, flopping onto her back as she clutched him to her chest. For a second, she thought of all the bugs crawling around in the night, but then she realized she didn't really care — at least not as much as she would have before spending weeks in the woods. There couldn't possibly be anything as creepy in the garden as the things she'd found wandering her tent...

She sighed, staring up at the stars. Without even having to try, she could hear their song, their beautiful twinkling washing over her in waves. If only everyone could hear them! How could you hate anyone while listening to such beautiful music? Maybe the songs wouldn't solve anything — it had taken the goddesses a thousand years to reforge their peace, after all — but she had to believe. Something so beautiful *had* to matter. Maybe it wouldn't be easy, but if she didn't trust that, what else was there? If the sun couldn't light the sky, there would be no day.

She reached up with her free hand, taking hold of Vilodai's Eye. The songs and those…voices swirled around each other, almost harmonizing before they spun out of sync again, like two whirlpools briefly overlapping. With both of them in her mind, it felt like being in the cave again, her mind floating in the pool. She lay absolutely still, hoping some secret about Vilodai would present itself if she listened closely enough, something she missed or an answer to her questions.

She disappeared into the spin of sound, letting go as it swirled around her. As she stopped listening so actively, it seemed her mind was finally free to really *notice*. Vilodai's rhythms weren't anywhere near as prevalent as Essomuai's songs. The songs truly came from *everything*, the goddess holding a memory of each plant, animal, and stone. Vilodai's vibrations, meanwhile, seemed to be outnumbered at least ten to one. And they weren't…memories; they didn't tell stories like Essomuai did. Instead, they were like the wall of the fort, like they wanted to *speak* to her.

Even as they all chattered around her, she tried to pick a single voice, hoping to separate it from the noise. Finally, she noticed the bedrock like she had in Akashan, and she *tugged* on it, trying to bring it closer. It felt familiar, like a whale beneath the surface, and yet…it was different. She could feel its contours far beneath her, stretching wide beneath the grass and soil as it held them. Its vibration seemed to reach for her, like a horse looking back at its rider. How many centuries had it laid there, straddling the land and sea?

As she listened, though, she noticed something softer, closer. It was a rhythm just like the rock but in miniature, a fly buzzing above the whale. In fact…it wasn't below her but right above her. She cracked an eye open, looking at the cat. At first, she'd thought he'd only been purring, but she could hear the same voice whispering, just like Parimu in Akashan…

What is this? she thought. *Is it—*

She started, a strong vibration suddenly filling every part of her as Vilodai spoke into her mind.

Welloshara, the goddess said. Images flashed into her mind: a desert, a mountain, a giant cave. The cave was dark, but there was a light there…a pillar standing in the center. It was made of a shining metal, and as it grew larger in her mind, six pieces broke away, flashing with light, the colors changing from gold to green to blue, from silver to grey to white. The pieces of metal — or were they crystals? — seemed to float onto the floor of the cavern, where they began to spin.

Kouselumakan, Vilodai said.

Oddly, the images in her mind didn't stop; they simply continued. The crystals spinning until they flew away, disappearing into the darkness, the glow still visible as they arced across a black void.

The image finally ended, and Sumi lurched up from the ground, her breathing heavy. As she gulped in lungfuls of cool air, an impression was left behind, the meaning of the goddess words echoing in her mind — *mind* and *voice*. But what was a mind? Was it like hers or something else? She was afraid she already knew the answer to what speaking was… The whispers, Vilodai trying to join the stones. And now the goddess was speaking directly to her? She suddenly remembered the stone in her hand, letting it go. She had to be careful with Vilodai. And yet, she couldn't help thinking there was some secret in those rhythms, something she'd need to save her people…

Amis growled at her from across the garden, having scurried away when she bolted upright.

"It's alright," she said, wiggling her fingers. "Sorry I spooked you."

He huffed, turning around before settling in the grass a few feet away from her. She chuckled. Of course, that silly cat would hold a grudge, but how to make it up to him? A snack was out of the question —

somehow, he'd gotten even fatter staying with the Tellemuirs.

"I know!" she said, sitting up. She took a deep breath, listening to Amis's song before flashing into his form. Amis swiveled his head around immediately, letting out a curious meow as he sniffed the air. Sumi meowed back, and Amis was immediately off his stomach, racing over to scratch whiskers with her. Just as he reached her, though, she flashed back into herself, scooping him up and spinning him around. He meowed loudly, licking her face as she laughed.

"Gotcha!" she cried before clapping a hand over her mouth, realizing she might wake the others.

She plopped back down on the grass, the cat apparently mollified for the moment as she went back to scratching his chin. She chuckled quietly in the dark, letting the songs fade back out of her mind. But as they did, she noticed she could still hear Amis's song, like it was still...echoing in the air. She closed her eyes, listening. Her own song was basically back to normal, so where was that echo coming from?

She reached for the stone where it was hanging against her chest. As she put her hand to it, she felt a vibration, an echo that seemed to harmonize with Amis's song. That was just like Akashan too... She listened to those voices again — the whispers in the darkness — and she could feel the slightest echo of the song in them, too. It was already fading, and it hadn't seemed to reach the bedrock, but it was definitely there...

She let go of the necklace, rubbing her chin. *Welloshara* and *Kouselumakan.* There was something there, and she would find out what. She lay back down on the grass, looking at the stars as if the answers would be hidden there — and perhaps they were. She was in the realm of the goddesses now, after all, and they had been here far longer than humans had. She didn't know what the difference was between voices and songs, but if she could get them all to sing, maybe she'd find her way.

12

You act like the responsibility is all mine! Would you tell the vole to start peace talks with the bobcat? I think you've drunk from the same stream too long, old friend.

-Excerpt from the ninth letter
Hiyelleom to Essolurei

—:—

By the next morning, a dense pocket of clouds had rolled in off the bay, their dark bottoms drumming a steady rain onto the street. Sumi walked with her hood up, heading east down Laeryia Boulevard. She was wearing a new face, one she'd made up — she'd already pushed her luck far enough walking around the terraces as Seriai — but she was still grateful for the added cover. She was more confident than she'd ever been in her powers, but it still felt odd to go long periods of time as something she'd just imagined.

The face she was wearing — whoever's it was — had just popped into her mind, like a combination of her mother and her school teacher growing up. Strangely, though, the face had its own song and snippets of a life attached to them. But this woman wasn't real…right? Erso had always told her there were all kinds of doors in the sacred halls, but how could Essomuai know someone's entire life if it was invented? It made her think of Vilodai's words, the crystals breaking off from that strange pillar. Could every thought and daydream have its own world hiding behind it, slipping into some mirrored version of their lives?

She shook her head. There was little time for philosophy on top of everything else. Finally, she reached the old wall, passing under its shadow into the city center. As she passed the hospital, she paused, her eyes tracing the third floor to the room where she'd gone as an umbrella. Was Tethel still there? She suddenly felt horribly guilty for not having thought of him while she was gone. Hopefully, the doctors had been able to heal him. Still, she made a mental note to check on his grandmother — at least whenever it was safe to return to the women's group…

She moved on, making slow progress as she walked, every landmark seeming to make her stop and stare — the banks, the warehouses, the sheer size of the port as it teemed with boats. She'd seen it all a thousand times, but that was before she'd seen other ports and other cities. Now she could see what made Berill special, what made it hers. Although she saw its pain, too… There seemed to be twice as many beggars as when she left, drifting at the edges of the sidewalk, hoping someone might stop in the rain to give a coin.

It wasn't just the beggars either. She passed by a small factory in the warehouse district, the morning whistle blowing as workers filed in through the large bay doors. The men and women marching in seemed bone-tired, too, their strength out of step with the intimidating brick building. Smoke billowed from the chimney on the roof, gouts of black that spilled out over the bay in an unrelenting stream, just like the progress Berill kept feeding into the Continent, whatever it had to wring from the workers to do so.

Even Fort Street — Berill's trophy case of gems and glass — seemed unrecognizable. She felt like the lamb in *The Lost Sheep*, finally coming back from the forest to find she didn't like the taste of grass anymore… When she turned the corner into the Lournoy, though, her heart did a somersault, the library at least still filling her with joy. No matter what the Berillai had done, this place was different. It had *saved* her, showing her who she was when no one else could.

Suddenly having what could be a very bad idea, she ducked into an alley, glowing as she removed her disguise. She left her hood up, walking quickly toward the library. The others wouldn't like it, of course, but she secretly hoped she would see the Master Librarian again. And if she did…she hoped he remembered her.

She walked up to the library entrance, pulling open the heavy door. Had that really been her all those months ago, climbing these steps and looking for answers? It felt like someone else's life entirely. And yet, as she walked in, it was like she'd never left, the hazy blue light of the speaking stones instantly taking her back to childhood afternoons with Nela.

She stared up at them as she passed, thinking of the cave and— Sumi staggered, only barely catching herself on the stone wall as her mind flooded with the buzz of voices. It sounded like the stones, only much, much louder. She shook her head, squinting at the blue light. Why was she hearing them? She hadn't touched her necklace, had she? She groped under her blouse for it, but she found it had slipped under her chemise against her skin, the stone vibrating in sync with the glow of the stones. She'd thought the speaking stones would have been out of commission somehow — why else would the Berillai abandon them as decoration? She pulled the necklace off her skin, the voices disappearing from her mind.

"Miss," a voice asked, "are you alright?"

"I'm sorry," she said, pulling her eyes away from the stones, "I'm fine. I just—"

There was the Master Librarian right before her eyes, one hand gently on her elbow as the other gripped his cane. Their eyes met, and she smiled, his eyes widening in surprise.

"Why, Miss Elerair," he said, smiling back, "if the seas haven't spit up a pearl! I was worried you'd forgotten us."

"Never!" she said, squeezing his hand before he let go of her elbow. "I was traveling, but I can't tell you how much I've missed this place."

"Traveling, eh?" he asked. "You do have the look of a woman who's gone and met the world."

"You could say that," she said, chuckling.

"Come, come," he said, beckoning her to follow as he shuffled back toward the front desk. "I can't have a scholar like you stuck in the lobby."

He heaved himself onto a stool, his thick glasses magnifying his eyes as he watched her eagerly.

"Tell me," he said, "where did you go? Did you finally see that family up in Anushai?"

"I did," she said, "though I'm surprised you remember so much about little old me."

"Well," he said, chuckling, "luckily, I'm not old enough to forget my favorite scholars. Not yet, anyway, though my wife would tell you otherwise."

He wiped his brow with a handkerchief, smiling as he no doubt thought of his murderously adoring wife.

"Anushai did always seem to have quite the hold on your old friend, Arteir Pallinayum. But at any rate, we've missed you here. We still haven't found a brighter young scholar to replace you."

"I missed you too, sir," she said, smiling warmly.

"Please," he said, chuckling, "no more sirs, dear. Only abominable men actually enjoy their titles. Since we're friends now, I have to insist you call me Peloris."

"Alright," she said, nodding, "Peloris it is. But you'll have to call me Sumi, you know."

"I will if my memory holds out," he said, laughing as he stroked his beard. "So, tell me, what brings you back to our humble temple of knowledge? Your reading list last time was most interesting."

"Well," she said slowly, "I suppose I'm looking for genealogies? I'm looking for some of my…relatives, people who might have a similar connection to Anushai."

Peloris froze, his finger pausing in the middle of his filing cards.

"Perhaps…" he said, speaking in a lower voice as he met her eyes, "there's something you might like to see in my private collection?"

She looked to either side, but there was no one else in the hall.

"Um…okay," she said, nodding slowly. "As long as it's not too much trouble." She bit her lip. "Hopefully, my request isn't a…problem?"

"No, no," he said, "nothing to worry about. Genealogy is just a — how do I put it? — prickly topic in this kingdom. And the articles on record tend to be a bit…sanitized by design. I'm sure you'll want to see my collection. Over some tea, perhaps?"

She nodded, but he was already in the process of pushing himself out of his seat. He reached for his cane, ringing a bell on his desk as a porter appeared from around the corner.

"Some tea to my office, please," Peloris said, "and call for an archivist to man the desk; I have a meeting."

"Right away, sir," the porter said, bowing. The Master Librarian shuffled to the far end of his desk, beckoning for Sumi to follow him down a dark hallway between the desks.

"At least I got you to accept first names," he said, grinning. "I can't get these porters to stop with the sirs. Every time I finally train one, they transfer them to the palace archives. Most inconvenient."

The Master Librarian led her down the hallway, shuffling past office doors whose glazed windows glowed in the blue light of lanterns. Finally, they reached the end, Peloris stopping at a door on their left as the porter miraculously came around the corner with a full tea tray. He stood at attention as the older man searched through his pockets, finally coming up with a key.

Peloris pushed the door open, revealing what had to be the loveliest room in the kingdom. It was no bigger than her bedroom at the cottage, but it seemed to go straight up, easily three stories tall and lined on all four sides with bookshelves. There was a small gap on the western wall with a blue-light fireplace, but otherwise, the place was very near bursting with books. There was a desk with two chairs in front of it — presumably for guests — though only one of them was free of books. The only other thing in the room was a flat table along the eastern wall covered in maps and silver tools — rulers, protractors, and compasses of every shape and size.

Peloris moved toward his desk, hastily clearing papers so the porter could set down the tea tray. Sumi poked her head into the room, the Master Librarian waving for her to sit in the open chair. She sat primly, waiting for the porter to close the door before she sprang back up, pouring tea for both of them. The tea smelled like spring, its floral scent filling the room as it settled into their cups. Peloris simply watched her for a while, sipping his tea — though it was still far too hot for her — before he finally spoke.

"So," he said, "forgive me if I'm off the mark, but am I right in presuming that you're a Shapewalker?"

She tensed, her eyes widening as she looked up from her tea, her heart thumping in her chest. Had this been a trap all along? What a fool she was! Her mind jumped to the silver instruments on the table. Could she change her form and still escape?

"It's alright," Peloris said quickly. "I'm a friend."

Their eyes met, and she felt like she could feel her pulse behind them, throbbing through her skull. Still, there was something in his eyes, something worth trusting. Slowly, she nodded.

"I'm sorry for being so direct," he continued, "it's just... Well, I've found it can take hours to get to the point with your kind when you dance around it."

"How did you know?" she asked, her throat suddenly dry. She looked him over for a keyhole but found none.

"Ah, right," he said, nodding. "You'll have to forgive me again, I always forget how surprising your kind finds that, seeing as I don't have that — what do you call it? — glowing buzz about me."

"A keyhole?" she asked.

"Quite right," he said, smiling. "Anyway, to answer your question, I've spent most of my career studying Shapewalkers. I was an expert in history and genealogy at the university. It was actually my studies into the lineage of House Berill that got me my first archival job here. But as I'm sure you can imagine, you can only study so many birth and marriage records before you start putting two and two together. I had my suspicions when you were researching Continental magic those many months ago, but when you came back and asked about genealogy, well,

I suppose I couldn't resist."

"Huh," Sumi said, staring at the bookshelf behind Peloris's head. This man was a renowned scholar, so maybe not just *anyone* could figure it out, but it sounded so simple when he said it. "And…it doesn't bother you to know about us?"

"No, no," he chuckled, "quite the contrary. I suppose I would fall into Pallinayum's camp. I'm a scholar, and I like the unknown. I've also met too many of your kind to be afraid any longer. It's like fearing the rain. But I *would* like to help. By the time someone comes to me, it's usually because they've asked themselves some very important questions. Questions that are safer to ask someone you can trust."

She met his eyes, and he raised his eyebrows. When she didn't say anything, he smiled.

"I presume," he said, "that your search for genealogies means you're looking for more of your kind?"

She couldn't stop herself from laughing. Apparently, this library really would be here for her exactly when she needed it. She'd been joking about the goddess of libraries, but maybe Wellonai really did have another daughter hiding somewhere between the pages of a book.

"As a matter of fact," Sumi said, "that's exactly what I'm looking for. I suppose I just didn't think it would be so…easy."

"I suppose easy is all in the perspective, my dear. I'm part of a little group of, let's say, like-minded individuals. And I've been allowed to recruit over the years — circumspectly, mind you. I think they'd be interested in meeting you. But I've also known them to disappoint. Sometimes, realizing your own kind is so close at hand isn't as reassuring as you think. Tell me, what is it you hope to find?"

Sumi opened her mouth to speak but stopped. This was the part where everything began to sound absurd — ancient magic, goddesses, all of it. But this *was* what she had been sent to do. No matter how hard it was to say out loud, it was the truth. She closed her eyes, reaching for Essomuai. She felt the golden glow in her heart, heard the librarian's song, the deep quiet of the stone around them. She could do this.

She opened her eyes, starting from the beginning — the very beginning — the creation of the world, Vilodai, their exile to the Isles of Dawn. Peloris opened his eyes wide at first, but then he started taking notes, nodding furiously as she talked. By then, she didn't feel afraid anymore. Between his fascination and her passion, the story seemed to pour out of her until she reached her own life: Nela, Anushai, finding the fountain. Finally, she finished, gasping for breath as she gulped down her tea.

"Absolutely…fascinating," he said, blinking at her over his glasses.

"You don't think it sounds…silly?" she asked.

"Far from it," he said, smiling. "In fact, you may have answered a question I've been asking myself all my life." He spun slowly in his chair, taking out a leatherbound book from the shelf behind him. He opened it, revealing a large map of the Isles.

"I've never been a religious man — not that I doubt the more…divine elements in your story — but our myths never made much sense to me. More importantly, the artifacts we found on our digs in the Isles didn't match the histories at all. I suppose now we know why."

He looked up at her, smiling again. Maybe it was the scholar in him, but he didn't seem bothered by hundreds of years of Berillai beliefs being tossed out in a moment. Perhaps he could help her explain it to the others, then… After all, Vilodai *was* Umilai; it would just take some getting used to.

"At any rate," he said, closing the book, "I think you certainly ought to join us for a meeting; we have one tomorrow night. But I should warn you, some of the people in attendance might surprise you."

He fumbled through his pockets, his coat apparently full of them, until he found a small key.

"Knew it was in there!" he said. "Anyway, a secret for a secret — it's only fair."

He unlocked a drawer in his desk, pulling out a thick green notebook.

"These are my personal notes," he said, turning through the pages, "a sort of private genealogy of the kingdom. Nothing particularly incriminating in here, mind you, though my wife is under strict instructions to raid this drawer when I die. Still, it should help paint a picture."

He turned the notebook around, sliding it across the desk. It seemed to depict a sort of family tree. There was a thick trunk in the middle with little bubbles sprouting along the sides, sticking out over time. The bubbles had names from all over the Continent, but the central trunk all had the same name — Pont'dulairn.

Her eyes shot up, locking with Peloris's.

"The Vice Peer?" she asked.

"Indeed," he said, nodding, "one of you."

She looked back down at the names on the page, the bubbles suddenly seeming full of possibility.

"And these names?" she asked.

"All the foreign brides taken into his house," he said. "They've made something of a tradition of it in their house, as you can see. I originally became interested in this as I tried to map the blood of the Berillai. It wasn't long until the Pont'dulairns realized the implications of my research and…enlightened me. I suppose I'm lucky they brought me into the fold instead of taking other measures. This is, of course, quite sensitive information."

"How…can this be?" she asked, her mind whirling with the implications. This was…enormous, but how did it square with the rest of Berill, with all the pain her kind had gone through?

"I know," he said, smiling sadly, seeming to understand. "I suppose we've done what we can, but that's part of why I'd like you to come tomorrow. We need fresh eyes. We've been too content to take small steps, and I want more. I may not have much longer to live, but I want to leave this kingdom better than I found it. They need to hear your story, Miss Elerair, but more importantly, I think you have the heart to change these people. So… Will you join us?"

She took a deep breath. Of course, she had to go. The truth was the truth, and she needed to speak it, even if she'd thought she'd be doing so with people like her. But maybe this was her true audience, the people who most needed to change.

"Of course," she finally said. "Tell me where to be, and I'll be there."

13

If you close yourself off to the possibility that things could be different, the pattern has no choice but to repeat. You think by winning the next war, the Berillai will somehow admit you were right all along? They'll just create something worse than a train, and we'll be right back where we started.

-Excerpt from the tenth letter
Essolurei to Hiyelleom

—:—

Parimu walked down the dusty road to Pauper's Gardens, flowers clutched tightly in his hand. Was it just him, or were the trees somehow more towering than last time? It had been more than ten years, of course… Otherwise, though, the place seemed unchanged, frozen in time. The city still hadn't reached that far, and the only thing taller than the trees was the smoke from the crematorium, lifting in an endless column.

He probably should have been helping the others with their search, but he couldn't seem to bring himself to do it. Even the way he had discovered the keyholes, it all reminded him of what he used to be — a hunter, a killer. Maybe one day, if Sumi discovered how to teach him the songs, he could find his kind that way instead, without the taint of his past.

Still, it wasn't like he'd seen nothing on his trip through the city. He'd even ridden the trolley, so eager to *feel* his people that he no longer seemed to mind the metal deathtraps. And now…he felt he understood them in a way he never could before. Looking back at his life — and Jalicyne's — he could see now why they came to the city. The jobs in the factories were grueling, the risks tremendous, but these people were *hoping* for something, some change in their lives, and he found himself wanting that change, too. Shapewalkers hadn't taken Jalicyne from him, ignorance had, closing themselves to the value of humans and Shapewalkers alike. And that's why he'd come back, wasn't it? Sumi could show them a way to change, to transform. It might take years, but if she could save him, she could save them all.

He made it to the end of the road, the smokestack finally coming into view over the canopy. As he came into the field, he found the grass already waist-high, the years of ash and bone giving life in the wake of death. He could make out men in the distance, moving through the ash with rakes. But this time, he didn't ask for permission, simply walking into the field. They'd only thought him strange the first time, and besides, he knew where he was headed. He pushed through the grass until he was in the center, roughly the same place he'd left the flowers last time.

He sat down in the grass, no longer worried about his trousers. For the first time in his adult life, he was in Berill without a uniform. He sat cross-legged and closed his eyes, putting the flowers on the ground in front of him. He listened to the wind moving through the grass, the birds chirping from the trees. Even the gentle grating of the rakes seemed like part of the forest, blending into a wall of sound. Maybe that was what Sumi's songs were like, the world weaving together. He waited until he felt himself blending into that sound, and then he spoke.

"Hi, Jalicyne," he said, smiling as he imagined her watching him, how silly he must look. "I guess we talk all the time now, but I still wanted to come. I don't know if any part of you is still here, but I brought flowers."

He undid the twine around the bouquet, fanning the blooms across the ground. Last time he'd brought roses, but now, he had wildflowers, like the kind that had grown everywhere in the summer in Emillon.

"I wanted you to know that I'm back in Berill. I…understand why you came here now. I don't know what will happen next, but I'm going to try and help them. Thank you for teaching me, and thank you for being my friend. This might be dangerous, but whatever happens to me, I know I'll see you again. And when I do…I hope I'll have done you proud."

He didn't wait for her response this time. He stood, leaving the flowers on the grass as he headed back to the city. Besides, whatever came next, she was with him all the time. And hopefully, when everything was over, it'd be her voice welcoming him home.

———

Two hours later, Sumi finally made it back to Parimu's. She'd been fit to bursting with all the things she had to tell them, but then, of course, she had to walk all the way back from the library. And then — life seeming to march on no matter what happened — she'd stopped to buy some bread so she could contribute to dinner for once. Still, as soon as she was through the garden gate, she flew up the steps, bursting through the front door in her excitement.

As she swept into the kitchen, though, she came up short, staring at the boys as they stood at the stove together, muttering over a pot with a cookbook held between them. She set down her bag, and they both whipped around, not having heard her come in.

"Are you…cooking together?" she asked.

"It's not what it looks like," Erso said quickly.

"We…uh…couldn't do lamb two nights in a row," Parimu added, "and well, yes."

"Aww!" she exclaimed, rushing over and grabbing them in a big hug. They both resisted slightly, but she ignored them, basking in the harmony of their songs as she took in a deep breath.

"Wait…" she asked, a strange smell filling her nose, "what *is* that?!" She peeked her eyes open, twisting out of the hug to stand over their…concoction. Bright red liquid bubbled in the pot where large chunks of grain were floating. It smelled…earthy, like a cross between the docks and Vilodai's cave.

"It's meant to be a stew," Parimu said, limply holding up the cookbook.

"But the recipe called for mutton," Erso said, "which I vetoed, of course."

"So, we used a canned fish," Parimu continued, "but when we added the peppers, it turned…this color."

"I thought maybe we could add extra grain to balance it out," Erso said, "but it just puffed up way too big."

"Huh," Sumi said, taking the chef's spoon and bringing a scoop to her nose. Up close, it…burned a bit, making her crinkle her nose.

"Well, looks — and smells — can be deceiving, right? I'm sure it'll be lovely."

"Sure, sure," Erso said. "Just cause you're Essomuai's angel doesn't mean you can't tell it to us straight."

She rolled her eyes. Yes, behold the sacred messenger of the gods. She ladled herself a bowl, giving Erso a look as she marched it to the kitchen table. They both watched her in stunned silence, unmoving as she took up her spoon and took a bite. It was certainly…strange. They had combined what should be totally normal ingredients, ending up with something a bit like fermented squid. Still, some combination of the stew's saltiness and her own ravenous hunger from her walk made her take a second bite, and by the third and fourth, she thought she might actually like it after all. She looked up, smiling at the others.

"Well," she said, "what are you waiting for?"

They both scrambled over, Parimu filling two more bowls while Erso started slicing the bread.

"Whoa, there," Erso said, walking over with a plate. "Remember to breathe, admiral."

"Noh-timf," she said between mouthfuls as she took up a piece of bread. She covered her mouth, trying not to laugh as she swallowed. "Honestly, though," she said, "it's not that bad. Tastes like squid."

"Great," Erso said, rolling his eyes. "I should've just suffered through the mutton."

Parimu came, sitting opposite Erso.

"Well, I'm glad it's edible, at least," he said. "Unfortunately, this is all I have to show for my time in the city. Did you two find anything?"

"Yes!" Sumi cried out, clapping a hand to her chest. "I can't believe I almost forgot! I think I might have found quite a lot, actually."

"Really?" Erso asked, pausing with a piece of bread near his mouth. "I walked to Wembly and back today and still didn't see a thing."

"Actually," she said, "I think there may be a reason for that. I have reason to believe most of the Shapewalkers in the city might be fairly important, people you wouldn't bump into on the street — like that carriage you saw the first day."

"Like who?" Parimu asked, leaning forward.

"Well," she said, "Vice Peer Pont'dulairn, for instance."

Erso coughed, choking on his bread, and Parimu dropped his spoon.

"I know," she said quickly, "I barely believe it myself, but while I was at the library today, I met with the Master Librarian. He has all these private marriage records of the royal bloodlines. It makes sense when you think about it. I only have Nela to attach my blood to the Continent, but the family tree I saw of Pont'dulairn…there's dozens."

"Huh," Parimu said, staring into the table. He finally looked up, meeting her eyes. "I don't know whether that makes me feel better or worse."

She reached out and took his hand, gripping it.

"I know," she said. "I don't know why they haven't done more. But Peloris — that's the librarian's name — he thinks we could help them.

Whatever their motives were in the past, he thinks telling them my story could help. About Essomuai, about where we came from."

"I wonder..." Erso said, still staring into space. He looked up at Parimu. "That trick I played on you last year, with the Vice Peer's wife, and all those changes he's making to the police. You think this could be why?"

"Maybe," Parimu admitted. "I thought he was only for commerce, but he *has* been pulling police off departments like mine for years."

"And you're sure this isn't a trap?" Erso asked, turning to her.

"I trust the Master Librarian," she said, nodding firmly. "They have a meeting tomorrow night, and if there's a chance of finding a bunch of Shapewalkers in one place, we have to try."

"Where's the meeting?" Erso asked.

"In the Lournoy," she said, "at the Vice Peer's house."

"We're going," Erso and Parimu blurted out at the exact same time. They looked at each other, and then all three of them started laughing.

"Alright," she said, holding up her hands in surrender. "We'll all go. At least they'll be impressed by my bodyguards."

14

*Keteraln presented some interesting letters from the desk of the DoR.
It appears his correspondence with the king has increased of late. He
proposed we broker a small meeting, seconded by Pristelorn.*

-Meeting Minutes of Dialasera's Rose
Weremin 793 PD

—:—

The next day passed at an excruciating speed, at once lethargic and
frantic, the hours somehow passing between vain attempts at fixing her
clothes and perfecting her disguise. Finally, as the sun set, Sumi stood
with Erso on the porch, waiting for Parimu to return with a hired carriage.
She started pacing again, Erso chuckling to himself as he smoked his
pipe, though the nervous tapping of his foot gave him away.

She stopped, pulling at the hem of her cloak again, making sure it still
looked how she wanted it to. She'd shaped it into silk, hiding the dust of
the road and adding lace in a few places. She'd also lowered the bust of
her dress just a bit, which made her flush again just thinking about it…
But they were going to the Lournoy! These people would be fashionable,
and for once, she needed to hope she looked the part.

"It looks as perfect as it did a minute ago," Erso said without turning
around.

"I hope so," she said, looking up. "How do you go around in shaped
clothes all the time anyway? I'm terrified they'll give up on me halfway
through the meeting."

"You'll be fine," he said, waving a hand. "You'll get at least two days
out of those. Besides, if your clothes are going to turn back, you'll feel
a little shake. Might actually show up in their song, too. Trust me, though,

you'll be fine."

"Right," she said, nodding, "bigger fish to fry. Is this face alright, though?"

"Not as pretty as you," Erso said, glancing at her disguise, "but it'll do. You look perfectly respectable, miss."

She heard the squeak of a wheel and turned, finding Parimu riding toward them beside the driver of an open-air carriage. He waved, pointing to the house as the driver pulled up on the side of the street.

Once they were all aboard, they rode through the city in silence. Even the driver seemed to sense their mood and kept to himself, only muttering occasionally to his horses. Still, the trip went by all too quickly, giving her almost no time to tame the butterflies in her stomach before they pulled up in front of the Vice Peer's house. Seeming to materialize out of nowhere, suddenly, a pair of footmen were there, helping her down. She only had time for a glance at the giant stone facade before they were ushered into the hall, one of the footmen disappearing with their cloaks as the other led them deeper into the house.

The footman promised to take them to "the Long Library," which, of course, meant there were other libraries that weren't as long. And there were certainly enough places to hide them… In their short walk, they passed a number of cavernous rooms, fireplaces and lamps lit despite the lack of occupants. Part of her wished she could pay attention to all the statues and wall hangings, but it took all of her strength just to walk straight with her pulse pounding in her throat. Finally, they reached a thick wooden door carved into a herd of deer. The footman gave them a short bow and rapped on the door, the sound of footsteps approaching.

After a moment, a well-dressed butler opened the door, revealing a large library. It looked almost as if it had been added onto the house, not at all in the Berillai style, though it was beautiful. Even from the door in the corner, she could see a blazing fire and a wall full of books that seemed to wrap around the room.

"Mistress Sumilnyeon Elerair and her chaperones," the butler announced in a deep voice, snapping her back to attention as he bowed her through the doorway. She had been expecting some kind of hushed, secret conclave, but what they stepped into seemed more like a posh party. There were about two dozen people inside, a mix of men and women standing in small groups in gowns and suits. At least she'd shaped her dress…

As they stepped through, every eye turned to them, and she hastily curtsied, suddenly feeling very small. Was a curtsey even the right etiquette when meeting peers? It felt like the palace in Anushai all over again. Why didn't she ever bother learning anything important?! She stood there as Erso and Parimu came up behind her, both of them bowing, albeit at seemingly different angles.

She looked around the room, trying to smile her most winning smile, and a few of the faces nodded to her or smiled in return, though most of them simply watched. Thankfully, though, she finally noticed the Master Librarian in a chair by a matching fireplace on the other end of the room. He smiled warmly and waved his cane before pushing himself out of the chair.

"Please, please," another man said nearby, "no need to be so formal. Help yourself to some drinks, and feel free to take your usual forms, we're all friends here."

Sumi turned to look at him, and her breath came up short. He was tall with a wide smile and a face she'd know anywhere from the newspapers — Vice Peer Pont'dulairn. She smiled back foolishly before turning to look at Parimu and Erso. She raised her eyebrows, but they simply shrugged, apparently indifferent to taking their own forms. She nodded, closing her eyes as she glowed, turning into herself — albeit with the same fancy dress from before. Erso reappeared in his best suit, and Parimu showed up in his uniform of all things.

"See?" the Vice Peer asked as he stepped up to them, "isn't that better?" He started on the right, shaking Erso's hand.

"A pleasure," Erso said simply, nodding.

Then he took Sumi's hand in both of his, the gesture suddenly reassuring and terrifying at the same time.

"Vice Peer," she said, bowing her head.

"Please," he said, waving a hand, "like I said, we're all friends here. Call me Kemarin."

He moved on to Parimu.

"Now, this is certainly a surprise, Detective. I wasn't sure I'd ever get to meet you, least of all in a place like this."

"Er…thank you," Parimu said, nodding.

The Vice Peer stepped back, gesturing to the rest of the room.

"Everyone," he said, "please make our guests comfortable. Take a few more minutes to refresh your drinks, and we'll get started."

He turned back to them, gesturing to a bar along the interior wall.

"Why don't you chaps grab some drinks before we start? I'd love to chat with Miss Elerair here for a moment."

Ever loyal, Erso and Parimu paused for the fraction of a second it took for her to nod before they wandered over to the bar, the rest of the guests quietly resuming their conversations.

The Vice Peer offered her his arm, returning to the group he'd been chatting with when they arrived. One was a man in a trim grey suit who introduced himself as Bowern, while the other was a stunning woman. She had a Three Sisters look about her, standing at least a head taller than herself with blonde hair and a flowing maroon dress.

"My wife, Elisal," Pont'dulairn said warmly.

"How do you do," she said with a slight accent as she curtsied. Besides the librarian, she was the only person in the room without a keyhole, but she seemed unfazed by the company she was keeping.

"Oh, my apologies," the Vice Peer said, waving for his butler, "I almost forgot a drink for you. Is kessembul alright?"

"Of course," Sumi said, nodding quickly.

"Excellent," Pont'dulairn said. "Now, Miss Elerair, I can't tell you how excited I am you've joined us tonight — not to mention how glad I am that you're alright. Your escape caused quite the stir last year. Still, I want to assure you that we'll find some kind of accommodation for you and your friends."

"Erm…thank y—" she began to say, but he continued right on.

"We are all absolutely fascinated by your stories. I think we all have a bit of a penchant for all things Continental, given our…pedigree. And Peloris has told me you have the most interesting things to say about the old goddesses and all that."

She nodded, her mind whirring with how to respond. What she had to tell them was far more than stories, and what she wanted could well be more than they were willing to give. Luckily, just then, she felt a touch on her elbow, and the Master Librarian was there, smiling up at her.

"Hello, Sumi," he said, "I'm so glad you could make it."

"Thank you for inviting me," she said, bowing, "it's lovely to see you again."

"Kemarin," Peloris said, turning, "I think we best leave the girl some time to speak to the group at large. We all need to listen well to what she has to say."

"Of course," Pont'dulairn said, nodding absently as the butler arrived with a tray of kessembul flutes. He reached out and grabbed one, handing it to her. She took a careful sip — it wouldn't do to lose her head — but the wine *was* good. It wasn't as sweet as cloud wine, but it was fizzier, with bubbles that could float you up to the ceiling. But she knew she wasn't here for wine. Beyond the fancy suits and marble floors, she was here to reach these people, to *change* them.

"Alright, everyone!" Pont'dulairn said in a loud voice, clapping his hands. "We have a full agenda tonight, so let's begin."

Everyone began to arrange themselves on the chairs and sofas in the center of the room. The Vice Peer pointed her toward a green sofa by the bar.

"Why don't you sit with your friends over there?" he asked. "That way, the whole room can see you."

The Master Librarian winked at her before shuffling back toward the fireplace. She nodded, heading to the other side of the room where Erso and Parimu were extricating themselves from a pair of older women. One of them laughed behind a gloved hand before squeezing Erso on the arm. The woman could have been her mother, but still, she felt a strange pang of jealousy, if only because it reminded her of losing him. But she'd rather see him with other women than lose him altogether. He could leave her, but she couldn't imagine being done with him, not after all they'd been through.

"I see you've found a friend," she said in mock anger, primly joining him in the middle of the couch.

He looked at her, bewildered.

"My dear," he whispered, "she's at least fifty."

She grinned, shrugging as she took a sip of her kessembul. He rolled his eyes, blowing out his mustache. Ribbing him did make her feel better, actually, as if there wasn't a room full of rich people staring at them. Still, as the room grew quiet, every eye on her, her hand began to sweat around the glass.

"Well," the Vice Peer said, smiling, "welcome, everyone. Thank you for joining us tonight. To begin, perhaps a bit of context might be useful to our new friends."

He gestured toward the fireplace on his right, where there was a long tapestry above the mantle. It depicted a stunning woman, tall and regal. She wore a crown of heathers in her hair and a flowing silver dress, surrounded by men on horseback. Her eyes were on the distance, her hands clinging to a thick bundle of branches.

"My great-grandmother by several dozen, Dialasera, was likely the first Shapewalker in our kingdom," he said. "As soon as the Mesop War was over, the chieftains offered their highest-born daughters in marriage to seal the treaty. King Rummon, of course, was dead, and his brother — then *King* Laeryia — was already betrothed. So, the honor of marrying her went to my foremost ancestor, the First Duke Pont'dulairn.

"Since then, our numbers have only grown. For centuries, we had no formal organization, though we tried our best to keep our secrets. It wasn't until my father that we formally built our association, Dialasera's

Rose. The work is difficult, but we have two essential goals. One is to protect as many Shapewalkers as we can — sometimes working with the DoR, other times avoiding them depending on the...level of their abilities."

She glanced at Parimu, whose fists were clenched, his eyes unmoving on the Vice Peer. She reached over, squeezing his arm.

"The second," he continued, "is to build a bridge between Berill and the Continent. It is difficult work, of course, and we have had to be cautious, but if you've read about my latest bill, I think we are *truly* on the verge of real change. Still, cautious or not, we will always do what we can for our own kind, so please know that you are most welcome here. I can promise, too, that we're extremely interested in all things Continental. So, if you wouldn't mind sharing your story with us, Miss Elerair, I think you'll find a most captive audience."

Sumi nodded, taking in a breath. That was about as good of an invitation as she'd ever receive, though it seemed harder to jump now that she'd walked up to the edge of the cliff. Still, who better to practice her heresies on than a secret group of Shapewalkers living in Berill?

"Thank you again for having me," she said, ignoring the lump in her throat. "I suppose this group will be more open to what I'm about to say than most. I assume you all know the legends of Anushai and the three goddesses?"

She was met with a number of nods and smiles.

"Good," she said, feeling her face mirroring their smiles, though she didn't quite have the feeling to match it. "This may sound a bit fanciful, but those are...our true gods. The Shapewalkers, all of us, were created by the first sister, Essomuai. There...is no Umilai, no Alomus." She looked to Peloris, who was nodding eagerly by the fireplace. "I'm not sure where they came from, but I think they're just misunderstandings, names we made up on the Isles because we forgot."

There were a few whispers at that, but mostly, she was met with silence. The Vice Peer was stroking his chin and nodding, his wife staring into the carpet. Was it too much? Was it not enough? Standing before these people, her limitations felt all too real. Essomuai had shoved two thousand years of history into her mind, and she was supposed to just explain it with words? She probably never would have understood a fraction of it if she hadn't seen it for herself. She was going to try and show them the songs tonight, but without *hearing* them, would they really understand? She was about to speak again — anything to fill the silence — when Peloris cleared his throat.

"You see," he said, shuffling in his chair to face the wider group. "As many of you know, I've long advocated for a more — shall we say, thorough? — review of our history. As soon as I heard Sumi's story, it seemed to hold the answers to many of my questions. If you don't mind," he added, turning back to her with a smile, "perhaps you could share with them a bit of the history — Elomikarus and the Southern Empire."

That blessed man! Maybe there was hope; maybe with him to guide her, they would see the truth in her story.

She nodded, and then, she began, from the beginning. Perhaps the endpoint — which gods existed, and which didn't — was simply too large to absorb. But the rest was a *story;* it was people and places that you could see in your mind, a space where her ideas really *lived*. And somehow, blessedly, her audience seemed to change as she told it. No longer staring into space, their eyes were on her, following every word, no doubt picturing Elomikarus, his palace, all the hidden facets of their world. She fell into the rhythm of the story, her mind starting to hear the songs without her meaning to, the threads of her dreams seeming to connect her to Essomuai. Even Vilodai's necklace seemed to thrum against her chest. And in that moment, for the first time, she realized one simple truth — Vilodai had *loved* Elomikarus. He had been so afraid of her wrath, but he was her child, and she was glowing with warmth at hearing his story told properly.

She wasn't sure how long she spoke, though she had to stop several times to sip her wine, anything to keep her voice afloat as her throat grew weary. She told them everything: the Isles, Rummon, even her own story — her trip to the fountain and the goddesses she found there. Finally, she stopped, breathing heavily, and she found Erso's hand squeezing hers as if whispering that she'd done well.

For a moment, there was silence, but a good kind, the feeling of her story still floating in the air until finally, the Vice Peer's wife spoke.

"These songs of…Essomuai," Elisal said, her mouth stumbling over the Anushai name. "Perhaps you could show us?" Still, her eyes looked eager, reflecting the firelight.

Sumi smiled. That's what she'd been waiting for — hoping for, anyway — a chance to show them the goddess. On her own, she was limited, but with Essomuai, the whole thing became clearer, dreams suddenly close enough to touch.

"I'd love to," she said. "If you wouldn't mind volunteering, I thought perhaps I could show you a shape from your song. Would that be alright, Lady Pont'dulairn?"

Elisal nodded, standing up from her chair, her hands clutched tightly together.

While she was preparing the night before — or tossing and turning in her bed for hours, anyway — she'd decided the best way to show off the songs was through the most important person from someone's past. She'd never forget how it had felt to sit across from Empress Hiyelleom in Nela's form, what a treasure it had been. And hopefully, since Elisal was human, it would be all the more moving. She had no way to summon her loved ones for herself, not even in a mirror as a Shapewalker could.

She stood from her own sofa, facing Elisal.

"Essomuai is in all of us," she said, "and each of us has a song that Essomuai can sing — even humans. If it's not too intrusive, I'd like to show you someone from your past."

Elisal nodded eagerly.

She took a deep breath and closed her eyes, letting Elisal's song pour into her. She'd gotten so used to quieting them, controlling when they filled her mind, that it still came as a shock when she really stopped to listen. It was like a river, an entire life flooding your heart in the blink of an eye. Suddenly, as if it had always been there, Elisal's life was surging through her. She saw the moment Elisal entered the world, her father speaking her name as the light bent into her tiny eyes. Even more than being born, being named recreated her somehow, lighting the fire that was still burning, connecting all her days.

And as the song flowed, Elisal's loved ones seemed to coalesce, the memories piling on top of one another like an overexposed photograph. They swirled around each other: her mother, her siblings, their palace, but most of all, her father. He had been the King of Rachelar, but to Elisal he was still just 'papa.' He had been a stern man, but he'd always had a smile for his little Elisa, taking her into the mountains with an easel to teach her how to paint. He had eyes like cold water, and his beard tickled when he kissed her good night. She could smell the cigar smoke lingering on his jacket, the whiskey he would drink each night. And then, she felt his death, the memories soaked in searing grief. Still, the love lingered, his presence never leaving, even with miles and decades between them.

Sumi breathed out, transforming into the king. She opened her eyes, watching as Elisal's hand went to her mouth, whispering in Trierlien as she sank into the couch, the words filtered through Essomuai.

"*Offnul hensen teilen, Papa,*" Elisal said — *I hoped it would be you, Papa.*

Elisal shook her head just as Hiyelleom had as if trying to force herself to wake from a dream. She reached for a handkerchief, dabbing at her eyes.

"Thank you," she said quietly in Berillai, "thank you."

Sumi nodded, flashing back into her original form.

"That is…a most astonishing ability, Miss Elerair," the Vice Peer said, a hand on Elisal's shoulder. "I never had the opportunity to meet my father-in-law, but I think I speak for both of us when I say we are truly grateful to see him now."

He turned to check on his wife again, but his voice seemed to break the spell hanging over the room, the others whispering to each other. She sat back down beside the others, feeling wrung out but somehow…satisfied. It had worked; she'd shown them Essomuai, and the rest would have to follow after. Finally, the Vice Peer turned back, his arms wide.

"What a display," he said, nodding to the Master Librarian, "thank you, Peloris, for bringing us Miss Elerair. I think I speak for all of us when I say this group is at your service. Whatever you need: a place to hide in the countryside, resources, whatever you require. We would all do well to have you with us."

She looked back at him, blinking in the dim light. After everything in her story…*that's* what he thought she wanted? It was kind of him, true, he didn't owe her anything, but that was very nearly exactly what Hiyelleom had offered her. Perhaps it had been naive, but she'd thought someone like her — Berillai and Shapewalker — would see. See the need to make their home safe, to be who they really were. The Master Librarian cleared his throat again.

"I think, Kemarin," he said, his quiet voice somehow filling the room, "that a different kind of help is in order. Please, Miss Elerair, if you'd share the plans you described to me."

"Right," she said, nodding gratefully before turning back to the Vice Peer. "I can't tell you how much I appreciate your kindness, truly, but I *do* have something else in mind."

She took one last deep breath, forcing herself to look right into the Vice Peer's eyes.

"All of this pain and suffering — the dead on both sides, the hundreds of years we lost on the Isles — it's all part of a cycle, and the goddesses want it to stop. *I* want it to stop. I want to change Berill, and I hope you'll help me."

Pont'dulairn had taken his seat again and was watching her with his fingers tented in front of his mouth. He didn't say anything, so she continued.

"I think," she continued slowly, "that the answer is in the songs, in what I showed the Vice Peeress. If we can show Essomuai to the people,

I don't think they'll fear us anymore. I know the rest won't be easy, and I'll need your help in the Peerage, but I think we have to try. Until the humans know we aren't monsters, nothing else will change."

The Vice Peer ran a hand through his hair, finally seeming to shake off the vision of his father-in-law. He sat up taller in his chair, seeming to speak less to her than to the room.

"I think we can all agree that it is time for change," he said, which received more than a few nods. "But, my dear, the situation in Berill is very…delicate. If you want peace, I promise you, my military bill is the best way forward. If we can control the navy, there will be far less death, far less suffering."

She glanced at Parimu, his face ashen, and suddenly she felt surprisingly…angry, the words leaving her mouth before she could stop them.

"And our kind?" she asked. "Will your bill make it no longer a crime? Will it change the memory of those we've hung?"

The Vice Peer grimaced.

"Yes, our kind die every day, and it sickens me, but what would you have me do? Do you have any idea the factions moving in this kingdom? How quickly they would come down on us if they knew?"

Sumi felt a heat rush up her neck, part shame at her outburst and part frustration. The fact was, she didn't know about the factions of Berill, didn't know anything about writing laws, but she was Berillai, and she knew her people. She had seen the good and bad in them, and she knew this magic could change things. It had to.

"I'm sorry," she said, "I don't know anything about politics, about how hard you've worked on your bills. But I know the people, and that's why I want to take the magic straight to them. That's why I want to hold a parade."

The Vice Peer scoffed, his mouth falling open.

"A parade?" he asked, looking at her like she had two heads. Elisal touched her husband's arm with a stern look, but he shook her off.

"I'm sorry, Miss Elerair," he continued, "but that is simply preposterous. To do what you propose is to invite death on us all, not to mention erasing every bit of progress we've made these last thirty years!"

"Well, I don't know," one of the other guests began, "I think if we—"

"No!" the Vice Peer snapped, his face growing dark. "This is not up for discussion."

Sumi blinked, suddenly cold. She wanted to shrink into herself, to disappear under that gaze. Maybe it had been foolish to come here. She knew how it sounded, knew it seemed fanciful. But…she thought after hearing her story, after seeing the magic, they would understand. The Vice Peer went on, his voice growing icier with every word.

"I will not have my life's work, my father's life work, undone for a daydream. My offer still stands to harbor you, girl, but you must promise me not to do anything foolish."

"Kemarin," the Master Librarian said sharply, pushing himself from his chair. "I think we have much to discuss amongst ourselves. Let's let our guests retire for now, and we can continue this in private."

The Vice Peer snapped his head toward Peloris, his eyes still afire, though something in him immediately cooled under the Librarian's equally fierce gaze.

"Fine," he said. He took a deep breath and sighed it out before standing. "Thank you for joining us tonight. It might be best if we did take some time to discuss what you've told us. Please hold off on what you're planning until we can get back in touch with you."

"Of course," Sumi said, standing. "Thank you."

She bowed hastily, blinking hard as she tried to hold back the last bit of dignity she'd lose if she cried. At least she could avoid seeming like a child and a fool. *Thank you*, she mouthed to the librarian before turning to go. He remained standing, nodding to her, though his smile was gone. Erso offered her his arm, and she took it gratefully, allowing him to pull her back out into the hall. As the butler closed the door behind them, loud voices started up again.

They swept through the mansion in silence behind the footman and back into the night. One tear slipped from her eye, and she was glad for the darkness to hide her. She felt like she was standing beneath a mountain, unsure of how to begin the climb. Maybe Peloris could help them, but it seemed more likely they would have to begin again — a new plan, a new path. She knew Essomuai waited for her at the top, but at the moment, she just felt small, like an ant that would never live to see the peak.

15

If you could only see them on the high holidays! I've never seen farmers give so much from their own lands. It's nearly double the alms day from the gardens. Perhaps it would change your mind about these so-called 'bloodthirsty' enemies.

-Excerpt from the seventh letter
Essolurei to Hiyelleom

—:—

Erso followed Sumi into the dark outside the house, Parimu close behind them. Somehow, their cabby was still there, their destination apparently promising enough to wait for a second fare. Halls knew they needed more than a ride home, but he'd take his luck where he could, and it beat walking home. The footman helped Sumi up before offering his hand to Erso, but he simply tipped his cap, climbing up to the seat on his own.

Once they were all seated, the cabby smiled at them, oblivious to their silence.

"Where to next?" he asked. "Hope you don't mind my waiting around, but I figure fine folks like you could always use a dependable ride."

Sumi looked up, but her eyes were empty, lit only by the sheen of her tears in the lamplight.

"Back where we came from," Erso said quickly. He couldn't do much, but he could at least handle the cab. The driver nodded, flipping the reins as he turned in a wide arc. Sumi leaned against the side of the carriage, staring down at the street. She was wearing her disguise again — the footman had at least let them put those back on before kicking them to the curb — but even without her own face, she looked…finished.

Erso sighed, pulling off his hat as he ran a hand through his hair. He wasn't surprised, of course. Sumi and Parimu were glaring exceptions, but otherwise, all the bloody Berillai were money-grubbing cheats, apparently even the Shapewalkers. He couldn't seem to muster any disappointment at that, though he felt Sumi's well enough.

The worst part was her plan wasn't half bad. The Vice Pompous Blighter had given her a tongue-lashing, sure, but there really was a certain logic to the parade idea. You couldn't put a wig on a goat — the Berillai would always be, well…Berillai — but if you wanted to stop being a monster, what else were you supposed to do? As mum always said, a crowd would never take a poet if they couldn't get a clown.

Not that the parade would get any easier now. They'd have to find a new barrel of Shapewalkers somewhere, not to mention doing the whole thing right under Pont'dulairn's nose. Erso wasn't particularly political himself, but he knew men, and Pont'dulairn was a dangerous one. He might wear the suit of a muckety-muck, but he had the eyes of a killer. And all of that was assuming Sumi could lick her wounds and carry on. It was one thing to disappoint him — he was a world-class cynic, after all — but Sumi *believed*. That was her magic, the whole reason he'd followed her across the damned Continent. But now… She looked like an egg half-cracked and already boiled besides.

He spared a look for Parimu. He'd been hoping the man could help him console Sumi, but he seemed in pretty rough shape himself. Fair enough. The meeting wasn't likely to sit well with him either, what with Pont'dulairn more or less admitting Parimu's boss had been in on the whole thing. Maybe he wouldn't have a month ago, but he found himself feeling bad for the bloke. He hadn't been a state-sanctioned killer himself, but it would be like finding out Beysal was a bloody Fida'lalean or something.

He shook his head, turning back to Sumi. There were enough thoughts in his head to fill his halls twice, but he had to make sure she was alright. He raised a hand, ready to squeeze her shoulder when he stopped. What right did he have to do that? But then again, she bloody needed him for once, and he'd promised himself he'd play the part. Bloody gods above, was he glad he'd snuck both of those whiskeys in the library — even if it only proved how damned unfit he was for her. Damn it all! He squeezed her shoulder, leaning in as he lowered his voice.

"Listen," he said, "I'm sorry the Vice Peer was such a git, but you did really well tonight, truly. If I had to dance in front of that many bears, I'd forget my steps for sure."

She looked up, wiping away another tear as she sniffed, showing him the smallest smile he'd ever seen on her face.

"Thank you," she said, "but I think I was the only git in the room tonight."

"Nah," he said, waving a hand through the air, "if having a vision was easy, they wouldn't sell telescopes. Besides, I think the room was more split than you think. Your librarian chap looked ready to box it out, and I wouldn't bet on Pont'dulairn just cause he's young."

She actually chuckled at that, thank the halls, though the smile never reached her eyes.

"Maybe," she said, nodding thoughtfully. He was about to ask her what her plans were — get her focused on the future and all that — but she looked at Parimu instead, worry furrowing her brow. Maybe he did have to break her heart if only to teach her to stop putting everybody else first all the time.

"Are you alright?" she asked Parimu. "That couldn't have been easy to hear."

The detective looked like he could crack a rock in his palm, but he softened as Sumi spoke, pulling his eyes off the floor of the carriage.

"I'll be alright," he said, nodding. "It doesn't change anything, not really. I've never understood any of this, nowhere near as much as I should have. But," he added, letting out a long sigh, "the things I did, I did on my own. Even if I'd been lied to, I still made the choice. So what if I'm a fool as well?" He shook his head. "No, it's time to act. If you'll still have me, I'll do whatever it takes to see your plan through."

"I'm not sure how much of a plan I have left," she said. But she reached out, taking Parimu's hand. "But whatever it is, I'd never do it without you by my side."

The detective nodded gratefully, his eyes no longer on the floor as he turned back. Erso nodded to himself, taking out his pipe. The work wasn't done — they were all just eggshells waiting to crack — but it seemed their ship still had some float left yet. He only had to hope it was enough to ride out the storm.

———

Later, as the night grew quiet, Sumi found herself in the garden again. She leaned against the house, where she could just see a sliver of the sea under the stars. Why did this place have to be so beautiful? For the first time in her life, she found herself wishing she could love her home just a little bit less, find it a fraction less perfect so she could let it go. Because here, in the quiet, she could finally admit to herself that Essomuai had picked the wrong person. Loving a place didn't make you qualified to save it, and being desperate enough to reach out to a god no one believed in didn't make you wise. Maybe Erso was right, and Peloris *would* fight for her, but who was she to ask him — or anyone — to follow her?

Even with all the magic at her disposal, the only idea she'd come up with was a childish parade. The Vice Peer's plans had taken decades of planning, and who was she to get in the way of that? She wanted so badly to show them the beauty of Essomuai, but now it felt like her meddling would only make things worse. Suppose she did the parade herself? Or at least some kind of display… It'd probably end with her being hung, but maybe that would be for the best. If it didn't work, Pont'dulairn could write her off — just another rogue monster in the kingdom. And if it did… Well, she'd have accomplished something without putting anyone at risk with her harebrained schemes.

She sighed, putting her chin on her knees. On the Continent, her sadness had felt so far away, like she'd left it behind. But now, with it threatening to sweep her away, she could see it had been there all along, waiting for her. As if her little adventure could fill the hole inside her. As if the part of her she hid was worth loving. But even Erso wouldn't be here without some misguided need to be noble. And who was she, anyway? One powerful man told her *boo,* and she was already in retreat? When they'd gotten home, the others had scurried about the kitchen, pouring tea and putting out biscuits, tiptoeing around her. It should have been the other way around, with her putting on the brave face, but she was too weak.

She felt a tiny thrum from her necklaces and dug them out from beneath her blouse. She held them in her hand, closing her eyes. *This* was good. *This* was true. She had been right to reject a false peace, had been right to go to the fountain. But maybe this was meant to be the end of her journey? She had brought the information home, had spread it, and now the gods deserved a real champion. Someone like Elomikarus, brave even at the end, not some mousy girl pretending to be a hero. She had put the sisters back together, had freed them of their prison, and now they needed someone worthy of their power.

She blinked, her eyes growing heavy. She'd had a thousand thoughts in the last hour but still no answers. Still, she forced herself to stand, finally looking for her bed. Hopefully, she had stayed awake long enough for sleep to hide her worries, to fill her mind with silence. In the morning, either she'd have the strength to fight again or the wisdom to know it was over. She stepped into the house and left the garden behind, the silvery shadows of the moon slipping away until only the darkness remained.

PART TWO

16

Meeting canceled due to weather. As per the group's bylaws, a replacement meeting can only be held when there are sufficient police absences. I will propose the 6th of next month in a letter to the other chairs.

>   *-Meeting Minutes of Dialasera's Rose*
>   *Ruvarinan 769 PD*

—:—

Peloris sat in his carriage, smiling in the morning sun. He was far too old for his liking — his head ached, and his eyes were bleary — but he smiled all the same. That was the most work he'd done in a single night since he was an archivist! His body would protest for a month, of course, but his mind reveled in it. He had always thrived at night, true, praying by candlelight to his god of books, but more than that, it felt good to spit in the face of death.

Human or Shapewalker, without fail, one day, you would die. But Ciersein was forced to be quiet, sneaking about the shadows. While you lived, on the other hand, the world was yours to shape as you saw fit, to dance upon and shout with glee. Life was noise and chaos, and he'd loved every bloody second of it. He'd be ready when the time came, an old husk with nothing left but piss and vinegar. But *today,* he had work to do — perhaps the most important of his life — and he would see it done.

He leaned forward, rapping on the door to his driver.

"A little faster, will you, Leonar?" he called out.

"But the bumps, sir!" the driver called back.

"To hell with the bumps!" he called back. "We've places to be!"

A bumpy carriage ride probably wouldn't do any wonders for his aches, but he needed to see Sumi as soon as possible. She had a good heart — an unfortunately rare thing in the world — and his plans would mean nothing if they lost her. Not that he thought himself evil or anything…but there was a difference between a hardened old man and a woman full of hope. A soul like hers could make the whole world brighter, like kindness trapped in a bottle. If you let them shine long enough, it was nearly impossible to reverse the good they'd done. He just had to get there before the bitterness of the world could crack the glass.

It was a brave thing she'd done, coming to that meeting. Perhaps he should have warned her more, but those soggy old bastards needed to hear the truth. He refused to filter her message for politics, and even knowing how Pont'dulairn would respond, it was the rest of the room he'd brought her to speak to. Kemarin was a good lad in his own way, but he was just like his father, and he had a skull thick enough to crack iron. But it was time for change, and this girl was the key. He'd spent his whole life searching for a story like hers, and if he didn't shout it from the rooftops, Ciersein could bloody have him.

The carriage zoomed under the wall, heading into the western neighborhoods. The girl had mentioned that she was staying with the detective, and with how long he'd worked for the crown, his address hadn't been hard to find. Still, he didn't often get to venture this far out, living in Sendorin as he did, and he found himself leaning against the window, staring at the passing houses. Each trip might be his last, and he planned to savor all of it.

Funny how nostalgic he'd grown for Berill. He'd tried to escape it often enough in his youth — something Lenara was more than happy to remind him of when she wasn't chiding him for his sweet tooth. But it was home, after all. And now, as it hurtled toward an uncertain future, it seemed new again. Perhaps he should feel jealous of the youth, getting to see what came next, but he found he didn't regret a thing. Even if he'd been born now, he'd still only want to spend his life with his books and his wife. In the end, whatever you had was enough. He only had to hope to leave Berill a better place.

They finally reached the right place, the carriage pulling in front of a quaint little cottage. Peloris climbed down from the carriage with a groan, pointedly ignoring the hand Leonar had offered. He could probably use the help, but when you were feeling fiery, you had to seize it. So what if he fell flat on his face? He happened to know for a fact that the Domelgaines had strong bones, and he didn't have much dignity to lose besides.

"Thank you, Leonar," he said, smiling.

"Sir," the man said, nodding, his face blank. Well, he'd crack him someday. Helping Sumi may be the most *important* thing he did before he died, but he'd make damned sure he didn't stop breathing before getting Leonar to smile.

Peloris set off down the little stone path that led up to the house. The stairs left him more out of breath than he'd like, but finally, he was knocking at the door. Sumi's Amoriai companion appeared in the window, cocking an eyebrow as he opened the door. He hadn't had much of an accent the night before, true, but he *looked* Amoriai anyway. Still, wrong or not, he wouldn't forgive himself if he missed his last chance to practice the language.

"*Yusill emto Amoriai, neshto?*" he asked — *You seem to be Amoriai, no?*

The man chuckled, shaking his head.

"*Mustaka em'toskal shuwes,*" he answered. *Full of surprises, I see.*

Peloris nodded graciously before switching back to Berillai.

"I wondered if Sumi was in. I have some news she might like to hear."

The man — whose name, Erso, he finally bloody remembered — glanced toward the second floor. So, she had taken it hard, then...

"I'm in no hurry," Peloris added quickly, "I'm happy to wait until she's ready."

"Alright," Erso said, nodding slowly. "Why don't we get you some tea or something, and I'll see if she can join you."

The other one, Detective Parimu, stuck his head into the hallway.

"Oh," he said, "um...welcome, Master Librarian. I'm sorry, I didn't realize we had company."

"Just came by to see Sumi," Erso said. "Mind brewing some tea?"

"Not at all," Parimu said, beckoning him toward the kitchen, "please."

Erso nodded, climbing the stairs as Peloris moved into the kitchen. He eyed a comfortable-looking seat at the head of the table and plopped down onto it. When he was younger, he'd never use rank to take a good seat, but when age afforded him that luxury? Well, that, at least, seemed fair. Anyone who'd avoided Ciersein's claws as long as him deserved a comfortable spot, all that 'Master Librarian' nonsense be damned.

"Sorry to barge in on you like this, Detective," he said, watching as the younger man sped about the kitchen, lighting the stove and rifling through the cupboards for mugs.

"No trouble at all, Sir," Parimu said over his shoulder. "But please,

Relsenair is fine. I don't think I particularly qualify as a detective anymore."

"Well, we'll see about that," Peloris said, smiling.

As the detective carried on with the tea, he took the chance to glance around the kitchen for pastries. Lenara was already furious at him for staying out half the night, but if she was going to be angry either way, he should at least sneak in a little snack. Unfortunately, there didn't seem to be much. Unless... He spotted one of those red tins of navy biscuits by the window. They were dry and more or less devoid of sweetness, but he'd take anything in a pinch.

"Not to be that old man," he said as Parimu approached with the tea, "but could I trouble you for a biscuit as well?"

Parimu followed his eyes to the tin on the window sill, chuckling.

"You're more than welcome to them," he said. "But they're…uh…hardly a popular choice."

"I'd hope not," Peloris said, laughing, "but really, I don't mind. I may not have been in the navy, but I've had plenty of tin biscuits, eating whatever I could stuff in my pockets. Maybe I shouldn't be so easy to please, but after the night I've had, I'm afraid I'm rather peckish."

"Right," Parimu said, returning with the open can, "about that. Did things…get any better last night?" He unconsciously glanced upstairs. "I think we could use some good news."

"Oh, yes," Peloris said, smiling, "I'd say so. I wouldn't ask for biscuits if it was bad news, believe me."

Parimu nodded, looking like he could finally breathe again. Not much for joking, that one… Still, he seemed loyal, and Sumi flipping the DoR was no small feat. More importantly, it seemed his years on the force hadn't made him stingy, the detective piling an empty plate with biscuits before setting it by the teapot.

"Do you mind if I join you?" Parimu asked, gesturing to the chair beside him.

"Seas below, man, yes!" Peloris said, laughing. "I'm a guest in your home, and an uninvited one, at that. By all means, make yourself comfortable — act like I'm not even here if you can. I may work for the crown, but the Queen's book peddler is hardly a sergeant-at-arms."

"Right," Parimu said, thankfully taking a biscuit without being prodded further. Discipline was all well and good, but what good could come from the navy browbeating its men so hard? Leonar was just as bad. He probably didn't have time for another project before he died, but perhaps he could speak to an admiral…

They sat in silence for a time, eating their biscuits while they waited.

They really were awful, though that didn't stop him eating one after another… Luckily, just as he was about to take his fifth, a series of bangs sounded from upstairs, followed by feet rushing down the steps. Sumi hurried into the kitchen, wrapped in a shawl and trying to tuck her hair behind her ear, Erso close behind.

"I'm so sorry to make you wait," she said, curtseying.

"Please, dear," he said, waving his hand. "I was just having tea with Mr. Parimu here. Come and sit; we should chat."

She nodded, taking the seat opposite Parimu as he sprang up to make more tea. Erso took the seat on the far end of the table, nearest the window. He was sly, that one, out of the way but always there like a wolf watching over its cubs. Not that she'd need protection from an old man… Still, whether she knew it or not, this young woman understood loyalty, the only currency that really mattered in their cut-throat world.

"Thank you for your help last night," she said, nodding in thanks to Parimu as he set a mug beside her hand. "I'm sorry I performed so poorly. I hope my…plans didn't cause any problems for you."

She sighed, reaching for a biscuit — a truly desperate act with how awful those bloody things were!

"Sumi," he said, squeezing her hand, "you were *brilliant* — exactly what I was hoping for. To be honest, it's I who should be apologizing to you. I should have warned you more, but I didn't want you thinking about politics. What those old codgers need is the truth."

She smiled sadly for a moment before it faded away.

"But what about the Vice Peer?" she asked. "His decision seemed pretty final."

"Let me worry about Kemarin," Peloris said, waving a hand. "He likes to think he's as scary as his old man, but he doesn't have all the say. He didn't come around last night, but he's not the one you were meant to talk to anyway. You see, several other members of the council were very moved by your speech, and they'd like to help with your parade. They've recruited others, and I think we'll have fifteen at the very least."

"That's incredible!" she said despite herself. "But…" She paused, her mouth going to a thin line again. "I'm not sure if I can go through with it."

It was exactly as he'd feared, then… The irony was her doubt only proved she was the real thing. There was no self-aggrandizement to Sumi Elerair, no politics hiding behind her promise to serve the people. She may need a bit of mending — all tender hearts did from time to time — but no amount of coaxing could breathe life into a heart frozen over.

"And why ever not, dear?" he asked gently.

"The Vice Peer is right," she said, looking into her mug. "I can't let the others risk their lives for something so silly." She looked up, forcing herself to smile. "Though I'd still love to meet the others if only to see how else I can help."

"Sumi," Peloris said, holding her gaze, "Kemarin doesn't know everything. I've spent a long time looking for someone like you. Hope might sound foolish to someone who's never felt it, but I assure you it is not."

"But what if we fail?" she asked. "Or ruin the treaties he's been working on? Wouldn't we be better with a leader who understands all that?"

"My dear, if he thinks those treaties are enough to stop the killing, then he's the naive one. We have to start somewhere, and the best place is the truth. Your idea is simple, yes, but that's why it will work. It conveys three basic truths: Shapewalkers exist, they live in Berill, and they are not here to harm you. Maybe we *will* fail, but what is failure anyway? It all depends on what game you're playing."

She smiled genuinely then, her face shining, setting his weary heart at ease.

"Maybe you're right," she said. "That sounds just like something my Nela told me once."

"Sounds like a smart woman," he said, smiling. "And of course, I'm right, even if my only magic is not dying. I may not be the sharpest you'll find, but I'm right about you. You're our leader, Sumi. Speak to their hearts, and they'll follow you anywhere."

She squeezed his hand, nodding.

"I'm not so sure you aren't magic," she said. Then, she took a deep breath, standing. "Alright," she said, "we'll have to see about this leader business, but let's go meet your friends."

17

I do so wish you a happy birthday, and congratulations on Sumi's graduation from school. However heated our exchanges become, I am truly grateful for your letters.

*-Excerpt from the eleventh letter
Hiyelleom to Essolurei*

—:—

It wasn't until they were all settled into Peloris's giant carriage that Sumi remembered she looked a mess.

"Oh, dear," she said, patting her messy bun. "I can't see them looking like this!"

"You're fine," the Master Librarian said, patting her arm. "Just look at me, like I slept in my clothes — which...I suppose I did."

"You do look the part," Erso said, grinning at her from the opposite seat. "Like a sort of wild oracle; perfect for the leader of a magical uprising."

She kicked him in the shins — not too hard, but enough to make him wince — and closed her eyes. She summoned up the first dress she could think of, a fancy-looking one she'd seen in a shop window on her way through the city. She glowed, feeling the folds of silk spilling over her, her hair unfurling into shiny waves. She opened her eyes to find Erso staring at her.

"What?" she asked, tilting her head down to look at the dress. She gulped, her hand going to her chest. It looked just as beautiful as it had in the shop window, but the neckline on this was decidedly...low.

"Oh, nothing," Erso said, his shock fading into a sly grin, "it looks great."

Parimu nodded once before pointedly looking out the window. Peloris seemed the most unfazed of the three, though she would have surely pinned him for a lech given his age.

"Most fashionable," he said, nodding. "My wife has one just like it. Did you find it at Boslemin's?"

"Actually, yes," she said, grinning. She really needed to meet that wife of his…

"*Very* fashionable," Erso nodded.

"Fine," she said, rolling her eyes, "it stays. It's not worth bothering with anymore anyway." She swiveled back toward Peloris. "So where are we meeting everyone?"

"A tea shop on the east side," he said. "Thank the gods — or goddesses, I should say — but no more stuffy mansions. Most of this group has their official homes in the country, though we'll probably want to start meeting out there soon."

"Why, of course," Erso said, fluffing his suit coat, "we haven't been to our country home in ages, it just takes so long to open after winter."

"Excuse him," Sumi said, shooting him a warning look.

"No, no," Peloris said, "I love it. This is exactly what our group needs — someone to kick the beehives. Just maybe let Sumi go first, eh?"

"A wise man," Erso said, nodding his respect. "But once Sumi has them on our side, I'll need you to show me where the bees are kept."

———

They finally pulled in front of the tea house, the low-slung building looking remarkably like a terrace cottage with its vine-covered stone. It seemed a bit too cozy for the posh group they were about to meet, though it would certainly help them keep a low profile. She crawled out after the others, Leonar keeping her from tripping in her frilly dress. At least she looked the part now, though the dress did nothing to stop her palms from sweating. She'd speak just like Peloris wanted, though hopefully when she was done, they could start to figure out who was taking charge.

Peloris guided her through the door, though as she walked in, she nearly froze, an army of people waiting to receive her. Peloris had said sixteen, but with them filling the tiny tea house, it seemed like a thousand, the air aglow with songs and keyholes. Before she could stop, though, Peloris was behind her again, guiding her toward an elegant older woman at the front of the group.

"Lady Croylinin," he said, "First Duchess and Peer."

"Oh," Sumi said, dropping her outstretched hand as she dipped into a curtsey.

"Don't be silly," the woman said, chuckling. She extended her hand, and Sumi took it, giving it a single gentle shake. Still, even in that brief moment before letting go, the woman's hands felt like silk! If only she'd thought to shape her hands along with her dress…

Lady Croylinin turned to her right, gesturing to the man beside her.

"Luckily, I'm the only Peer here — it'd be far too stuffy otherwise — but this is my cousin, the Third Duke Karileen."

"How do you do?" the man asked, shaking her hand warmly. He was easily half the height of Lady Croylinin, though his voice somehow boomed above the noisy room. "Mestaris here had some lovely things to say about you. My brother, the Peer in the family, usually votes with Turimane, but I say it's high time for some fresh ideas."

"Thank you," Sumi said, nodding, her head swimming from all the names. Although if Lady Croylinin had good things to say about her, maybe all hope wasn't lost. All she needed was the right person to hand the reins to.

Peloris took her by the elbow, moving her down the line. The next two men were navy captains, both vaguely familiar from the night before. She would absolutely never remember all the names — the captains apparently named Erinon and Krudal — though at least she could pull names from the songs in a pinch. Still, names hardly seemed to matter anymore, with everyone smiling at her. It seemed as though the night before had never happened, left behind in the gloomy library like a bad dream.

Peloris kept her moving, introducing her to Dr. Gerrinal, a surgeon from the Royal Hospital who was joined by his apprentices, a man and a woman named Yurayna and Eden. After them was a young woman who nearly gave her a start, looking almost identical to Seriai with her small frame and round glasses.

"So pleased to meet you," she said. "I'm Meloy." She gestured to two men standing beside her. "And these are my colleagues, Cusert and Relton. We're the Master Librarian's assistants, and he's told us all about you."

Finally, they reached the end of the line, meeting a group of four wearing fine livery. As it turned out, they were Lady Croylinin's servants — two maids, a butler, and a valet — all of them Shapewalkers. Sumi eagerly shook each of their hands, feeling relieved to finally have someone of her own class. With the exception of Kestorael, the butler, they all seemed to be about her age, smiling warmly as they greeted her.

"Alright," Peloris said, clapping his hands together after the final introduction. "That's the first part out of the way. Why don't we actually have some of this tea, and we can discuss our business?"

The room burst into barely organized chaos, everyone bobbing about as they tried to sit at the single long table set up for them by the fireplace without completely chucking propriety and rank. Somehow, she landed a spot roughly in the middle across from Peloris, with Erso and Parimu at her sides. For a minute or two, there was a symphony of clinking as the tea was poured before Peloris clapped again, calling for quiet.

"So," he said, "I hope you're all comfortable. We're here to discuss our plans for a parade. And please, speak freely. As most of you know, this is the duke's tea house, and we'll have nothing to interrupt us today. Miss Elerair, if you'd be so kind as to start us off? I know your reception wasn't the warmest last night, but I promise you, this group is more than amenable."

She nodded, taking a deep breath. Every idea she'd ever had seemed to be jumbling about her head, but thankfully, she'd brought her notebook. She pulled it out of her pocket, opening it to the back where she'd been sketching.

"Thank you all for coming," she said. "Like all of you, I'm as much Berillai as I am Shapewalker. But this is my home, and I came back to change things, to end our hiding. Still, I know how these ideas might sound. So, after you hear me, just remember, you're welcome to leave at any time. There won't be any hard feelings on my part. But to me, this feels like the only way — Essomuai's way. This magic can't only change us; it has to change our people, too."

Surprisingly, she saw a number of nods.

"This is like the legends from Anushai, right?" Meloy asked. "Elomikarus attacking the city?"

"Exactly!" Sumi said, nodding. Perhaps it was Meloy's training at the library, but it seemed as though Peloris had spread her stories beyond those in the room the night before.

"Our ancestors used their magic to turn back the Southern Emperor, true, but those images were also terrifying. When I was at the fountain, I saw the Anushai dancing in beautiful shapes and using them to calm Vilodai's rage. My plan is like that. If we can show our people how beautiful our magic is, they'll have to forget the scary bedtime stories and see us for what we really are."

Captain Erinon took a long puff on his cigar, stroking his beard.

"It's hard to imagine walking the streets without any cover, but I still think you're right. I've seen what the Admirals are cooking up, and they'll make the wars of the past seem like a bar fight. We need something new, and more fighting isn't it."

A bit of murmuring broke out at that, everyone adding their thoughts on how dangerous the parade would be. Which was exactly why they needed a leader. Even if they wanted it to be peaceful, they couldn't control what the other side did.

"Well," Dr. Gerrinal said, adding his deep voice to the crowd, "I do train my staff in field surgery, and we could probably fix you up if it comes to that."

"Hard to fix an arrow through the throat," Erinon said. "Not that I disagree. Probably hard to shoot a shape in the sky anyway."

"I think it's brilliant," the duke said. "And I'll take any risk to see the look on the Queen's face."

"Well, that raises a good question," Captain Krudal added from the other end of the table. "Do you reckon we ought to warn the Queen first? She might not like a surprise, given her feelings on our kind."

"I think perhaps not," Parimu said, speaking up for the first time. He seemed to just notice that he'd spoken, shutting his mouth for a moment before he continued. "She and I have…discussed the topic before, and she doesn't take our kind lightly. It might be better to let the people see the show before she has a chance to shut it down."

"Forget the Queen," Lady Croylinin said, "it's Pont'dulairn I'm worried about."

Sumi raised an eyebrow, meeting Peloris's eyes.

"*Should* we worry about the Vice Peer?" she asked.

Before Peloris could answer, Karileen spoke up.

"Kemarin's a wily one," he said. "He's normally very protective of our little group, but after the red line he drew around this project, there's no telling what he might do. Right now, seems he'd sell his own mother if it got that bill passed."

"He'll come around," the Master Librarian said, shooting a look at the duke. "But we can worry about the politics later. For now, let's let Sumi share the rest of her plans, and then we can vote. Sumi?"

"Of course," she said, nodding. "And thank you, everyone, for being so engaged. If we're gonna pull this off, we'll need all of our insights."

She smoothed out her notebook, touching her necklaces as she took a breath.

"I know I called it a parade, but this is…something more, and we don't have to do it alone. To do what our ancestors did, we'll need an incredible amount of power. Some of you saw it last night, the power of the songs. I'll need to teach you all to hear them, but if we can link together like the Anushai did, we'll be able to make much larger shapes than any of us could alone."

"You really think your songs can do that?" Lady Croylinin asked. "I've never been anything bigger than a horse."

"I *do* think it's possible," Sumi said, although she ignored the fact that she'd only been able to teach Erso so far… "We'll have to practice, but that's what's different about us now. We have Essomuai, and with her comes her power. I felt it when I danced in the fountain, making an entire world of her memories."

The crowd seemed a bit awed by that last bit. A number of them took pointed sips of their tea, while others simply sat there, blinking as they took it all in.

"I know it's a lot," Sumi added. "We'll get to that part soon, but for now, why don't we go through some of these ideas?"

She picked up her notebook, going through it page by page as she showed them what she'd sketched out. Suddenly, her ideas didn't seem so foolish, the room buzzing as suggestions came from all sides. Somehow, everyone seemed to believe. Finally, when the teapots were empty and the scones devoured, Peloris knocked his cane against the wooden floor.

"So," he said, looking slowly around the table. "It seems we've sparked your imagination. After hearing all of that, who's still in?"

Immediately, about half of the hands went up. The rest came in a slow trickle, but eventually, they all joined until only the Peer and her servants remained. Sumi looked at Lady Croylinin, feeling her jaw go stiff.

"Oh, relax, child," the Peer said, smiling as she raised her hand. "I like your plan, I just like to feel the water first."

Her servants, at least, looked relieved, quickly putting their hands in the air. Hopefully, that meant they actually wanted to do the parade for themselves and not their mistress… Still, it was a unanimous vote, and sixteen felt like an impossible wealth of support after all that time in the wilderness. She met Peloris's eyes, and the older man smiled, winking at her. This had been his intention, all along, of course, to force her to lead. She still felt he was wrong about that, but there'd be time to sort that out. Until she found someone better, she was what they had.

She stood, bowing to the group.

"Thank you all," she said. She didn't know what else to say, so she said the Captain's Oath, exactly as Grandpa had taught it to her. "Slow or fast, we sail together. Whoever holds the helm, you are my sails."

"Here, here!" Captain Erinon said, tapping his teacup with his spoon as the others clapped. Then, thankfully, the pressure let up, and everyone began to move about, talking to their neighbors. Meloy waved at her, coming around the table to kneel beside Sumi's chair.

"I loved your ideas," she said. "But if you don't mind, I had a suggestion for the first section."

Sumi nodded eagerly, turning to a fresh page as she scribbled out some notes. She'd nearly filled the whole page when Lady Croylinin spoke up, her voice carrying across the room.

"Sumi," she said, "before we begin this…adventure, do you think you might show us again what you did last night for Elisal?"

Sumi looked up and found that the whole table was eyeing her, leaning forward in their chairs.

"Would you all…like a turn, maybe?" she asked.

More than a few heads began to nod.

"I think we could manage that," she said, smiling.

———

Erso stood in the corner, watching as Sumi went down the line of chairs, transforming into something different for each member of the group. The forms looked a bit stodgy if you asked him, though fancy blowhards would have memories to match, he supposed. Still, even if the shapes weren't interesting, it was fascinating to watch Sumi choose them. He listened to the songs alongside her, but she never chose who he thought she would. A few selections were obvious, of course — parents and the like — but more often than not, it was someone he'd almost missed: a nanny, a neighbor, a cousin they hadn't seen in fifteen years.

Without fail, though, he could tell she'd chosen well, the people across from her gasping or grabbing her hands. For the sixth person, Sumi even turned into a dog, the woman in front of her crying, no less — which was at least slightly reassuring… He'd never trust them completely, of course. A rich man could cry over a dog and laugh as he stabbed a fellow in the back, but these *were* the ones who had chosen Sumi, defying Pont'dulairn in the process.

Still, hopefully using her powers this much didn't knock Sumi off course again. She seemed…better, more in control, than she was before the fountain. But after the week she'd had, he felt more protective of her than usual. Funny that he wanted to protect her while plotting how to leave her, but just because a dog protected the barn didn't mean he ought to sit at the dinner table.

Parimu had stayed right behind Sumi to watch, but after the first half, he stepped over, joining Erso in the corner. Not that he folded his arms or leaned like a regular bloke. Instead, he stood at bloody parade rest, ever the policeman.

"What do you think?" Erso asked, nodding at Sumi. "Trustworthy?"

"I suppose so," Parimu said, running his eyes over the group. He shook his head, glancing back at him. "Can't say for sure, though. I was taught to catch thieves, but it seems like the really dangerous people in this kingdom all wear suits."

"Here, here," Erso said, chuckling.

"You know what's strange, though?" Parimu asked, scratching his chin. "It's been fifteen years since I've been in the navy, but those captains still make me nervous, even though we were probably helmsmen at the same time. Don't get me wrong, they seem like decent gents, but their uniforms give me the willies."

"I feel the same way about actors," Erso said, nodding in what he hoped was a sage manner.

"Huh," Parimu said, nodding along. "Wait...actors? I didn't think they were much for discipline and all that."

"Oh, they aren't," Erso said, "but I feel the pressure all the same. When I'm around old friends of my parents, it's like I have to compete to be *more* myself somehow — more dazzling, more everything. It doesn't really matter what the dance is, I guess, it's always hardest when you start making up your own steps."

"Hmm," Parimu said, nodding again. "I like that."

"Wait," Erso asked, "I actually said something intelligible in all that?"

"I'm afraid so," Parimu said, chuckling. "I won't tell anyone, though."

Erso shook his head, slapping Parimu on the shoulder. It still surprised him how much he enjoyed the old goat. Hopefully, if they all survived this thing, they could be drinking buddies or something, contemplate the stars and all that. Not that he was supposed to be drinking anymore, but hell, you couldn't be an optimist all the time. They both went back to watching Sumi. She had her eyes closed, listening to the next song, but it probably wouldn't be long before she reappeared as a prized horse or something, knowing this lot.

"You know," Parimu said quietly, "I'm not the only one who needs to learn a different dance." He turned to face Erso, searching his face. "Sorry if I'm overstepping, but you don't need to pretend you don't deserve this life. The girl loves you, and you'll be worthy of her if you let yourself."

Erso felt his jaw lock, his tongue somehow frozen in his mouth. So, the detective *was* more savvy than he let on... His eyes flicked over to Sumi. Unfortunately, if his plans were this obvious, then Sumi could almost certainly tell. Still, there was nothing he could do now but go on pretending. He shook his head, finally forcing a smile onto his face.

"Thank you, mate," he said as Parimu visibly relaxed. The poor bloke must have thought he'd bite his head off — for a bloody compliment, no less! He slapped him on the back again, chuckling. "But don't worry about me. It's good advice, but it can wait for the parade. You don't go digging for skeletons in a rainstorm, after all."

Parimu cocked an eyebrow at that. So, not an expression the Berillai shared, then… Well, they ought to have it with all the bloody skeletons they put out. Still, what mattered was Sumi, and he'd simply have to do better at pretending.

He nodded, moving toward the librarian, the man holding court at the end of the table with a bottle of wine. Sumi would probably be a while yet, and he couldn't drink dirty tea water forever. Besides, he'd need a spot of wine to work up the courage to rescue her from the rich folks. He wouldn't interrupt yet — she still had a wide smile on her face — but she was starting to get those tired lines on the sides of her eyes. He may just be the guard dog, but he knew who filled his bowl, and he'd look out for her, the rest be damned.

18

Terolin is almost certain the third pillar was destroyed, but if that were the case, why would there still be so much activity in that section?

-Setorin's Log
3724-73

—:—

Twenty-seven Years Ago

Kemarin found himself awake well before dawn the next morning — although awake was a relative term. He hadn't slept much, to begin with, tossing and turning as he thought about Elisal. At least now it was late enough to give up the charade of restfulness. He sat up against his headboard, watching as the sky grew bluer over the mountains until the sun appeared over the ancient city. Was this how Maldegurn looked through her eyes?

To him, this trip had only been an obstacle, something standing between him and his destiny. But it seemed he'd forgotten his true purpose, the meaning behind his family's plans. They really *were* different — he knew that all too well — but if he couldn't see the people in these princedoms, then what were they fighting to change the Continent for?

He grimaced, replaying the day before in a different light. Bloody gods above, but he'd been so arrogant in the library! Thinking he knew something about her father from the briefing book as if politics alone could create the beautiful, complicated woman before him. He was such a political creature himself, it was easy to forget how much more there was to life. Even without a kingdom, she was still a woman trapped in her uncle's home, orphaned and lost. And if he couldn't see that, then even marrying foreign bloodlines would be little more than a tired tradition.

Elisal would never have him now, but he could at least make amends —and at least hope he'd be worthy of the next Elisal he met. His parents would be angry when he returned without an engagement, but there was no value in slinking back to Berill with an easily captured princess thrown over his shoulder. He would find a worthy wife when he was worthy himself. He dashed to the writing desk, starting a letter.

Mother and Father, he wrote,

This letter may only precede me by a day or two at most, but I'd have you know of my failure in advance—

He wrote on, the pen flying, explaining his intentions to them almost as much as he was to himself.

―――

A few hours later, Kemarin found himself at breakfast, grateful for the strong Amoriai coffee. They were back in the formal dining room, the entire party present and seated in their little pockets. He paid only the bare minimum of attention required for conversation, though no one seemed keen to press him on it. In truth, most of them seemed hungover, seeming to assume the same of him. Mostly, he watched Elisal from across the room, though with a far different gaze than from the day before. He no longer felt like a hunter, some hawk looking for an easy morsel. Instead, he *really* looked, searching for whatever it was that made her so...*her.*

It was only because he was watching so closely that he caught her cousins' conversation. They had been gushing, not too quietly, about how many romances had blossomed in the garden the night before. Although, perhaps 'gush' was too positive a word... Volcanoes didn't gush so much as spew.

"Yes," the younger Tauschfeig daughter, Lilara, said, "I do think *most* of us will be married by the end of the season, anyway."

A few others in her vicinity laughed, giving themselves away as they glanced at Elisal. For her part, she seemed to be pretending not to hear, staring forcefully into her plate, though her face began to flush.

"Well, all the real princesses, anyway," added Surklein, a lesser cousin from Klenocht.

Perhaps he shouldn't have been surprised, given what he knew about royalty, but it seemed a bit vicious for your own cousin. Unfortunately, they were ruled by their own fear. After all, if Elisal could lose everything, it only proved how easily their own fathers could end up on the wrong end of the knife. Still, it only made Elisal all the more beautiful. She should have been the most desperate of them all, but she put her honor first, even as the others snatched up the first Berillai they could to save themselves. The last thing she would want was him butting in now, but the longer he listened, the more he realized he'd never be able to stand by.

"Yes, quite," Prince Hefturne said. "If only the charity cases would be satisfied with what they've already received."

He was on his feet before he realized it, his chair squeaking as the entire room turned to stare. He threw his napkin on the table, marching toward Elisal. She didn't look up right away, but when she finally glanced at him, the anger was clear on her face.

"Would you mind speaking to me in the garden?" he asked.

She stared back at him for a moment before nodding as she finally stood, taking his arm as the room stared on.

———

They said nothing for a time, simply walking toward the garden. His arm felt stiff, suddenly all too conscious of the fine hand resting on it, a hand like a violin, perfectly crafted and tuned with precision. His heart still pounded with anger at the others, of course, but her presence was most…distracting.

They reached the garden, and Elisal released her grip, wandering over to a short iron fence that ringed the patio. She looked out at the grass while he leaned his back against it, facing the palace. He listened to her breathe, looking up at the ramparts as he waited. Finally aware of his foolishness, there was nothing for him to say. If she wanted him to speak, she would say so.

"Thank you," she finally said. "And I'm sorry for last night in the garden. It appears I misjudged you."

"No," he said, smiling, "I think you had the right of it. I'm as foolish as the rest."

She looked at him from the corner of her eye but didn't turn from the garden.

"Still," he continued, "I'm glad I could do something small to make up for how I behaved. It's not much, but at least those cretins know who my father is, and hopefully, they'll remember this little chat we had after I go."

"Ah," she said, sounding strangely disappointed, "leaving so soon, then?"

His eyebrows quirked up at that. What did that mean? Foolish though it was, hope seemed to flower in his heart.

"Are you…sad to see me go, then?" he asked carefully.

"Perhaps," she said, grinning. "Don't let it go to your head, though. I simply find you more interesting than my…present company."

His mind whirred. Was this an opportunity? He didn't want to be arrogant again, presuming too much. But he didn't want to miss his last chance, either. Everything moved so fast with royalty. Even if Elisal was the only one in the palace with a backbone, her aunt and uncle would still find a way to marry her off before the end of the season.

He turned toward her, swallowing as a lump suddenly appeared in his throat. Still watching him, she met his eyes, searching him for something. He took her free hand, so delicate and warm. She blinked in surprise but didn't pull away. And if that was the only opening he got, he'd bloody well sprint through it.

"Perhaps," he asked, "you'd like to marry me?"

She chuckled, but with none of her earlier contempt.

"Is that how you Berillai do it, then?" she asked. "So quick to pick one deer on the hunt?"

"No," he said, smiling. "This is no hunt for me — not anymore. In fact, I wrote my parents this morning and told them I'd be returning without a wife. But…you showed me something. You proved me wrong and saw the false things in me. I need that in my life, a conscience, a mirror to show me when I'm the fool."

He took a deep breath. "I know you hardly know me, but I'm sure I know myself — at least more than most men, anyway — and I know I'll be good to you. You aren't a deer to hang on the wall; you're a treasure, and I want you to escape this place with me. Don't do it for politics or for revenge. Do it for yourself. Do it because I will love you more than you've ever been loved."

They stared into each other's eyes, that keen gaze seeming to melt him down to nothing, inspecting the tiny bits of his worthless little soul. He held his breath, but finally, her mouth quirked up just a bit, and he smiled, her 'yes' entering his heart before she even said it.

19

Kesoteranumal - an image appears of a woman sowing seeds as she walks, but the plants are growing ahead of her instead of behind.

-Excerpt from The Arguments
Seventeenth Cycle

—:—

Two days — and a frenzy of packing — later, Sumi found herself hurtling down a dusty road toward Lady Croylinin's estates. They'd been in the carriage for hours already, but she still found herself peeking out the windows at the countryside. They weren't far from the river, tracing the foothills as emerald green fields spread out in every direction. It was funny to think she'd traveled the world before visiting Croylinin lands, though it was probably too late in the game to be surprised by anything anymore...

She glanced at Erso, where he was leaning back against the opposite seat with his arms folded, his hat tilted low over his eyes. She couldn't tell if he was sleeping, his eyes shaded by the brim, but after a moment, his mouth twisted into a grin. You could never tell with him... At least he still thought her mooning over the view was endearing. Hopefully, if she was lucky enough to hold onto him a few more months, he'd still think it so.

She leaned back into her own seat and went over her checklist again. There was probably a limit to how much she could actually prepare for what lay ahead, though a list at least let her *pretend* to be in control. They had spent the last two days in a flurry of preparation, trying to get as many supplies as they could before leaving the city. Fabric for banners and costumes, stage makeup, and a tragically expensive reel of gold thread — paid for by Peloris, thankfully. Most of the parade would rely on Shapewalking, of course, though they'd need to look the part before the first transformation — not to mention needing a failsafe if she couldn't get the bloody magic to work…

The rest of the time had been a frenzy of packing until Peskold, Lady Croylinin's valet, had shown up in front of Parimu's with a carriage and a pair of tough-looking guards. Perhaps it was standard for wealthy people to guard their carriages, but she couldn't help but think of Pont'dulairn and the dangerous plan they were about to undertake. They'd made one more stop at the Master Librarian's house — thankfully, his wife had agreed to watch Amis, even if the poor creature would never forgive her for all the moving about — and then they'd sped out of the city.

As she sat staring into her notebook, she caught the murmur of Parimu's voice from on top of the carriage. Hopefully, he was alright up there… It was an awfully long ride to spend in the driver's box, but he'd insisted on getting a feel for the others — which was a good idea, of course. If this was going to work, they'd need to go from strangers to friends in record time. She just hoped he wasn't doing it for her sake. It wasn't like she and Erso were about to be sneaking secret kisses at this point… Just then, a knock sounded on the roof, and Peskold called down to them.

"Coming up now," he said, "Linindal will be on the left."

Linindal… To think they'd be staying at a house with a name. She just hoped she didn't make a fool of herself… Surely, once they were staying in the private home of a Peer, everyone would realize there were better leaders in the group. But until then, she'd just have to figure out the magic — and how to teach it — and someone else could take over.

She put away her notebook, looking out the window as they climbed the last hill, revealing the estate. It was stunning, a wide field stretching between a ring of forest, its grass tall and green from the spring rains. There was a pond off to the side glistening in the sun, its surface dotted with lily pads and reeds. And there, finally coming into view, was the house, set back on a stretch of manicured lawn at the rear of the clearing.

It was certainly as large as she'd expected, though it was nothing else like what she'd thought. She'd assumed it would look like a castle, covered in stone and arrow slits like the Peerage. Instead, it was like a giant library, covered in red brick and copper roofs, the metal long ago fading to a soft green. It even had an observatory, a single tower on the far edge of the building capped in a copper dome.

They turned off the road and onto a drive flanked by tall hedges. It was lined with mysterious bronze statues depicting animals that either didn't exist or were strange chimeras of ones she did know: a boar with wings, a fierce-looking snake with legs. The metal looked ancient, the bronze having taken on a smoky green cast. Was this how a storied Shapewalking family decorated their grounds, with statues hinting at the possibilities hidden in their powers?

As they emerged from the hedges, Peskold pulled the carriage around a wide circle drive, parking in front of a sweeping staircase. There was a fair bit of wrangling to do with the luggage — and some well-earned stretching — but afterward, Sumi found herself at the threshold to Linindal. Peskold bowed, opening the door onto a massive three-story entrance hall. It was lined with windows, letting in the afternoon light, and a wide staircase that wrapped around the sides.

Sumi stared in a daze. It felt like seeing something she'd dreamt, the snippets she'd heard of Lady Croylinin's life circling swimming through her mind. Still, places in the songs were like a bass line — crucial but drifting beneath the surface — and it left her staring at the details, trying to remember where she'd seen them before. She finally tore her eyes away, shaking her head as Peskold pulled out a long piece of parchment.

"So," he said, "let me see which rooms we have you staying in." Apparently, the entire group would be staying here, though where that many rooms were hiding only made the place more impressive…

"Sumi," he continued, "you'll be in the Rose Room. Erso is in the…Blue Room, and Relsenair is in the Garden Room."

He nodded, stepping over to where a rope hung from the wall. He reached out to grab it before he stopped.

"Ah, right," he said, turning around and wringing his hands together. "I'm afraid I forgot, old habits and all that… Lady Croylinin has sent the majority of the staff to the city for the week, so we can practice in private. It'll only be the four staff members who can shape and the wagon guards, though they'll be out of the way in the stables. I'm afraid that means you're on your own for maids and valets."

"I think we can manage," Sumi said, smiling as Peskold visibly relaxed. "If I need anything done, I'll just call for Erso."

Erso turned from a wall hanging he'd been inspecting, cocking an eyebrow at her.

"Yes, well, thank you for understanding," Peskold said. "It's certainly difficult for me — we try to maintain standards here, after all. Why don't I show you to your rooms? You'll have some time to freshen up before tea in the drawing room."

"That'd be lovely," Sumi said, following the older man toward the stairs.

As she thanked Peskold and shut the door, Sumi immediately realized why she'd been given the Rose Room. This had been Lady Croylinin's childhood bedroom, the place of all her happiest memories. It was here where Sumi had plucked her sweetest memories to transform into at the tea shop: playing with her dolls, writing in her diary, bedtimes with her grandfather, the original Duke Croylinin.

She set her bag down by the door, running her hand along the wall. It was papered from floor to ceiling in a cool cream color, with hundreds of hand-painted roses in full bloom. Even the bed had a rose stitched onto its quilt. Thankfully, though, other than the giant bed, the room was relatively small. She'd peeked into the boys' chambers as they passed, and she'd never be able to sleep in their cavernous rooms.

She stepped toward the bed and flopped onto it, sinking into the downy mattress. Duchesses probably didn't flop, but she was no duchess, and she may as well make herself at home. Besides, this was the best way to stare up at the ceiling. There was a mural there with dozens of winged horses circling around a brilliant sun. Imagine looking up at that as a girl, knowing you could shape into anything you wanted! She wouldn't trade her bedroom in the cottage for anything, but part of her *did* wish she'd known what she was — or at least what she'd someday become. She smiled. If they succeeded, maybe she'd be the last little girl who had to grow up without magic.

Just then, clocks up and down the hallway began to chime, and she scrambled off the bed, taking a desperately needed trip to the privy before racing back down the hall. Peskold had said tea was at the top of the hour, but it felt like she'd been in her room for all of thirty seconds! Mostly, she tried not to get lost, following the valet's instructions to the drawing room. Apparently, it was 'just beyond the fireplace in the great hall,' but in a place with great halls, she could easily wander for days before she found her way.

She flew down the stairs before crossing back over the entrance hall to the door Peskold had indicated. It opened onto another hallway, but thankfully, she immediately heard voices coming through a door on her left. She sighed in relief but froze the moment she touched the handle. Were you meant to just walk into rooms in a fancy place like this? Her mind whirred to the only thing that was useful — *The Borimol Plains* — but in those houses, there was always a valet to let you in! She forced herself to take a deep breath, rapping lightly on the door. Thankfully, it swung open immediately, revealing Kestorael, the head butler.

"Well, hello, Sumi," he said, smiling as he bowed her through.

"Welcome to Linindal."

"Hello, Kestorael," she said, bowing her head in thanks. He was a sweet, gentle man. He was getting on in years but still stood straight and proud. He reminded her of Mr. Feirshin in a way. More importantly, he wasn't at all what she'd feared after the butlers at the Imperial Palace… None of the staff were. Perhaps it helped that they were Shapewalkers?

She stepped through the doorway and finally found a cozy room waiting for her. After a week of intimidating libraries and fancy carriages, this seemed like a room that was actually meant to be lived in. It was still enormous, of course, but it overlooked the garden and had dark wood paneling, perfect for getting lost in a book on a rainy day. Lady Croylinin was seated nearest the fire in a high-backed chair with the others — or just the women, rather? — arranged in a square around her on various sofas.

"Oh, Sumi," Lady Croylinin said, "please do come in. Help yourself to some tea." She gestured toward the far wall, where a large spread was set up on a cart.

"Thank you, Lady Croylinin," she said, curtseying, "and thank you again for hosting us."

"No trouble at all," she said with a wave of a ring-studded hand, "can't have everyone breathing down our necks in the city. But please, use my given name, Haleone. Peloris is insisting we do away with propriety while we're here."

"Alright," Sumi said, nodding, "Haleone it is, then."

She looked around the room where the others were shuffling in their seats as they watched the exchange. By the looks of it, they were struggling to relax around the duchess as well. She still felt full of eels herself, but she probably ought to set a good example for the others… She moved over to the cart, taking a muffin before pouring herself some tea. Lady Croylinin — or Haleone, rather — pointed to the chair opposite her beside the fire.

"Why don't you sit there, dear," she said, "better to address the group that way."

Sumi took the seat, trying to hold her teacup as primly as possible as she set down her muffin. She took a slow sip of her tea, eyeing everyone else in the room. Meloy, the librarian, was sharing a sofa with Edeln, one of the surgery apprentices. The other apprentice, Yurayna, sat opposite them, looking terribly pretty in a dress she must have shaped for the occasion. Neristala, the lady's maid, stood by the door with Kestorael. It felt wrong that the servants weren't sitting with them, but at least they were in the room… She didn't want to overstep, especially if she was going to have to pass her leadership to Lady Croylinin, but if they were going to march in the parade, they ought to be a part of things.

"Where did all the men get off to?" she asked.

"I'm afraid Karileen's rounded them all up," Lady Croylinin said, "something about smoking cigars. No doubt they've found my late husband's whiskey as well."

Lady Croylinin seemed to blame the duke, but she wouldn't be surprised if it was Erso's idea. Before she could stop herself, she rolled her eyes, which immediately got the women laughing.

"Yes, they certainly are a different breed," the duchess said. "I suppose we'll have to figure out why we have three goddesses but still ended up with men!"

The group chuckled politely at that, but not a moment later, Lady Croylinin was leaning toward her, eyes narrowed.

"But tell me, Sumi, I'm sure I'm not the only one who's dying to know — have you managed to tie down either of those young men you travel with?"

"Um…" she stammered, the fire beside her suddenly feeling very hot. "You mean Erso and Relsenair?" Parimu was handsome in a way, but she wouldn't exactly call him young! Although he was easily ten years younger than the duchess… Still, what was she meant to say to that? She didn't want to say Erso was up for grabs, but what kind of claim could she really make on him the way things stood?

"I suppose there's a…bit of a romance between Erso and I," she said, "though I'm not sure how serious."

Not serious?! What a foolish thing to say about the love of your life. As if it would make it hurt any less when he finally left…

"Oh," Lady Croylinin said, nodding as she licked her lips. "Now that *is* interesting."

"Does that mean the detective is single, then?" Meloy asked, immediately covering her mouth as if she hadn't meant to say the words aloud.

Sumi stopped, smiling. Her own love life was mortifying to consider, but if she could find someone for Parimu… She opened her mouth to reply when the door burst open — so much for her silly knocking — the Master Librarian shuffling in. Somehow, his entrance was both dramatic and glacial. He must have tried to push the door hard enough to step through with his cane, but luckily, Kestorael was there in a flash, holding the door for him.

"Well, hello, everyone," he said, peering up at them from beneath his bushy eyebrows.

"Nice to see you, Peloris," Sumi said, standing as he made his way to a couch. "Not smoking with the others?"

"Heavens, no," he said, making a face as he dropped onto the sofa next to Yurayna. "Awful stuff. My wife loves to break me of my vices, but unfortunately for her, that's one I never fell into."

"It's true," Meloy said, nodding. "He once fired an archivist for smoking."

"In the stacks, mind you," Peloris said, chuckling as he raised a hand in self-defense. "Still, I think I've made up for it with how many Shapewalkers I've hired."

Meloy nodded eagerly at that, a clear beneficiary of the hiring practices at the library…

They went on like that for a while, the conversation flowing far more easily with Peloris in the room. Finally, as she was about to finish her tea, a whole mess of footsteps thundered down the hallway, the men stampeding into the room. Karileen led the way, still telling some story in a loud voice. He was followed by the captains and their first mates, with Gerrinal, the surgeon, bringing up the rear with Erso and Parimu. Sumi immediately sought Erso's eyes and cocked an eyebrow at him, but he simply shrugged, parrying her attack with his most dashing grin.

There was a good bit of shuffling, but between the long sofas and a few extra chairs that lined the walls, everyone but the servants were eventually sitting. There was another wave of activity as more tea was poured, but before long, they were all sipping their drinks in a surprising state of quiet.

"Well, everyone," Lady Croylinin said, "I suppose since I'm the host, I may as well begin."

Sumi perked up in her chair, nodding. That would be a tremendous help. She'd brought her notebook, and she'd be here for the magic parts, but they really did need a master of ceremonies or something, anyone to keep morale up while she flailed about with her half-baked ideas. Besides, Lady Croylinin was a peer; she'd know the politics better than anyone.

"Our time here is short," the duchess continued. "We have just over a week until the royal stay ends on Pont'dulairn's bill. We have to march before then, or we might miss our chance to affect a once-in-a-generation law. I want our kind in their rightful place when this is done, so I hope you'll agree we must do *incredible* things. For the next week, let this be your home as well as mine, and together, we will see this through."

Sumi's eyes widened as she nodded along. Once in a generation! As if they needed any reminder of how high the stakes were. Still, they really were lucky to have a peer on their side. Maybe this way, her idea could be used for more than just inspiration — it could actually help politically where she'd only thought it would hurt.

"Most inspiring," the Master Librarian said, leaning into his cane. "But Sumi, dear, why don't you tell us what you have planned for us while we're here? I've no doubt your plans will be more than incredible."

"Right," she said, pulling out her notebook. She'd written a loose schedule, but mostly, it felt like cover until she figured out how to link them into a giant shape. She had her own schedule for figuring that out…but in the meantime, they could at least practice the basics. She wasn't sure what everyone's capacity was for Shapewalking, but if she got them practicing with Beysal's exercises, that should at least help open them up. The rest would be about being on display — walking in formation, stage presence, whatever other thousand things would get them ready to do the impossible. At least it was a start. As Grandpa always said, 'If you want to train a fish, you'd better start with a bowl.'

"Thank you all for coming," she said, turning her eyes around the room. "We have a lot of work ahead of us, but I hope we can enjoy getting to know each other, too. I have a little schedule written up, though nothing is set in stone. We'll do a bit of everything each day — blocking out the parade, basics on Essomuai, maybe a bit of stage presence. At the end, we'll try to link ourselves together with the goddess's help. If we can do that, I think we'll be ready."

She paused, taking a deep breath. She looked around the room, looking for questions or suggestions, but everyone just nodded. Peloris, for his part, was beaming at her in a way that made her feel at least a fraction less a fraud.

"Alright," she finally said, "let's begin."

20

Some would rather know where they came from, but I find it baffling that more of us don't ask where they went.

-Setorin's Log
3725-36

—:—

After a considerable amount of wrangling, Sumi finally stood looking out over the field, surveying the little pockets of Shapewalkers scattered about. She felt like a general surveying her troops — though maybe generals wouldn't grin quite so much... Still, seeing them spread out like that made all her fanciful sketches feel like they might actually be possible. They'd started out not even knowing if they'd find another Shapewalker, and now they had nearly twenty! Combine that with Essomuai, and they might just show the city something it would never forget.

She'd just called for a break after their first exercise, and everyone was milling about the refreshments — which the staff had very thoughtfully transferred from the drawing room. Unfortunately, everyone still stood with their original companions — the surgeons, the librarians, the navy officers — but maybe Lady Croylinin could help with that? Either way, there was time for that yet.

For their first exercise, they'd paced out the field into a square — roughly the width of Laeryia Boulevard — before walking through their order for the parade. There had been a good bit of jostling at that, the others seemingly torn between prestige and how dangerous they thought it might be at the front. In the end, Erso had unfurled his banner, which they all agreed should be carried first by 'Sumi and her two companions.' Then, thankfully, Peloris settled the rest. After the three of them, it would be the navy men, then the duke and duchess, followed by the library staff and the surgeons in the rear for medical support — though gods forbid that proved necessary.

After the break, they'd start their exercises with Erso — a Beysal-style meditation, followed by a few acting lessons to make sure they would look their best in front of the crowds. She grabbed herself another tea from the refreshment table and was flipping through her notebook when a familiar voice called out behind her.

"Oy! Where you lot keeping the Shapewalkers?"

She whipped her head around, finding Beysal himself standing at the edge of the field with a pack slung over his shoulder. Even at a hundred yards, it was undeniably him, like a bear that had somehow learned to walk.

"Beysal!" she shouted, somehow remembering to set down her teacup as she ran toward him. He braced for her hug just in time, grunting as she launched into him. He managed to spin her in a circle, but as he set her down, she felt her neck get hot, her embarrassment finally catching up to her. But curse her dignity, Beysal was *here!*

"Good to see ya, girly," he said, patting her shoulder as he caught his breath. He looked around at the others standing in their little pockets. "Quite the operation you got going on here."

She nodded. "Trying to do my teacher proud," she said. She watched the others for a moment before turning back to face him. "Wait, how are you here?!"

"Well," he said, "when Erso wrote to tell what you were planning, I knew I couldn't miss it. Luckily, the little bastard also telegrammed to tell me you'd be at this palace. Anyway, I have to admit, Berill's not half-bad." He gestured at the sprawling fields around them. "At least, I can see why the sheep like it."

"Well, Berill could certainly use another bear," she said, chuckling. "But are you sure you want to do this? It could get dangerous, and…with your family. Did…you get my letter, too?"

"I did," he said quietly, smiling sadly. "I appreciate everything you said, but you can't blame yourself for what happened in Amoriai. This is the life we live, girl, and we're in it together. Besides," he added, pointing at Erso, "he's mine too, and I'm not letting him into this scrape without me."

"But what about Kel?" she protested.

Beysal sucked in a breath. "Kel will be alright," he said as if he needed to will it into being true. "If anything happens…well, he's got a good mother, and I'm sure he'll understand someday. I wasn't there the night

Erso's folks died, but I'll be there this time."

She met his eyes, and she saw something unfamiliar in them, a sort of…ferocity.

"Okay," she said, nodding, "you can stay."

"Thank you kindly, Sergeant," he said, grinning as he saluted her.

He dropped his bag and took her by the shoulder, leaning in as they walked toward the others.

"To be honest…I also think I need to see for myself about all this Essomuai business." He puffed out a breath, shaking his head. "You'd think I'd be used to the mysteries of magic and all that, but it's like the bloody stories. This…could change everything. *You* could change everything."

"I don't know about that," she said. "But I have wondered, why didn't your people ever discover the songs? Why me? I'm nothing special, and I hadn't even had my powers a year when I discovered them."

"Yeah, you would think that, wouldn't you?" he asked, chuckling. "What's that saying again? 'If diamonds knew they were valuable, they'd hide better.' Listen, if you're foolish enough to give me any grandchildren with that big lug over there, you're gonna need to accept how special you are and teach those kids the same."

She started. Just how much was Erso telling him in these letters?! Apparently, not enough if he still thought she had a chance… She smiled sadly. Maybe Beysal would still be like family after this, even if it was only as her teacher. Beysal, for his part, didn't seem to notice her discomfort, letting go of her shoulder as he ran a hand through his beard.

"You do have a point, though," he continued. "I was thinking the same thing the whole way here. How *could* so many bloody people miss it? It must go back to Anushai — always acting like Essomuai was just an idea. So, what were we to do? Maybe there were others who felt the goddess, but they didn't know what to do with it. Besides, it's not like we don't have our own gods — whatever those are worth, now… I guess we needed someone like you, with fresh eyes and old stories. You're a gift, you are."

She ignored the compliment, but otherwise, he *was* right. Essomuai showed her some of that in her dreams, but to think that Geomongiar had been so successful… Maybe it wasn't just him, though, but Essomuai herself, too. It seemed she wouldn't put the songs in your mind unless you sought them out. Maybe they really had needed someone like her — not someone special, but someone who had been so lost that she'd need to reach out to a goddess that might not exist… But she *was* real, and that changed everything.

Beysal stopped while they were still a ways off from the others, lowering his voice.

"Do you think," he whispered, "you could *show* me?"

She should have been used to the request by now, but it still took her by surprise. She'd never realized she'd have something to show her own teacher. Still, she couldn't help but smile.

"Of course," she said, "I'd love nothing more."

She took a deep breath, opening herself to Essomuai as fully as she could. It felt like going back to the fountain, her access to that place even stronger after her trip to the cave. She still didn't understand how to bring that power out, to share it with the others, but she was glad to touch it all the same. The closer she could be to the goddess, the better, the secret surely hiding somewhere within that golden place. She listened to Beysal's song, letting it fill her ears. When she opened her eyes, his keyhole was glowing brightly, and she touched it, taking them away in a flash of light.

For the first time, she felt like she actually recognized this place. The bright field of gold, so foreign to her the first time, now felt familiar. What she'd always called the golden nowhere *was* Essomuai, the field where she'd danced for Vilodai. But did that mean she was in the fountain? Even from so far away? But now there was something else…something that hadn't been there last time. There was a kind of thrumming in her body, something *beneath* the songs. It seemed almost like— Suddenly, she wasn't able to think anymore, the light coalescing in front of her and pulling her toward it.

As she reached the light, she saw it was Beysal, standing before her with his eyes closed. He looked so peaceful, so different from the first time with Parimu — though he had come here willingly, eager to touch Essomuai. She closed her eyes, too, allowing Beysal's song to dance behind her eyes. It was like a beach along the sea, both limited and infinite, a single lifespan made of a billion little moments.

She saw his mother, the bruises on her face. She saw his father and felt a hot anger welling up inside of her. She felt the power in her fists when she fought the other boys growing up. But then she felt the joy in her hands when that power changed, using it to build instead of destroy: cutting and painting at the theater. She saw Erso's mother again, the familiar song filling her ears for a moment but different, somehow, like the key had changed, filtered through Beysal's mind instead of Erso's. And then…she felt the night they died, the light almost disappearing from her heart. Finally, she saw Erso himself. They had spent so many days together — magical days, drifting through the summers together until Elo appeared, and then Kel, a bright light filling his life.

She opened her eyes instead, finding herself there again — the Sumi that was Beysal. The other Sumi opened her eyes and smiled, a toothy grin of pure joy. She so rarely smiled like that in her own body, but it felt right to her now. Perhaps she should try it more… She laughed, light pouring from her mouth. For some reason, she felt so much more present than the other times, still intact despite the light filling her mind.

"This is incredible," Beysal said, his own voice coming from the other Sumi. He looked up, staring into the endless golden sky. "What is this place?"

Somehow, the words were already in her mind — *wellonaiyam.* "We are we," she said, translating from the goddess tongue.

She wasn't sure how time worked in this place, but they ought to get back — the others were waiting. Although, maybe there was time for just one shape… She put her hands out and reached for Beysal, flashing with golden light as they became an enormous bear. She pushed out with her mind, a forest forming around them with trees as far as the eye could see. They ran through the forest, laughing and roaring, climbing up trees and splashing through ponds. They found a cave and rolled on its floor. In the end, they simply stood, closing their eyes and feeling the light. *Thank you*, she thought. She breathed, slowly letting go of the bear until the light was gone.

They reappeared on the grass, and Beysal started laughing.

"Great gods of the halls, girl, that was incredible!" he roared, scooping her up into another big hug. He spun her around twice before dropping her. Then he froze, holding her by the shoulders. "Oh dear, but your life," he said. "I'm so sorry. I knew you'd had a hard time of it losing your grandmother, but I had no idea how it *felt*."

"You too," she said, cupping his face. "It's hard to live someone else's pain, but it's good, too. You're a good man, Beysal, and I'm lucky to know you."

He nodded, smiling. "You're the real thing, Sumi, and if anybody can do this, you can. Wherever you lead, I'll follow."

They stepped apart, turning around to find a crowd around them. Everyone who'd been casually talking before was gathered around, staring with wide eyes.

"What…was that?" Meloy asked, taking off her glasses and wiping them on her skirt.

"Such a bright flash," Captain Erinon added, "like being inside a…a lighthouse or something."

"Did anybody else see something in it?" Gerrinal asked. "Like a…bear, maybe?"

Sumi chuckled, scratching her head. She was hoping to lead up to this lesson, but she had no choice but to explain it now.

"I'm not really sure what to call it," she said, "but we linked through Essomuai. I guess that's what we're building up to. Once we work on stilling our pools and growing together, we'll all need to join like that, only outside of that light, in the real world." She unconsciously felt for her necklaces beneath her blouse. Vilodai's stone was still there, vibrating along to their songs again. That thrumming… "I'm still working out the mechanics, but *this* is how we'll power the parade."

Everyone still looked properly bewildered, but they broke back apart into their respective groups, talking in hushed tones about what they'd seen. Well, it was a start… Erso broke away, marching up to them.

"You came?" he asked Beysal, stopping a few feet away with his hands on his hips. "I specifically told you *not* to come."

Beysal laughed. "Yes, well, if you didn't want me to come, you shouldn't have put the name of the estate in your telegram."

Erso scowled. "That's what I get for being honest, I guess," he said.

"You and the girl worry too much," he said, waving a hand. "I'm not senile yet, and I can go where I please. If I start leaving the risky stuff to sprouts like you, then I'll really be old."

"Beysal," Erso said, rolling his eyes, "you *are* old."

With that, the wrestling commenced. Sumi had her turn at rolling her eyes then, but mostly she just laughed as the two grown men floundered around in the dirt. The rest of the students, on the other hand, all stopped to watch, Lady Croylinin looking particularly confused.

"Um…uncle from Amoriai," Parimu offered.

"Oh, why, of course!" Lady Croylinin said, nodding as if that explained everything perfectly well.

"You bet your behinds I'm from Amoriai," Beysal said, getting up from where he'd finally pinned Erso as he wiped the dust from his hands. "Apologies for humiliating your teacher like that — he's great, but he is also my son, and I gotta keep him in line and all that. I'm Beysal, and I'm the best hall runner on the Continent, so listen sharp, and I'll get you lot working proper in no time."

Perhaps it shouldn't have come as a surprise after they watched him flip a grown man to the ground, but everyone did suddenly look a bit sharper. They all stood straighter, at some semblance of attention, and even the duchess primly folded her hands. Luckily, before the magic could fade, Beysal immediately took charge, pointing people to different parts of the field where they could train in smaller groups. While everyone wandered over to their places, Relsenair crept up to Beysal.

"Um…hello," Parimu said, extending his hand with his fingers too wide, "I'm Relsenair Parimu, and…uh…I believe I owe you an apology."

Beysal heartily pumped his hand and began to laugh. "Now that *is* interesting," he said. "You're the bloke that searched my house, right?"

"Yes," Parimu said, nodding. His shoulders slumped a bit, but he didn't look away. "I'm so sorry. I don't expect your forgiveness, but—"

"No, no," Beysal said, smacking Parimu hard on the arm, "I'm glad to see you."

"You— you are?" Parimu asked, cocking an eyebrow.

"Of course," Beysal said, "about time somebody took a run at us. Gotta stay sharp somehow. Bloody Fida'lalean don't know their *himark'en* from their *esh'anf* if you know what I mean."

"Um…right," Parimu said, smiling nervously.

"Anyway," Beysal continued, ignoring Parimu's confusion, "I think we're all living proof that there's still good ale at the bottom of the barrel, eh? No surprise with little miss here to set us straight."

All three of them looked in her direction, and she cocked her head and waved.

"I'm sure you'll both get on well," Erso said, chuckling. "Don't know if I'm thrilled or terrified, though. Beysal doesn't really need any more encouragement."

"Bah!" Beysal said. "You're just sour I pinned you again." He rubbed his hands together, turning toward the little groups of people on the grass. She wasn't sure if he had done it by instinct or not, but he'd actually successfully broken up the little factions. By pointing randomly to places on the grass, everyone had been wonderfully mixed up.

"Alright, everyone!" Beysal roared across the grass. "Everybody have a bloody seat!"

21

Sisorulamaera - appears to be one of the unitaries as only a color appears, a calming sort of orange that feels like a sunset.

-Excerpt from The Echoes
First Cycle

—:—

As Beysal called for them to sit, only a few immediately complied, dropping to the ground and folding their legs in front of them. The rest looked around at each other, not wanting to be the first, but likely afraid to be the last, too. Lady Croylinin looked like she might try her hand at wrestling, but luckily, her maid, Neristala, hurried over and dropped a blanket beneath her before scurrying back to her own spot on the grass.

Beysal began holding court, standing in the center as he explained the intricacies of Mu'lalat. It all must have been quite a shock to them because there were a number of bewildered expressions. Even more than the large Amoriai man shouting at them, what would it all mean for how they viewed their powers? She'd told them about Essomuai, true, but Beysal needed them to relearn *how* they used their magic. They'd all learned well enough to avoid detection — in some cases being taught since children — but had they ever learned from the Continent, from the culture of being a Shapewalker?

After his introduction, Beysal moved between the groups, starting them on individual meditations. To his credit, after only a few minutes, he had everyone closing their eyes and focusing on their breath. Erso moved up beside her. She met his eyes, and for a moment, he looked like he used to when they'd meet in the woods. But then, he sighed, folding his arms.

"Sorry I've unleashed a monster," he said.

"Hardly," she said, "look at them." Even if the rest of their plans failed, getting two dozen rich people to sit on the ground was probably a memory Essomuai would never forget. Maybe the next Sumi, two thousand years from now, would see this all in a dream.

"If only I'd played my cards right, he'd be my uncle, too."

She felt her neck get hot as soon as the words left her mouth. What on Wellonai had made her say that?

He frowned, looking at her again.

"Some day," he said quietly, "you'll have to realize I was the one who needed to play his cards right."

She wanted to ask him what he meant by that, but somehow, she couldn't. When she finally worked up the courage to demand the truth from him, it would be the end.

"Yeah, yeah," she said, knocking her shoulder against his as she walked away. She wound between her students, ready to offer any help she could. As cuddly of a bear as Beysal may be, she somehow had the feeling the others would be too afraid to ask him questions.

———

Beysal kept his students going for about an hour, and to their credit, most of them had actually kept their eyes closed. Still, Sumi could tell they were starting to fade, the fidgeting and stretching growing worse by the minute. So, with a nod from her, Beysal clapped his hands together, moving next to her in the middle of the group.

"Alright, everybody," he said, their eyes fluttering open like they were waking from a dream. "I think that's a good start for today. Tomorrow, we'll get you dancing proper."

"That's it?" one of the first mates asked — Sermian, she thought his name was.

"What do you mean, 'that's it?'" Beysal asked, cocking an eyebrow. "It may not seem like much, but letting go is hard. If you don't have a foundation, you'll never build a bloody house. Like so."

He held both hands up, pointing his index fingers in the air. The others looked at each other, but she didn't dare take her eyes off him. She'd only seen Beysal run the halls the one time, and she didn't want to miss it. She may have Essomuai, but what Beysal did was an art form. He began to dance, swinging his arms back and forth like an upside-down pendulum.

"I was gonna save this for tomorrow," he said, his hips starting to sway to the rhythm, "but I may as well give you lot a taste now."

He glowed, reappearing as a butterfly, though a far more splendid one than he'd shown her in Amoriai. It was gigantic, too, with long rainbow-colored wings. Suddenly, the butterfly glowed again, and Beysal reappeared as a bird, snatching the same butterfly out of the sky and swallowing it whole. Some of the students gasped, but just as quickly, he glowed again, reappearing as a tree with the bird on one of its branches. Finally — because apparently, no demonstration of Beysal's could ever have enough drama — the tree burst into flames, the heat flashing across her face. As it burned to ash, the smoke itself began to glow, returning Beysal to his original form.

For a moment, there was only a stunned silence, the demonstration surely well beyond anything a Berillai Shapewalker had ever seen. Beysal took a little bow, which finally reminded everyone to clap.

"When are we gonna get to try that?" Meloy asked, her hand clutched to her heart.

"Soon enough," Beysal said, a mischievous smile on his face. "I always say these powers can jump out at you in a single day if you're open to it, but I think we have a bit more to learn than usual. Sumi, I yield the floor."

"Right," she said, putting her hands back down mid-clap. "As I said back in the drawing room, the last thing I want to do today is a bit of acting. I know it sounds strange, but we'll need a bit of stage presence with the whole city watching. Erso?"

He rubbed his hands together, stepping up beside her.

"So," he said, "my mother was the actor, not me, but she taught me everything she knew. And one thing she always said was to 'play to the back row.' When we do our parade, we want to present the same face to everyone, no matter how big the crowd. That'll mean big smiles, so I'm gonna teach you all a bit of clowning."

A few mutters rose up at that, but he kept going.

"I know, I know," he said, raising a hand. "But it's not as bad as it sounds — I'm not gonna make you wear lipstick or anything. You just gotta learn how to hold yourself." He clapped his hands twice, looking every bit his mother wrangling her stage hands. "Let's get in two rows, and I'll show you how it's done."

Like everything that afternoon, precedence made it harder than it should have been. Still, they eventually got into rows, even if Lady Croylinin was in the front beside the duke. When their eyes were back on Erso, he started pacing, his hands behind his back.

"Alright," he said, "first thing you gotta learn is how to carry your head. Now, I know what you're thinking: 'Erso, I've carried my head my whole life, what's there to learn?' But your head naturally wants to dip low, toward the ground. Makes sense on a normal day, nobody wants to trip, but when you're in front of a crowd, you need to stand tall and show your face. Like this."

He turned sideways so they could see his profile, tilting his head back as he jutted out his chin. Then, he took a deep breath, motioning with his hands as if he could trace the air going into his lungs.

"See?" he asked. "Just like that, tall and proud. Now you all try; follow my hand." He held two fingers in the air about a foot above his head. They followed with their eyes, unconsciously tilting their heads back by a few degrees.

"Good, good," he said, "now stick those chins out like you wanna bite the air." A few eyebrows were raised at that, but they all complied. "That's it!" Erso shouted. "Now hold that right there and take a few deep breaths, see how good it feels, how easily the air goes in."

Somehow, they *did* look prouder. Their eyes betrayed their confusion, but somehow, they *did* look prouder, like soldiers on review. Erso held them there for a few moments before letting them take a break.

"Excellent," he said, "really good. Now, don't cling to it — you don't want to look rigid — but if you keep this mind out there, you'll have a huge head start. Let's try again."

They went through a few more rounds — Erso popping around to make corrections — before he clapped again.

"What a talented bunch!" he said. "But if you're gonna tilt your head back, you have to put something on your face worth looking at. So, I wanna see your best smile. And I'm not talking about the one you make when you get an ugly scarf; I want a real, genuine smile."

He opened his mouth, pointing his fingers at his cheeks as he flashed a brilliant smile. That was another gift from his mother, though it was a wonder he'd kept it through all his years of wandering and drinking. He kept talking through his teeth, somehow keeping his cheeks pulled wide. "Just like this," he said. "I wanna see both rows and a good lower lip, like a milk saucer."

Sumi found herself smiling as she watched him, her face unconsciously mimicking him. Just a second of smiling like that, though, and her cheeks began to burn. It sure took a lot of endurance to be happy all the time... For the most part, the students were doing the same, looking beautifully happy.

"Well done," Erso said, waving for them to release. "Just make sure you practice those in the mirror tonight. Now, for my last lesson, I want to get you moving. Humans have hips for a reason, and I don't want you looking stiff out there. When you're in front of the crowds, I want you leading from your hips with your shoulders swinging after. Let me demonstrate."

He turned again so they could see the way he moved. He glided across the grass, swinging his hips wide before following with a flourish of his hands. Then he stepped back to the side, clearing the grass in front of their two rows. "Now you try," he said, waving his hand for them to move forward.

"Now wait just a damn minute," Captain Erinon said, holding up a hand. "I want to show our stuff, same as everybody else, but I won't look like a fool doing it."

"I agree," his first mate said. "When I hear parade, I think precision, uniforms gleaming. We want to show that Shapewalkers have honor, not that they're a bunch of…well, a bunch of damned clowns!"

"Alright, hold on," Erso said, turning back around to the group, "nobody's gonna look like a fool, we're just trying to wow the crowds."

Suddenly, everyone began to argue, their voices rising to shouts as they all somehow ended up on different sides. The librarians were for the clowning — which wasn't much of a surprise — while the surgeons were arguing with the sailors on whether or not military dress would be *more* dangerous. The servants stayed out of the fray, though they were muttering amongst themselves.

Sumi looked on, blood thumping in her throat. What was she meant to do? Captain Krudal called Dr. Gerrinal a coward, and more than a few of the others looked ready to throw punches, Erso included. She looked to Parimu, but he'd lost all his color, his eyes darting from group to group. Beysal was between Erso and Captain Erinon, even his giant arms barely holding the two back. She looked around for the Master Librarian and finally found him off to the side, his hands resting calmly on his cane. She locked eyes with him, but all he did was nod. Did he mean for *her* to wrestle them all to the ground?

"Everyone!" Lady Croylinin yelled, her voice scaring a few birds into the air. Suddenly, everyone stopped, which couldn't have come a moment too soon the way the captain had begun rolling up his sleeves.

"I think we need another good talk about the direction of this parade," she continued once the silence settled in. "We *all* believe in change — we *hunger* for it, even — and in that, we are allies. All we need to do, then, is determine the best means for accomplishing that."

Sumi found herself nodding along. This was what they needed, someone who could bind their group together before it tore itself apart.

"While I share Miss Elerair's conviction that inspiration is a necessary fuel, it stands to reason that we must determine what exactly it is that inspires."

Sumi frowned at that. She thought she'd found something inspiring in her plans. After all, there was nothing that spoke more strongly to Essomuai than beauty and joy.

"Berill," the duchess continued, "is already a land of marvels. Even if all of us are of mixed blood, it is the Berillai who covered the Continent in trains and ships. What we need to show is the future of what a fully realized Berill could be. If we—"

Peloris shuffled up beside her, taking her hand.

"Sumi, dear," he said in a quiet voice, "I think it's time you trust those instincts of yours."

She met his eyes, frowning. Did he really mean for her to interrupt *a peer*, a speaker who could run circles around her? But then, Lady Croylinin's words broke through again, sending a chill down her spine.

"—are we to show ourselves worth of ridicule or the awesomeness of our power? Sumi said it herself, we are of the *gods.* "

There were appreciative murmurs at that, especially the navy men. This was getting out of control. She knew she couldn't lead the parade herself, but this wasn't at all her vision! The awesomeness of their power?! That would only terrify the Berillai, not to mention how far that sounded from *eshernulam.* She looked at Peloris again, and he smiled, nodding once more. She would never find the words to counter an argument like that, but maybe she could find something else, something…more than herself.

She took a deep breath, squeezing her forehead as the songs came back into her mind. They were all jumbled together, but the more she focused on her breath, the more she could pick them out. She focused on Lady Croylinin's, trying to absorb as much of it as she could.

"So," the duchess finally said, "what say you?"

Voices began to rise from all sides, but she was ready.

"Lady Croylinin," she said in a loud, firm voice — a strange blend of Nela and Grandpa that hardly sounded like herself. Everyone suddenly froze, turning toward her. She felt like there was a stone in her throat, but somehow, she pushed on.

"I think…" she said slowly now that every eye was on her, "that your arguments are sensible. We would do well to look sharp during the parade. *But,* " she continued, "we can't lose the joy of this parade. We're here to show that Shapewalkers are not the enemy, and the less we look like an invading force, the better. Tell me, do you remember when you took your granddaughter to the circus?"

Lady Croylinin's mouth fell open before snapping closed. She licked her lips as if they'd somehow gone dry during her speech.

"Yes, of— of course," she said, nodding.

"And what was her favorite part?" she asked.

"The…well, the clowns, I suppose," she admitted. "She talked about them for weeks."

Sumi nodded, smiling. "The Berillai are our people," she said, "and we are no danger to them. Our goal should be to captivate, not scare. Our kingdom *has* accomplished incredible things, but the next step will only come if we take it together. I promise you, I won't let you look foolish, but we have to bring them joy. Do you trust me?"

The duchess met her eyes, though there was a coldness in them she hadn't seen before. Still, after a moment, she nodded.

"Yes," she said, "I do."

"Good," Sumi said, turning to the others, "because I trust all of you, and I also trust your expertise." She turned toward Captain Erinon. "Like you, captain," she said. "Tomorrow, I'd love it if you showed us some marching techniques. That's just the thing to make us look sharp as we move down the boulevard. Would you do us that honor?"

"Of course," he said quickly, dipping his head.

"Thank you," she said. She glanced at the sun, where it was already angling sharply toward the trees. "Now, I think we've done more than enough for today." She looked toward Lady Croylinin. She needed to keep her vision intact, but she didn't want to look like a horse bucking the bridle, either. She *would* need the duchess's leadership. "Haleone," she said, "if you wouldn't mind, I suggest we adjourn."

Everyone looked around at each other for a moment.

"Well, you heard her," Lady Croylinin said, heading toward the house. "We have a fabulous dinner planned, and I, for one, am famished."

The others began to follow, though, thankfully, at least a few smiled at her as they left, including Meloy. She turned to the librarian, who was still watching.

"Well done," he said, smiling.

"You think?" she asked, watching the others climb toward the house where it hid behind the hedges. "You sure it shouldn't be you making those speeches?"

"I'm sure," he said. "Like I told you in Berill, *you* have to lead us, Sumi. It's your vision, and it's your heart. If that isn't a leader, I don't know what is. *Stay firm.*"

Stay firm… She still wasn't the leader he thought she was, but she supposed she did owe it to Essomuai to protect her vision. She was the only one who knew the goddess — at least for the moment — and until she could get the others hearing the songs, she'd have to do, poor substitute that she was.

"Come on," Peloris said, offering his arm. "You'll feel better after dinner."

She took it, nodding as she helped him up the grass, the songs still dancing through her mind.

22

*It truly is a long time to be alone. Everyone jokes about the dying man
casting his voice into the void, but I still can't seem to avoid the urge.
Even if I fail, I have to believe this trip will serve some purpose.*

*-Setorin's Log
3811-92*

—:—

Parimu leaned toward the mirror in his room, still fussing with his bow
tie. He'd shaped it just like Erso had taught him, but something about it
still didn't look right. Not that he would know what a bow tie was meant
to look like, anyway… He'd worn them once or twice with his dress
uniform, of course, but he probably looked just as foolish then as he did
now. He'd felt dapper enough at the time — no doubt dreaming about
sweeping Jalicyne off her feet — but like they said, you couldn't put a
sheep in a top hat and call him a lord.

He growled, yanking the knot out with a huff. His breath had fogged
the glass, and he couldn't even see the damned thing anymore. Perhaps
if he started from the beginning… He took the ends in his hands again
and was forming his first loop when he heard a knock on the door.

"Come in," he said stiffly, forcing the words past the silk snake
cutting off his lungs. The door swung wide, revealing Sumi in a puffy
dress.

"Well, don't you look handsome!" she said, smiling.

"I don't know," he said, lifting his sorry excuse for a bow tie so she
could see. "Erso helped me design it, but I can't get the tie right."

"Let me see," she said. He tilted his chin back, and she stepped in,
turning him toward the light.

His face grew hot, realizing how undignified it was to need help
dressing. After all, it'd been some thirty years since his mother last

helped him tie a tie… Perhaps he should have been just as mortified to let a respectable lady touch his neck like that, but he could never manage to feel that way around Sumi. She was too much like family now, and in many ways, she was all the family he had left. Hopefully, she still felt the same. The more songs she listened to, the more likely it was she'd realize how flimsy he really was.

"There," she said, smoothing his lapel and stepping back, "that should do it."

"Thank you," he said, finally letting out a breath as he stepped away from the mirror. "There probably wasn't anything wrong with it in the first place, but it all just feels so…" He struggled for the words, gesturing around at the cavernous bedroom.

"I know," she said, holding up a handful of her ballgown. "It feels like playing dress-up."

She eyed the clock on the bedside table.

"We have a bit of time if you'd like to sit in here a while. I was just coming to tell you that you're my escort tonight. I think Erso and Beysal snuck off to drink with the guards or something."

"That sounds lovely," he said, gesturing to a pair of chairs by the fireplace. It was a bit absurd to have a sitting room by your bed, but it would be a lot more private than the parlor. Sumi curtsied, floating gracefully across the room despite the thirty pounds of silk around her waist. He joined her, patting down his pockets as he sat. He felt something in his breast pocket and pulled it out, realizing his pipe had made it through the transformation.

"Actually," he said, "do you think I could smoke in here?"

She grinned. "I won't tell anybody," she said. "But honestly, I don't think they'd even notice in a house this big."

The hallway outside was quiet — not that he'd be able to hear much through the thick door. Still, he stood, popping open one of the crystal window panes before returning to his chair to stuff his pipe. Sumi sat and watched him but didn't say anything. Another strange talent of hers… He wasn't sure if it was conscious or not — or driven by her powers? — but she always seemed to know when there was something he needed to get off his chest. Still, he didn't speak right away, lighting his pipe and taking a long drag before he leaned back, massaging his temples.

"Sorry I'm a bit off," he said. "It's just…hard to feel comfortable here. Not that I don't want to be here, of course."

"It's alright," she said, smiling. "I feel a bit like a sheep out of pasture myself, though I do feel lucky we've found so many Shapewalkers."

"That's true," he said. "And I'm grateful, it's just… Why didn't they stop me? They all knew, and they just let me—" His jaw tightened, his mind filling with memories of all the nooses he'd tied. It was getting better — the more he talked to those he'd failed — but when his blood was up, he couldn't seem to keep them from his mind. "It doesn't take away what I did," he finally said, forcing out the words, "nothing ever will. But if they could have stopped me…"

"I know," she said, gripping his hand where it clung to the edge of his chair. "But you're not alone. I'm guilty, too, all the suffering I let pass right under my nose. None of us are innocent, but we're prisoners of the cycle, too. I know the others aren't like us, but I trust Peloris, and I think he brought us people who are ready to change. Just give them that chance."

His jaw was still clenched, but he nodded. She was right. He'd never leave his guilt behind, but he *had* changed — they could all change.

"Just promise me something?" he whispered, squeezing her hand.

"Anything," she said, meeting his eyes.

"If we do this," he said, "we do it for them, the people I've hurt. Not for the Peers, not for trade, but for *them*."

"I promise," she said, gripping his hand more tightly. "No matter what."

"Alright," he said, nodding as he took a grateful pull from his pipe. And it seemed that was all he needed, the tension slipping away. Sumi really was incredible. If only the others could see it. They probably thought the icy coolness of the duchess was what leadership looked like, but Sumi had a strength that never seemed to break. And he would do whatever it took to serve her, even wear a damned bow tie in a palace…

"You know," he added, grinning, "this might seem a bit petty after everything we just said, but I do wish they'd show you a little more respect."

She laughed. "Now you're just being biased. Though it is hard having Peloris in one ear and Lady Croylinin in the other…" She sighed, looking at the fire. "I want to honor Essomuai, but I know we need a real leader, too. Still, I know something good will come out of it. We brought *twenty* Shapewalkers together, after all."

He suddenly realized he'd clenched his jaw, his calm slipping away as quickly as it had arrived. It was fine — honorable, even — to forgive these people. He knew well enough he didn't deserve an ounce of the forgiveness he'd been shown. But to hear the doubt they were putting in her mind… She was worth a bloody barrel of peers, and he'd be damned if anyone thought otherwise.

"We already have a leader," he said, trying to keep his voice from shaking with anger. He leaned forward, looking into her eyes. "Sumi, you are the *only* light in this darkness. You think we're all guilty, but these people did *nothing* as their own kind died, just as I did. I may be the worst of us, but without you, there would be no hope. Don't let them take that from you. I'll *die* for this parade, and I'll do it gladly, but it's *you* I follow, not them."

He sucked in a breath, shaking his head.

"I'm sorry," he murmured. "I…didn't mean to—"

"No," she said, nodding, "you're right. I *don't* know anything about politics, but I know you, and you're one of the bravest men I've ever met. It isn't easy letting go of who you are, but you've fought for me — you've fought for this. And if you're with me, I should be fighting too."

She looked like a captain then, someone who could fight back the waves. And before he could stop himself, he was humming an old navy song, *The Captain's Stand.*

Not wind, nor hail, nor winter's gale, your mast will never bend.

You are my deck, you are my sail, we stand until the end.

"Until the end," she answered, smiling. "My grandpa always loved that one."

They both leaned back, sitting in silence for a moment, though it wasn't uncomfortable. In fact, it was the best he'd felt in days.

"Hey," she said, "enough with being serious, we should be celebrating. Let me have a puff of that pipe."

He eyed her but handed it over. He wasn't one for questioning the captain, after all. She leaned forward with a grin, taking it and carefully sticking the end in her mouth with the stem between her fingers.

"Ish thish right?" she asked through clenched teeth.

"Yes, ma'am," he said, fumbling in his pocket for his matchbook. "Let me just stoke the flame again for you, make sure you get a good pull."

She sat there, unmoving, watching as he struck the match and relit the blue polis Erso had given him. He could tamp it, but the bowl should be good enough for a quick taste.

"Just breathe in?" she asked when he was done.

"Not quite," he said. "Take a slow draw and keep it in your mouth for a bit. Taste the leaves, then breathe out."

She nodded, closing her mouth and sucking on the pipe. She immediately started wheezing, coughing up big puffs of blue smoke.

"Oh, that's foul!" she said, sticking out her tongue as she handed him back the pipe. "I finally found something worse than mouse blood."

He raised an eyebrow at that, but she was already chuckling and wiping tears from her eyes.

"Not a word of that to Erso," she said, pointing a finger at him, "he'll never let me hear the end of it."

He raised his palms in acquiescence.

"And don't go laughing at me for being a girl, either!" she warned. "I'll have you know that Berillai priestesses smoked pipes on the Isles of Dawn."

"I don't doubt it," he said, chuckling as he took his own draw on the pipe. "With your visions, you probably know more history than anyone alive. Although…the detective in me would say that means you can basically make up anything you want."

She scoffed, kicking the side of his leg with her dainty slipper. He blinked, looking down at the pink satin. That was even more surprising than her dress — she never went anywhere without her boots. She followed his eyes.

"I know," she said, tucking her foot back under her, "that's the worst bit. Just make sure we don't get chased tonight, alright?"

Just then, the large clock in the hallway chimed the hour.

"Alright," she said, pushing her way out of the chair and smoothing the folds of her dress. "Off to the gallows."

———

He followed Sumi down the winding stairs, his shoes echoing in the giant hall. Sunset had passed while they were in his room, and the house seemed transformed, with candelabras shining off the marble floors. It felt more like a keep now than a country estate, and it was hard not to picture themselves a hundred years in the past. They crossed over into the dining room, finding most of the guests milling about with glasses of wine, the servants moving about to refill them. At least this room felt more festive, the table covered in candles with a roaring fire in the grate.

Everyone looked up as they came in, with a few raising glasses, but thankfully, they skirted around the giant table toward Erso and Beysal, where they stood talking to Meloy. Not that he was much use to Sumi when it came to conversation, but he'd certainly prefer to dip his toe in the water before he was forced to really swim…

"Meloy," Sumi said warmly, squeezing the woman's shoulder. Sumi always said she was nervous around people, but she made everything seem so…effortless. Meloy beamed at them, stepping back to widen their circle.

"I was just telling these two about my research at the library," she said.

"On top of…special projects for Peloris, I also study boat design."

"Oh, really?" Sumi asked.

"I was as surprised as you were," Erso said. "Can you believe there's more than one kind of boat?"

"Har-har," Sumi said dryly before turning back to Meloy. "Really, though, that's fascinating. What do you study about them?"

"Industrial design," she said, "some of my modifications have made it onto navy boats, iron bilges, and things like that."

"Do you think you could draw one for the parade?" Sumi asked. "I'm afraid if we leave it up to me, it'll either be way too huge or like something a five-year-old would draw."

"Oh, I'm looking forward to this," Beysal said, laughing. "You know, the first thing Sumi asked me when she came to Amoriai was if she could be a boat. I think this'll be a match made in heaven."

"Well," Sumi said, "a girl's gotta have something of her own. You always get to be a bear, and Erso runs around like a dandy."

"On behalf of dandies everywhere," Erso said, "I'm truly offended." The others chuckled, but Parimu found himself frowning. Those two had been acting strangely the past few weeks, but gods above, he hoped they could just work things out! No one could get Sumi smiling more than Erso, and all of their worries just seemed to slide right off his back.

Sumi opened her mouth with some retort when Peskold came over with a tray of wine.

"Wine for you two?" he asked. "It's made here at Linindal with wild blackberries."

They each took one, and Parimu nodded his thanks.

"What about you?" Sumi asked the footman. "Won't you get to join us?"

"Afraid not, ma'am," he said, smiling. He gestured to the other servants, who were similarly making the rounds. "The only other staff this week are the cooks, and they're under strict orders to stay in the kitchen. That leaves us for hosting. But don't mind me, it comes naturally."

Sumi frowned. "Well, as long as you're sure," she said. "But make sure you spend some time with us after, alright?"

"I surely will," he said before drifting over to the next group.

Meloy continued her talk of boats, but Sumi's eyes stayed on the servants. As long as they were comfortable working, he saw no problem with it. He knew himself how hard it was to adjust now that he wasn't a detective. Although…he had just asked her to do this for the *real* people, hadn't he? If the servants were left out — even the Shapewalking ones

— what hope did the rest of them have?

He looked down at his wine, carefully swirling it in the glass. Worried it would be too sweet, he took a cautious sip, instead finding it delightfully tart. Sumi finally did the same, her eyes popping open.

"Wow," she said, "this is delicious."

"Certainly the best wine I've ever tasted," Beysal said.

"To enjoying the finer things before prison," Erso said, raising his glass.

"Terrible wine in prison," Beysal added with a grin. He, unfortunately, could only gulp. He'd face his fate like the rest of them, of course, but how could they joke about it? Prison terrified him, probably all the more so because of how many people he'd locked away in them… He wanted to think more on that, but just then, a tiny bell chimed from the center of the room. Lady Croylinin must have seen Erso raise his glass because as he turned, he found the duchess at the head of the table, her own glass raised.

"I'd like to propose a toast," she said, "and then, by all means, let's get on with the food. I'm sure you're all as famished as I am from our romp in the grass."

Everyone turned, dutifully raising their glasses.

"To…Essomuai," she said, "and the glory of her creations."

"To Essomuai," everyone said loudly.

"Alright," Lady Croylinin said, waving a hand at them. "Take your seats. There are name cards, and I tried to mix things up a tad. Just try to have some fun tonight."

There was a good bit of scurrying and shuffling, but in short order, everyone found their name card. His place was between Edeln, the other apprentice from the hospital, and Meloy. As he looked around the table, it finally dawned on him that they'd been mixed by gender. He felt a cold sweat on his forehead. The duchess had dropped plenty of hints about her matchmaking, but surely that wouldn't apply to him, would it?

He glanced at Sumi, who sat opposite Lady Croylinin at the other head of the table. At least it was a place of honor, but there were a handful of empty spaces between her chair and his own. He turned, looking for Erso when he came face to face with Edeln, a wide smile on her face.

"Mr. Parimu," she said, "since we're to be companions for the night, why don't you tell me something of yourself?"

Oh dear, he thought, suddenly feeling a lump in his throat. It *was* a rather fetching smile, but perhaps that meant there were more designs on his person than he'd thought…

"Please," he said, clearing his throat, "call me Relsenair."

She inclined her head, still smiling demurely.

"I suppose there isn't much to tell," he continued, forcing himself to take a sip of his wine. How did his throat become so dry, anyway? "I was in the, um…navy, and then… Well, I suppose I was lost until Sumi found me."

"Ah," she said, nodding, "now that sounds fascinating. You'll have to tell me your side of things; I'm afraid we've only heard about the…spiritual side of it all."

She took a sip from her own glass but continued to look at him as if he were the most interesting thing in the room, a notion he needed to disabuse her of, surely.

"Please," he said, waving a hand, "I'd much rather hear about you. I always had such an admiration for surgeons, the things you accomplish. How did you become an apprentice?"

She only smiled more widely at that, flushing a bit as she began to tell him about the hospital. It turned out she had come from a village just like his, though further east than Emillon, on the coast north of Strussfaran. He nodded along, trying to focus as he realized he'd forgotten how to swallow.

As soon as everyone was properly settled, the servants emerged from the kitchen, serving two plates at a time. As they set one down before him, he finally noticed the battalion of silverware around his plate. He had a vague memory of using a proper soup spoon at a naval banquet, but what in blazes was that second fork for? Still, it was hard to think of propriety as his mouth began to water. There was a trio of lamb chops fanned out on the plate, surrounded by a bed of potatoes and tall stalks of roasted chard. It smelled like…home.

He shook his head, turning back to Edeln as Lady Croylinin spoke.

"Well," she said, "do tuck in. As you can see, we're eating banquet style with such a small staff, but don't stand on ceremony. Enjoy."

The clang of silverware began to fill the room, but Sumi cleared her throat.

"Actually," she said, "if you wouldn't mind? I don't want to push propriety too far but seeing as how there's no other staff in the house, I'd love it if the others could eat with us."

The staff froze on their way back to the kitchen, their eyes darting between each other and the duchess. Parimu was sitting close enough to Sumi to see her jaw tighten, but she never took her eyes off Lady Croylinin's.

You can do this, he thought, silently trying to lend her some strength. Perhaps it was his little outburst in the bedroom that had put her up to it, but if the servants were risking their lives, they surely deserved the same treatment. Although Lady Croylinin looked as if she might ask for a duel, her stare unwavering as her mouth formed a thin line. The Master Librarian, meanwhile, never stopped eating his lamb chops, a tiny smile on his face. Perhaps Sumi had pressed her hand too far? He was about to stand to offer to eat with the servants in the kitchen when Lady Croylinin spoke.

"Yes, well, I don't see why not. If anyone's earned a seat at my table, it's you four." She didn't turn around to face them but raised her hand in the air, beckoning them. "Come now, serve yourselves and take the seats by Miss Elerair."

To a one, all the servants blinked in surprise. Kestorael, the butler, was the first to regain his composure and quickly gestured for the others to follow him. They disappeared into the kitchens for a moment, returning with their own plates.

"Oh, and Kestorael," the duchess added, "do be a dear and lock the door. Even cooks can get nosy."

The older man nodded, looking relieved as he took a key from his pocket, locking the doors on either side of the fireplace.

"Now, Erinon, you were saying?" Lady Croylinin said loudly, clearly signaling that everyone was to resume as if nothing had happened. The conversations that had previously been suspended slowly picked up again like wounded birds trying to regain flight. But before long, a happy hum returned to the room.

"Thank you," Pretanin, the other maid, said quietly to Sumi. She smiled before turning back to her plate, her jaw falling open in rapture as she looked at her own spread of lamb chops. He knew well enough from his time in the navy that just because a captain had meat didn't mean the sailors did. This may well be the first time they'd gotten to eat a full spread like this, even surrounded by the countryside's bounty as they were.

Sumi began to chat with them, and soon they were all laughing, tight jaws giving way to smiles. Even when they eventually scrambled back up to clear the plates and serve dessert, there was a certain spring in their step. He looked down at Sumi, nodding as he caught her eye. There was power in this — a shared meal, the feeling of family. In the end, this was what they were missing, and this was what Sumi — what Essomuai — had to offer them. If you could share a meal, you could share a kingdom, and that meant there might be hope for them after all.

———

After dinner and a painful hour in the drawing room — Lady Croylinin staring daggers at her the whole time — Sumi slipped back upstairs, eager for her room. Her hand had nearly shaken on her wine glass each time she met the duchess's eyes, but the dinner had still been a joy. Sitting with Peskold and the others, talking and laughing… She was glad she'd done it. Perhaps she'd looked a fool, but Parimu was right.

In fact, it was the look in his eyes that had given her the courage. Her necklaces had seemed to thrum at his intensity, the songs forcing themselves into her mind as he spoke. And with how hard it was for him to speak, how could she ignore it? Some people loved to spout off whenever they felt the slightest thing, but with people like Relsenair — or Nela, for that matter — once you saw the spark, it was already a forest fire. But like Grandpa always said about his beautiful, occasionally furious wife: "Fire makes steel, and steel makes a good ship. If I'd wanted a porcelain doll, they were a copper a crop."

If only she could be sure Peloris knew what he was doing! She still didn't feel like she knew enough to really lead the others. How did you contradict a peer without giving offense? How did you keep a group together when you challenged its greatest authority? Still, she saw her responsibility now — to Essomuai, to her vision — she just had to hope she could steer their ship through the dark.

Finally reaching the refuge of her room, she leaned against the door and closed her eyes, flashing away her frilly dress. Then she set about undressing, unlacing her boots, and brushing her hair before switching to her nightgown. She supposed if she were Erso, she could have just shaped directly from the dress to the nightgown, but that felt lazy… Besides, her nightgown had sentimental value. Nela had stitched the flowers on the neckline herself, the beautiful yellows and purples like a field in Anushai. It was the last thing Nela would ever embroider for her, and any number of moth holes was worth that feeling.

Once everything was done, she climbed into bed — even if she wasn't likely to sleep much. There had still been a fire in the hearth when she arrived — though she couldn't imagine how the poor servants had scrambled after dinner to see them relit! — so she stared up at the rippling light as it played off the canopy above her bed. She was walking a tightrope here, balancing between Peloris and Lady Croylinin, but the most important question was unfortunately still unanswered. How was she supposed to teach nearly twenty other Shapewalkers to hear the songs in a matter of days?

She closed her eyes, listening to the melodies filling the room. The song from the fire, the garden outside, even the bedspread, they all made it feel like Essomuai was there with her, as if she'd dipped herself back into the fountain. It felt like she hadn't dreamt of anything in weeks, but she needed far more guidance now than before the fountain. Essomuai had shown her the truth in those dreams, of course, but even with two goddesses around her neck, she felt no closer to who she needed to be.

Essomuai, she prayed, *show me how to join them. How did your children do it? Woyel beyesh jildel kelm.*

She let her mind go quiet then, falling into absolute stillness as she let her breath align to the rhythm of the songs. Her necklaces seemed to thrum along with her, and eventually, she slipped away.

23

Intorulenomal - an image appears of a mountain surrounded by giant trees. I do find it odd they repeat these particular parts of the cycle, but it appears to be in their nature. They seem to relish reliving old wounds, even if they no longer seem to cause any adverse effect — though the final cycles do seem to brighten things considerably.

-Excerpt from The Arguments
Third Cycle

—:—

Kemarin Pont'dulairn sat in his peerage office, scratching out notes on tomorrow's bill. Finally unable to focus on the words any longer, he paused, squeezing the bridge of his nose. Great gods below, but he felt useless! Ever since the Elerair girl came, it felt like he had a boulder on his chest — as if the royal stay hadn't put him on edge enough already... Still, seeing as how masochism seemed to be his truest instinct, he'd forced himself outside to work on a bloody sanitation bill, of all things. But like father always said, politics was momentum, and there was no better way to hide your fear than pushing out trivial bills during a stay.

He began writing again, but it wasn't long until he found himself staring at the suit of armor across from his desk. He was like a damned three-wheeled carriage, derailed at the slightest distraction. Still, he kept staring into the suit of armor as if it held answers. Sometimes it did... If nothing else, it was a good reminder that the clock of power ran faster than you could count. Nothing in this office was truly his, and that meant he had to act while he held the keys.

Even his father, who had held the Vice Peer's chair some twenty years before him, hadn't left a single trace behind in this room. There was something poetic in that. Even when a Croylinin and a Maserint held the seat before his own term, that same suit of armor had stared down at them. He could stoke his fire in the same hearth and walk proudly by the Hall of Blades, but in the end, he was nothing but another quill mark on a three-hundred-year-old desk. It was only out there, in the kingdom, where his changes had some hope of lasting.

Just as he was about to pick up his pen again, Terosan came into the room. He was technically just an undersecretary in the office, but that was just an excuse to give him a reason for barging in at any time of day. Pont'dulairn immediately stood, reaching eagerly for the report in Terosan's hand. It was ciphered, of course, but easily enough that he didn't need a reference to read it. Though after seeing Kollenail's personal ciphers, their own notes now felt rather crude by comparison…

"And the other thing we discussed?" he asked, handing the cipher back, which Terosan dutifully tossed in the fire.

"The librarian's definitely gone," Terosan said, leaning against the door, "few of his apprentices, too. Gerrinal isn't at the hospital, though that could be normal — guess he still does naval rotations. Strangest is Croylinin. She's got a whole mess of servants at her house in the city, but as far as I can tell, she isn't there. Nobody's used the front door all week. I posed as one of their delivery chaps, but the cooks said they don't know where she's gone."

Pont'dulairn tilted his head back, looking up at the ceiling as he sighed.

"Very well," he said, "thank you." He was hoping he'd quashed the parade business, but it seemed they'd need a firmer hand. He'd bet everything on this bill, and letting a bunch of monsters march down the street would be as good as tearing up his slip before the race began. He bloody well wouldn't outlive Welaya, and he didn't have another twenty years to set things right.

Not that he should be surprised. Of course, Domelgaine would try something. As his father had always said, the librarian was 'too bloody smart by half,' and with that came a certain wiliness you had to constantly manage. Although Haleone Croylinin was a bit of a surprise… He'd always pegged her for the type who valued power over sentiment, but even his perceptions had their limits.

"I've got to run," he said, getting up from his desk and pulling on his coat. He pointed at the drafted bill on the desk. "I missed dinner, but I promised Elisal I'd be home before the sherry's gone — she has cousins in from the Sisters or something. Will you run that bill to Oeskidara? Tell him I need his signature by morning."

Terosan nodded, picking up the bill and carefully folding it before stowing it in one of the many pockets that lined his coat. Then they both walked out together. His official secretary, Lestorn, got up quickly from his desk when he realized the peer was leaving as well. He was a sharp enough man, though he was a peerage appointee, not at all reliable in the way Terosan was.

"Anything else I can do, sir?" Lestorn asked.

"No, no," Pont'dulairn said with the wave of a hand. "Just watch the office for the next hour and send a runner over with any extra correspondence, would you?"

They pushed their way past the guards and their constant bowing until they finally reached the street. Terosan nodded once before slipping away, off to do far more than the one task he'd been given. Pont'dulairn watched him go for a moment before turning toward home. He was lucky to have Terosan. He'd done the lad a favor when he was younger that he could never possibly repay, but after all these years, he knew his loyalty was real. Besides, you needed someone moving the pieces while you thought about strategy, or you'd never get your head out of the water.

He passed the library and turned left, passing the rows of stately mansions. He didn't always like living in Lournoy. It always felt...exposed, the whole city growing around you like a barnacle. But there were advantages, too, and the five-minute walk to the peerage was fairly high on the list. A valet opened the front door for him as he approached, taking his coat and hat. He turned an ear toward the sitting room but didn't hear anything, so he snuck off toward his study. He tried to never directly disobey Elisal, of course, but if he didn't think about this parade business for at least a few minutes, those bloody cousins of hers would make his head pop!

When he reached his study door, though, he found it unlocked. He pushed it open, finding Elisal at her own desk, tall and elegant as she wrote. He did sometimes wonder what father would have thought of that. When they'd gotten married, she'd insisted on Sisters tradition, having a desk right by her husband's. He had bristled at first, but twenty-five years later, he'd grown to love it. Somehow, he found himself more focused when she was in the room, the scratching of her quill and the warmth of her presence putting him at ease.

"Ah, husband," she said, looking up. "I thought I might find you sneaking in here."

"Guilty," he said, closing the door behind him. He shuffled past the edge of her desk, leaning in to kiss her before moving to his own. He set down his briefcase, taking a deep breath. It always smelled better when she was here, too. She wore her usual perfume, of course, but she always threw incense on top of the logs, too, as her family had always done. He never had figured out what it was that she burnt, but it smelled of pine and spice and certainly went a long way in pushing back the musty smell of his books.

"What about your cousins?" he asked, turning away from the fire.

"I made your excuses," she said without turning around. "But," she added with a chuckle, "I promised them you'd personally serve them breakfast. If you sneak off without your eggs tomorrow, you'll have a *wubrose* on your hands."

He smiled tiredly, leaning his head on his hand.

"Very well," he said. "Thank you, darling."

"Kiterosht minahl guterenk," she said. His Trierlien still wasn't perfect, but he knew *that* phrase well enough. Something like, 'you're a fool, but I love you.'

Now, what to do about the Elerair girl? Her powers *were* impressive, but why was she so determined to throw them away? Shapewalkers in the capital, in a bloody parade, no less! He pulled out his private maps, looking over the coalitions he'd colored in. How fragile it all was. His mind worked through the probabilities, watching in his mind's eye as the colors changed on the map, loyalties shifting in her wake. The moment these Shapewalkers came to light, the men he'd muscled onto his bills would turn on him like rabid dogs. He was the one pushing for the Continent, after all. And while the others were fine with lining their pockets, they'd sing a different tune with monsters in their backyard.

He *had* to put a stop to this — the only question was how far he wanted to go. The Elerair girl was remarkable, true, but he owed her nothing. She had come to him, and he'd refused her offer, begging her to see reason. The others, however, had earned his loyalty over the years. Perhaps there was a way to eliminate only the girl and her companions? If Croylinin was gone from the city, then she must be at Linindal. Would she go so far as to offer her home to the girl? Surely it was too great of a coincidence to ignore.

But how quietly could he handle something of this scale? If even a whiff of an attack on a peer's estates came out, the Queen would be looking at him far more closely than he'd like. Even Kollenail was just a fly compared to interfering with another peer. Should he go directly to Welaya? If he was her ally in rooting out the Shapewalkers, with her own missing DoR in their midst… Yet even that would set his plans back years, at least.

No, he'd need to do this himself. Still, a simple show of force should do, especially if he showed restraint. Croylinin was proud, but she was no fool. The girl should be enough… Take the head off a snake, and it was just a length of meat. And perhaps he could avoid violence altogether? The girl was a wealth of knowledge, and he had only to hold her long enough to get through the royal stay. Besides, she deserved better than Kollenail, surely. Not only would killing her make him a monster in the others' eyes, but that could very well make him a monster to himself.

He took out a piece of parchment and his best cipher, laying them by his seal and blotter. He was just dipping his pen in the ink to write out his orders when Elisal stepped over, standing in front of his desk.

"What of that sweet young woman from the other night?" she asked. "Have you apologized yet?"

"Dearest," he said, "I told you I have nothing to apologize for, she—" He paused, finally looking up and seeing the look on Elisal's face. Her eyes seemed to glow in the firelight, and she looked as if she meant to see right through his skull to where his mind churned.

She leaned forward, setting something heavy on his parchment. She moved her hand, revealing Kollenail's signet ring, the symbol of the thorns on its side. She held all his trophies — if he could really use that word for such a morbid prize. But she knew who and what he was, and still, she supported him, a wonder in itself.

"You are a brilliant man," she said, her expression softening just a hair, "but you lose yourself, driving men like horses. You forget what it is to let them drive themselves. What men *believe* is what shapes their hearts, husband, and those who believe the wrong thing can never be brought to see the light."

Then she reached beneath her dress and pulled out another ring, this one on a long chain. She placed this beside Kollenail's. It was nearly twice as large and set with a massive ruby. It was her father's, and in all their years of marriage, he had never once seen it leave her breast.

"My father is gone," she said, "and you are my heart now. I will never leave you, but I *will* demand you keep your promise. Whatever you choose, let that be foremost in your mind."

His mind flashed to that garden in Maldegurn all those years ago. She had promised to be his conscience, and she had. She turned to go, pausing for a moment at her desk to seal the letters she'd left folded there. He stared at her, bewildered, his eyes wide. He knew his wife ran as deep as the ocean, but she so rarely broke the surface that a foolish man could forget. He was still sure he would have never found a woman of her like anywhere else on Wellonai.

"I will see you in your room," she said, turning and sparing him a smile as she left, more valuable than all the world's riches.

Yes, she was his conscience. Still, a man sometimes had to look his conscience in the eye and choose the necessary path. Elisal may not like it, but he would keep her in his heart. There would be no unnecessary violence, and the girl *would* live. Perhaps when all of this was over, he could mend fences with Domelgaine, but for now, they needed the bridle.

He reached out, taking the two rings and putting them in his breast pocket. *I hear you, my love*, he thought. Then he went back to the parchment. Snakes could bite quickly, and his sword would have to be quicker.

————

Peloris sat in the drawing room, staring at the fire as he sipped his claret. Dinner was already two hours past, but the room still hadn't emptied out, everyone no doubt staying on for the wine and conversation. He was just a crusty old man, of course, so he was expected to be glued to his chair, but he couldn't easily justify leaving a full dessert tray and a warm fire for another night of worthless sleep. Speaking of which… He swiveled his eyes to the tray, where there was still a tart for the taking. *Forgive me, Lenara*, he thought with a grin as he waved for Peskold.

Eventually, all the hangers-on disappeared, the hard work in the sun making their eyelids heavy even if they wished the night would never end. Just another benefit of his age, apparently. He had done absolutely no hard work whatsoever, which at least allowed him to play the night owl. Finally, the captain got up to go, looking like he was a few barrels deep but bowing to Haleone all the same. As the door closed behind him, the duchess looked his way. Apparently, she was as ready for the charade to be over as he was.

"Peskold," she said to the butler, "you may leave us. Just make sure Pretanin has whatever she needs in my dressing room before you turn in. Tell her I won't be long."

"My lady," he said, bowing his way from the room.

She watched him a while longer, her hands folded neatly in her lap. He waited, his permanent smile just at the edge of his lips — not mocking, not foolish. He supposed he could try to look nervous, but he wasn't. This conversation was all part of the plan, after all, even if the duchess didn't see it that way. Not that he thought it would be an easy conversation… Haleone had backbone, which you couldn't say about every peer. She was a good egg, too — deep down, anyway. A bit ruthless, perhaps, but less so than the others. She may balk, but he sincerely hoped she wouldn't. Even if they had to do the parade without her, he'd see it done, but it'd be better with her aboard.

"Do you know why my father built Linindal?" she asked, finally breaking the silence as she reached for her wine.

"I don't, actually," he replied. "Though you know I love my house histories."

"Well, then, I'm sure you know my family has held these lands since the first century. We had a keep closer to the river, but my father built this house as a sort of…temple to our kind, a place where our power could be on display. You saw the statues in the drive, surely, but even the observatory was a link to Shapewalking and his grand theories about where we came from."

He nodded. He supposed he'd wondered that himself enough times. He hadn't known Lord Croylinin very well, but he'd certainly been an…eccentric.

"Brilliant man, your father," Peloris said, smiling a bit more widely. "That's precisely why I thought you'd want to join us in this. I don't know about the stars, but Sumi did have many of the answers your father always sought."

"Yes," she said, taking a long sip from her wine. "The girl has *some* answers. But this isn't exactly what you promised me either, is it?"

He cocked his head, raising an eyebrow. They both knew very well what game they were playing, but she'd have to be the one to say it.

"I may lack the…entirety of my father's intellect, but I'm alike him in many ways. Far more so than my mother, at any rate. And you know full well that I think it patently ridiculous that the most powerful of us are forced to hide in our own kingdom. If the girl proves anything, it's that our people hold the power of *gods* in our hands. I have a feeling you may have promised a great many things to all of us to see this parade done, but you're mistaken if you think I'll let your sentimentality drag me into a sideshow for children."

At least she didn't say it was a sideshow for old men! Children were wonderful, exactly the audience he was hoping for. The trick would be getting her to see that.

"Surely you wouldn't have the humans fear you? They already do that, and we know what's come of it. Don't you see the elegance in the girl's plan? Joy is the only antidote to fear I know of."

"No, not fear," she said, "but I would have the humans *respect* me. We should have more to choose from than monster or court jester. Power is the only currency that matters, Peloris. Just look to the Anushai if you think there's some sort of reward in this world for virtue."

He sighed, shaking his head.

"Would you have yourself become a god? I hate to remind you, my dear, but you're a Berillai Peer. You're already one of the most powerful creatures in all of Wellonai, and if you can't use that power to some good, what do you think you'd do with more?"

She paused with her hand on her wine glass, meeting his eyes.

"I didn't see the city until my tenth birthday," she said. "My father hid me here until I manifested my powers. There was no guarantee he could bribe the DoR if I accidentally transformed at the wrong time. Even the Vice Peer could have his child hung by the docks. And you call that power? I seek change, yes, but I'm far from wanting more of the same. I will change this kingdom, but strength must come first."

Peloris nodded, bowing his head to her as he put a hand to his chest in sympathy. Poor girl. He couldn't imagine what she'd been through, what *any* of them had been through. But that was all the more reason to seek something better.

"I don't pretend to have known your father well," he said, "but I'm not sure he would have agreed with you on that score."

She opened her mouth, but he held up a finger, digging in his pocket for the papers he'd brought. It took another minute of fumbling with his second pair of glasses, unfortunately, but there was a price to pay for living so long.

"You may recall that among my many responsibilities is the collection of Peerage memoirs. I really enjoyed your father's when I read it, so much so that I had a copy made for my personal library. Perhaps you'll remember this bit."

Even magnified to several times its size, he had to squint in the dim firelight, but luckily, he'd put most of it to memory.

"'To what do we owe our strength? Is it the bounty of these lands or the steel of our swords? No, I say! It is in our goodness, the fact that we bring something more to these lands than what lay here before. We are the fire in the cave, the symbol in the storm. If we are not just, then let us be nothing at all.'"

He folded the paper, looking back up at Haleone. Her mouth had formed a thin line, but as he finished, the faintest smile appeared.

"It was in the very same memoir that my father said, 'if boulders were afraid to smash pebbles, there'd be no sand.'"

"A colorful writer, your father," Peloris said, chuckling.

She stood, turning toward the fire with her hands behind her back. Even in the dim light, though, he could see the muscles bulging in her fists. Finally, she sucked in a sharp breath, turning to face him.

"Fine," she said, "I see your point. But do you really expect me to leave my brain at the door? I knew this would make an enemy of

Pont'dulairn, but I was thinking I'd have something to show for it when it was over. You expect me to babysit the girl for free?"

"No," he said, groaning as he pushed himself out of his chair as well. He strained his back, forcing his eyes to be level with hers. "I expect you to do it because it's *right*. But I'm no fool, either. You may also be aware that I manage the Royal Surveyor's Corps. I've had some private readings done of your lands the past few years, and I think you might like to hear what my stone speakers have to say about the silver veins in this area."

She blinked, apparently genuinely surprised. But as the saying went, if you couldn't ask the lamb to leave the meadow, you'd better come with an apple.

"Something to think on, then," he said, smiling. "Good night, my dear."

He turned, heading toward the door. He couldn't leave with much grace — he was too stooped for that, unfortunately — but he could leave hopeful. He just had to trust that people really were as good as he gave them credit for. He hadn't been proven wrong yet — not completely, anyway — but nothing in this world was ever certain. Still, a craftsman didn't stop measuring his wood just because he was experienced. He just went ahead and sharpened his saw.

24

The records say there were three other pillars on the eastern side of the blast burrow. That would fit the diagram, though those were surely taken much earlier. It doesn't answer any of my most pressing questions, but it's interesting to note the pattern repeating here.

-Setorin's Log
3831-71

—:—

There was nothing between Sumi and the dream this time. It seemed she had stayed open to the songs even as she faded into sleep, and it was almost as if she could see the dream beginning, the threads of Essomuai's magic weaving through the blankness until she was surrounded by color and sound. There was only a moment of knowledge before the end of herself. She was Saldal, the Great Mother of Grass House, and she was surrounded by chaos.

A tidal wave of humanity surged past her, the humans running for the mountain, though it would do them little good now. Still, the black-sailed ships in the harbor promised death, the memories of Elomikarus's power still fresh for every southerner who had fled here. Her soldiers stood firm, but they seemed so silly now, like playthings compared to the approaching army.

Mother, she thought, reaching out with her mind. Her siblings were already there, the chatter of their thoughts filling her as they all sought the pillar. She could feel its golden core, like a heartbeat beneath the mountain, connecting to the gold within her heart. The whole city was thrumming with it as if Essomuai hoped she could somehow spirit them away. Saldal bonded her mind to it, hoping to see some path that led away from death.

She stretched out her awareness, looking through the pillar until she was amongst the ships. It didn't take long to find the Southern Emperor. He stood on the first bow, his sword free as if he meant to take the beach himself. She could not see inside his heart — so it *was* true that his *welloshara* was of a different sort — but he had a smile on his face. This man felt no fear. Not at what he would face on the beach and not at what he planned to do.

Mother, she said again in her mind, *seontesharemai*.

The humming of the pillar grew louder in her mind, the infinity of Mother's *kouselumakan* filling her.

Reolekasara, Essomuai answered. Images began to fill her mind, but she knew this word, had been raised on it since Mother had brought her to this world. She was right. They must sing. Even as death threatened to pour onto the beach, they had vowed to sing until the end.

"Tudal!" she cried out to her sister, the one they'd chosen to lead them. "We must sing!"

Her sister turned from the head of the shape they had arranged themselves in, the ancient pattern of strength — the Mother of Mothers, forever lost to her children but speaking to them still. Tudal met her gaze, her eyes searching, as worried as her own must be. Her wide sleeves of green silk were tied beyond her elbows, though she held no sword. She was prepared to die this day. Still, she nodded.

"Saldal is right," Tudal said to the others. "We must sing. Join me now, in the old way."

Saldal closed her eyes, keeping her connection to Mother as the song began. As always, Geomon was first, singing in his deep bass the Song of Stones. As he followed the progression, his many children joined him, their voices singing of the hidden mind of stones, the ancient search for life. Tudal was next, her voice thick like the soil, her light filling the empty space between them.

Heyal and Teon came in at once, baritone and soprano blending in perfect harmony. A river rushed through her mind, water pouring through the world as a blue sky soared overhead. Essomuai's world was forming, and its life was bursting in her veins. As the third cycle came around, her own turn approached, her heart fluttering as she took a breath. The air smelled of death, of fear, but this was her home, and for the moment, she was still alive. She sang with all her might, singing the Song of Life as Yeonmol joined her with his Dance of Shadow. Plants sprouted in her mind, growing and dying as the seasons changed, life and death intertwining in the golden field.

Soon, they were all singing, the cycle pulling out and rushing back like waves on the ocean. Mother thrummed with joy, the world within her glowing ever brighter, joining them in its light. She could feel them all there — not just her siblings but their children, too — each and every spirit mixing into one.

Dilaremusae, Mother spoke into their minds — *dance the dance that is*.

There was a tug on her heart, and Tudal was suddenly there, pulled with her mind as she began to weave them. This was so many more than they had ever joined with, but somehow, the sacred shape stayed whole, its light growing as it flowed toward her sister. Suddenly, the light was all around them like a second sun as Mother's essence poured out from the mountain. Even as she disappeared, Saldal sang on with all her might. Mother's infinity wrapped around her, and in the span of a breath, she was gone. The dance had begun.

25

Vestorilunaral - a stone shatters, cracks forming along its base until it breaks into the shape of the diagram. This seems to be a strange hybrid between a unitary and an invulsion, though that makes me question its purpose.

-Excerpt from The Echoes
Second Cycle

—:—

Erso woke with a groan, the bright morning light apparently keen on splitting his skull open. He reached for his aching back and found hard stone beneath him. As he forced one eye open, he began to laugh, though that only made the pain worse. Bloody hall of curses, was he sore! Memories slowly started to filter in, though what he could remember didn't explain much… He'd apparently fallen asleep in a giant empty fountain — hopefully somewhere near Linindal. He shielded his face from the light, turning his head, where he found Beysal beside him. That's right… They'd been drunk as lords going in circles about…Sumi.

His heart skipped a beat, but he shook his head, reaching out and pushing on Beysal's shoulder. The man was snoring like a ship engine, but he started at Erso's push and split his eyes open, laughing hoarsely as recognition came over his face.

"Great halls, lad," he said. "Why do I let you talk me into this nonsense?"

He rolled over, great hulking bear that he was, and pushed himself upright, leaning against the rim of the fountain. Erso stayed on his back, staring up at the giant statue in the center. It was even stranger than the ones in the drive, some kind of hodgepodge creature dancing on stairs made of moons.

"I seem to recall you pulling out the whiskey after dinner," Erso said, grunting as he tried to shift his weight off of a sharp rock, only to find an even larger one digging into his back.

"Yeah, yeah," Beysal said, waving a hand in the air while the other massaged his brow. "I don't mean the whiskey." He coughed, clearing his throat. "I mean arguing with a stubborn fool like you all night until we somehow slept in a bloody fountain! Why didn't we just sleep on the leaves?"

Erso laughed. "I'm not taking the blame for this. Remember the time you made us sleep inside that log?"

"Yeah, that's fair," Beysal said, chuckling. "It seemed like a good idea at the time. Woke up with a bloody frog in my boot, though."

He glanced down at his own boots, worried there'd be a frog, but he'd apparently been too drunk to take them off.

"Hey, at least we didn't drown," Beysal added, nudging him in the ribs. "Why d'ya think the fountain's empty?"

"Probably heard you were coming," Erso said, "didn't want a bear swimming in it."

"You're probably right," he said, rubbing his beard. "Well, at least they're sure to have a king's breakfast waiting for us. You'll think on what I said last night, though, yeah?"

Erso groaned — far louder than before — as he forced himself to a seated position, leaning against the base of the statue.

"Isn't one bloody night of going in circles enough for you?" he asked. He tried to lick his lips, but they were dryer than the Void. "Just let me handle this. Besides, you said yourself the gods are real. You think they're gonna let me drag their best angel through the dirt? It's for the best, just let it be."

"I'll let it bloody be when you admit you're wrong," Beysal said. He groaned again, forcing himself up the side of the fountain where he sat on the lip, his elbows on his knees. "I was too deep in my cups to say it right last night, but I'm not leaving this fountain until you hear me out."

Erso rolled his eyes but opened his palm, waving for Beysal to go ahead. How much worse could it get anyway? He'd done the crime, might as well see to the headsman.

"So," Beysal said, meeting his eyes, "you wanna talk about gods, eh? So what if you're a miserable lout, don't you think the gods find that delightful? Essomuai's got a song for everything, after all."

"Fine," Erso said, "but Sumi—"

"Sumi nothing, boy!" Beysal shouted. "You act like Peritrine invented grapes to plague you personally. So you got some edges that need dulling, who doesn't? Even if you were the bloody saint of the sands, you'd still find a way to hurt this girl, lad. Just be glad it's you that gets to hurt her, the one who's gonna bloody love her best. Elo found me in a damned ditch, but I would kill for that woman. Don't let trying to be some knight keep you from being the miserable brute who's gonna make her happy."

Erso sighed, putting his head in his hand. This was going to be a long morning and an even longer day. Beysal would probably be right if he were talking about anybody else, but how was he supposed to willingly let Sumi throw her life away on him? It would always feel wrong, selfish even. It wouldn't be easy to let her go, far from it. It'd be like letting out every drop of his blood, but he'd do it. Even if he had to fight Beysal. He sucked in a breath, bracing for another round.

———

Sumi closed the door to her bedroom, hurrying down the hallway to find Parimu. Her dream hadn't been a complete answer — not yet — but it was a start, and it filled her with hope. She could still feel Essomuai's power passing through her, so much like the Fountain and yet…different. The Elders had summoned her through the song, bringing the goddess into the world, and if she could use even a fraction of that power, she knew the parade would work.

She passed Erso's room, pausing with her hand above the doorknob. Part of her wanted to tell him the good news, but… She shook her head, moving on. He'd be asleep anyway. Not that she was running away! Besides, it was Relsenair who couldn't hear the songs yet. Erso would be excited for her either way, he always was, but it would be best to tell the others when she was sure it would work. Still, her head was so full of random thoughts that when she reached Parimu's room, she forgot to knock.

"Relsenair," she said, "you'll never—"

She stopped, freezing with her hand on the door. Parimu was awake, thank Essomuai, but he was sitting on the edge of his bed in his shirtsleeves, oiling his sword. He froze, too, the pair of them like the sheep caught wandering the clover.

"Oh," she said, "I'm…uh… Well, sorry to barge in like this. I just…uh…had some good news."

"O-of course!" Parimu stammered, hastily standing as he put his sword away. "Please come in. I don't have tea or anything but make yourself comfortable."

"Okay," Sumi said, chuckling as the air finally came back into her lungs. "I guess I'm lucky you didn't run me through."

"Right," Parimu said, forcing himself to smile as he scratched the back of his head. "I suppose I don't have to oil it every day, but it's an old habit. Helps me feel more ready to face the day."

Somehow, she got the feeling he would have rather been caught in his skivvies than with his sword out. She was about to take a seat by the window, but she stopped, turning back to Parimu.

"Actually," she said, "would you mind if we took a walk? I think I might have found a way to teach you the songs, but I wouldn't mind a little privacy."

His eyes lifted at that. "Of course," he said, quickly shrugging on his coat. "The others mentioned a nice fountain in the woods; maybe we go there?"

A minute later, they were through the Great Hall and making their escape through the gardens. They were stunning, a maze of hedges and flowers that no doubt depended on another army of servants. But enchanted or not, Parimu moved quickly, his urgency to learn the songs apparently no less than hers to teach them. They were about to reach the tree line when they heard voices. Parimu stopped looking back at her. They were allowed to walk the grounds, surely, but who else would be out at this hour?

The voices grew closer until Beysal and Erso appeared on the path, their eyes widening as if they'd been the ones caught in the cookie jar. Although, calling their eyes wide was perhaps an overstatement… They both looked a bit worse for wear, their eyes obviously bloodshot even at a distance.

"Well," Beysal said, recovering first, "fancy running into you two. We were just looking for some breakfast."

"In the garden?" Sumi asked, grinning.

"Fair enough," he said, laughing. Erso stared into the plants as if he wished he could disappear. Beysal slapped him on the back, shaking his head.

"But don't blame the lad. I never get to drink properly anymore, and I think I pushed us a bit too far. Still, a bit of morning air always helps set things right. Lovely fountain back that way, too, by the way."

"Yeah," Erso said, scoffing, "lovely. Pretty comfortable, too."

"Oh, good," Parimu said, "that's where we were heading. How far into the woods is it?"

"Just past the tree line," Beysal said, pointing over his shoulder. "But what about you two? Didn't think you'd be out here walking things off."

"Just a bit of practice," she said, forcing herself to smile. Parimu eyed her but held his tongue.

"The hero never sleeps, I see," Beysal said, motioning for Erso to follow him toward the house. "If I see anything promising in the kitchens, I'll try to save you some!"

They moved on in silence, quickly reaching the trees.

"I'm sorry I lied back there," she said. "It's not because of you. I'm just…afraid I might still fail."

"Don't worry about me," Parimu said, holding a branch up so she could pass. "Ships have captains for a reason. Besides, it'll work."

It would work, wouldn't it? Just hours ago, she'd seen the magic through Saldal's eyes. She knew it was real; she just had to find it. They finally reached the clearing, the fountain empty as it sat under the shade of the canopy.

"So," Parimu said quietly, "where do you want me?"

"We may as well get comfortable," she said, gesturing to the wide stone rim. "We'll have to figure this out together."

He joined her on the fountain's edge, though he didn't look comfortable exactly. Still, he'd sat, and the rest was up to her.

"I had a dream last night," she said, the light returning to her mind. "I was one of the Elders in Anushai, making the signs that defeated Elomikarus. I know this will sound silly, but they *sang* the songs, like actually sang them. They all took a part, so I'm not sure if it will work with just two of us, but…will you try to sing with me?"

"I'd love to," he said. "I know I can't hear them yet, but if you can sing them first…"

"Alright," she said, smiling. She cleared her throat, trying to remember how the song had sounded in her dream. It wasn't singing exactly, it was just sounds, but they *had* sung along. Perhaps if she could hear the rest, it wouldn't feel so strange. She opened herself to the songs, allowing them to pour into her mind. The trees surrounding them, which had already seemed so full of life, began to burst with it, the leaves and birds and bugs all lifting up their songs as one. And beneath it was Essomuai's song, every melody swirling together as they were joined by that single golden thread.

Listening now, though, she could recognize the layers of the song, the parts each Elder had sung. She noticed Geomon's first, the bass line of the stones holding up the others. It took a few cycles, the song repeating in her mind, but she finally noticed Saldal's part. What had she called it, the Song of Life? She closed her eyes, watching as the plants grew in her mind. The cycle began again, and as it did, she hummed along. And then, she started singing, her own voice mixing with her ancestors'.

She stood, keeping her eyes closed as she breathed in deep, singing with all her might. As she found her harmony, she felt her own voice disappear, the others growing louder in her mind as the song drew near. She wasn't sure how long she sang, maybe a dozen cycles? But it could have just as easily been hours. Finally, she remembered herself, closing her mouth as the song faded away. It was hard to let go, feeling like she could disappear into that music. She opened her eyes, finding Parimu watching her, his eyes wide.

"Did you hear them?" she asked, clasping her hands together.

"Uh…maybe?" he said. "Or maybe not. It was beautiful singing, I've never heard anything like it, but not *the* songs, I don't think."

"Drat," she said, sitting again. "I guess I should've known it wouldn't be that easy. Still, it felt…different, like the songs were singing with me."

"Maybe I should join you," he said. "Not that I want to subject you to my singing voice."

"Could be," she said, nodding. The song wasn't complicated exactly — it was almost entrancingly simple — especially when it was split into parts. "Let me see if I can find a part to teach you."

She leaned against her knees, pressing her forehead with her fingertips. As she did so, her necklaces fell from her dress, spinning as they dangled in front of her. Beneath her, ants wandered across the pavilion, weaving between clumps of grass pushing up between the stones. They were just like her, wandering, hoping for something more while the goddesses swirled above her. If only she could be as sure she'd find something on the other side.

She reached out, taking the necklaces in her palm. As she held Vilodai's Eye, the goddess's thrumming filled her mind. But it was different than before… It was louder than she'd ever heard it, spilling outward in a strange echo of the songs. The stones around them shook with it, vibrating to Vilodai's power. And beside her, there was…a larger vibration, a rhythm that went deeper than the stones. She turned, staring at Parimu. It came from him, echoing with the vibration of the songs.

He was looking out at the trees, waiting patiently for her to figure something out. But as he noticed her, he turned, smiling nervously.

"Is everything alright?" he asked. "You look like you saw a ghost."

"I think…I feel something," she said. She dropped the necklace, and the vibration left her mind. "It's…a rhythm, like Vilodai's, and it's coming from you."

"From me?" he asked, looking down as he touched his chest. "From the mountains?"

"I don't think so," she said. "You never came into the cave. It must have always been there, but with her eye…" She picked up the necklace again, another wave of vibrations crashing into her. "Like that," she said, shaking her head. "It's happening now. It's an echo, like it hears the songs, the same way the necklace hums when I change shapes."

He blinked, frowning. She hadn't told him that, had she?

"I mean," she stammered, "it's nothing to worry about. It's been happening for a while."

"Right," he said, nodding slowly. "I mean, she did create the humans, right?"

"*Welloshara*," she said quietly. The goddesses, the stones on the terrace, it was all connected somehow — *they* were all connected somehow.

Parimu looked at her, his face concerned.

"There's something I need to tell you," she said, her neck burning with shame. He'd been nothing but loyal, and she hadn't told him the whole truth. "Something strange keeps happening with Vilodai, and…I didn't tell you. I'm sorry. I thought I could avoid it, but…I think I need to understand it."

He nodded, keeping his eyes on hers. He didn't look angry, he looked…steady.

"When I passed the fort, the stones in the wall, there were these…voices. They seemed like they wanted to join together, but I was afraid of what would happen if I let them, something like…Elomikarus."

"And that word?" he asked, sounding it out. *"Welloshara?"*

"It means 'mind,'" she said, "but not like the mind in your head. It's…got something to do with the goddesses, before they were born, I think. But I think they're connected: you, me, the stones. These rhythms…it's like they want to echo the songs. It's like…a keyhole, but for things."

"A keyhole," he repeated. "In the stones?"

"Maybe," she said. "I don't want to do anything dangerous, but this vibration, it's coming from you, and it sounds like the songs. What if we sang again, but with the necklace? Only if you think it's safe, I mean. I—"

"I'll do it," he said.

She nodded. She thought of Elomikarus again, the stones beneath them suddenly feeling like bombs ready to explode. But she didn't think the eye was meant for that; she'd left that power at the mountain.

"Thank you," she said. "You're very brave, Relsenair."

He chuckled. "Maybe," he said. "It can't be any more dangerous than loading a cannon, right?"

"Somehow, that doesn't reassure me," she said, smiling.

They stood, going around the other side of the fountain — anything to get further from the house without leaving the pavilion. Somehow, she thought the vibrations would work better with the stone beneath them. They stood facing each other, and she took off her necklace, holding it in her hand.

"Ready?" she asked. He nodded. "I don't know if this will work, but in case it does...try to keep your heart open."

She took a deep breath, closing her eyes as she opened herself to the songs. This time, she knew what she was listening for, and the voices of the stones crashed into her mind, colliding with the songs as they fought for space like the ocean trying to fill a jar. But then, the voices came together, realigning to her necklace as they reached for her. She slipped into the whirlpool of sound, trying to hold onto herself as she reached for Essomuai, trying to follow the cycles of the song.

She finally found Saldal's part, the Song of Life, and she sucked in a breath, unwilling to let the song escape her. She sang with all her might, her own voice mixing with the others in her mind. As she sang, the vibrations grew louder, the rhythm of the song rippling from her hand into the stones around her. When she cracked an eye open, though, Parimu was still standing there, completely unchanged. Still, she didn't stop, balling up her fists as she sang louder. She wouldn't give up. This was sacred. This was good. She had to make it work.

Welloshara, she thought as she sang. What was a mind? How did it work? *Welloshara.*

Kouselumakan, a voice said in her mind.

Her heart skipped a beat, nearly jumping out of her skin as Vilodai filled her mind.

Kouselumakan, the goddess said, *welloshara*, repeating the words from the garden. The voice...and the mind. The image of the pillar entered her mind, shaking as it filled with light. And then, she *heard* it. A rhythm shaking as it spun around the others, and it came from Parimu. It wasn't a keyhole, it was...his mind, his *welloshara.* How hadn't she noticed it before? It was a part of him, hiding beneath his song even as it echoed to its melody.

And if that was the mind...then was she the voice? She wasn't sure how, but somehow, she directed her singing at his mind, reaching for it even as her lungs began to burn. Her own voice began to fill her mind as if she were singing both within and without, her voice growing louder as it traced the cycle of Essomuai. The vibrations intensified, the song seeming to bounce off Parimu like sparks escaping from a forge. If she just pushed a little harder, it felt like she could—

"Sumi!" Parimu cried out. "I can hear them, I can hear the songs! Oh, gods above, they're beautiful!"

"Join me!" she cried, her voice strained as she fought for air. There was no time to teach him, but somehow, he already knew. As the cycle began, he sang with her, somehow knowing that Yeonmol's part should go with hers, the songs of life and death intertwining. Their voices joined together, harmonizing as they echoed through the tiny minds around them. Something shifted in the air, and suddenly, the songs grew louder, like a wave crashing into the world.

She opened her eyes, finding great gouts of light pouring from their hearts. They kept singing, and the light joined between them, swirling where the two crashed into each other. She could feel his mind, the outline of his soul blending with her own. It felt like moving a boulder, but somehow, she stepped forward, moving toward him. The light shot up around them like a geyser, the clearing invisible behind a curtain of gold, a storm with them at the center.

Parimu, she said in her mind.

Sumi? he asked, only just realizing she was there.

Dance with me, she said.

The light began to shift, and suddenly, she knew she could shape it, like shaping herself but bigger, the power far deeper than her own pool. It wasn't quite as infinite as it had felt inside the fountain, but it was massive, like the tide rolling in. She felt the warmth of the sun, and she reached for it, joining with Parimu as they became a tree, stretching toward the sky as one of the ghostly trees from Vilodai's Heart. They swayed above the canopy, and she could feel Parimu with her there, both of them looking out at the horizon as they floated in the wind.

Thank you, she thought, reaching for them all — Parimu, Vilodai, Essomuai. *Thank you.*

26

Why here, though? It's so clearly a backwater, but it must not have been at the time... I can speculate all I want, but at this point, I suppose I have to see it for myself.

-Setorin's Log
3677-04

—:—

Sumi burst into the dining room with Parimu, a thick stack of papers in her hand. The others looked up in surprise, freezing with bacon and eggs hanging from their forks.

"We have an announcement," she said, smiling despite the duchess's glare. Peskold approached, no doubt to usher her to a chair, but she simply handed him the stack of parchment, motioning for him to pass them out.

"We summoned Essomuai," she said. "And I learned how to teach the songs."

"With…sheet music?" Meloy asked, holding hers up. Erso was sitting next to her, and their eyes met. He smiled, shaking his head.

"Not exactly," Sumi answered, "though the sheet music will help."

Assuming it was legible, of course… She and Parimu had spent a painstaking hour by the piano in the sitting room, making a rough transcription of every cycle. Still, it had been ten years since Nela had forced her to take those piano lessons, and she'd never been particularly good. But if it got them singing, the rest would take care of itself.

"It comes down to Vilodai," she went on as she tried to explain — as nearly as she could without the goddess tongue — what they had discovered about voices and minds. She left out the bit about the necklace, praying no one ever discovered the other stones. But by the end, the others had started nodding, somehow understanding her rambling about keyholes and minds and the way they used the songs.

"Not to be…overly skeptical," Lady Croylinin said slowly, sharing a strange look with Peloris, "but you expect us to sing? And you expect us to sing this here?" She held up her sheet music, her mouth moving as she scanned the page. "There aren't even any words, they're just…notes."

She'd given the duchess Tudal's cycle. It wasn't too difficult — none of them were, really — but it was essential. She met Lady Croylinin's eyes, and she realized she wasn't afraid anymore. Politics be damned, Peloris was right. Now that she'd heard the songs, nothing could possibly matter more.

"I know how it looks," Sumi said gently. "But it's only a reference. Once you hear the songs, nothing else will matter. I know you're afraid, but you have to trust me."

The duchess's eyes darkened, but as she opened her mouth again, Peloris reached out, laying a hand over her wrist.

"I'm going to the practice field," Sumi said. "Anyone who wants to learn the songs can join me there."

She turned on her heel, marching from the room.

———

For a moment, as she stood in the field with Parimu, she thought they might not come. But somehow, it didn't seem to matter. She had the songs now, truly had them, and even if it took her the rest of her life, she would find Shapewalkers who would listen. And one day, when she had enough of them, they'd bring Essomuai to Berill.

Luckily, though, it wasn't long. Two figures appeared at the top of the stairs, one of them visibly bear-like even in the morning light.

"Sorry we didn't come sooner," Erso said as they approached. "We had to watch the show."

"Rich people in a hurry," Beysal said, chuckling. "Like a bloody barrel full of weasels."

"So, they're coming?" she asked.

"Oh, I'd say so," Erso said. "Thought the captain was gonna choke, he's eating so fast." He stopped, meeting her eyes. "You really did it, huh?"

She nodded.

"Well done," he said, smiling. "I knew you would."

He lifted his hands like he wanted to hug her, but he coughed instead, running a hand through his hair. She nodded, turning back to the stairs as Meloy appeared.

"We're here!" she cried, waving a hand. "Don't start without us!"

As she rushed down the stairs, the others appeared: the surgeons, the captains, even the duchess, walking slowly with Peloris at her side. As they reached the bottom, they formed a semicircle with every eye on her.

"Thank you for joining me," she said. "I suppose Relsenair and I could give a demonstration, but I want to give you the opportunity to hear the songs as soon as possible. Would anyone like to go first?"

Their eyes, glued to her a moment ago, darted to either side. They had all rushed down from breakfast, but going first with the strange new magic? Not to mention the strange Anushai girl putting noises in your head...

"Does it hurt?" Meloy asked, raising her hand.

"Not at all," Sumi said, smiling. "It might feel a little strange at first, but it's the most beautiful music in the world. Even if my sheet music doesn't look like it."

There were a few nervous chuckles at that, at least, but they still looked like lambs at their first shearing.

Captain Erinon stepped out of line.

"Seas below, I'll do it!" he said. "A captain should be the first to shore anyway."

"Thank you," she said, motioning for him to stand a few feet across from her. As he did so, she carefully slipped Vilodai's Eye into her hand. As the rhythms poured into her mind, she noticed now the subtle differences from the fountain. She was surrounded by people, each with their own tiny rhythm, but they were standing on grass, too, the closest stone beneath her, the bedrock lurking like a whale. She could sense how far it spread, beneath the pond and past Linindal, holding up the entire hillside. She gently shook her head, turning to the group.

"Now," she said, "I'm going to sing to Captain Erinon's mind, his *welloshara*. The part I'm going to be singing is Saldal's. If you look at your sheet music, you'll see you each have your own part to sing. Once you can hear the songs, it'll be easier to pick out, but try to keep that in mind."

The rustle of parchment answered her as everyone pulled out their music from wherever they'd stored it. She should probably ask if they all read sheet music, but that could wait. She faced the captain and closed her eyes, allowing the songs and the voices to flood her mind. There was still some nervous whispering from the group, but as she picked out the captain's mind and sang, the field became silent. And as his rhythm started to thrum with Essomuai, she knew it would come. She opened her eyes just in time, the captain falling to one knee as he clutched his chest.

"Incredible," he forced out, wiping away a tear. "I wish my father could have heard them."

She turned back to the others, their eyes wide and fearful. Those poor creatures! Of course, they wouldn't know what to think… They still couldn't hear the songs, and they'd seen the captain fall to his knees.

"Captain," she said, taking his hand and helping him to his feet. "Would you sing with us and help us show the others?"

"Gladly," he said, turning back to face the group. Parimu stepped up beside them, nodding.

"Thank you," she said. "I think I assigned you Geomon's song. It's the low one that sounds like stones." She gestured toward his first mate. "If you need the sheet music…"

"No, no," he said, smiling, "I don't think I'll ever forget how this song goes."

She closed her eyes, letting the first cycle wash over her. As it came around again, she tapped the others.

"Now," she said.

She took a deep breath, but before the first note began, it felt like she could already see the golden light before her eyes.

PART THREE

27

Esherniskolera - an image appears of a cloud, lifting from a field like fog as it drifts away. Undoubtedly the word is related to eshernulam, albeit perhaps as an opposing cognate. It should come as no surprise the word seems to have grown from Itorunai's pillar.

-Excerpt from The Arguments
Twenty-fifth Cycle

—:—

Sumi folded another blouse, packing as quickly as she could even as her mind lingered on the parade. She heard a knock on the door and opened it, revealing Erso in his workman's clothes again, his own bag in hand.

"Ahoy," he said, flicking the bill of his cap.

"The captain's got you ready to be a sailor, eh?" she asked, waving him in.

"What can I say? The man can march."

And he could that. The last two days had passed in a beautiful blur, but even with all the incredible shapes they'd made, the marching with Captain Erinon still stood out.

"Well," she said, "at least your clowning hasn't convinced anyone to join the circus."

Erso pretended to scoff, wandering to the other side of the room where he planted himself in one of the tiny rose-embroidered chairs.

"It may not be as important as whatever it is you contribute to the parade," he said, "but you'll be glad for that clowning. Somebody had to loosen those *al'gerahn* up. Like ma used to say, 'if you move like a block, you look like a block.'"

"Wise woman, your mother," she said, chuckling at the thought of the duchess following Erso on the field. Still, somehow it had all worked.

They'd sung the songs, they'd made the shapes, they were one, and they were ready. Or as close to one as they'd ever be… The first time she'd held all their minds had felt like holding a barrel of fish in her hands, everyone's thoughts flailing about. Still, it hadn't threatened to fall apart like a normal joining. With Essomuai, it was…different, infinite.

"I just wish we had more time," she said, folding her other dress.

"Five days is tight," Erso said, "but when you're ready, you're ready."

She nodded, putting away the dress. In five days, the royal stay would expire on the Vice Peer's bill, and Peloris thought it best if they held the parade before then. He seemed to think it was the kind of bill you only passed once. But even more than that, she knew that when the parade was over, she'd lose Erso. And then…

"Bit of advice," he said, pushing himself up from the chair. "If you want more time, don't waste it on packing." He took the sock from her hand, tossing it into her bag. "Mu'amashdar don't need clothes, my dear, they shape them."

She forced herself to smile, shutting the suitcase.

"Good advice," she said, picking up the bag. She paused, meeting his eyes. He was so close, sitting just on the edge of the bed.

"But…" she said quietly, "I guess I wish *we* had more time. To fix this."

"I know," he said quietly. "But everything'll work out just how it should. Just trust me on that. After I watch the city cheer your name, we'll sort this out. I promise."

She watched him, finally nodding.

"Alright, then," she said. What else was there to say? She could wait. Even if it was over, and she had to love him the rest of her life without him there, she'd do it. There was no one else she wanted by her side at the parade.

"Come on," he said, standing. "Your entourage awaits."

———

As they reached the great hall, Peskold was waiting for them, his cloak on with a paper in his hand.

"Good morning, Miss Sumi," he said, nodding as he marked something on his sheet. "That's everyone, then."

"Oh dear," she said, frowning. "Are we last? I hope you haven't been waiting long."

"No, no," Peskold said, waving a hand. "I mean, we *are* waiting, but I suspect everyone hurried down from excitement."

As he led them out, Erso gave her a look that seemed to say, 'I told you not to fold your socks.' Kestorael was waiting on the steps, and as they came through, he pulled a giant golden key from his pocket, locking the door behind them.

"That seems rather final," Sumi said, smiling at the old butler.

"Well," he said, shrugging, "the cooks are still here, but it's tradition."

Sumi nodded. There was honor in that. As much as she'd fought — and would fight again — to get them a seat at the table, they clearly cared for their mistress, and she cared for them, too, in her own way. Besides, if you were going to be a Shapewalking servant, who wouldn't want to serve one of the oldest Shapewalking families in Berill?

There were seven carriages waiting in the circle drive, and everyone was milling about them, talking as the guards stored the luggage and checked the bridles. Lady Croylinin and Peloris were nowhere to be seen, apparently already hidden away in the stately white carriage at the back of the line. As the others noticed her, though, they stopped talking, turning to watch.

"Um, hello, everyone," she said, waving. "I guess I wasn't told I needed a speech." She at least earned a chuckle or two at that, but they *did* deserve a final word for all their hard work. "Thank you all for coming here this week. I can't believe how much we've accomplished, and I can't wait for what's to come. We'll be splitting up now, but soon, we'll make history together. I'll see you at the meeting spot in three days."

She bowed, and a few of them clapped, Beysal letting out a whoop.

"Come on," Erso said, taking her bag. "We have you in the place of honor."

He led her to the carriage in front, where Peskold was already holding the door for her. She smiled at him gratefully, climbing into the cool darkness of the carriage. Erso followed after, sitting opposite her as he closed the door behind him.

"Just you?" she asked, arching an eyebrow at him.

"I know," he said, shrugging, "it's a shame. But Beysal wants to ride with Parimu — seems he's trying to replace me or something."

"Well," she said, "at least you don't talk in your sleep."

He scoffed, clutching at his heart as the carriage jerked, swinging out of the drive. She watched as they passed the statues, the gates, and the grounds, and before long, Linindal was behind them, leaving nothing but the open road and Berill waiting beyond the horizon.

The next hour went by quickly, split between looking out the window and talking through the parade with Erso. He'd said he wanted to walk through the plan one last time, though, in truth, he just seemed afraid of having nothing to say. He was talking faster than normal, flipping out jokes like cakes at a cafe. Still, it *was* fun. It almost felt like old times, even if those 'old times' had only been a few weeks ago.

Still, eventually, even the plans were talked through, and they both stared out the window until Erso slumped down in his seat, his hat tipped over his eyes. Sumi folded her arms, leaning into the corner so she could look straight out the window. They were nearer the river now, only a few miles from the bridge to Moranal. The grass was taller there, and it danced in the wind, running to and fro on some unknowable current. She didn't remember there being so many birds last time, though… There seemed to be hundreds of them, crying as they launched from the grass, swirling above the carriage. Wait, was that really the wind? It was almost like…

"Erso," she said, reaching out to tap his knee. "I think—"

She never got the last words out, the carriage lurching as the earth erupted in front of them. She could think of nothing, seeming to float for a brief second before she slammed into the door as the carriage began to roll. For one final second, everything was still, nothing but darkness and a humming in her ears. It felt strangely familiar…like Vilodai was tapping at her mind. But then all was chaos. Erso was there, pulling her from the carriage as shouts rose from all sides. She blinked, suddenly realizing she was standing on the side of the road, her vision swimming back as dust filled the air around her.

She turned, looking at the front of the carriage when she emptied her stomach. The horses… They were dead, caught up in what remained of the harness where the blast had gone off. The front of the carriage was a mess, the wood split and smoking, some of the wheels gone — the driver nowhere to be seen. But what could have caused— Suddenly, the shouting grew louder, and she turned, finding men on horseback all around them. There was still shouting from all sides, though she couldn't make out the words above the clanging swords, the guards desperately trying to fight back. She turned to look for Erso, to get him to safety, when something slammed into her head, and all was darkness again.

28

I'm sure now I won't run out of fuel, but what if I had? It makes me shudder to think. When you're digging for diamonds, it's just as easy to get buried by rock as it is to find what you came for.

-Setorin's Log
3913-55

—:—

Erso walked through the wreckage of the caravan, the smell of spent gunpowder stinging his nose. Why was he walking through this charred rubbish again? Did he think he'd find her hiding beneath an overturned carriage? She was gone, maybe even dead. No! He wouldn't — *couldn't* — accept that. But she had been right there… He'd pulled her out of the fire himself, but then there had been horsemen everywhere, two rushing him at once, his own sword barely quick enough. But then, it was just…nothing, the men riding away as quickly as they'd appeared.

He returned to the back of the line, where the others were congregating around the librarian's carriage, the surgeons trying to help the guards who were still alive. They'd rallied to protect their precious duchess well enough, though not for free… Even if they were only after Sumi, the horsemen had hit from all sides — to create more chaos, no doubt — and there were some dozen men dead on the ground. He walked up to the largest group, where Croylinin was holding court.

"We need to get back to Berill," she said. "I've no doubt the Vice Peer is behind this, and the sooner we get back, the sooner we can negotiate. If we—"

"How did he know when we'd be here?" Erso asked, his voice not sounding like his own.

"I didn't tell him if that's what you're implying," the duchess

192

answered, staring coldly down her nose at him. Beysal shot him a warning look, but he didn't care.

"One of the guards, then?" he asked, staring right back. "Was one of them bought? They knew which carriage she was in."

"Now hold on," the librarian said, holding up a hand. Was it a trick of the eye, or was the old man standing straighter than he normally did? "I don't think anyone betrayed her. We're up against another Shapewalker here. He could have had us watched by a bird for all we know."

Erso ground his teeth, swallowing his words. Unfortunately, they were right. And he'd thought Berill was dangerous before… Now they had bloody mu'amashdar on both sides.

"Well, however it happened," he said, "we need to get her back."

Parimu, standing on the other side of the circle, nodded.

"We don't know what their intentions are," he said. "And if we don't go after her, it might be too late."

"We have to remain calm," the duchess said. "He's probably just holding her, and it won't do to be dramatic with no information. Until we know what Pont'dulairn is thinking, we can't make any other moves."

"Damn it!" Erso yelled. "We ride now!" He forced himself to pull in a ragged breath, softening his voice. "Or I ride. Alone if I have to. But I'm going after her. I don't care about your bloody politics. Your kingdom means nothing to me without her."

The librarian met his gaze and nodded. He may be old, but there was a fire behind his eyes, too, like the one raging in his own chest. Good. He hoped they could all feel it. They were damned worms next to Sumi, and the fire could take them all if she was gone.

He turned, swinging his sword clean through the nearest horse's harness. The animal spooked a bit, but he calmed it, pulling himself onto its back before it could bolt. As he swept around, he found Parimu, Beysal, and a handful of guards — the ones who were still walking, anyway — climbing onto whatever horses they could get their hands on. The duchess wouldn't like her men running off, but one look at their faces told him they wanted their own revenge when this was done. Still, that would only make about a dozen men against who knew how many. Well, a dozen minus one…

"Not you," he said to Beysal. The man opened his mouth to protest, but he pushed on. "For Kel. Keep the others safe."

Beysal met his eyes, nodding. There was a limit to how much he could take from that man. Besides, he needed someone to watch the surgeons. They didn't know what else Pont'dulairn had planned, and they'd need the doctors if Sumi was hurt. As for himself, he didn't care if there was nothing left to stitch together. He just had one more request, and then he was ready to ride his horse into the ground. He turned back to the librarian.

"Can you get to a telegraph?" he asked. "Negotiate if you want but find out where they're going. If we don't catch them now, I'll be there when they reach the city."

The man simply nodded again; no questions, no protests.

"We'll see you in the next town," he said. The man had a soft exterior, but his insides were iron. Good.

Erso spared one glance for the others on horseback before he kicked his animal, shooting into the fields the way the others had gone. He might need Parimu to find the trail once they hit the tree line, but for now, if he didn't take the lead, his blood would boil over. He'd been a bloody fool to ever think he could be without Sumi for a single minute. But whether she kept him or not, it only mattered that she lived, no matter how many he had to cut through to see it done.

———

Sumi came to, her head a mix of pain and blankness. She groaned, putting a hand to her temple, finding her hair wet with blood. She blinked her eyes open but found herself in darkness. She was lying on some kind of metal floor, and it was shaking? No…it was *moving*. As she listened more closely, she heard the clop of horse hooves and the jangling of reins. So, she had been hurt in an…attack? From who, Pont'dulairn? She tried to think, but her mind moved like sludge. A wave of nausea crashed over her, and she clamped her eyes shut. Erso had been there, hadn't he? They must be taking her somewhere safe. But then…what was this metal box?

Finally, she blinked her eyes open again, finding that they'd adjusted to the semi-twilight of the carriage. She groaned, forcing herself to roll over, but as she tried to sit up, she found the space wasn't tall enough. Where was she?! Her heart began to pound, making the throbbing in her head worse. She could see a tiny scrape of light to her side, the outline of a door. She reached for it, but there was no handle. She pounded on the metal.

"Help!" she screamed, though her voice was like gravel. "Let me out! Let me out!"

Suddenly, the carriage stopped. She gave up her shouting, sucking in ragged breaths as she heard footsteps drawing nearer. She heard the scrape of metal, and a latch slid open in the door, flooding the box with light. She squinted, holding up a shaking hand to block it. A face appeared, a man she'd never seen before.

"Please do be quiet," he said. "There's no one here to help you, and you'll just make yourself hoarse."

"Wh-ho are you?" she asked, her tongue feeling like the Void.

"Never mind that," he said, smirking. "But you've certainly made the wrong enemies."

"And…the others?" she asked.

"Fine, except for the fools who fought back," he said. Her mind flashed to Erso, her heart pounding again. "I've been told to tell you your life is in no danger. But if you make things difficult, I'm told the discipline is up to me. So shut your mouth, or I'll shut it for you."

Enemies… Pont'dulairn? She opened her mouth to speak, but the latch slammed shut, sealing her in darkness again. So, the Vice Peer was stopping the parade by force, but he didn't want to kill her? Why not? But the ones who'd fought back… Oh, gods above, let Erso be alive! If they'd lost anyone… But if they *were* alive, they'd come for her. She had to get out of this box before she lost anyone else.

She shut her eyes, trying to listen to the songs. Only…the songs were gone. Not hidden or separated from her, just…gone. She reached out, touching the metal ceiling above her. Was it silver? But even when she'd been hit by Parimu's arrow, Essomuai had still been there, pushing through the haze with her songs. How thick would it have to be to completely cut her off?

It finally sunk in: she was alone. And without her goddess, she was nothing once again. She had made the others risk everything, and she had failed them. They would come for her, and they would die. She began to sob silently, her chest shaking against the metal floor as it rocked from side to side, the carriage rushing to a place where there was no hope left.

———

Kemarin Pont'dulairn sat in his study, his brow furrowed as he reread the same letter for the fifth time. His eyes passed over the words, surely, but no understanding entered his mind. But how exactly was he meant to read all this drivel while he was waiting for the only message that really mattered? He dropped the letter, running his hand through his hair. It would all go to plan; he just had to remain calm. He stared into the fire, letting his mind go blank. Once the commander started a battle, he couldn't think about loading the cannons. All he could do was stare at the sea and see the thing through.

He had just turned back to his letter when he heard a *thunk* against the window. He stood quickly, just catching the tail of a bird as it circled once and flew back toward the east. There was a metal cup on the windowsill, and he eagerly fished into it, pulling out a string with two green beads. He breathed a sigh of relief, slumping into his chair and leaning his head back. Thank the heavens! The first meant the girl was captured, and the second meant the duchess was unharmed. So, it *had* all gone to plan. Five more days, and he'd be done. The stay would end, the bill would pass, and the rest would take care of itself.

There was a knock on the study door, and he bolted upright, stuffing the string into his pocket. He sprang around the desk, yanking open the door to find Telonderan, Elisal's secretary.

"Apologies for disturbing you, my Lord," he said, bowing low. "I was wondering if her ladyship was present. She asked me to send a letter and come with the response posthaste."

"Oh," Kemarin said, nodding slowly. "I believe she's in her sitting room in the east wing. Have one of the footmen show you."

"Certainly, my Lord," he said, bowing again as he backed away.

Pont'dulairn shut the door, standing there blinking for a moment before he went back to his desk. As soon as he sat, he shook his head, taking his papers back up. It was all well and good to be distracted when something important was in the offing, but now there was work to be done — and far too much of it to be staring into the fire like an old man.

He probably got a solid ten minutes of work done after that, but when he went to seal the letter he'd written, he heard the quick pitter-patter of footsteps coming back down the hallway — Elisal's slippers, by the sound of it. He got up, adding another log to the fire. She always liked things on the warmer side, and perhaps if he was already standing, she'd give him a sorely needed embrace. He leaned against the mantel, waiting as the door opened. Elisal looked as beautiful as ever, the diadem he'd gotten her from Mesopyn perched in her golden hair and her favorite green dress clinging to her shoulders.

"My wife," he said, spreading his arms wide for her as she entered the room. She paused by the door, her eyes falling casually on him as if she'd been hoping he wouldn't be there...

"Husband," she said, stepping in and lightly kissing his cheek.

"Come," he said, motioning toward the sideboard, "have a drink with me."

She said nothing, so he glided to the table, pouring two glasses of cloud wine. He'd been saving the bottle for the passage of his bill, but capturing the girl was just as good. At this point, dodging any roadblock was a victory.

"Are we celebrating something, husband?" she asked, her eyes boring into him as she took a delicate sip of her wine.

He paused, eyeing her warily over the top of his glass. To Elisal, words were like blood. She would spill some if she needed to, but every drop would be precious. But what could she be referring to? The only matter of importance was hundreds of miles away.

"Perhaps I'd like to toast that you remain my bride after all these years," he said, winking at her as he raised his glass.

She scoffed, shaking her head as she tilted her chin back and drained her glass in one gulp, shoving it back into his hand.

"I wanted to give you one last chance," she said, "but it seems you'd rather have me play the fool than the wife."

He opened his mouth, desperate for any word that would do, but she was too quick for him.

"I know about the girl," she said, her tone laced with acid, "so don't try to wriggle free like you Berillai love to do. I don't care about your excuses, just send the order to free her."

"Dearest," he said, setting both glasses down. "I won't do you the disservice of denying that something needed to be done, but I promise you the girl is safe. You have to trust me. I'll release her when the bill is passed, but to do so before would be madness."

"Madness?" she asked, narrowing her eyes at him. "*Stebohl lend diestarin,*" she added, shaking her head and turning toward the fire. "I meant what I said when I promised to be by your side, but I will not be married to some *zendeskiehn.*"

He reached for his wine, his mouth suddenly dry. He'd never read the damned book, but only when she was truly angry did she quote from the *Sepondelarn*, the Trierlien book of legends, and the comparison — whatever a *zendeskiehn* really was — would not be a good one. He felt a sudden stab of fear, an image pushing into his mind of her watching him in the Peerage from the viewing platform, a smile never again gracing her lips. Sometimes she just didn't understand, but he needed her, and he knew that more than any other truth. He just had to make her see.

"Darling," he said hastily, stepping toward the fireplace, "if you'll only listen to reason. I assure you—"

"How dare you!" she said, halting him in his tracks as she turned, brandishing a finger in his face. "You think I'll let all your promises turn to nothing? All your sweet words — 'my heart, my conscience' — were not empty to me. The kind of men who speak of *reason* are the kind who killed my father. You told me you were more than that. These people are your friends, they are your allies, and you would truss them like pigs? For what? So your precious bill can pass? Any bear can have claws, but a mother must also have milk. You stand by your friends, Kemarin Pont'dulairn, or I will."

"Elisal," he stammered, "surely you don't mean—"

"I mean what I say. Come to me when you have made it right, or else I will free the girl myself, and you can watch me in her parade."

Before he could speak, she spun on her heel, leaving the room and slamming the door behind her, the force of it shaking the pictures on the wall. He stood there, stunned for a moment before he finally made his way to his desk, slumping into his chair. Before he could think, he had a fresh piece of paper in front of him, his pen scratching out orders to release the girl. But what good would those do? The sun was already low, and that bird would be the last until the morning. And even if he did release her, what of the rest?

She'd asked him to be different, and he had failed her. Had he become a man who would do anything to see his plans done? He hadn't killed the girl, true, but he had imprisoned her all the same. And Elisal had asked him for far more than that. She had seen the girl's magic, and she'd found herself able to believe. She'd asked for him to lend the girl his *strength*. But who was he without his plans? Was he truly his father's son?

He was afraid to answer that question, but the inscription in the marble of the fireplace seemed to answer it for him. Built by his great grandfather, it had been inscribed in the Mesop high tongue, etched with their family's creed:

'Klems mün boloyt khort, khort klmesk münt. One for all people, until all people are one.'

He was Berillai, and he was a Shapewalker. This was his kingdom to build or destroy, and yet, all he knew was blood. Without the bill, he saw no path forward. But without Elisal, he would be a man without a conscience, rudderless. Could he salvage his plans *and* fix things before he lost her? He leaned back in his chair and stared into the fire. He felt adrift, with no land in sight, like a ship banished to an empty sea.

29

Terisolenmurselam - easily one of the longest words I've yet to uncover. It appears only at the end of the cycle and appears to be a full narrative. I'll record it in the appendix — the vision itself seemed to last an entire hour. Even then it could be a fragment, perhaps it's a path towards new emulations?

-Excerpt from The Echoes
Fifty-third Cycle

—:—

Eventually, the sun fell, plunging the world into darkness. Sumi lay on her back in the box, watching as the sliver of light disappeared from the hatch. They had ridden for hours, her head still swimming. In between bouts of tears, she'd tried everything she could — prayers, singing, the pool — until there were simply no tears left. She was dried up, spent, finished.

Finally, the rocking of the carriage stopped, and she heard voices, what sounded like dozens of men moving past her box. Where were they? She forced herself to listen past the ringing in her ears, but there was nothing that held a clue. Somewhere in the distance, she heard an owl. So maybe they were in the woods? But in north Berill, that could be anywhere.

Suddenly, the latch in the door slid open again, the same man appearing, his profile lit by torchlight.

"We're stopping for the night," he said, shoving a burlap sack through the hole. "Eat something, and keep your mouth shut."

He slammed the hatch shut, leaving her blinking in the darkness again. Without realizing it, she'd slid her body against the opposite wall. She stayed there a moment until her heartbeat slowed, and then she edged toward the burlap sack. There was a water skin, a hunk of stale bread, and a wedge of cheese. She ought to be proud, ought to refuse anything until she was released, but she began shoving the bread into her mouth, barely stopping to breathe before she inhaled the cheese. Then she attacked the water skin, drinking so quickly she began to cough. But as soon as she was done, she pushed away the bag in disgust, hugging the wall with her knees against her chest.

There was still a splitting pain in her head, but with food in her system, her brain seemed to partially emerge from its fog. She tried to gather her thoughts, take stock of what she knew. The others hadn't reached her, and night had fallen. They hadn't killed her yet, and they were stopping for the night, which meant they were still far from their destination. And that meant they might feed her again, would have to open the latch… Could Essomuai sense her through a hole that small? If only she'd thought to try it earlier!

She slammed her hand against the floor, a sharp pain blossoming in her knuckles. Still, she did it again, slamming her hand against the roof and the walls again and again until there was a hand beating on the other side.

"Shut up!" a voice yelled — not the man she recognized from before. "Keep your hands to yourself, or we'll tie 'em for you."

She froze, not moving or breathing until she heard footsteps walking away. She sucked in a sharp breath, balling up her fist as the pain began to shoot through her hand. She held it against her chest, biting her lip as she waited for the throbbing to subside. But as she held her hand there, she felt a lump beneath her blouse… Her necklaces!

She pulled them out, the pain disappearing as she fumbled for the golden pendant. She closed her palm around it, clamping her eyes shut as she looked for the songs in her mind. But there was nothing… Perhaps there was the faintest buzz from the metal? But it wasn't at all like feeling Essomuai's presence, not even behind a veil. She just…wasn't there. Still, every bit of gold was part of Essomuai, right? Unless, cut off, it was just golden again… She took a deep breath, squeezing her forehead. She'd just have to wait for the slot to open again. Unless she could make it open…

She started to bang on the walls again with both hands. She yelled, too, slamming her back against the floor as she shook in as many directions as she could. Part of her was terrified of what that man would do to her, but she would try anything. It wasn't long this time before the pounding answered from the other side.

"Hey!" the second man yelled. "What did I bloody tell you?!"

She heard him fumbling with the latch, and she closed her eyes tight, ready to reach for the songs the moment it opened. But suddenly, there was another voice, the two whispering heatedly until she heard footsteps leaving again. Finally, she heard the first man's voice, quiet but laced with malice.

"Clever," he said. "He told me you were a smart one. But you listen now. That's the last time I open this door until you learn to behave. And don't think I can't teach you a lesson with it closed. The next time you make a sound, I'll light a fire under this box, and I'll add a log every time you so much as breathe too loud."

As the man left, she couldn't even find the courage to cry. She didn't know him, but she knew he'd do what he said. She really was a fool. She thought a parade could change the world? A world where your enemies were willing to cook a woman in a box? She shuddered, crumpling in on herself again. She reached for her pendant, wanting Essomuai close even if this was the end. But as she did so, her hand brushed her other necklace, and a thousand voices sprang up in her mind, *welloshara* reaching for her from every side.

Vilodai? she asked.

There was nothing for a long time, only the drone of those voices, but then she heard it, a…rumble, distant but powerful.

Serushalenomay, it said, *daughter.*

Sumi squeezed her eyelids tight, a tear slipping down her cheek.

"Thank you," she whispered, clutching the stone with both hands. She kissed it, impossibly grateful to not be alone. After so many months of having Essomuai in her mind, she'd forgotten how alone she could feel. Was that really how her life had been after Nela died? The memories were already hazy, like someone else's life. And it was. She was a different person now. She had found her goddess — both her goddesses — and she had two mothers now. She might not be able to feel one, but the other had no fear of silver; had no fear of anything.

I need help, Sumi thought. She didn't know how to explain what had happened, but she pictured herself trapped in the box, the sides shimmering with silver. She felt a quaking from Vilodai, so powerful she thought the box might shake around her. Somehow, she knew that Vilodai was shaking in her mountain, her anger threatening to split the rock in two.

Keloskeromae, Vilodai whispered, the image coming like great spouts of fire, somehow turned to liquid as it spilled over the edge of a mountain. It felt like an infinite amount of rage could be held in that word, like one word would never suffice — fury, destruction, vengeance. The image shifted, and Vilodai spoke another word — *eskotelusara.* Her fire reached another mountain, melting its rock until it fell, until it was nothing but ash. *Destroy them*, it seemed to say.

"I can't," Sumi whispered, those horrible images of Elomikarus appearing in her mind. She pictured the wastelands he'd left behind, bodies crumpled on the battlefield, broken and bloody. Even with these men threatening her life, she knew she couldn't kill them. "I can't," she said again, her eyes filling with tears. But she knew what it would cost her, too. The others would come, they would die saving her, and it would be her fault. She was a coward; she was nothing. She let go of the stone and hid her face in her hands, shaking in the tiny prison she had made for herself.

————

Erso sat on his horse, flexing and unflexing his hands as he waited for Parimu. His horse was flaring its nostrils, shifting its forelegs from side to side as it smacked at the bridle. They'd run hard all day but still hadn't caught up to the men who'd taken Sumi. Now, they'd reached the end of the road, the trail disappearing into the grass, but they were losing the sun, and before long, they might lose the trail altogether. Parimu was ahead, trying to pick up the trail where it had crossed a stream.

"Anything?" Erso asked as Parimu walked his horse back over the water.

"They went east to the tree line, but they climbed a ridge, and I can't see anything else in the dark. I think we need to stop, pick it up in the morning. They'll have to stop soon, too, should give us a chance to catch up."

Erso ground his teeth.

"If they stop, we need to be there," he said. "We'll have a better chance at this in the dark."

The rest of the men were quiet. They'd been happy to let them lead when their blood was hot, but they looked haggard now. Parimu climbed back on his horse, nudging his mount closer.

"I know," he said, taking Erso's shoulder. "I want her back, too. But if we keep going, we're gonna lose the horses."

"Then we fly," Erso said, staring into the other man's eyes. "If we go as owls, we'll spot their camp in no time."

Parimu shook his head. "You saw their numbers. They have us two-to-one, not to mention silver. If we go on our own, we don't have a chance at getting her free. We hit fast, we get Sumi, and we get out."

"Fine," Erso said, looking away. "Then we ride at dawn. But we still ought to know where they are. I'll scout it out and come back."

He tossed Parimu his reins and swung off the horse. He glowed, turning into an owl. As he launched into the air, Parimu turned the others toward the trees. He raced on to the east. As much as it pained him, he would keep his word — if he did anything foolish, those men might just keep moving through the night, and then she'd be truly lost. But he would bloody find her, and come morning, he'd set her free.

———

Peloris sat at a table in the back of an inn in Apaskine, reading over the latest telegraph. Unfortunately, it didn't hold much more information than the dozen before it, no one in his network having heard about a captive girl. Of course, that was to be expected. Kemarin played things close to the chest, especially when they were dangerous. Still, even a shadow of a hint would be enough, something for them to go on if Erso failed.

He raised his hand, signaling for another wine. They'd already been there for half the day — much to the chagrin of the telegraph operator — but he'd stay up until he had something useful. Someone *had* seen Terosan Pinal, Pont'dulairn's unofficial right hand, leaving town the night before. He just needed to know where he was going… He sighed, dropping the piece of parchment in front of him. Haleone picked it up, just as she had all the others, even though she knew by now that they were ciphered — yet another point of consternation for the poor telegraph clerk.

"Still nothing, I presume?" she asked. There wasn't a hint of arrogance in the question. After he'd bullied her into riding for Apaskine, the duchess had seemed to accept her fate admirably. He was normally a subtle man, of course, but now that the girl's life was in danger… Well, if he didn't mind getting blood on his hands, he didn't mind bruising an ego when it really mattered. But if he really had gotten Sumi killed… He grimaced, a sickening feeling blossoming in his stomach again.

"I'm afraid not," he said, turning as the innkeeper arrived with the wine. He nodded graciously before gulping half of it down. "Send the telegraph chap back over if you don't mind," he added to the man. This time, the innkeeper simply nodded. They were already a few hours after the end of the poor lad's hours of operation, but they were paying enough silver to put a new roof on the place, so no one was too keen to object.

"Anyone else you want to try?" he asked Haleone, pulling out another piece of blank parchment, which he began to cipher for the boy.

"No," she said, shaking her head and sighing. "What good will it do? How many secret societies do you think you can operate inside another one? Everyone I know is already involved on one side or the other…"

He chuckled. True enough, that. Still, it was time to prepare for other measures. Elisal Pont'dulairn had been vague in her reply, but he had a feeling she might become more amenable with time if he sniffed around long enough. And if the girl wasn't back by dawn… Well, there was one more cipher he had stored in his head, one he'd only used once or twice and hoped he'd never use again. The poor boy might die from fright when he realized he was messaging the royal line, but if it kept the girl alive, he'd do what had to be done, even if it got the rest of them killed in the process.

30

He seemed to think copper might be the unifier, which is just as well since I certainly don't want to transport that much mercury. At any rate, I've brought about a hundred length. Still, I can't exactly expect a warm welcome, not with how much we've all changed.

*-Setorin's Log
3844-33*

—:—

Sumi woke on the floor of her prison, her shirt damp with sweat. When had she fallen asleep? It was still dark, but there was no telling what time it was. She groaned, her muscles stiff from being trapped for so long. At least her head didn't hurt as much — not that it did her much good. She was no closer to escaping, no closer to saving her friends. Outside the box, it was completely quiet, save for the hoot of an owl. *Who-whooooo,* it called, surprisingly close.

"Hoot, hoot," she whispered, wishing she could see that owl, wishing she could be one herself. If even one bar of its song entered her mind, she'd be free. She closed her eyes and held Vilodai's necklace, listening to the voices she couldn't bring herself to use as she waited for the end.

Erso hooted once more before he took off, shooting off the branch and soaring out of the camp. He could feel the exhaustion in his wings, but he pushed on. There was a blue tinge to the sky behind the mountains in the east, and they needed to attack before the men woke up. He just hoped Sumi had heard his calls. *I'm coming for you,* he thought as he crossed over the forest, *just hold on.* He hadn't seen her, of course, but there was no question they were the same men, just as there was no question who was in that box.

His blood boiled thinking of her trapped there, alone and afraid, in a box no bigger than a coffin. He still had a long ride ahead of him, but he would kill every last one of those men. He finally reached the end of the woods, arcing over the stream to where he'd left the others. To his surprise, they were up already, each of them sitting on their horses as they faced the direction he'd flown. He cried out, their eyes turning to him as he landed, flashing back into himself. Parimu held his mount, nodding to him as he climbed on the horse's back.

"Did you find them?" he asked.

Erso nodded, pointing toward the woods.

"About fifteen miles east," he said, "in a hollow by the mountains. Holding Sumi in a bloody silver box."

Parimu's jaws tightened, and he turned to face the others.

"Is everyone ready?" he asked. "Once they see us, we'll be in the heat."

To a man, they all nodded.

"We'll come in from the north," Erso said. "The hollow slopes up the hill there, and Sumi's at the bottom. We'll have to cut our way through, but we'll have the high ground."

"You three take the ridge," Parimu said, looking to the men with bows. "The rest of us will ride in a wedge. Get to the box and hold the line until you see Sumi on a horse — in and out."

They nodded again, so Erso waved a hand, kicking his horse to a gallop. In a moment, they were through the stream and into the woods, racing over ground just barely visible in the blue light of dawn. He'd be at the front when they arrived, and he'd cut the way through to her. He had failed her, but he wanted it to be his face she saw when she was safe. After everything he'd done, he owed her that much.

———

Pont'dulairn turned off of Fort Street just as dawn was lighting the horizon. He turned onto his own street, his house standing in darkness. Not total darkness, of course — the kitchens were already bustling, and the coachman's lights were lit — but the only light that mattered to him was out. Elisal's room faced the street on the third floor, and there was nothing behind those curtains. Although perhaps it was best that she still slept, it didn't seem like he'd have much to show for himself by the time she woke anyway.

After trudging through the city half the night in disguise, he'd finally tracked down one of Terosan's boys who was still in the city and sent him off to find the others. Still, it would be a long flight, and Terosan could be well on his way to the city by then. He ground his teeth, turning down the drive toward the kitchens. It wasn't as if the girl wouldn't reach the city eventually — he'd ordered them not to harm her, after all — but how many hours could you expect someone to stay in a box before they were past friendship?

Not that he'd cared about that before… He could see the right of what Elisal had said, surely, though his mind still whirred with how to hold it all together. He should have seen the girl's charisma from the start — not something the others would let go of easily, least of all the damned librarian. But they *were* his allies; perhaps he should have worked harder to bring them into the fold… There had to be a way he could control the damage enough to give them their little parade without losing his bill. He just had to think…

But would that really suffice in Elisal's eyes? Even now, he couldn't abandon his need for her, like a plant forsaking the sun. Besides, even if father had inspired him, Elisal was the one who got him to this point, had seen the opportunity in a military bill after all his years of trade pacts. But how was he supposed to just abandon their life's work for a fairy tale? The world was more than magic, it was blood and steel, and without him, it would be mostly the former.

He finally reached the kitchen doors and gave the whistle to signal he was home but in disguise. Apparently, it was the whistle of a Sner Hen. He'd never seen one, but it was a staple in Mesop country, and it had been the signal for generations of Pont'dulairns. Pendulen stuck his head out, his chef's hat already on and a blood-soaked towel over his shoulder. He didn't bat an eyelid at seeing Pont'dulairn with another face, simply bowing as he held the door open.

"Welcome home, sir," he said. "Bit late for business, no?"

Pont'dulairn chuckled.

"I suppose so, my friend," he said, stepping into the house. "It seems we're both butchers this morning."

He moved toward the hallway, flashing into his own form as he pulled off his cloak. The valets wouldn't be up for another hour, but he'd rather freshen up with his own face before he saw them.

"I hate to be a bother," he said to Pendulen before stepping out of the kitchen, "but if you could send some tea before the maids are up, I'd be grateful."

With that, he left the kitchens, hurrying toward his study. There was always a way if you looked hard enough, he just had to find it before it was too late.

———

Erso cursed under his breath. On his belly in the brush, he was at the top of the ravine, looking down at the enemy camp. They hadn't arrived in time, the men moving about below as they tended to their horses. Still, they hadn't mounted yet, and surprise was still on his side. If only he hadn't left his bloody rifle in Berill! He looked at Parimu, who nodded, beginning the agonizing process of crawling back out to the road.

"Alright," Erso said quietly when they reached the others, "they're awake, but only just. Two dozen or so, horses are hobbled in a single line on the east side."

"We'll strike with archers first," Parimu said, drawing a quick picture of the ravine in the dirt. "We'll have you three on the edges here and here. Two straight volleys and we ride in. Just pick your shots well; we need you to drop at least a few before we're in the thick of it."

The archers nodded solemnly. Every man had trained in the Berillai navy, so they should at least know their business. They just had to hope it was enough to make a difference.

<hr>

Sumi awoke to screaming. She started, banging her head against the metal box. *No, no, no,* she thought. Those were the sounds of fighting and dying, of her friends coming to die.

"Erso!" she screamed, banging on the walls. "Erso, no!"

She kept banging, but the din outside only grew louder, the screams and swords far louder than she could ever hope to be inside her little box. She clamped her eyes shut, reaching for her necklace.

Vilodai, she thought, *Vilodai, please help.*

The voices of the silver flooded into her mind, but for a moment, she was afraid Vilodai wouldn't come. She had rejected her help, had been too proud to take the power. But then, the rumbling came. She could feel the goddess's simmering rage, its fire wrapping her in its warmth.

Kouselumakan, Vilodai roared, *Welloshara.* The Voice and the Mind. It always came back to those words. Parimu, the songs, the giant bedrock beneath the earth, and…Fort Merricut. Vilodai had tried to *join* the voices of the wall. She had dropped the necklace then, afraid of what would come next. But now…

She shut her eyes, listening to the buzzing metal. She listened as she had with Parimu until she could *feel* the silver. Even though the box was solid, it was made up of hundreds of voices, like the grain in wood, overlapping where the silver had been melted down. The ripples of silver formed a picture in her mind, like waves on the sea. And as they did, she felt another rumbling from Vilodai, quicker this time, the goddess seeming…eager. She didn't know what would happen when her eagerness and wrath collided, but for once, she was ready to find out.

Show me, she thought to Vilodai, *show me, and help me save them.*

Vilodai's rumbling grew more intense, surrounding her until she felt like she was back at the mountain.

Keyansuyosul, Vilodai roared. She didn't know that word, but maybe if she saw the image, she— There was a flash of pain in her forehead, her temples throbbing. She cracked an eye open, finding the box full of light. She could *see* the silver, not its shiny outside but the minds within it, glowing like a speaking stone. They shimmered to the rhythm of their voices, their glow overlapping where the minds flowed together.

How? she asked. She pictured Elomikarus and the giant stone he had carried. He had seemed to read the earth, parting it with his stone like water.

Etkolositara, Vilodai said. An image appeared in her mind of two people standing back to back before walking in different directions. *Different from the one before.* So she didn't have the same stone, but with Vilodai's Eye…

Kouselumakan, the goddess said again. The Voice. So, she had to…speak? She set her jaw, watching the fragments of silver. She'd had the songs then, but she'd shaped Parimu's mind, hadn't she? *Spoken* to it, pushed the songs into it.

Join, she told the silver in her mind.

For a moment, it resisted, holding to its rhythm.

Join, she said again. *Join, join, join!*

Vilodai rumbled in her mind, the rhythm of the goddess filling her until she could hear nothing else. The silver wavered, buckling under the weight of the goddess's power as it began to form together. Sumi rolled onto her stomach, ripping the cord from her neck so she could hold the necklace firmly in her hand. The silver was one, shining so brightly she almost forgot about the darkness. She reached for Vilodai, pulling her strength into the world. She couldn't explain it, but it was like the songs, her ancestors pulling Essomuai's light from *somewhere,* something they'd called a pillar. She filled her heart with Vilodai like it was a song until she thought she might burst from holding so much power.

Change, she commanded, and the box exploded, blasting apart in all directions.

She stood, looking out over the chaos of the battle. She could see the men before her, on horses and on foot, but to her, everything shone with the blue of Vilodai's light. She could feel the minds of the men, but they were dwarfed by the immensity of the stone beneath them, like an ocean unto itself. All those men were turned toward her, frozen in tableau, their swords covered with blood, the liquid glowing blue from the mix of minds the steel had run through. There was one man in the center, a pistol in his hand. She knew his face, had seen his eyes the night before through the latch in the door. He raised his pistol, aiming at her heart.

She pulled at the stone beneath her with her mind, her unspoken command shaped by the force of Vilodai. The stone exploded upward as the gun fired, throwing her in the air as it formed a giant pillar beneath her, her wagon prison flying into the trees. The bullet thudded uselessly against the stone, and she landed on her feet, looking down on the men below.

She felt Vilodai's wrath boiling inside her, her arms shaking as she struggled to hold it back. Freed from the silver, part of her mind could hear the songs, but they were like mosquitoes compared to Vilodai, the immensity of her power greater than a mountain. Every single one of those blue lights could be snuffed out in a moment, their minds eviscerated by Vilodai's might. It would be the work of but a moment, the earth itself nothing before her power. She could finish this, finish them all, crack Berill like an egg if she wanted.

"No!" she shouted, the earth shaking around her, cracks forming in the ground. *I. Will. Not,* she thought to Vilodai. There would be another way, there *had* to be another way.

"Stop!" she shouted to the men, but they had stopped long ago, all of their weapons suddenly on the ground as if they'd forgotten they'd been holding them at all. She gritted her teeth until she thought they'd crack but forced herself to let go of Vilodai. *Thank you*, she thought, and then she dropped the stone, her vision of the world returning to normal. Still, she felt that if she looked hard enough, she could find the minds again. But for now, she saw only men, terror in their eyes.

"We are Shapewalkers," she said, her chest still heaving, the bloodlust thick in her mind. "Sent to build, not destroy. Tell Pont'dulairn we're coming. Not to fight Berill, but to change it. Leave, and be grateful that I spared your lives."

There was a moment of silence, but then they fled, running for their horses. The animals' eyes were wide with fear, pulling desperately at their reins. But somehow, the men mounted them, racing away to the north, to Pont'dulairn. She picked up Vilodai's Eye, putting it in her pocket as she climbed down from the stone. But as soon as she touched the ground, she collapsed, her knees buckling as her head swam. Suddenly, someone was there, holding her. She opened her eyes, blinking in the light as her eyes struggled to focus. It was Erso. His face and arms were bloody, but he smiled.

"You're safe," he said, clutching her to his chest. "Bloody halls, you're safe." He began to weep, his chest shaking with sobs. She felt like a rag doll, but she put her hands on his back, holding him weakly as he cried.

"I'm sorry," he said. She tried to form words, but her mouth was dry, exhaustion wringing them from her tongue.

"No," she muttered. "Not…your fault."

"No, it is," Erso said, shaking his head where it was hidden in her neck. "Not just this — *all* of it." He pulled back, looking her in the eyes, his own glistening with tears.

"If I thought for a single second I could live without you, I was a damned fool. The thought that I could lose you… I don't deserve you, Sumi Elerair, but I will never leave your side again."

She touched his face.

"Okay," she said, and they kissed. She could taste the salt of his tears. It was like their first kiss, a thousand possibilities held within it.

When she finally opened her eyes, Parimu was there, smiling down at her in Erso's lap.

"I'm glad you're safe," he said. He didn't look much better than Erso, but it was like the battle had never happened, the blood covering him a mere coincidence from walking through the woods.

Between the two of them, they got her to her feet, and she turned, facing the motley group of guards that had rallied to save her. There were as many men dead on the ground as standing, but four of them still lived, watching her with wide eyes. From the hillside, two men were scrambling down with bows in their hands.

"Thank you all," she said. "I can never tell you what your courage means to me — to all of us. I promise your sacrifice won't be in vain. If you'll join us, we're riding for Berill."

31

Risonumarayan - an image appears of a clam shell. It sits beneath the water, though the waves appear to open its shell as they pass. However, within it, another shell appears.

-Excerpt from The Arguments
Nineteenth Cycle

—:—

Kemarin walked quickly toward the Peerage, two letters in his pocket. By the end of the day, he'd send one of them, but despite agonizing over them for two sleepless nights, he still wasn't sure which one. Would either of them be enough to save his skin? And what of Elisal? Would she still be proud of him if the end came? She'd taken the news of the girl's freedom as if he'd been talking about the weather, her brows arching as if to say, 'And what of you, Kemarin Pont'dulairn? Have you really lent her your strength?'

If only his strength was still worth lending… If what his men said was true, the world he'd fought so hard to lead may well be ending. The world was dividing again into a before and after, the time of trains and cannons giving way to *gods*. The girl had told him as much, of course, but he'd dismissed her, her stories sounding like nothing more than sentiment. But the power to crack the earth like an egg… It made him wonder what else was true. Like the treaty signing in Relimora all those years ago, the tall tales he'd dismissed in the name of science.

He finally reached the doors, waving his way past the guards. He didn't have time for silly formalities, not on a day like today. It was time to act, to change, to ride the wind. But since the girl — if he could even call a divine weapon 'girl' anymore — escaped, there hadn't been a single trace of her. He'd sent letters to Linindal and the library to seek a truce, but there had still been no answer. But with the royal stay lifting in two days, they had to act soon, didn't they? And that meant changing his plans before his old ones proved useless.

He moved through the great hall, sparing a glance for the Sea Blades. How had his ancestors found the strength to wield the gods? Standing now where they stood, with the future in his hands, he wasn't sure how they'd learned to jump. Perhaps they hadn't; perhaps they'd been pushed. The girl wanted Shapewalkers to have their proper place in the world? Well, that was undeniable now. With the girl's powers, castle walls would fall like sand. The world would see it as a threat, of course, but those with magic had no choice but to demand their proper place now.

As he opened the door to his office, Lestorn was there, rummaging through a large stack of letters. He blinked in surprise. Had the man really not expected him? It may be Queen's Day, but they had a damned bill coming up!

"The furthest ocean," Lestorn said hastily, looking up.

"Is the deepest," Pont'dulairn answered, nodding. What would beady-eyed Lestorn ever do if someone didn't know the words? The man would be dead before he could blink. But that's what the ciphers were for, after all. You could rummage around his office all you wanted; it wouldn't do you much good.

"I might have some letters," he said to Lestorn as he walked by.

"Certainly, sir," he said. "I'll keep my runners handy."

As Lestorn closed the door behind him, he sat, sighing in relief. Blessed quiet. It wouldn't make his decision any easier, but it was better than nothing. He reached into his pocket for his letters when his blood ran cold.

"Hello," a voice said. He looked up, his hand reaching for his knife. It was the girl, come for him at last.

"It's alright," she said, holding up a palm. "I'm not here to hurt you."

He stayed tense, his fingers inches from his blade, his eyes glued to her.

"I promise," she said, "I just want to talk."

"Alright," he said, nodding slowly. He relaxed his arm, gesturing to the sofa by the window.

"Please," he said, "have a seat. Can I…send for some tea?"

"No, thank you," she said, smiling of all things! "I have a few more places to go yet."

She sat demurely, gently smoothing her dress as if she didn't have the power to snap him like a twig.

"If you'll allow me to begin," he said hastily, "I think an apology is in order. I'm…sorry for how I treated you. Above all, our kind ought to be friends, and I betrayed that trust. And thank you for sparing my men — you didn't have to."

She simply looked back at him, her eyes appraising. He felt a chill run up his spine. Was she communing with the goddess now? Asking if she should really spare him?

"Thank you," she said. "I do want us to be friends. I'm sorry anyone had to die on either side. Just promise me you'll care for the families of the men who were killed?"

"Of course," he said. "Always."

She nodded. There was another moment of silence, each second like an hour to him, but the girl simply looked out the window as if the gardens were the most interesting thing in the world. He needed to take this opportunity. She was here, before him, and for the moment, he was — if not forgiven, then at least tolerated. But how to ensure his place in the future she was building?

"Tell me," he said, "how else can I help?"

"I'm glad you asked," she said, turning back to him. "That's why I've come." The girl — or Sumi, rather — did smile an awful lot. Perhaps she would need him, someone to navigate the shoreline while she looked at the stars.

"The parade will be tomorrow," she said. "I don't object to your bill, truly, and I'm not trying to make things complicated for you, but…it's time we ask for more, and I hope you'll support us in that. We plan to speak the truth, but our voices will be much louder with you by our side."

He nodded, smiling. It was impossible his smile looked as genuine as hers, but it *was* sincere. Maybe not the type of sincerity she was used to, but it was the smile of a man whose horse had just crossed the finish line.

"You know, I couldn't agree more," he said.

She blinked in surprise, raising an eyebrow.

"You see," he continued, "as I'm sure you agree, I'm afraid I became a bit…overzealous about my bill. It's like the old story, *Seran and the Clam.* I was so sure I'd get the pearl, I forgot to hold my breath. But now, you've helped me see what I was missing. It *is* time for change, and an immense one at that."

He patted his left pocket, where his letter to the admirals was waiting. Until he saw Sumi, he'd truly thought he'd use the other letter, but this one felt right now. "Sumi, with your immense power, there's nothing we can't—"

"Vice Peer," she said, cutting him off. "I'm afraid you've misunderstood me. There *is* no immense power. This parade is for peace, and all we need are the songs. But the others have learned to hear them, and I wanted to give you the same chance. I suppose I thought if you could hear her, you'd understand."

He thought of the stories his men had told, of the ground quaking at her voice, the stone rising from the earth like a tree.

"But…" he started, "what you did in that forest. The stone… It's like the story you told us, with Elomikarus. If we had that power, we—"

"That," she said, "is not a power for anyone to use." She narrowed her eyes and looked out the window for a moment, muttering to herself. "Perhaps we *can* speak to the stones, but…" She shook her head, rousing herself. "Never mind. That was Vilodai, and she was only trying to protect me. She — all three of us, actually — want peace for all people, *eshernulam*, and we'll make sure no one has that power ever again."

He thought of the girl's story from that night in the library, the mountains to the south. Perhaps he could… But no, the goddess would be there, waiting to destroy him. Without her, he had no conduit, no way to crest the wave.

"So…" he said slowly, "just a parade."

"Just a parade," she agreed, smiling. "But I think you'll find it's far more than that. Would you mind…if I sang to you?"

"Please," he said, bowing his head. As much as he feared it, he still longed for her true power, but perhaps if he heard the other…

"It may work better if you close your eyes," she said.

He met her eyes, studying them. He supposed if she really wanted a knife in him, she would have done it already, could have killed him a hundred different ways without coming here to meet him.

"Very well," he said, closing his eyes.

She took a deep breath, and then she began…to sing. There were no words, only a haunting melody, though her voice was surprisingly good. From what he understood, she'd been a shopkeeper before the gods chose her. Perhaps there was a lesson in that, but not one he wanted to dwell on… As he listened, he began to notice a pattern to the song, and he began to nod along to it as it went through its third cycle. Her voice started low, lifting higher. Almost like…plants coming up from the ground. He could almost see them, like tiny golden orbs rising in the sky, almost like—

He gasped, a bloody *symphony* pouring into his mind. The girl sang on, but suddenly, there were what seemed to be dozens of voices joining her, seemingly infinite layers joining her own. What had seemed like the edges of a picture before glowed brightly in his mind, the plants suddenly joined by an entire *world* knitted out of golden thread. He felt his jaw slacken but couldn't seem to care, enraptured by the music.

"You can hear them now," she said, though it was hard to focus on the words as the songs threatened to sweep him away. "You can listen to any of them — even your own if you listen closely enough."

He might never have discovered it if she hadn't said so, but he realized he *could* shift his focus. He wasn't sure how, but he...looked inward, the other pieces of the song finally falling away, reducing from a flood to a trickle as they hummed at the fringes of his mind. The song within himself was strangely familiar like he'd heard it before. As he listened, images appeared in his mind, only this time like memories, like a dream half-forgotten.

He saw his childhood, his family estates, all his days with Elisal. And then...his father. He saw the day his father stepped down, when the Vice Peerage was as good as his, the mantle heavier than a mountain. And the words his father had burned into his memory forever.

"Kemarin," he'd said, "life is longer than any man. But plant a single seed, and you will grow a forest."

Tears came to his eyes, but he couldn't stop them. He finally understood. He wiped his eyes, laughing in spite of himself. Perhaps the girl was right after all. It was good he had written two letters. It would have to be the right pocket, after all.

32

We know now, of course, that most minds lack overlapping signatures, especially something on the scale of a pillar. I can see how some might fail to have a use under our present condition, but that still doesn't explain why this one was left behind.

-Setorin's Log
3625-71

—:—

Kemarin moved quickly down Laeryia Boulevard, Terosan close on his heels. The Queen's summons had come far more quickly than he'd expected, and this wasn't an appointment he wanted to be late to. Still, he was determined to use the front gate, which meant a very hasty walk around the palace. Far too many commoners used the peerage entrance these days. Not that he minded particularly himself... But Peers were allies, not *servants* of the crown, and all his actions had to embody that distinction.

The guards were ready for them when they arrived — the gates pulled open with a line of guards flanking the path on either side. Although judging by the archers lining the fence, Kollenail's death hadn't left Welaya feeling particularly friendly, either... The palace high marshal stood by the gate, a tall white feather rising from his hat.

"Vice Peer," he said, bowing his head. "Her Majesty is honored by your visit."

Pont'dulairn nodded, stepping onto the path. "I suppose you'll want to see my tattoo then, eh?"

"Yes, sir," the high marshal said, tilting his head again formally.

"Of course," Kemarin said. He handed his briefcase to Terosan, carefully pulling back the sleeve of his suit. There, on the inside of his wrist, was the Pont'dulairn crest in silver ink. Strange bit of magic, that. Apparently, it wasn't enough silver to hamper his transformations, but no matter what he turned into, that tiny crest would appear somewhere on his body. His father had taught him early on how to control it. If you were a horse, for example, you could force it under a hoof. They could have made fakes, of course, but father had always seen it as an honor, a mark of their dual role in the world.

"Thank you," the high marshal said, stepping over to look at Terosan's as well. Terosan's wasn't a house sigil but something simpler, like the palace guards, but at least essential peerage staff could opt for the tattoos instead of the endless passphrases. Truthfully, he'd only seen the man's tattoo once, some kind of strange diamond shape with a sunburst in the middle. He wasn't sure what it meant, though perhaps Sumi would… He took a deep breath, nodding to himself. If he didn't fail the girl now, perhaps he'd get the chance to ask.

As the high marshal led them toward the palace, he noticed a few groups of people watching from the street. *Good.* The pageantry was for their benefit, after all, even if they'd see something far grander tomorrow… When they reached the palace doors, the high marshal handed them off to the head butler, Terosan disappearing to wait with a valet. Surprisingly, though, Welaya was already there, waiting for him in the grand hall. Standing in the center of a giant tile moon, her dress flowed around her, her crown perched delicately on her hair. She *was* beautiful, but there was far too much of her father's cruelty in that gaze for him to forget her true nature.

"Your Majesty," he said, pausing with a sharp nod. She had never seemed the type to mind that Peers didn't bow, but there was a fire in her eyes today.

"Vice Peer," she said, nodding curtly herself. "I was surprised by your request. You've certainly become a hard man to find these past few years…"

She let that last bit trail off, hanging in the air. Yes, it would take a good deal to earn her trust at this late hour… He'd been acting for the common good, of course, but there were few in this world who could avoid taking political attacks personally.

"Yes, well," he said, "we're long overdue. We have much to discuss, if you think we might find somewhere more private?"

He glanced around the palace, hoping she'd take the hint to have as few listening ears as possible.

"Very well," she said, inclining her head. "Perhaps my study, then."

"That will do nicely," he said, smiling, "thank you."

She nodded to her side and turned, indicating that he could walk by her side. Even when they acted as equals, she had her precedence, and he had his, he supposed. Each little bit of the dance was important in one way or another. They left the entrance, staying on the ground floor as they followed a hallway to the east side of the palace. Only four guards came with them. That may be as much privacy as you could expect with a queen, but it was just as well. He'd have to get used to saying the truth soon enough.

Thankfully, the walk was a short one. The study was in an interior room on the ground floor, facing a courtyard garden. He had seen her father's study once, but the royal study was a traveling room, each ruler picking whichever room was most comfortable to them. That was useful information itself, of course. Her father's study had been imperious, towering over the palace on the third floor and full of dark paneling. But this room spoke of a humbler air. She may be more dogmatic than her father, but in many ways, she likely still saw herself as serving the old man's wishes. Not unlike himself...

The head guard showed him to a seat facing the window, offering him tea before he joined his fellows in the hallway. Welaya sat regally in a high-backed armchair. It must have been a favorite of hers, looking like a slightly softer version of her throne. It was angled slightly toward the fire, and there was a book on the side table. He was tempted to read the name on the spine — knowing what the Queen read for leisure would have been even more useful — but he kept his eyes trained on hers.

"So," she said, her manner decidedly more casual once they were alone, "why have you come? You make your hatred of me clear enough in the peerage; why request to see me after all this time?"

He nodded, smiling sadly.

"I appreciate your candor," he said, "but I wouldn't use the word hatred. I admit we've had starkly different visions for this kingdom — for all of Wellonai, really — and I regret when those debates have grown...heated. Still, I hope you believe me when I say I mean to be a friend to you."

Her face was blank, but she opened her palms. He was free to go on — she would hear him out, at least. He took a deep breath, reaching into his pocket where he'd put Kollenail's ring. *You better be right, girl*, he thought. Either way, the die had been cast. There was no turning back now.

"If I may?" he asked, showing her the ring as he made to stand from his chair. She nodded, and he stepped carefully toward her, placing the ring on the table beside her. It took a moment, but, of course, she recognized it, her eyes widening. A silver ring with a sapphire thorn — there was only one of its like in the kingdom.

"You threaten me?" she asked quietly, not turning from the ring.

"No," he said, keeping his gaze on her. She finally looked up, meeting his eyes. "I *am* a friend to you, Your Majesty, though perhaps of a different sort than you'd like."

He reached into his pocket again and took out Kollenail's last letter, the one he'd stolen from his folio before they burned the carriage. It was still ciphered, but she could access those easily. It was in the man's own hand, and it would be evidence enough.

"Commissioner Kollenail was planning to assassinate you," he said. He placed the letter beside him, afraid to step toward her again. "I am partly to blame, I admit. After my changes to the police, I think they thought you too weak to rule. But it's much more than that. We have long been a nation of warriors, and some men simply cannot put down the sword."

"Why tell me this now?" she asked, her gaze penetrating. She seemed to believe, but she still didn't understand. "Kollenail has been missing for over a month. What do you have to gain by telling me this?"

Kemarin chuckled. It wasn't funny, of course, but something about facing the truth always made him laugh. What a fool he'd been.

"An excellent question, Your Majesty. I suppose I want you to know just how much of a friend I am. We may have our differences, but when the time came, I was on your side, not his. I promise I'll defend your crown and your right to wear it."

He took a deep breath, tapping his fingers together as he stared into the fire.

"But…I suppose I've come to admit where I've been wrong, too. And I hope if you'll hear me that we can both learn from my mistakes."

He took a sip of his tea, rubbing his hands together.

"Kollenail and I saw the world very differently, but I never really appreciated what it takes for men to lay down the sword. I thought I could bind them with commerce, making war too expensive. But what we have here, Your Majesty, is a matter of the soul — the hearts of men. The Continent is not our enemy, and it's time we stop being theirs."

"And you think this enmity was my choosing?" she asked.

"Hardly," he said. "We were handed this situation, but it *is* our choice to continue it."

"And what exactly is it you ask of me, Lord Pont'dulairn?"

"Nothing I don't ask of myself," he said, chuckling. "You see, I came here to tell you I'm a fool, perhaps the greatest fool of all."

She narrowed her eyes, but he pressed on. He *needed* her to see, to understand what he had failed to for so long.

"I've been lucky in life," he said, "far luckier than I've any right to be. But all my bills, my reforms — they allowed me to ignore the bigger picture. You see, Your Majesty, change is coming, *real* change, change that is far greater than you or I. And now, we have to ask ourselves, will we fight it, or will we let it pass? I suspect, if you let these seeds be planted, you might like what grows from them."

"Out with it, then," she said. "I've had enough of this bloody tiptoeing. What's your next reform? What *grand* change do you wish to run me over with?"

"I'm afraid it's not that simple," he said. "Tomorrow morning, there's going to be a parade."

"A…parade?" she asked, blinking. "A parade for what?"

"Shapewalkers," he said.

She sucked in a sharp breath, just a single moment of losing her composure before the immensity of her royalty reasserted itself. Still, she was her father's daughter, and he could see the fear in her eyes.

"You mean to tell me," she said, "that a pack of those…things have not only entered our kingdom, but they want to hold a parade? To what end? To overthrow the crown?"

"No, Your Majesty," he said. "They haven't entered the kingdom, they were always here."

"Impossible," she sputtered, her voice rising. "This kingdom has always purged those vermin. Our very police hunt them! This cannot be!"

"It *is* possible, Your Majesty," he said firmly. "It is the way things have always been. Even serving your father, Drekkles knew only so many could be captured. Only so many were…worthy of capture. From the beginning, Shapewalkers have lived among us, and not all of them in low stations."

"Like who?" she asked. "I demand you tell me at once."

He was standing at the betting line now. The pieces were on the table, and the chips were in his hand. He thought of Elisal and her song. He thought of the promise he'd made her: to give the girl his strength, to let go of ambition in exchange for something greater. He closed his eyes and began to glow.

He opened his eyes, meeting Welaya's. She had shrunk into her seat, looking like the little girl he'd met so many years ago, her hands shaking on the arms of her chair. But she didn't call for her guards. Her mouth moved, but no words came out.

"You see," he said, a perfect imitation of the woman before him, "we have *always* been here. Since the beginning, when my house stormed that first beach. But we became a part of this land and everything that goes with it."

"Have you come to kill me?" she finally asked, her voice hoarse.

"Far from it, Your Majesty," he said gently. "If I wanted you dead, I would have let Kollenail do it. I'm here to protect my kind and because I'm the only one that can be, the only one who can reach you. I beg you, tell your guards to stand down tomorrow. The others don't mean you any harm, and if you let them march, I think you'll see that."

"The only one that could come here..." she whispered, repeating his words. "How did you get in here then?" she asked. "What of the tattoos?"

"Real, of course," he said, showing her his wrist. "The silver never fades."

He took a deep breath, changing back into himself before he stood.

"I'll see myself out," he said. "But think on what I said. The future is ours to decide, Your Majesty. Will you choose hope or blood?"

With that, he left, the Queen staring blankly as the guards escorted him away. His heart was racing, and he had to make a fist to keep his hand from shaking. But whatever came next, he had bet his entire hand. He only hoped he'd done Elisal proud.

You better be right, girl, he thought as he reached the entrance hall. *And even if you are...Essomuai help us with what comes next.*

33

Gesorulansara - certainly my favorite invulsion. It only lasts an instant, but you can watch an entire desert become a field from a single seed.

-Excerpt from The Echoes
Seventh Cycle

—:—

Somehow, in spite of all her planning and all her sleepless nights, the day of the parade arrived. Sumi stood in Parimu's garden as the sun came up, holding Amis as she stared out at the city. She ran her eyes along the shoreline, over the rooftops, and up the hills toward the terrace. Somewhere up there was her cottage, where her story began, in the city where it could very well end. Still, there was nowhere else she would rather be. She loved this place, and she would risk anything to save it. After so many days of doubt, she was finally sure, finally ready to accept what came next.

She heard a noise and turned, finding Parimu's blurred image in the kitchen window, stooping down to light the stove. She ought to get back in and finish preparing with the others. She was already dressed, of course — though she'd hardly slept long enough to justify taking off her clothes in the first place — but there was still plenty to do: packing up the banners, closing the house, getting to the meeting point. First, though, she had to say her goodbyes. She turned Amis around, lifting him to eye level.

"I love you," she said, scratching his whiskers, "my brave, fat little knight. I'm going to do everything I can to come back for you, but if I don't, just stay in the garden, alright?"

Late the night before, she'd dropped a letter in the post for Alip. If they failed, she'd given him Parimu's address and instructions to come looking for the cat. And if they succeeded… Well, then she'd finally be able to come clean and explain the whole thing. She put Amis down, tossing him the large sausage in her pocket. There was no way he'd be able to finish the whole thing, but as long as there was food, there was little chance he'd leave.

She went into the kitchen where Parimu was knocking around the pots and pans, pulling things out of the larder. He turned, flashing her a smile.

"I wasn't sure if a big breakfast would help or hurt," he said. "But I guess I'd rather not gamble on an empty stomach."

"Good thinking," she said, nodding her thanks as he handed her a mug of tea. She took a seat at the table, closing her eyes as she breathed in the fragrant steam, listening to the sounds of the kitchen. With death breathing down her neck, it made moments like these feel all the more precious. After all, these were the moments that made up a life, the little notes that wove themselves into the songs.

She sat that way for a long time, Parimu bustling around the stove as they shared the space in contented silence. Finally, she heard Beysal and Erso upstairs, banging around like they may well be wrestling already. Parimu stepped around the counter, dropping a heaping plate in front of her. It was basically everything left in the house: biscuits, sausage, eggs, even some rice. So, she wasn't the only one preparing to not return…

She stared down at the food, a tear suddenly coming to her eye. She stood, wrapping him in a hug.

"Thank you, Relsenair," she said, "for everything."

He actually hugged her back, holding her for a long moment before he stepped away, scratching the back of his head. He took a deep breath, meeting her eyes.

"You know," he said, "I'm the one who should be thanking you. Just promise me something, will you?"

"Anything," she said.

"No matter what happens today, don't turn back. Even if we lose someone, you have to finish this. We know the cost as well as you, and if we're gonna spit in Ciersein's eye, let's make sure the bastards feel it."

He was right. Maybe she was ready for the gallows herself, but when she thought of putting the others at risk, her blood still ran cold. But like he said, they all knew the cost, and for their sacrifice, she owed them courage.

"I promise," she said, holding his gaze.

"Alright then," he said, smiling. He nodded, returning to the stove as the others started down the stairs. Beysal popped into the kitchen first, looking surprisingly fresh for how late she'd heard them in the garden.

"So," he said, joining her at the table, "it's the big day, eh?"

"Here we are," she said, smiling.

Erso leaned in to kiss her cheek before sitting beside her. Parimu came back with more plates, each one piled higher than the last.

"Wow," Erso said, his eyes wide. "I'm impressed. An army's-worth of food and not a single ounce of squid."

"Ignore the lad," Beysal said, rolling his eyes. "I reckon even when he carries my bones to *Su'selo'mae*, he'll still be cracking jokes."

"What can I say," Erso said, shrugging with a piece of toast in each hand, "in the end, we all must be true to our nature. You, for example, are a large bear, and I am a funny, charming gentleman."

"Sure, sure," Beysal said. "Just pass the butter during your speech, give you something useful to do."

Erso grinned, though it never reached his eyes. Ever since the woods, there'd been a fire behind his eyes, one she hoped wouldn't make him do anything reckless... She was glad to have him back, of course, but he still seemed consumed by regret. No matter if she told him a million times there was nothing *to regret,* if he thought she was in danger, there was no telling what he'd do.

"You know," he said, stuffing a sausage in his mouth, "my mother always said you should never eat before you go on stage."

"She also wore a corset," Beysal offered, chuckling.

"I forgot about that," Erso said, turning to Sumi. "Care for a last-minute corset, my lady?"

She kicked him under the table — nothing hard, but enough to earn a yelp for her trouble. They mostly ate in quiet after that, stuffing themselves until the clock chimed in the hall.

"Well," Erso said, standing up and brushing the crumbs from his pants, "don't want to be late to our own party, eh?"

"No, that wouldn't do," she said. She looked to Parimu. "Shall we leave the dishes for the victory party?"

He chuckled. "I think that'd be a fair reward for all our hard work."

They all sprang up from the table, shuffling around the kitchen until everything was more or less stacked in the sink. When they were done, Erso ran upstairs, returning with the costume bag over his shoulder.

"Sumi," he asked, "do you have a second to join me in the garden?"

She looked at the others, who had odd smiles on their faces.

"Um...sure," she said. He led her through the kitchen, saying nothing as he took her to the garden fence.

"What's going on?" she asked. "Is there something you need for the parade?"

"There *is* something I need," he said, smiling as he turned to face her, "but not for the parade." He fumbled around in his bag for a moment. "I know you Berillai do some nonsense with salt and clam shells, but I guess an Amoriai tradition will have to do."

He finally pulled out a big clump of wheat and handed it to her. She raised her eyebrows, holding it to her nose like a bouquet as she sniffed the golden buds. They were earthy, the fine strands tickling her nose. What had he meant about clam shells? Berillai did marriage proposals with stuff like that, but… She looked at the stalks of wheat, where they were joined by a sparkling circle. A ring had been put onto the wheat, binding it together. It was gold with a sparkling piece of glass on top in the shape of a rose. She stared up at him, her eyes widening.

"It's not my mother's," he said, "lost that in the fire. But it's still from our family — passed down from Elo's grandmother. We'll have to figure out something else for Kel, but I guess we have a while yet to sort that out."

He cleared his throat, chuckling.

"Sorry, getting off topic. I…uh…well, I wanted you to know if this works out, I'll make an honest woman of you. And if they don't…well, you have my promise either way. Beysal brought the wheat without asking, stubborn mule, but I guess he was right. I know I failed you before, and there's still a lot of broken things in me, but…" He took a deep breath, closing his eyes for a moment before he looked at her again, cupping her cheek. "You're my life, Sumi Elerair. Broken or not, I'm yours today, and I'm yours tomorrow."

"Yes," she said, grabbing his hand from her face and squeezing it.

"I didn't ask the question yet," he said, chuckling.

"Yes," she said again, grabbing his head and pulling him into a deep kiss.

She heard clapping behind her and turned, finding the others at the back door.

"You both knew?" she asked, shooting them a dirty look. "You were smiling like rats in the larder."

"Guilty," Beysal said, holding up his hands. "Have to keep some secrets from the boss."

"Well, thank you both," she said. "I couldn't think of a better gift for today."

She held tightly to the grain, slipping the ring off and onto her finger. Luckily, it fit like a glove. She'd never thought of her fingers as particularly dainty — not like Nela's — but maybe that meant she'd be marrying the right man.

“I hate to ruin the party,” Parimu said, glancing back at the kitchen clock, “but we’d better get going.”

She nodded, looking at the others.

“Well,” she said, “let’s go have a parade.”

34

The others have been so eagerly destroyed... It's enough to make me hope I never find it, though a naive part of me still hopes I can hide it once I do.

-Setorin's Log
3984-93

—:—

Sumi moved quickly through the alley, adjusting costumes on the other Shapewalkers as she passed. They were east of the palace, the Master Librarian's carriage blocking the entrance. A few people glanced in from the street as they passed, but no one stopped or stared. Were they even visible in the shadows? They all wore white costumes with spun gold in their hair, though the alley was a deep one. Not that it mattered... Soon, they'd be on full display, marching straight down Laeryia Boulevard with the whole city watching.

"Alright, everyone!" she called. "Circle up!"

Erso was at her side in an instant, taking her hand — the one with the ring on it — as Beysal took the other. The others joined them until they stood in a tight circle, jammed between the walls of the alley. She looked at them all, nearly two dozen Shapewalkers staring back at her. More than a few had pulled her aside, worried about the new archers above the palace gates, but no one had abandoned them, even the duchess.

"I want to thank each and every one of you for being here today," she said. "I know we're all nervous, but you've already shown tremendous courage. When the goddess called for us, you answered. Just try to enjoy it and smile as wide as you can. The people will know we mean no harm. We've practiced, and now we just have to go out there and show Berill. But before we do, I'd like to sing one last time."

228

They nodded, most of them closing their eyes. She listened to the songs, waiting until the cycle began, and then she led them off, starting with the Song of Life. The others joined her, their voices growing until she could feel the stones of the alleyway vibrating with their power. They only sang one full cycle, but even so, she could feel the golden light in the air, ready to pour from their hearts. They stood in silence for a moment, basking in the echo of the song.

"Alright, everyone," she said quietly, "let's begin."

They set out from the alleyway, turning into the street in procession. Sumi was in the front with Erso and Parimu beside her, holding the banner. *Eshernulam,* it read with the Berillai translation underneath. The streets were already crowded, and at the sound of their boots marching on the cobblestones, people began to turn and look. As they reached the first set of street lamps, she paused, waiting for the others to turn out of the alley. The carriage came out last, Peloris waving his hat from where he sat with his driver.

She nodded; it was time to begin. She reached out in her mind, taking in the songs behind her. She could sense their minds, the *welloshara* still vibrating from their singing. Even the gold in their hair seemed to hum with music, the tiny pieces of Essomuai longing to connect themselves to the whole. The street had grown quiet as people stopped to stare, the traffic freezing around them in the street. She took a deep breath, calling out in a clear voice.

"We are Shapewalkers!" she yelled. "We are not your enemy. We come for peace, to create a land for all peoples!"

"For Essomuai!" the others called out behind her. "For Vilodai! For Wellonai! For Berill!"

With that, the shaping began. They started separately, and she felt the hum of the shifting around her, their songs blossoming into a beautiful chaos as they turned into their favorite creatures. She could sense Beysal behind her as a bear, reaching high with his paws as others swooped back and forth over the procession as birds. Sumi took her own first form, becoming the Angel of the Sea. Meloy and Edeln would be joining her as angels in the back, forming a triangle around the surge of animals. Sumi held her sword high, feeling her dress become longer as it flowed along the ground. Erso and Parimu had both become lions, using their jaws to hold the banner.

The crowd began to thicken, with a dozen more people appearing on the sidewalk every moment. Carriages were pulling to the side of the road, and shopkeepers were coming out of their shops, stunned looks on their faces. She'd spent her entire life in this city, watching anonymously from these same sidewalks. But now, they were watching her, her secret no longer her own. Still, all she could do was smile and hope they'd understand.

They moved into the next stage of the parade, beginning to coordinate their forms, though they wouldn't fully join until the finale. She focused on her face, appearing as a clown in pink makeup, bounding about the street as she smiled and waved at the children. She felt like she could feel Essomuai's joy, her massive well of gold sitting just beyond the edge of sight. But she felt Vilodai, too, the necklace in her hand thrumming with pleasure at all the people, all her children she had never seen.

They reached the edge of the palace, the gates rising on their left. It was time to begin the next phase, but as she spared a glance at the archers, her heart thudded in her throat. Their arrows all had silver tips, the metal shimmering in Vilodai's Eye even as they swallowed the songs around them like pits of silence. Her body wanted to run, but there was no turning back. She had to believe — believe the guards could see the smiles on the children's faces, could see they meant no harm.

She reached for the goddesses, feeling them where they waited in the southern mountains. From Essomuai, she felt only calm, an image forming in her mind of golden children dancing on the earth. She loved them, but she had made them to reach a broken world. She may lose them, but she was with them to the end. Vilodai, on the other hand, seemed to thrum with eagerness, ready to fight if the moment came. Sumi suddenly felt all too aware of the bedrock beneath the street, the bricks and cobblestones around her that could offer violence if the need arose. But they hadn't come to give the Berillai something to fear. No matter what happened, they couldn't fight today.

The crowd had grown too large for the sidewalk, spilling out into the street as the people jammed together. And as they passed, the crowd turned with them, following behind like the wake of a ship. This was more than they could have possibly hoped for; they just had to keep going. She kept the smile plastered to her face, finishing the clown's dance as she prepared for the third phase. She lifted her hand, signaling the beginning of the songs, but something was wrong…

She heard shouting from the fence and turned just as the thwack of a crossbow rang out, the rhythm of the silver rippling through the air. *Oh, gods above,* she thought, watching as a single bolt raced through the air, a bright flash exploding from the rear of the parade. She felt a searing pain from Essomuai as Edeln fell, her song shaking against the silver's hum.

"Hold!" Parimu yelled, the others standing firm as the surgeons dropped their forms, rushing Edeln to the carriage as they'd planned. Part of her wanted to turn back, to abandon the parade before anyone else was hurt, but she remembered her promise. She had to stand firm. Even if they were all slain this very moment, the people had seen them dance, and they would remember.

"Sing!" she shouted, signaling the others. She sucked in a breath, belting out the song with all her might. Even before the first cycle finished, the others had joined her, no longer needing to wait since they knew the song by heart. Still, even as she sang, preparing for the merge, she kept looking back toward the wall. Why had there only been one shot? And why Edeln? She felt a chill as she realized. There had been three angels at the beginning of the parade, three women for the Queen to seek out…

She watched as the closest archer knelt, his crossbow trained on her, the world seeming to slow as she heard the shot ring out. This time, the silver came for her like a wave crashing down over her head. Her eyes widened, preparing for the end, but suddenly she was thrown to the side. She rolled on the ground, pushing herself to her hands as she fumbled to her feet. Parimu was there, an arrow sprouting from his middle, the searing pain of Essomuai echoing off his song.

"Relsenair!" she cried, but Beysal was already there, lifting him up. Even as tall as he was, Parimu looked like a doll in the other man's arms. He ran Parimu to the carriage, Peloris waving for them as he pushed his driver to the front. She felt a quaking in her heart, Vilodai reaching for her through the necklace. She clamped her eyes shut, nearly falling to her knees again as the goddess's wrath tried to push its way in.

"I can't," she whispered, "I can't." She could never control that much power, not in this place, not with all these people. How many would die if she defended herself? What hope would Shapewalkers have if she failed? She shut her eyes, bracing for more shots, when Erso appeared, his arms around her and his hands covering her head. But something had changed… Suddenly, the crowd was louder, pouring into the streets around them, somehow missing the crossbow, laughing even as the clowns fell into disarray. A voice screamed from the fences.

"Hold your fire, dammit! Not with the crowd, hold your fire!"

"Sumi!" Erso shouted over the crowd. "It's time! We have to sing!"

She turned toward the others. Their eyes were wide, terrified, but this might be the only chance they ever got.

"Sing!" she cried again, and they sang.

There were only sixteen now, but their voices still rose above the crowd, syncing with Essomuai as the cycle spun on. The surgeons would save Edeln and Parimu — they had to — but *she* had to dance, had to finish the parade. The others began to glow like a second sun, and she pulled their light toward her, spinning it from their hearts like golden thread. She pulled until Essomuai was there with them, until she could hardly feel her body anymore, the others' souls filling her mind. And then she danced.

She turned them into water, crashing through the street as a giant wave as if the ocean had reappeared a hundred yards to the south. The crowd ooh'd and aah'd, the children laughing as they leapt for the sidewalk. It felt like painting, like she could sweep her arm through that light and make anything with a brushstroke. And even with sixteen, their canvas was so big that almost anything felt possible. She made a whale, crying as it leapt from the water, its back shining in the sun.

She moved forward, the light somehow following her intention even as it spilled in all directions. She glowed, changing the water into a field. It was like the one in Vilodai's Heart, only real, the golden grass waving in the wind as it appeared. And as the parade crawled forward, new grass appeared, emerging in the place of the fading grass behind them. She thought of the prayer: *If even one traveler should pass, let your color make them smile.* She pushed upward, covering the field in flowers, their glistening petals like gems in a crown.

She moved her awareness outward, taking in the crowd. Their faces had become still, their eyes wide and staring as their laughter turned to rapture. Still, there was no fear — only awe and wonder at so much magic. She felt movement at the gates and pushed further, taking in the archers. They were moving, rearranging around...the Queen. Welaya had come, and she was standing on one of the platforms, surrounded by guards. Their eyes were on their queen, their hands tight on their crossbows. Even with the crowds, would they be ordered to shoot?

Sumi paused, stopping the parade outside the gates. Even with all that golden light, she somehow found herself, lifting her own form as she appeared above the field, dressed as the Angel of the Sea. She faced the queen, bowing low. Let the crowds see she was no threat. She was Berillai and Anushai, Shapewalker and human. Like everyone in the parade, even with her magic, even with her blood, this was her home. She finally stood, locking eyes with Welaya as she rode the waves of grass. The crowd turned with her, their eyes eager as they noticed the queen.

Someone began to chant, and the whole crowd joined them,

beseeching, begging her to let the parade go on.

"We-la-ya!" they chanted. "We-la-ya!"

Would she let them have their magic? Their peace? There would be a lifetime of work after this moment — new treaties to be signed, new laws to be passed, agreements and repairs and healing — but if they could just have this moment, the rest would feel so incredibly *possible*. They had all known pain, had all known loss, but with something to believe in, they could reach for that change and see it through.

Welaya looked back at Sumi over the gates, over a chasm of generations pulled apart and riches won and lost. The Queen looked, and then…she nodded. It was the smallest gesture, a simple inclination of the head, but it was done. Welaya turned, leaving with her guards as the crowd erupted. Sumi smiled, slipping back into the light, ready to begin the parade in earnest. This was no longer a dice roll — it was a celebration. She released the others, and they took their own forms, cheering and dancing as they moved into the parts of the parade they weren't ever sure they'd get to.

They all turned into sheep, a nod to the ancient Berillai, swooping around each other in a figure-eight. Then, they became a herd of horses, wearing the royal colors as they pranced through the streets, the crowd surging beside them as if they were part of the shape. Finally, they reached Fort Street, and they circled for the finale, preparing for the shape she'd dreamt of long ago, never knowing if it was even possible.

They began to sing again, and she reached out for their minds, feeling their joy, their *triumph* pouring back to her. She pulled at their light again, taking them with her as she lifted their shape into the sky, becoming a giant rainbow. She could sense the entire city around them, and they lifted over it like a balloon, drifting effortlessly into the sky. It had been her final dream that showed her it could be done when she'd watched Saldal make her giant sigils in the sky. Essomuai made them into water and light, a mist that was everywhere and nowhere, the sun spinning off their backs into every possible color. The crowd roared below them, their shouts filling the air. *We did it*, she thought, to herself, to the others, to the goddesses. *We did it.*

———

Slowly, Sumi returned them to the ground. Their light, still pulsing to the rainbow's song, knitted back together, mist and light taking shape until they stood on the cobblestones, human again. She turned, looking for Erso, and when their eyes met, she ran to him, throwing her arms around him. The crowd was still all around them, cheering and clapping from the sidewalks, some of them still chanting Welaya's name.

They joined in the middle, holding hands as they took a deep bow. The crowd roared and finally, realizing it was over, began to part, the people drifting away as if waking from a dream. As the rows of onlookers opened up, Peloris's carriage finally pushed through, stopping in the center. Beysal was up front with the Master Librarian, and their eyes met, his face grim. *Parimu!* She ran to the carriage, wrenching open the door.

Edeln was sitting on the first seat, wrapped in a blanket with her arm all bandaged up. The others, though... The surgeons were huddled around Parimu, where he was laid out on the opposite seat, their hands working furiously on his side. The crossbow bolt that had hit him was on the floor, dark blood blocking any hint of the silver. She couldn't see what they were doing, but there was sweat on their foreheads, and their hushed whispers were strained. Parimu was looking directly at the ceiling, his jaw clenched in pain, but his eyes slowly moved toward hers, and when they met, he gave her a weak smile, holding out his hand.

She finally unfroze, kneeling on the floor of the carriage beside the surgeons as she gripped his hand tightly in hers. It was clammy, but she could still feel his pulse thumping against her hand.

"I..." he started, pausing to lick his lips and swallow, "heard the...cheering. Did we do it?"

"We did it," she said, nodding as she smiled through her tears. "*You* did it, Relsenair. You saved me; you saved the parade."

He smiled again, that same weak smile, though it reached his eyes this time.

"Good," he said, bobbing his head slightly in a nod. "Good."

She rubbed the back of his hand as she held it tightly in hers. His eyes began to flutter as if he was drifting off to sleep. But then he looked at her again.

"Promise..." he said, swallowing again. "Look...for them."

"I promise," she said. There was no question who he meant. This man who had become something he'd never wanted to be to protect his people, to honor Jalicyne. This man who had recognized the monster in himself and turned it into magic. Even at the end, he thought of them, the people of this city, this place he loved to his bones even as he hated its trolleys and crowds.

The surgeons finally looked up from their work, realizing what was happening, realizing it was the end. Their faces ashen, they forced open the other door on the carriage, filing out as they made room for her. She inched closer, touching Parimu's face. His eyes were still on hers, but his breath was coming out in ragged gasps. She leaned in and kissed his forehead.

"You're a good man, Relsenair Parimu," she said, choking back her tears. "I love you, and I'll see you again."

He smiled at her, closing his eyes as if to blink, but he was gone. She put her head on his chest, a chest no longer rising, and wept into his shirt. Suddenly, Edeln was there, rubbing her back with her good arm. Sumi finally let go, turning and hugging the woman, squeezing her tight. Edeln rubbed the back of her head, cooing in her ear.

"Come on," the other woman finally said. "Let's let him be."

Sumi looked at Parimu. He looked like he was sleeping. She reached out and took his hands, folding them together. She would be there when his ashes came from the kiln, and she would scatter them in all the places he loved. She would hold him in her heart for all of her days, never letting go of this wonderful man. But Edeln was right…he deserved to rest now.

She nodded, opening the door for Edeln and helping her down. She shut the door behind her and turned, finding the carriage still surrounded by a crowd. The others had fanned out, greeting the people who remained, some of them taking requests and turning into random shapes for the children. There were hundreds of Berillai gathered around them — rich and poor, young and old. She blinked through her tears, seeming to see them again through Relsenair's eyes. There was so much work to be done, but she would keep her promise to look after them: the sick, the poor, the Jalicynes of this world.

Still, she knew she wouldn't have to do that work alone. They could begin together now, every flower in the field. *This* was their world — broken yet beautiful — and *this* was their life. It was just one moment, but it was a part of an infinity, a truth that had endured even when it was hidden in a cave thousands of miles away. No matter how long it took, the goddesses would wait for them, would call to them. Even in her rage, Vilodai would always yearn for her children, and Essomuai would always sing, reflecting back the impossible beauty of the world surrounding them. In truth, they were all Shapewalkers, surrounded by golden light. And in the end, there was nothing that couldn't be transformed.

Epilogue

Essomviloshuran - an image appears of a woman, her mind glowing brightly in gold and sapphire, a dozen others glowing behind her. This seems a recent addition, so late in the cycle as it appears.

-Excerpt from The Echoes
Final Cycle

—:—

Five Years Later

Sumi left the cottage in a whirlwind, a piece of toast clamped in her mouth as she dragged her daughter by the hand. Omu was four and a half now and getting her to leave the house on time was easily the hardest thing she'd ever had to do — hunting for goddesses included. She chuckled, winking at Omu as she locked the door. It was easy to get lost in the chaos of parenting, but she *did* love it. Marking her children's heights on the doorframe, telling them the same stories Nela had told her, all of it felt exactly as it was meant to be.

"Where are we going so early?" Omu whined — gods forbid someone disrupt her routine. "Why didn't I go with daddy?"

They started through the garden, which was surprisingly back to its former glory — or as close as they could get it, anyway. They wouldn't be winning the terrace rose competition anytime soon, but with three extra pairs of hands, the plants were at least staying alive.

"We have to run some errands," Sumi said, "but you'll see him at school. Besides, it's Umidiar; shouldn't you be excited?"

Omu's eyes glistened for a moment before she pouted again.

"I wanted to go with daddy more," she said.

Sumi rolled her eyes. Essomulnyeon was a daddy's girl through and through — which would have offended her if it didn't tickle her so much to watch Erso be a father. Besides, their son, Vilo'da'rein, was only two years old, but he, at least, still preferred his mother like a sensible child.

"I'll tell you what," Sumi said as she closed the gate. "If you want, I can change into daddy for the walk. Would you like that?"

You couldn't win every battle, of course, especially not against a four-year-old...

"Yes!" Omu yelled, jumping up and down. She loved Shapewalking more than anything, which would only make her harder to control once she could fly away from her chores... Still, Kel had turned out alright so far, hadn't he?

"Alright," Sumi said, grateful for a stalemate as she opened herself to the songs. Essomuai entered her mind, the entire world pouring into her as she filled with golden light. She heard the songs of everything: plants and stones, clouds and trees, but Omu's song was the loudest of all. Maybe it would mellow with age, but it was like a storm, crashing about with all the raw energy of the world. Essomuai seemed particularly tickled by the littlest Shapewalkers. In their obsession with bugs and plants and all the little details of the world, they seemed to share something sacred with the goddess — something adults would do well to learn.

She focused her thoughts on Erso — a song she knew by heart no matter how far away he was — and not a second later, she was standing there as her husband, bowler hat and all. Omu clapped, throwing her hands in the air to be picked up. She personally had a firm no-being-carried-on-Fort-Hill policy, but with Erso's muscles... She squatted down, lifting Omu up as the little girl buried her face in her neck.

They left the garden, turning east. One of her neighbors, Mrs. Udarrin, was in her garden, waving as they passed.

"Morning, Sumi," she said, smiling. "Would've thought you were Erso if I hadn't seen for myself!"

"Let's just keep this as our little secret, alright?" she said, chuckling. "He doesn't like me spoiling her, but all she ever wants is her dad these days."

"My daughter was the same," Mrs. Udarrin said, laughing. She waved at Omu one more time before heading back toward her house.

"Alright," Sumi said, patting her daughter on the head, "hang on tight. We've got places to be."

———

As the sun climbed above the mountains, they finally reached the school. She'd eventually gotten Omu to use her own legs, which had likely saved her life with how many bags she had slung over her shoulder. She could see Erso through the windows, moving tables with Beysal, Vilo no doubt watching from his blanket. Omu sprinted away the moment she saw her father, of course, but Sumi paused just inside the fence, closing her eyes as she flashed back into her normal form.

She walked up to the bronze statue by the entrance, reaching into her bag for a bouquet of flowers, which she put by the statue's feet. She leaned her head back until she met Parimu's eyes, his gaze looking out over the city he'd loved.

"These are for you, old friend," she said, running her hand over the statue's foot. "Happy Umidiar."

She heard the creak of a wagon wheel and turned, seeing Alip and Barine ride up, a mountain of barrels stacked behind them.

"Sumi!" Alip called, jumping off the wagon. Barine was extremely pregnant with their first child, and he helped her down, her cheeks rosy as she waddled over for a hug. She squeezed them both before moving toward the wagon, her eyes widening as she realized just how much there was.

"Alip," Sumi said, "you didn't have to bring *this* much!"

"Well," he said, smiling, "between the students and the orphanage, I figured it'd be better to have too much than not enough. Besides, if your stomach isn't bursting with fish by sunset, did you really celebrate Umidiar?"

"You'd think he's the one eating for two," Barine said, rolling her eyes. "Though he is big enough to fit two of me."

"Speaking of big," Sumi said, winking at Alip, "Beysal is here if you want a rematch."

Alip's smile disappeared, but then he wiped his hands on his pants, kissing Barine on the cheek.

"Sorry, darling," he said, "but I'll have to unload in a bit. Got a score to settle with a bear."

"Just make sure your back still works after you lose," Barine called after him. There was some grumbling at that, but Alip still had a spring in his step as he disappeared into the house. He really seemed to think he could win, though there was no way he'd found someone Beysal's size to practice on.

Barine looked at the statue, eyeing the flowers. She put her arm around Sumi, squeezing her shoulder.

"I suppose it gets easier, but the holidays always hurt, don't they?" she asked, a sad smile on her face. It had been nearly ten years since her brother had passed, though it probably only felt like a day.

"They do," she said, nodding. "But I know he would have liked this."

Just then, the gate opened, and Kerint, their youngest student, marched in, trailed by his sister.

"Good morning, miss," he said, nodding at Sumi.

"You're here early," she said, smiling.

"Mr. Milak'erat asked us to set up the fish stakes," his sister, Vendorin, said quietly. She was awfully shy, but she was a promising student. She'd learned to hear the songs without the help of Vilodai's stone, and at fifteen, she was already able to run the halls.

"Oh, alright," Sumi said. "If you hurry, you might be able to get some breakfast, too, before they eat it all."

The kids ran off, but as they opened the door, there was a loud bang from inside.

"We might want to get in there," Barine said, chuckling as she moved toward the house. "That sounded like my husband's head hitting the floor."

Sumi followed behind her, but she paused for just a moment, turning back to Parimu.

"A promise is a promise," she said, blowing the statue a kiss. Even when they were intent on wrestling each other to death, she would keep looking out for their people. The school, the orphanage — anyone in Berillai who needed them. It always felt like there were a thousand things to do — and no time to do them — but as long as she was alive, these people would have a place. And as long as there was a school, the children would have a feast on Umidiar.

———

Late that night, Sumi found herself back in the garden, looking over the edge of the terrace toward the sea. She was utterly exhausted but perfectly content — just how she liked it. The house behind her was dark and quiet, but it didn't feel empty. If only Nela could see them now. She looked out at the water and sighed contentedly, humming to herself. As she so often did without realizing it, she was humming Essomuai's song.

She could still hear it, would always hear it. She usually hummed a part of it to Omu as she put her to sleep after saying the prayer Nela taught her. She would run her fingers through her daughter's silky hair, listening as her breath grew deeper. She'd pick just one piece of the song — maybe the tune of a nearby tree or the song of an owl hunting overhead. And on rare nights, when everything was still, she would listen to the earth and hear somewhere deep below the echo of Vilodai. She would hum that rhythm to her daughter as well, a reminder that what was broken could always be rebuilt.

It was funny to think how seldom she used her magic now. She still shaped, of course — especially at school — but mostly, she was herself. They were *her* hands in her children's hair, *her* voice singing the songs, *her* lips that Erso kissed. After all, that's what the goddesses had wanted for them — to really live. There would likely be war again someday, and there would always be more than enough pain to go around, but as long as one person still believed, there was hope for *eshernulam*. And no matter what came her way, she would always sing their songs with pride — the Song of Life, the Song of Essomuai, the Shapewalker's Song.

<h1 style="text-align:center">THE END OF
THE SHAPEWALKER'S SONG</h1>

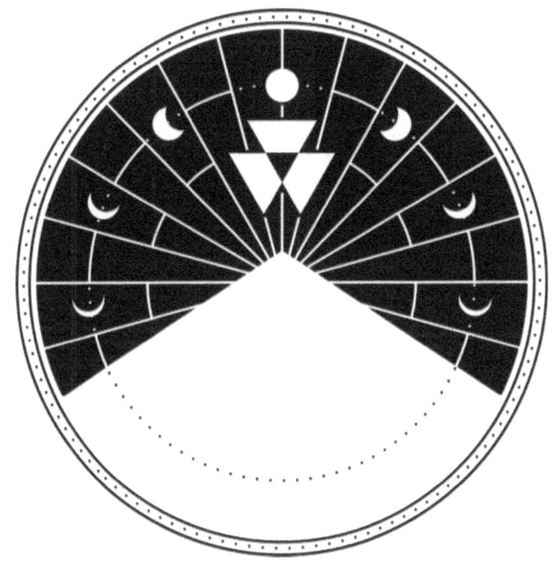

Alight, to the desert! The mirror of the sky awakes! How the earth shall tremble when the divisions are made whole. How the void shall shatter when the daughters are rejoined. It comes, it comes.

-The Coming of the Mind
Song of Kishtoran the Uniter